The Lady in the Veil

THE TALBOT SAGA

Allie Cresswell

Prologue

Yorkshire, February 1835

They were burning the heather on the moor. They did it every year, different half-acre patches, to do away with dead wood and encourage new shoots to come. In very early spring, before the snowdrops had faded, they chose a day. They chose it by some in-bred instinct, without consultation or pre-arrangement. It was a day marked on no calendar other than the one that every moorsman had written on his soul, when the colour of the air, the smell of the sky, the taste of the wind told him that the day had come. It must be a windless day—although never, on the moor, was there a day entirely without wind—when the black peat still sucked and oozed with snow-melt but the scrub was dry.

Inscrutable, monosyllabic Yorkshiremen—ragged, broken-booted, oaken-hearted—shambled out from scattered farmsteads and lowly hovels to surround the doomed area. They leaned on their shovels, eyeing the sky, the scrub, each other. Then three or four on the windward border bent and stuffed rags amongst the bare branches of heather, gorse and juniper and brought their tinderboxes within the lee of their bodies to set the rags aflame.

Instantly—before the heat, before the smell—came the noise; the crackle and fizz of wind-dried wood as the fire took hold. The land roared, the plants cried out, they zizzed and spat and hissed and snapped. The flames, at first, could not be seen. It looked as though the branches withered and crumbled from within, their sage-green and grey-brown stalks disintegrating to dust in the air. Wizened berries boiled their last vestige of juice in sticky, resentful globules. Old leaves curled and dissolved to ash. The only sign of heat was the mirage that hovered over them—oily, scented with rosemary and thyme. It rose up into a film that distorted objects seen through its lens, wild imaginings brought to life, ghosts and spectres, the Angel of the Lord in the burning bush. Then came the heat, a hot, singeing breath that made the men step back and wipe their brows and grip their shovels. The translucent fumes became tongues of flame, an orange-magenta-purple-blue miasma sweeping across the brush and furze. Last of all came the smoke—acrid, white—rising in a tower above the flame-ground, carrying ash and sparks and white-hot filaments of tinder.

Suddenly, things began to move. The men, with surprising alacrity, leapt over tufts to extinguish rogue outbreaks of flame. They hefted their shovels again and again on the crisping undergrowth and spongey ground. Rodents and rabbits scattered, bursting out from where they had been cowering, their fur scorched, their ears back. Birds wheeled above their old nest-sites and screamed their dismay. Creatures that could neither run nor fly were rendered, instantly, to cinders.

A hundred yards away from the inferno, two women stood and watched. Their clothing—good, but not ostentatious in style—and their elegant bearing marked them as ladies of a certain quality; they did not come from the cottages that ran, raggle-taggle, along the periphery of the moor. Of the same height and build, they might have been sisters, but whatever similarity or discrepancy there was between them was impossible to know, for one of them was thickly veiled.

This one, from beneath her shroud, said, 'It always seems so harsh to me, so wantonly destructive, to burn the heather.' Her voice was quiet and low. It was a young voice, but characterised by a sighing mournfulness beyond its years. 'The shelter, for all the creatures, torn away.'

'Yes,' said the other woman, 'it does seem cruel. The men are careful, Mr Harlish tells me. They beat the undergrowth first, to give the wildlife warning. But you are right, not all will escape.'

She wore no veil, indeed no head-covering of any kind. It was hardly seemly, for a lady to be without a bonnet, but there was, in her hatless state, a sort of defiance of the other's complete envelopment. Her hair—mid-brown threaded with silver at the temples—was carelessly caught up into a knot. Tendrils had escaped and she let them whip around her face. She wore no ornament, and her fingernails were rimmed with dirt. Notwithstanding, she was without doubt a lady; her bearing and her speech declared it. Lines etched themselves into the outer corners of her eyes where she squinted into the smoke. Had there been no smoke, though, she would still have had the lines. She was not a young woman.

They stood and watched for a while as the flames leapt from plant to plant, and crept beneath the knee-high canopy, eating up deadwood and fallen leaves, blackening the moss and sedges that must have thought themselves safe, so close to the saturated earth. The men, half-hidden in heat-haze and smoke, beat at the heather with their shovels; the thwack, thwack, thwack reverberated through the peat, making the women feel as though the ground was the flesh of the world with its beating heart beneath their feet.

'It is for a good cause, though,' the older woman continued. 'Where the old things have been torn away, new growth will come. It will make better feeding for the sheep and cows, and for the gamebirds. It *seems* cruel, but, in the end, it brings new life.'

The veiled lady gave a dry laugh. 'Is *that* why you brought me up here, Mama? To show me a metaphor?'

Her mother gave a rueful smile. 'Not wholly. But it is true you are too … cloistered, Georgina. You hide yourself away. It isn't healthy. This …' she reached out and caught hold of the veil that concealed her daughter's face, '*this* is quite unnecessary, especially here.'

'You say this to me *now*,' Georgina cried, stepping away so the gauze slipped from her mother's fingers. 'How you have changed your tune!' Her tone was mocking, playful, but it had a bitter edge. 'All my life,' she went on, the bitterness taking over, 'you have bade me be discreet. We were not to draw attention to ourselves. I was not to go to school but must be taught privately, at home. We could not accept invitations from our neighbours. Assemblies, the theatre … these things were denied me. Do you know I have never danced, except with Lucas? I have had no acquaintance beyond the Burleighs. So, yes, I have learned to be self-sufficient. I have taught myself not to need society. Which is fortunate, is it not, since you are to go away and leave me alone?' Her vehemence surprised even her. Her breast rose and fell, panting with passion. Her eyes, even through the thick stuff of her covering, flashed fire.

'You will not be alone, Georgina,' her mother said. 'You will be with your cousin George.'

'I will be with your cousin George, whom I do not know,' the young woman corrected. 'I had rather stay here, or with Mr and Mrs Burleigh. I do not want to go to London.'

'In spite of all the balls and assemblies and plays that have been denied you? You make no sense.' Georgina's mother—whose name was Jocelyn—could not keep the irritation from her voice. 'Here I am offering you all the things you tell me you have missed. But no. It will not do for you. You are perverse.'

The burning was almost done. A roughly square patch of blackened earth and tortured, twisted stumps stood where, only an hour since, had been a natural shrubbery of heather, Juniper, dwarf cornel, bog rosemary and cloudberry. The men laboured over it, as eager now to extinguish the flames as they had been earlier to set them. The women turned and began to follow the narrow pathway which had brought them to their vantage point.

'*I* am perverse?' Georgina burst out. She was walking behind her mother and, out of her sight, lifted her hands to her head. She might have torn her hair, if it had not been covered over. 'I am not the one who has changed.' She dragged her feet, allowing a yard or two to open up between herself and her mama. 'Mr Stockbridge has changed you,' she muttered.

Jocelyn stopped abruptly and turned on her heel. 'Yes, he has,' she almost shouted, 'and for the better. He has set me free. I have been very afraid, Georgina, especially since your father died, afraid of exposure … But Frederick has taught me that I have nothing to be afraid of, and that I should not be punished for the misdeeds of others.'

'*What* misdeeds?' Georgina cried, taking hold of her mother's arms and almost shaking her. '*What* have you been afraid of? If you could only *tell* me.'

'I cannot tell you,' Jocelyn sobbed. 'But I have been very wrong to burden you with it, Georgina.' She took hold of the veil. 'This is a prison I have put you in, my dear,' she said more gently. She made as though to lift the veil away but Georgina caught hold of it and wrenched it from her mother's grasp again.

'*Please*, do not take it off,' she rasped, backing away. She looked wildly around them, at the moor and the men who, very distantly now, were beginning to rest from their labours. 'People will see.'

'Who will see?' asked Jocelyn, looking significantly at the empty moor. 'And see what?'

'You know what happens,' replied Georgina, her tone tight and filled with panic. 'You know what happens when people see my face.' She lifted her hands and covered her face with them, raking it through the stuff of the veil. 'They stare and … *look* at me. All our carefully constructed obscurity is stripped away. And it is mortifying.'

'Their ignorance reflects on *them*, not on you,' Jocelyn said.

'It does reflect on me, though!' Georgina cried out. 'It reflects on me like the noonday sun. It lights me up as though a million candles shone. It sets me on fire like the martyrs of old, so that every eye is on me and people say, "Look! Look! Who is that girl? Can you see her? Did you ever see the like? What is the curse she carries?"'

'And I will tell them, "That is my daughter, Georgina Willow. She is no more cursed than *you* are."'

'You will not be here,' said Georgina coldly. 'And, in any case that is Mr Stockbridge speaking, not you. You parrot the new truth he has fed you. But the *real* truth, the truth *you* have brought me up to understand, is that my face will cause calamities. I am not fit to be seen.'

'No calamities will befall,' said Jocelyn, but she lowered her eyes. She still doubted.

1

London, March 1835

'My dear,' said George Talbot to his wife one morning as they sat at the breakfast table, 'I have received a letter from our relative, Jocelyn Willow.'

The subject of Jocelyn Willow was always a contentious one between the Talbots and George was not at all surprised to hear his wife say, with considerable scorn, 'The recluse?'

'She lives in retirement,' George corrected. 'She is not absolutely a recluse, my dear.'

'She may as well be,' Lady Jane retorted. 'I cannot begin to understand her. *I* could not live as she does.'

'No, of course not,' George murmured. His wife, indeed, was as entrenched in society as Jocelyn Willow was removed from it. Lady Jane lived for the at-homes, dinners, tea-drinking and card parties that were such anathema to his cousin.

'And then,' said Lady Jane, as George had known she would, rehearsing the old, old argument, 'she is a relation whose relationship cannot be defined! I am afraid I count her no relative of *mine.*'

Her husband bridled. Would Lady Jane *really* open this old wound again? He felt his temper rise, but controlled it. The presence of Miss Trimble, his wife's old school-fellow and long-time companion, prevented him speaking his mind.

Lady Jane looked for a moment as though she would fling another sally towards her husband's seat at the far end of the table, but seeing his scowl and his significant look in the direction of her friend, she desisted. Perhaps it occurred to her that Miss Trimble's presence had spared her a volley at least equal to anything she could have mustered. She threw her friend a pacific look.

Miss Trimble, sensing that her being there in the breakfast room was an annoyance to one party and a gratification to the other, simpered awkwardly, managing to communicate both apology and obligation in one semi-strangulated whimper. She made a great show of refusing more coffee from the pot poised by a footman—her vigorous shake of the head communicating that no, she couldn't possibly impose, a second cup would be gluttony, she was already surfeited by her hosts' kindness and it would choke her to consume a drop more than was absolutely necessary for her corporeal continuance—but then relented, accepting coffee, sugar and cream.

George remarked with artificial mildness, 'We have revisited this issue several times. It hardly matters, but Jocelyn and I are connected through my mother's first marriage to the Gilchrists of Spalding.'

'Such a very distant connection imposes no obligation on you,' Lady Jane felt herself safe to reply. 'What does she want?'

George consulted the letter. 'She is to marry again,' he said. 'A gentleman by the name of Stockbridge. Willow has been dead these eight or nine years, you know.'

'A stumbling, awkward fellow,' Lady Jane opined, dabbing her thin lips with a napkin. 'Death was a blessed release.'

George's temper flared anew. 'Willow was an excellent man,' he barked. 'He was injured in the service of his country and suffered grievously as a result. It was a wonder he kept his leg. The pain must have been unimaginable.'

'He left his widow prettily provided for,' Lady Jane said, as though this were more than ample compensation both for his suffering and his demise, and also disliking the image of Captain Willow's ulcerated limb that her husband had conjured into the breakfast room. 'Not to mention that she has her own fortune. I cannot imagine what she requires from us.'

George folded the letter and put it into his pocket. 'She wishes to send her daughter Georgina to us,' he replied. 'Jocelyn and Mr Stockbridge are to go on a wedding tour of some months' duration, to Europe. Possibly even further afield. Jocelyn is eager to travel, but she feels that Georgina is not equal to it.'

If there was one person more calculated to rile Lady Jane than Jocelyn Willow it was her daughter, although she could not quite say why. It could have been simply the light that came into her husband's eye when he spoke of her.

'It will be inconvenient,' she said, 'to have a country girl to take around, and such a one as she! She has been nowhere, met no one. Her manners …'

'Her manners will be unexceptionable, I can assure you,' George said. 'But in point of fact there will be no necessity for you to take her anywhere. As you point out, Georgina has lived a very retired life up to this and Jocelyn thinks it unlikely that she will wish to go into society at all. Indeed, Jocelyn believes it would be unwise.'

'Not go into society?' Lady Jane repeated. 'Why ever not? What is wrong with her?'

'There is *nothing* wrong with her,' George said, through clenched teeth. 'She simply wishes …'

'Excuse me,' Lady Jane interjected, 'but there must be something wrong, some deficiency of mind or of manner. Or,' she narrowed a speculative eye, 'something scandalous. What other reason can there be for renouncing society?'

'Oh, I don't know,' George replied, and Lady Jane should have been warned by the gimlet light in his eye, 'perhaps the pointless posturing, the artificial friendships, the mindless conversational exchanges, the pretence. It is all a sham! I am not surprised that an intelligent young woman chooses to avoid it. It is more surprising to me that so many apparently sensible people choose to expose themselves to it. Whatever the reason, Miss Willow very particularly does not wish to enter society and we will respect her wishes.'

'There seems no point in the girl coming to town, in that case,' Lady Jane said. 'Why does she not go to Europe with her mother? Society there might be more to her taste, and young women benefit just as much from exposure to foreign culture as young men do. Perhaps more. Europe is swarming with Americans these days. *They* are not so particular as to birth, you know. Any English gentlewoman suffices for *them*. Perhaps, under the circumstances, it would be a good thing to have her comfortably settled abroad.'

'Under what circumstances?' George asked. He directed a steely glare at his wife, daring her to elucidate.

Lady Jane met his eye but sealed her lips. As provoking a topic as Jocelyn Willow and her daughter was to her, it was a sensitive one with her husband; there was much that could—but never had been—said. Lady Jane had not infrequently tested his defensiveness, nudging and probing in the manner of someone with a mild but wholly benign curiosity. It was not benign, and he knew it. He had parried her every thrust as though his life were at risk. At the same time she had felt sure that the possession of his secret was burdensome to him; he *wished* to reveal it, *would* confide it, if only he could. It pleased her to know that her husband had this vulnerable spot and she liked occasionally to press it, to remind him that she knew it was there and could make it hurt if she wished. She found it infuriating, however, to be denied access to his secret. She was of an inquisitive—not to say nosey—disposition. Scandal, intrigue and gossip were meat and drink to her and to have this tit-bit, as it were, on her very table, was exasperating. She had exercised all her wiles and slyness to get him to reveal his secret, but to no avail. His habitual response, out of all proportion to the provocation, was to insist emphatically that there was nothing whatsoever to be known; no shameful secret, no awkward history, and he would horse-whip any man who suggested otherwise. His protestations only increased her interest and of course she had made energetic enquiries beyond the Talbot circle, but discovered nothing. The Willows were a quietly prosperous family who divided their time between houses in Wiltshire and Yorkshire. In both places they lived a very retired, unexceptionable life. Of the Gilchrists she could discover nothing; there seemed to be no surviving branch of that family tree.

It would be hard to say what, precisely, Lady Jane mistrusted; her suspicions were uncrystallised, vaguely troubling but not specific. Much stemmed from the Willows' rejection of society, a standpoint quite incomprehensible to her. She was sure that some unsavoury taint adhered to the Gilchrists—lowness, meanness, bumbling rusticity or a distasteful trade connection—but then why would George's mother have allied herself to such a clan? *She* had been well-born. George's admiration and affection for his cousin was marked; there was no one, other than his children, who could excite more passion in him. Was there some lingering childhood infatuation on his part, conceived in George's youth and never quite consigned—like the tin soldiers, ragged kites and exhausted rocking horse—to a box in the attic of his recollection? Lady Jane was not jealous, except possibly for her son, who would be superseded by the son of George's first wife. Jealousy was not in her nature, though she was often envious.[i] She supposed she was simply curious. George was an open book on every topic; his business dealings, his political leanings, his emotions. Only on this subject, the subject of his cousin Jocelyn and her daughter Georgina, was he close-lipped.

All this went through Lady Jane's mind as the ornate clock on the Adam mantel ticked and the flame beneath the spirit stove hissed and Miss Trimble crumbled her toast into smaller and smaller morsels.

George, having made his point, allowed his eyes to slide to where Miss Trimble sat, her gaze downcast and seeming intent upon her plate, but acutely self-conscious. It was embarrassing to have exposed her to this altercation and he felt heartily sorry for it. His wife's recommendation that Georgina accompany her mother on honeymoon must have recalled sharply to Miss Trimble's mind—as it had to his—those weeks of exotic luxury she had surprisingly found herself party to on the Italian Riviera. He himself had been surprised beyond articulation to discover that Miss Trimble was to be a fixture of his wedding tour. She, he thought, had been hardly less so. He recalled her, flustered and blotched with anxiety, on the ship—one of his own—that carried them from Portsmouth down the English Channel and into the Bay of Biscay. The captain's cabin had been especially fitted out to accommodate the bride and groom and the first mate's quarters put aside for Lady Jane's maid. But these had been hastily reassigned when it had become clear that a second lady was to be of the party and the maid had been bundled somewhere below, where she had remained, green-gilled, until they had docked at San Sabastiàn. It had fallen to Miss Trimble to prepare Lady Jane for her wedding night. The bride's maiden bashfulness had been less than the friend's! And then, in the sun-bright palazzos of Venice and the eye-searing blueness of the Rimini coast, how startled and bird-like Miss Trimble had been, mazed by the strange and precipitate circumstances that had brought her to such wonders from the obscurity of her father's parsonage. Recalling all these circumstances—her amazement, her gratitude, her air of being illuminated for the first time in her shadowed, obscure life—made him say with marked chivalry, 'Not every bride—or groom—appreciates the great felicity of a female companion on a wedding tour.'

On their return from their tour of Lake Garda, Venice, Rimini and Rome, Miss Trimble had not, as he expected, returned to her father's house, nor had she disappeared off to some respectable but lowly lodgings in an unfashionable quarter of town. No, she had remained, apparently a permanent addendum to the Talbot establishment. Now, after eighteen years, Agnes Trimble's presence in the London house or at the Talbots' country estate, in the Talbot brougham and at the Talbot table, was as customary to George Talbot as the familiar furnishings thereof. It would be easier to picture Ecklington Grange without its ornamental lake than to imagine his tea table without Miss Trimble. He was almost fond of her. She was certainly the kind of woman to provoke compassion, and he could afford to be compassionate.

George noticed that a shaft of sunlight had travelled across the table and now illuminated Miss Trimble in an unflattering brightness. She had no beauty and little wit that he had ever managed to discern. Her fine, brownish hair was dressed very simply and not very becomingly. She wore clothes that were plain, designed for longevity of wear and versatility of use rather than for ornamentation or in pursuance of any fashion. In the cruel illumination of the morning sunlight he observed that her skin was dry and dull, her pale lashes stubby, her nose too long and beaded with a suggestion of moistness. Her demeanour was trembling and timid. He knew she was a little afraid of him even after so many years as his guest. He had never, that he knew of, given her cause to fear him.

Miss Trimble, knowing that she was being scrutinised, slopped her coffee in her saucer and mewed with distress at her own carelessness. The footman dashed forward with a cloth and his exertions exacerbated her discomfort. The little scene was lit up like a play as the sun poured in, its malice intensified by the crystal water jug, the burnished silver coffee pot and the arctic whiteness of the cloth. The shine of tears and a fine beading of sweat on her upper lip joined the glint of dew on Miss Trimble's nose. A blush of shame spread up her neck to her sallow cheek. She looked as though she would like to flee the room, to dart beneath the table or hide herself behind the curtains. She rummaged fruitlessly in her reticule for a handkerchief, found none, but baulked at using her napkin, knowing it would be a serious transgression of etiquette to do so.

It dawned upon George why his wife always took the chair with its back to the window. This realisation filled him with a feeling that was almost tenderness for his perpetual house guest; Miss Trimble was poor, grateful and utterly harmless. He waved the officious footman away, motioning him toward the window.

'Adjust the blind, why don't you?' he growled. 'Can't you see Miss Trimble is being almost blinded?'

George passed behind Miss Trimble's chair, dropping his own handkerchief into her lap as he did so but making nothing of it.

'At this time of year, Miss Trimble,' he said, with a gentle tone, 'you might prefer the seat opposite. The sun would not be in your eyes.'

'She likes to look across at the trees in the park,' Lady Jane said sharply.

'Oh yes,' Miss Trimble stammered. Her voice was muffled by the handkerchief, but was in any case habitually so soft and low as to be almost inaudible. 'I *do* like to see the first flush of green in the treetops. But of course, Mr Talbot, if you think … any seat is just as agreeable. In short … I do not presume …'

'Whatever you wish,' George cut in, to save her further exposure. He turned to the footman. 'See that the drapes are better arranged in future,' he said.

'You might write and suggest that Georgina would benefit from Europe,' Lady Jane murmured. It was her last strike, but she knew her cause was lost.

'I do not think so,' George pronounced, as she had known he would.

Perhaps prompted by Miss Trimble's observation he had walked to the bay window and now stood with his back to the room, surveying for himself the new-furled green of the trees in the park across the street. 'I presume they have discussed all the possibilities. Jocelyn does not wish to take her daughter and thinks the girl too young to be left alone for such a long spell. I shall write and say that we shall be delighted. Perhaps, my dear, a line from you would be a kindness?'

'Very well.' But Lady Jane, although defeated, was not quite ready to concede the point. 'She is hardly a *girl*,' she mused, as though to herself. 'She is older than Robyn, is she not? Quite old enough to maintain her own establishment, I would have thought, as Robyn does.'

'I would not call a garret in Paris 'an establishment'.' George said mildly as he turned from the window and crossed the floor. The footman opened the door for him, but George hesitated on the threshold, thinking fondly of his elder daughter, the child of his first wife Bibi, dead now for many years. Robyn was studying at Pauline Auzou's[ii] art school for young women. He provided a generous allowance for her, but she insisted upon living a bohemian lifestyle in the manner of the other, less well-provided-for students. 'However, you make an interesting suggestion,' he said. 'I shall ask Robyn to come home for the duration of Georgina's stay with us. The two got on well as children. I am sure they will both be happy to be reacquainted. Good morning my dear. Good morning Miss Trimble.'

Then he was gone. Beyond the door, in the vast hallway, the suddenly increased volume of street noises indicated that the master of the house was going out; the front door was open and his carriage was being brought around. His voice was jovial and unaffected as he exchanged greetings with the men who were to attend him—he was always thus with grooms and drivers. He had a natural affinity with the lower class of men—rose up to them, melding with the voices of hawkers along the street and the shouts of children in the park. Then there was the swish of the whip, the jangle of harnesses, the sound of wheels on the paved square, and he was borne away to his day's occupations.

2

The door of the breakfast parlour closed and the footman resumed his position by the console table where the breakfast meats were arrayed. No one else would come down; the house was empty. Mr Talbot's two older children—Lady Jane's stepchildren—were away; Robyn in Paris and her twin brother Bobby in the Holy Land with his tutor, completing his *grand tour*. Lady Jane's own two children, Raphael and Beatrice, were at school. The ladies had clearly finished their breakfast but they remained seated at the table and so the footman could only wait whilst the kedgeree and the kidneys and the other dishes dried and spoiled beneath their domed covers.

Still Lady Jane made no move. She wore a dissatisfied expression; she had not emerged as the victor. She had uncovered no more of Jocelyn Willow's connection to her husband and had not succeeded in vetoing the plan for the Willow girl to come to them. She allowed that facilitating the second could well enable her to make progress with the first—what more natural than that the girl, away from home and thrown in to company with her hostess, would be artlessly forthcoming on the topic of her antecedents? Oh, but the burden of having *another* ward to watch over. Did she not already have her own two children and her stepchildren? Not to mention Agnes Trimble!

Dear Trim! At Lady Jane's hint, *she* sat and gazed upon the treetops, giving the impression of finding them a source of extreme interest and enjoyment. She would continue to do so, Lady Jane knew, like a puppet laid aside, until a word or a gesture should indicate that she was wanted.

There was immense satisfaction to Lady Jane in having about her a person who was wholly her own creature. Lady Jane herself was the youngest daughter of Earl Brougham.[iii] With several older sisters *she* had been the one—sourly—to fetch books, to tidy away the tea things, to tend to their ageing father as one by one *they* had entered into society, married and gone away. At last, left alone and facing spinsterhood, she had been her curmudgeonly father's only companion, subject to his caprices and a steadily decreasing level of mental capacity until a chance encounter had introduced her to George Talbot.

The year had been 1817. Her father had taken her to Chelsea, to Ranelagh Gardens[iv], prompted by a sudden urge to visit the pleasure ground of his youth. His outrage and dismay upon finding it demolished, with only a rough-strewn field of nettles and rubble where he had spent so many happy—and dissolute—hours in former years had brought a sort of convulsion upon him. She had looked on in helpless despair as her father had stamped and raged, his face turning from a wrathful white to an apoplectic red and finally to a dark, suffused shade of heliotrope. The coachman had been unable to persuade the earl back into his conveyance or to procure medical aid. A small crowd had gathered— snot-nosed boys and shabby-looking labourers, a gaggle of women on their way to the public wash house—none of whom had provided assistance or advice but who had merely stood by as though the earl were an escaped inmate from Bedlam. Lady Jane had scant love for her father or sympathy for his display of childish truculence but she did very much mind being the object of such public curiosity and embarrassment. She had been on the very verge of her own display of hysterics, which would have ill-become any young lady, when a sole rider—a gentleman—had come to her rescue. Dismounting quickly he had thrown the reins to a by-stander, barked a rebuke at the groom and hoisted the earl from the road. A coin flung in the direction of the least wily-looking on-looker had summoned a medical man and a brusque gesture had dispersed the other gawping by-standers to their business. The immediate crisis dealt with, the gentleman had turned on Lady Jane a smile of such winning pleasantness that it banished utterly her horror and dismay but replaced it with something almost as violent. She blushed, stammered her thanks, felt her heart fluttering with unwonted puissance in her breast and at last swooned, but not before taking the three or four steps required to ensure that his arms would catch her.

Their courtship had been short; three or four calls to enquire for the earl, a chance meeting at the home of a mutual acquaintance, a ball and a ride in the park had been all the intercourse needed to persuade Lady Jane that a marriage between them would add materially to her happiness and satisfaction. George Talbot was a widower, well-respected in the mercantile sphere, and wealthy. At twenty-six he was still a young man. To be sure, he was encumbered with two children—half Indian, if you please—and had no name of note, no title, no blood. He cared nothing for these things, insisting in his thoroughly good-humoured but altogether sincere way that he esteemed his master of horse more highly than any marquis he had ever met and that a duke was just a man like any other when reduced to his under drawers.

'I think I can meet most men of rank face to face and pound for pound,' he declared.

His attitude was singular but then he was unlike any gentleman she had ever met. In comparison to her sisters' husbands he was extraordinary; confident, worldly and uninhibited. His oddness was universally forgiven, however, even by the baronets and earls he despised; he was popular with gentry and common folk alike. And he was handsome, although grief, it was murmured, had stolen the full bloom of his beauty away.

Lady Jane was no beauty, she knew that, and at twenty-nine it was not to be supposed her personal attractions would increase. Her nature—she had been told, by her sisters and several governesses—was sullen, bitter and resentful. But George Talbot was of that irrepressibly good-humoured disposition that can overlook the surliness of others. Lady Jane decided that if he would live with her shortcomings—and she made little attempt, after their second or third meeting, to disguise them—she could accommodate herself to a man who, in the eyes of her sisters and her papa was nobody, even if a rich nobody. Where there was money—and there was a great deal in this case—inconvenience and incompatibility need be no barrier. She was a Lady, she was his superior in birth, but she was not stupid; it was unlikely that any other offer would come her way.

She had acceded to his proposal with ladylike grace and the sufficient quantity of blushing reticence before putting aside such silliness in favour of business-like pragmatism. So much good, she decided, would come to Lady Jane Talbot that had evaded Lady Jane Brougham, and she made her stipulations. The house in Grosvenor Square must be made-over; it was old-fashioned and gloomy, the furniture altogether spartan and the kitchens by no means sufficient to entertain *le bon ton* to the dinners and balls Lady Jane hoped to hold. She must have a house in Brighton for the summer season. Fashionable society flocked there now that the Prince Regent's pavilion was complete. She would not endure the dullness of Ecklington, the Talbots' country seat, for more than a few weeks at Christmas. She must have her own carriage. So much for the outward manifestation of all that would accrue to her on her marriage. As for the private expressions of marriage, well, the unpleasantnesses of the matrimonial bed had been endured by other women before her and she was sure she was equal to them; she set her face to endure it. A small voice she would barely acknowledge whispered that even *that*, with *him*, might not be so awful, but she rebuked it. To submit physically to the objectionable exigencies of the nuptial bed was one thing; to have her heart subjugated would be worse. She would not endure it; she would be nobody's vassal.

Yet, as the day of the marriage approached, and the itinerary for their lengthy wedding tour was explained, she had found herself quailing. She hardly knew George Talbot. She had spent a very few hours in his company and hardly one of them alone. His ebullience was wearing, his zest and enthusiasm for *everything* gave her a headache. He was so sure of everything—where they would go, which sights they would see, their routes and means of transportation. How would she contend with his boisterous, almost boyish fervour, alone, amongst strangers on the Lido? How could she counter his superior experience of travel, of society, of culture? He would lead, decide, guide and what would she be able to do but follow? It was insupportable. She must have, in her turn, a subordinate, someone to stun and dazzle and bemuse. Someone, potentially, to blame.

Her answer had been Agnes Trimble, a poor, shy girl she had known at school and with whom she had maintained a desultory correspondence since. Agnes was a girl who, like Lady Jane, had been left at home to care for her elderly father but who, *unlike* Lady Jane, would never be married, and certainly not to a man of means like George Talbot. She would be the perfect foil; even less nice looking than Lady Jane, the bride—however thin and angular—could only compare favourably. Agnes had little elegance of manner or address, less cleverness and no confidence at all; any of Lady Jane's *faux pas* could be passed off as Miss Trimble's. She would be suitably grateful and very discreet. She would be useful.

And so it had proved to be. On the wedding night Agnes' trepidation had exceeded Lady Jane's own. Her commiserations the next day, her proffering of hot water bottles and willow bark tea and *sal volatile* could not have been kinder. As they toured Italy, Agnes proved herself invaluable at reading up and then imparting salient points of interest about the ruins, the galleries, the palazzos and sepulchres they were to visit, whispering the name of this artist and that architect so that Lady Jane could appear knowledgeable and informed. When Lady Jane became fatigued, Miss Trimble's lack of strength was blamed. She became the perfect companion—subservient, unobtrusive, without pretention, disarmingly eager to please.

When the couple returned home, Agnes mooted a return to her father's house but Lady Jane would not hear of it. And so she had stayed ever since. Her usefulness had not diminished, through childbirth and child-rearing and on the death—at last—of the earl, Miss Trimble made sure to be useful. It was the least she could do, she said. She wrote and answered notes, reminded Lady Jane of appointments at the milliner's and dressmaker's, and accompanied her to these places, as well as to galleries and public occasions at which a lady did not like to appear alone. On the other hand Miss Trimble had no expectation of joining Lady Jane to evening parties, at-homes, dinners or the theatre. There was no awkwardness of that kind. She could be left at home as easily as she could be carried forth and seemed to have no particular preference for either; everything was to be just as Lady Jane liked.

And Lady Jane *did* like. She liked Miss Trimble's ability to converse, generally, on most topics, providing alternative points of view but never, in the end, disagreeing with Lady Jane's own opinion. She approved Miss Trimble's ability to fade into the shadows—the dun brown of her frocks and her shrinking demeanour seeming quite designed for withdrawing to a far corner with a piece of amorphous needlework or a book, whilst Lady Jane entertained proper company. Miss Trimble innately understood that there were times when she should leave the room altogether—without remark, without ruckus, without any reproachful backwards glance—when she sensed that would be pleasing to her friend. There were times, indeed, when Lady Jane believed that Miss Trimble *had* departed, so silent and still was she, that it was a surprise to see, after several hours, her friend still perched, still waiting, like a faithful dog, in a far corner of the room.

Miss Trimble sat now, in just that attitude of patient, respectful attendance, looking out over the park, and Lady Jane allowed her thoughts to return to the matter of George's relation.

He kept up a regular correspondence with the woman he styled 'his cousin' Jocelyn, for she never came to town. The letters were not shared, read aloud or précised; certainly they were never left where Lady Jane might peruse them although she had not infrequently stolen into George's study to see if one had been left out. Cousin Jocelyn had consistently declined Lady Jane's invitations to parties at Ecklington, their country estate, and to dine at the house in Grosvenor Square. Accordingly Lady Jane had never had the satisfaction of meeting her husband's cousin. This determined refusal to be known by Lady Jane was perhaps Mrs Willow's most heinous crime. George's claim that she should not take it personally—the Willows *never* dined from home, *never* paid calls, never went *anywhere* except to Yorkshire—buttered no parsnips with Lady Jane; such behaviour was simply incomprehensible.

Captain Willow *had* shown himself, just once, at the June 4th cricket match at Eton,[v] where his son Lucas and her stepson Bobby were enrolled. Though well-mannered and gentlemanlike he had not impressed her. His limp was so pronounced, his features set in a rictus which was hardly agreeable to observe. Her enquiries—perfectly civil—about his wife and estate, had been parried and at the conclusion of the sport he had abruptly taken his leave. She took it as a particular rudeness that when George had been invited to take the children of his first marriage to the Willows' house in Yorkshire, she—Lady Jane—had not been invited to accompany them. It had rankled. But then the reports that Bobby and Robyn had brought back with them had tended to make her think she had been spared. The house, they told her, was old and sparsely furnished. The weather was rarely clement. The regimes imposed were quite extra-ordinary, with as few servants as equalled none at all and such servants as there were sitting down to dine with the family quite on equal terms. Everyone was required to shift for themselves in the way of fetching hot water for washing and the provision of foodstuffs for the table. It reminded Lady Jane of an ill-fated scheme she had read of in Tennessee[vi]. Certainly, *she* was not the kind of woman to dig her own vegetables or fetch her own coals.

Her impression was that there was something barely proper about cousin Jocelyn, and of course any stain of impropriety must also leach onto her daughter. Such a mode of living! A determined refusal to engage with *any* society but the very lowest. How could it be respectable? To be intimate with mere servants! And it must be an unnatural mother who did not wish to secure for her daughter an advantageous match. But Georgina had been absolutely kept away from the marriage market. There *must* be something seriously wrong with the girl. Why else maintain this veil of obscurity, this shroud over her, over the whole family? Who knew what lowness, what vulgarity, what scandal Georgina Willow might introduce to Grosvenor Square?

Lady Jane's ruminations were interrupted by the approach of a footman with a note on a tray.

'From the master,' the footman murmured, proffering the tray, 'delivered just now, from his club.'

Lady Jane took up the note. Her husband's handwriting was always execrable and she squinted to make out the two or three lines the note comprised.

I think you mentioned that it was your intention to visit your dressmaker today. If so, or whenever you next find it convenient to do so, please ensure that Miss Trimble is supplied with two new gowns and any other apparel that might be wanting. You might think a new pelisse in order. The one I passed on the hallstand this morning is lamentable.

Your humble servant

George

Lady Jane crumpled the note in her hand.

'No reply,' she said to the footman. He withdrew, throwing a baleful look at his colleague, who still stood in attendance on the cold buffet.

Lady Jane gathered herself and rose from the table. Miss Trimble instantly threw off her reverie and rose likewise.

'I had thought to visit Madame Le Favre today,' Lady Jane began, Madame Le Favre being her usual dressmaker.

'Certainly, ma'am. I am quite at your disposal,' replied Miss Trimble with an eager expression, although she could have no suspicion of Mr Talbot's generous intention.

'But I have decided to wait for another occasion,' Lady Jane concluded, throwing the crumpled note into the fire. 'I shall retire to my sitting room. I have some letters to write.'

Miss Trimble looked a little crestfallen but said equitably enough, 'Very good my lady. Can I be of any assistance to you?'

Lady Jane looked at Miss Trimble's dress. It certainly was very dowdy, with sleeves of nowhere near the fullness that was favoured by fashion and only the smallest suggestion of lace at the throat. Now she thought about it, it was the same dress that Miss Trimble wore every day and whilst she did not have the need for a variety of clothes of course she did not have the money to buy them even if she had the need. George's offer was kind, and just like him. Lady Jane experienced a frisson of mingled shame and annoyance that she had not herself noticed her friend's need and had the gratification of offering to supply it. Now the credit could go to George, for of course Miss Trimble ought to be told the name of her benefactor. But that need not be today.

'I do not think so,' Lady Jane said at last. 'You may take a walk in the park, if you care to. I am sure Dickie would like it.'

Dickie was Lady Jane's lapdog, a bad-tempered spaniel that spent most of its time on her bed but which must, at least once a day, be coaxed outdoors.

'Certainly, ma'am,' Miss Trimble replied with a grim smile.

3

When George Talbot climbed into his carriage he had intended to visit Euston, the site of one of his most exciting investments. The railway station being constructed there would afford him untold benefits as a terminus for goods from Liverpool. He had invested heavily in the Liverpool and Manchester Railway[vii] and that, for five years, had opened up to him markets in the increasingly affluent mill and manufacturing towns of the north, but freight from there to the capital could only be economically carried via the tortuously slow canal network. With a depot in the heart of London, George's imports would be amongst the first to appear in shops and homes there.

Something about the morning's altercation with his wife, however, made him change his mind and he bid his driver take him straight to his club in the City[viii] where he commanded paper and wrote his note. He did not like to quarrel with his wife, and would by no means presume to teach Lady Jane her duty, but her peculiar lack of compassion did irk him. Poor Miss Trimble!

He quailed to commend Georgina to his wife's care; from what Jocelyn had written, the girl was sensitive, fragile, not to say troubled. He could not trust his wife to put as kind and considerate an arm around the young woman as she clearly required, and as he could wish. Lady Jane had not taken her stepchildren Bobby and Robyn to her heart, as he had hoped, though they had been but babies, hardly out of long frocks, when she had become their stepmama. Her feelings even towards her own children had been cool. Simply, she was not a passionate woman. Rather, she was a calculating one, and that gave cause for concern.

Once established in a chair in the library with a pot of coffee and a glass of sherry at his elbow, George got out Jocelyn's letter and re-read it.

I do not think you will recall Frederick Stockbridge. He was a tenant at Upton Park for a short time with his sister in the year 04. I was able to do them a small kindness and it seems that Frederick has never forgotten it, though it was but an insignificant thing. His sister sadly died not long afterwards, leaving a son, William, who Frederick has brought up as his own. William is a captain of Marines, a profession Frederick himself graced in former years. I had the great good fortune of meeting William whilst he was on furlough at Christmas. I must say he is an exceptionally fine young man, very handsome, gently-spoken. He could not have been more considerate in his attentions to Georgina; he made no comment on her singular behaviour. I was only too sorry that Lucas was not at home to meet him. He, as you know, remains in the Americas, assimilating as much as he is able of their farming practices before he attains his majority next year and assumes ownership of Chanbury Park. It is his house now, and although my Barnaby is in every stick and stone of it, I must withdraw. Indeed, I have withdrawn, and we are currently in Yorkshire, although we will return very briefly to Wiltshire towards the end of April, for the marriage.

The improvements you have commanded to the house here are all complete. The north wing comprises a new kitchen and ancillary facilities with additional accommodations above, plus quarters for a housekeeper. The new chimneys draw exceptionally well. How clever of you to devise them in that way. They are out of all proportion to the house, but they needed to be. I have decided that this house which, thus far, has had no name, shall from now on be called Tall Chimneys. Shall you find a tenant for it, in its new, improved state? I am not sure how often I shall be able to return here, or if it will be wise for me to do so. I must cast off the old and take on the new.

Frederick has no estate, for he has led something of an itinerant life, but means now to find a property and I relish the idea of fixing on something together—a new beginning for us both.

I think that it is not everyone who is fortunate enough to marry their soul mate, as you and I have been privileged to do. Your Bibi and my own Barnaby were our all-in-all, were they not? Their very heart beats were in rhythm with our own, their minds in complete alignment, their tastes in accordance, their tempers the mirror image. But they are gone. You have seen the sense and comfort in finding a new helpmeet and so must I, but it is not to be supposed that we can be so lucky twice. Frederick is a dear man; tending to be shy and taciturn where Barnaby was so genial, yet Frederick is sensitive to the feelings of others and I do not know that his feelings do not run more deeply than Barnaby's did. He is peculiarly attached to me, and quite willing, on that account, to take on my odd way of living, making no scruple about my intimacy with Mr and Mrs Burleigh and others of their sphere. On the other hand he is determined to open to me new horizons, and from the hour of our wedding my days of looking over my shoulder are to cease.

For yourself, I am sorry to hear you describe your marriage as made in haste and repented of at leisure. I am sure Lady Jane graces your home and your name elegantly. She is the mother of two of your children and you owe her much for that, for children are not brought forth or raised up without great labour and pain, I assure you!

Although Georgina could easily be accommodated by Mr and Mrs Burleigh I have decided to accede to your oft-repeated request to have Georgina with you for a time. It is natural that you should wish to know her and, although being in London will expose her to an unwonted degree, I feel that it is right to let her come to you.

As you know, this past twenty years I have believed it necessary to keep away from the world. Our whole society has encompassed only the Burleighs and some of Chanbury's tenant farmers. In Yorkshire we are more private still. I have been assiduous about repulsing approaches from the well-to-do families and even the rector has never so much as crossed our threshold. When we must go out in public Georgina and I both wear veils, but we have avoided this exposure if we possibly could. Georgina has entered thoroughly into this expediency without understanding the need for it, but now I fear that my paranoia is manifesting in her to an increased and peculiar degree. My fear of being recognised has become, in her, a fear of being seen.

She positively shies away from all intercourse with strangers and obscures her face even when we walk together on our own property. She has come to believe that there is something about her face that has necessitated our hiding away. She is partly right; poor girl, there is, in her appearance, something too likely to attract notice and cause remark. It has become, for her, a phobia; she hates her appearance.

I send her to you in order to separate her from the influence I unconsciously wield over her; all the habits and practices of our past. I would have her walk free of them, as I am doing, but I doubt she is ready for such a reversal. It must come gradually, and at her own volition. Public entertainments, balls, theatricals or concerts, all these will be anathema to her. My own opinion of London society is that it is a circus, a bear-pit. Georgina is not equal to it; she must remain in quiet but genteel obscurity. I will not have her paraded, George. I say this baldly that there might be no misunderstanding on the point. But if you can tempt her, just a little, from the shadows, I shall be your grateful, as well as your loving

Jocelyn

George sighed and folded up the letter. At this hour the club was quiet, most of its members being about their business in the City. It was a new club, quite recently established, and made up of new men. He had chosen it for the opportunities it might offer in the way of commerce; the members were, like him, traders, brokers and merchants, all successful or rising to success, and not particularly politically affiliated. This had proved a great boon, for the government had alternated of late so frequently and precipitately between Tory and Whig that anyone who had tied his colours irrevocably to the mast of either ship would have found themselves strangled in the halyard[ix]. George himself was a man with an eye to the future and a reputation for looking kindly on new-fangled schemes dreamt up by under-funded dreamers. Men like McAdam[x], Aspdin[xi] and Bell[xii] had benefitted from his financial backing. Cooke and Wheastone's[xiii] telegraph made him so excited he could barely speak. He was in favour of everything that favoured his business interests, which were broad, and forward-looking.

But he was also a humanitarian. He had been pleased by the abolition of slavery in 1833 and had supported the Factory Act[xiv] of the same year that had protected to some extent the rights of children in the workplace. Neither of these Acts had been good for business and many of George's associates had railed against them, but George—who had seen the conditions of slaves in the Caribbean and of children in mines and factories for himself—could not join them. He might have a business head but he had a father's heart. In his father's lifetime the Talbot fortune had derived almost entirely from trade with India, and this still formed the foundation of it. But George had invested in railways and manufacturing. He shipped cotton from the Americas to Liverpool to be woven into calico and then re-exported. He was interested in new inventions that would increase productivity, in anything that would improve transport and infrastructure; all these things, he believed, were on the cusp. He foresaw in the not too distant future a huge expanse in manufacturing, as mechanisation was introduced. Machine-breaking could not halt these things. Accordingly he had already bought up vast tracts of housing in the midlands and the north, improving and modernising slums to accommodate the influx of workers he anticipated, and he was building new houses aping the work of Bazley and Gardner in Bolton[xv] A new world was coming—a world of new men, new ways of doing things, new beliefs, new morals.

But that world was not yet come, and George understood Jocelyn's delicacy in relation to her daughter. He had not seen Georgina since two years ago, when he had gone to the Willows' estate in Wiltshire to collect Lucas, carry him to Liverpool and settle him aboard a ship bound for New York. Necessarily, he had paid more attention to the young man who was to be his companion on the road and the bearer of letters to his agents in America than he had to the shy, retiring young woman of the house. That was all he recalled of her; she had kept herself very much in the shadows. Now she was to come to his house and, he feared, be subjected to the hostility of Lady Jane unless he could do something to shield her. Miss Trimble, he felt, might prove a valuable aide in this regard. *She* would be a companion for Georgina—the differences in their age and circumstances notwithstanding—who would comprehend the need for discretion and understand the kind of obscurity that it would be best for the young girl to inhabit. Of course the notion of summoning Robyn home appealed to George: he was eager to see his daughter again. And it was true that she would neither take nor allow any nonsense from her step-mama. But she would hardly understand the need for delicacy in relation to her cousin Georgina. George could almost hear his daughter's remonstrance. 'But why should we not go about, Papa? Are we not to be trusted? Are you ashamed of us? Surely you do not expect us to stew and moulder here in the gloom of the house when the season is at its height?'

He opened the letter again and allowed his eyes to skim the lines. The words 'made in haste and repented of at leisure' stung him. Had he said as much to Jocelyn? But he could not gainsay them. He *had* proposed too hastily, his innate compassion blinding him to reality. He had mistaken Lady Jane's sullenness for unhappiness, believing that, once married and carried away from her father's unpredictable mental state, the sour cloud that sat over her head would clear and she would reveal herself to be an accommodating and gentle helpmeet. Her connections were good, and *that* could of course do no harm to a man like George. She had been of the ideal age for childbearing, and George did wish for more children. But most of all he had hoped—had perhaps assumed—that the unification of two lonely souls would be a remedy, the one filling the other, banishing heartache. How wrong he had been! In the great formulae of life it seemed that when one well of loneliness joined another, all that resulted was a deeper well.

George paused in his ruminations to see that the chair on the opposite side of the fire had been occupied. The man was tall, his long legs extended to the Turkey rug. His boots were of excellent quality and immaculately clean. His face was obscured by the newspaper but the hand that held the sheet was dark-skinned, its smallest finger adorned by a heavy gold ring with a large stone. At his elbow there was coffee and a snifter of brandy.

George shifted in his seat and gave a slight cough and the gentleman lowered his newspaper.

'Oh,' cried George, in delight. 'It is you, Mr Balfour. Do forgive me, I did not see you come in.'

Amory Balfour was a man who George held in great esteem. They had much in common. Like George, Balfour was successful in business, a broker whose acumen and shrewd understanding of the markets were gaining him universal respect. Both men had inherited their wealth, and whilst both had to a certain extent endured cold aristocratic shoulders to make their way, those turned against Balfour had been more obdurate. His parents—both slaves—had died on a plantation in the Indies. The plantation owners, childless themselves, had adopted him, brought him to England and educated him to be a gentleman. Nothing about Amory Balfour—except the colour of his skin—marked him out as anything other than thoroughly English, thoroughly genteel; but his one singularity had set some against him. Whilst George's response to aristocratic prejudice had been an onslaught of cheerful good humour, Mr Balfour had met it with *hauteur*, looking down upon those who would look down on him, surpassing them in lofty pride.

Mr Balfour had dined with George both in Grosvenor Square and at the club but lately they had been vouchsafed little opportunity for private discourse, so George was particularly pleased to see Mr Balfour before him, alone.

He got up from his seat and offered his hand. 'I am heartily glad to see you Balfour.'

Balfour also rose and the two exchanged a formal handshake. Amory Balfour was a handsome man, with dark hair sculpted close to his head, brown eyes beneath heavy brows, a generous mouth and a determined jaw. His suit—like his boots—was impeccable. He was aged thirty-five or perhaps more but was unmarried. This circumstance—in spite of his unbending and superlatively dignified air and his particular appearance— made him popular amongst London's hostesses, for a single, unmarried gentleman—especially a wealthy one—was always a boon at their dinners and at-homes. He declared himself a confirmed bachelor— declared it in his manner and his reticence, if not in words. Some society mamas with older, unwed daughters scoffed at that; he simply had not encountered the right girl. Others thought him quite right to keep his blood to himself. He troubled himself neither to contradict the first nor to be offended by the second, and held himself aloof from the machinations of both. The facility to make himself agreeable to young women did not come easily to him, if it came at all. There was about him a degree of seriousness, a certain stiffness of manner. He was earnest, not given to frivolity. George—possessing no racial bigotry, for he had himself been married to an Anglo-Indian lady—had wondered briefly whether his daughter Robyn might win Balfour's heart. She was a well-looking girl, clever, and knew the nature of the mercantile life. But she was artistic, and George did not think Balfour's interests lay that way.

'You were deep in thought,' Balfour said now, seating himself once more, folding his newspaper in precise quarters and disposing himself to conversation. 'I know how little I like to be disturbed in my train of rumination so I would not for the world have interrupted yours.' He nodded at the letter that George still held in his hand. 'You have received bad news?'

'Oh no,' said George, folding the letter and returning it to his pocket. 'In fact, quite good news, in itself, but …' he hesitated. Something about Amory Balfour invited confidence. His eyes were like deep wells, a safe depository of secrets, and now that he sat forward with one elbow resting on his knee the magnetism of his safekeeping exerted an almost irresistible pull in George.

'But?' Balfour urged, raising a querying eyebrow.

George sighed. 'It could incur difficult consequences, that's all. My cousin has asked me to take charge of her daughter for a time.'

'A child?'

'Not at all. Georgina is past twenty years of age. But she has lived a retired life up to this, and is somewhat … troubled. London will be a change that perhaps she is not prepared for, that's all, and it is a responsibility I feel keenly.'

Mr Balfour leaned back in his seat and it was almost as though shutters had gone down. He was, again, a closed, impenetrable fortress. 'I am sorry to say that on this subject I am unable to advise,' he said.

'What man is?' George quipped. 'Women are unfathomable.'

'Indeed,' Mr Balfour agreed, but rather as though he doubted it. Nothing, his quizzical eyebrow said, was unfathomable to *him*.

The two men discussed the markets for a time, and George motioned the waiter to refresh their glasses. Presently Balfour drank off his brandy and then consulted his pocket watch. 'I am due on the Exchange,' he said, rising to his feet. 'I must bid you good day.'

'Good day,' George echoed. 'I am so glad to have seen you. You must come and dine again very soon. Lady Jane would be delighted.'

George finished his own coffee and drank off his sherry before stepping out onto the pavement of the City. The by-ways were busy with traffic: boys delivering messages, city gentlemen hurrying to the Royal Exchange, hawkers, people on their way home from the market on Wentworth Street.[xvi]It was March, a fine, dry day, so he decided to walk to Surrey Docks to see what progress had been made on his new ship, a steam ship which was to be propelled by two paddles, as well as sail, and to view the newly-opened swing bridge over the south dock entrance.[xvii] He dismissed his coachman and set off down Bishopsgate towards London Bridge, walking briskly.

As always, the docks energised him. He felt galvanised by the seeming-chaos of stevedores unloading cargo, shipwrights, metalworkers, coopers and smiths. He almost envied the men who swarmed around him, hauling and hammering, loaded down with sacks and crates, their faces slick and grey with sooty sweat. They worked hard, no doubt, but they worked honestly, by the skill of their craft, and were not troubled by the rate of the pound or the vacillating policy of government. They lived an uncomplicated life.

Overhead, unwieldy structures of gantries, brackets and braces formed the tackle for lifting and shifting. Such ingenuity! George gasped at it although he had seen it hundreds of times. Chains rattled through pulleys, scaffolding towered, and all around echoed the reverberations of engines pounding in the workshops, the screech of saws, the hiss of steam, shouts and whistles, the incessant hammering from the skeletal hulks. It all seemed to come from a department of purgatory—the heat, the noise, the smell. The efforts of the men seemed a kind of penance. And yet, from it all, above it, rose the ship. A carcass of bare bones at first—like the fossil of some long-extinct, gargantuan creature, too large to be real—ugly and exposed. But then, gradually, it was clothed with the flesh of raw planking and sinewed with rope, muscled with metal and skinned with canvas. It would be reconstructed, reanimated—a colossal thing, beautiful, stately, powerful. It would lie ready, breath held, its life stopped up, until the day the engines should be lowered into it, and set to beat.

George wandered in awe along the dockside, greeting the foremen by name, exchanging nods with the other workmen, smiling his appreciation and gratitude and throwing pennies to the boys who carried the tar before seeking out his clerk of works. This was his own man, a Mr Ribbonshaw, an experienced shipwright who had been relegated to a drear corner of a draughtsman's office by a severe injury to his arm before George had brought him forth to oversee the building of his new vessel. Elsewhere, it was rumoured, Mr Brunel planned a ship of iron, which would be powered entirely by steam[xviii]. Both Mr Ribbonshaw and George were avid for information and dreamed, in time, of emulating Mr Brunel's scheme. With this in mind George had lately attached to Mr Ribbonshaw a young assistant already skilled in metalwork and engineering. Arthur Harlish was a Yorkshireman, one of cousin Jocelyn's protégés and educated at her expense, with an innate aptitude for all things mechanical—a man for the future, George believed.

At first Mr Ribbonshaw had objected to his assistant, expecting a feckless youth with only a theoretical understanding of shipbuilding.

'A lad who can draw a ship cannot necessarily build one,' he had grumbled, 'and a gentleman who speaks with a plum in his mouth will not be understood by the men.' But Arthur Harlish had allayed Mr Ribbonshaw's reservations. He was quietly-spoken but unashamed of his flat Yorkshire vowels. He was competent with compass and set-square, a good solid draughtsman, and his calculations could not be faulted. But ships on paper held little appeal for him. He was eager to get his hands dirty and would strip off his jacket and shirt to work in the foundry, take his turn on the saw, heft coils of rope and scale scaffolding. The men respected him. Whereas Mr Ribbonshaw was a man of small stature—though large girth—Arthur Harlish was tall and extremely well-muscled, his physique a testimony to his energy and prowess. He was a pleasing-looking lad, with a mop of brown curly hair, intense blue eyes and a wide, winning smile.

George ate luncheon with Ribbonshaw and Harlish in the tiny cubicle that served as an office; hot pies and a pint of porter brought from a local public house as they pored over the plans for the ship. Arthur ate two pies to George's one and could, George suspected, have managed a third if it had been offered.

'You have found good lodgings?' George enquired when their meeting was finished.

'Yes sir, at the home of a widow-woman in Rotherhithe.'

'That's splendid. And do you have news from home?' Home, for Arthur Harlish, was the gatehouse of the country house in Yorkshire. The property was owned by George but he had given it over to his cousin Jocelyn Willow. Arthur's parents maintained the place in her absence. 'Mrs Willow is currently in residence, I believe.'

'Indeed sir. She stays until Easter, I think, and will be married in April.'

'That's my understanding. Her daughter is to come to London. We are to have the pleasure of her company for a few months.'

Arthur's eyebrows rose. 'Is that so?'

'Yes. You have known her from childhood I think. What kind of young woman is she?'

Arthur hesitated, choosing his words. 'I have not seen her for some time. My studies kept me away. But it is my belief that after Mr Willow's death, a change came upon her.'

George nodded. 'So her mother informs me. Miss Willow is very retiring, is she not?'

'Yes … but at night, my mother says, she is known to walk.'

'To walk?'

'Yes, around the grounds and sometimes out onto the moor.' Arthur gave a half laugh. 'There are rumours, in the village, that Mother Shipton walks once more!'

'Mother Shipton?[xix]'

'Oh, it is an old Yorkshire tale. A woman bore an illegitimate daughter and they lived in a cave at Knaresborough. The child had gifts of prophecy and healing. Some said she was a witch, and a cardinal[xx] said he would burn her as one, but he died before he could make good on his threat. People said he had been cursed. The girl was ugly and covered herself for fear of being attacked. Miss Willow wears a veil, and so … But it is just superstition and nonsense, sir.'

'Of course. But Miss Willow, is she …?'

Arthur shook his head. 'It would be impertinent in me to offer an opinion, sir. And, I have not seen her these five years. What notice does a lad take of these things?'

George nodded. He liked the lad's loyalty, and his discretion. 'You will like to see her, when she is in town?'

'Very much sir, if it pleases her.'

George bid Arthur farewell and went on his way, walking at random through the wharves and docks. An hour or two was lost this way until, at last, he hailed a cab and had himself driven to an address in Chelsea, a quiet cul-de-sac with six or seven pretty houses on either side. These, though small, showed a delicacy of taste in their polished windows, scrubbed steps and pretty little gardens. Of all these tidy and respectable dwellings the one at the very end of the street—the quietest and most cloistered end, hard by a high railing beyond which was a small park— was the most neat, with curtains of especial whiteness fluttering at the upper window, a winter clematis in super-abundant but minutely pruned display clinging to the red brick wall and a wrought iron seat perfectly placed in the square of immaculate lawn. Such was the consummate prettiness of this house and its little garden that it was impossible to suppose it could be the home of any but the most fastidious lady. A large pear tree that grew on the park side of the railings but that leaned over the small garden and would, in season, shed its blossoms and its fruit there, and gave the house its name: Pear Tree Cottage.

George dismissed the cab, waiting until it had turned and disappeared back into the main thoroughfare before approaching the wicket gate. The street was quite deserted; no delivery boy or dray, no flower woman or peddler, no maid or manservant was to be seen. Lace curtains at the windows of adjacent houses gave no sign of anyone watching from behind them. His only observer was a robin, perched on the pear tree and looking at him with a head cocked and an eye very beady. George smiled at the bird, lifted the latch of the gate and strode through. The door of the house was blue, its brass furniture gleamed in the sun. A pot of primroses on the step added its welcome and George knocked perfunctorily on the door before seizing the handle and going inside. He entered not at all like a guest—even one whose arrival was expected and anticipated—but rather like a man going home.

4

At six o'clock Mr Ribbonshaw and Arthur Harlish finished their work and extinguished the lamps in their cramped little office. Twilight had fallen on the docks—an eerie, violet gloaming, the bright day giving way to a clear-skied, frost-bright night. The docks were deserted now, the men having already departed, leaving only two night watchmen by a low-burning brazier. Beyond its circle of warmth the ground sparkled with icy fire. Gantries overhead creaked and chains clashed from time to time against the stanchions. A little wind had blown up from the river and it sighed around the skeleton of the ship, but otherwise the docks were silent.

Mr Ribbonshaw secured the lock of the building whilst Arthur ran to the nearest thoroughfare in order to hail a passing hackney carriage. He returned quickly and saw his superior safely settled within, their priceless plans and schedules of work stowed in Mr Ribbonshaw's satchel. Then, with a word of farewell, the cab departed and Arthur commenced his own journey home.

At one time in the not too distant past, Rotherhithe had been a rural place, dominated by marshland, where small-holders scratched a living from sheep and cattle and from market gardening. But now, as the construction of Brunel's tunnel continued apace[xxi], any beauty it had ever boasted had been sublimated. Piles of spoil from the diggings, rough enclosures for horses and building materials, makeshift dwellings for the labourers and temporary forges for the repair of tools had encroached from the workings as far as the docks. Little streams that intersected the marshes had become dirty and sluggish, choked by rubbish, pooling into stagnant and malodorous ponds. Across the barren swathe Arthur could see the glow of fires, surrounded by angular lean-tos, sheds and ramshackle shelters. Contorted shadows and strange, twisted silhouettes loomed large, backlit by the glow, as men and women stirred cooking pots and passed flagons of drink between them. Itinerant labour congregated in the public houses; the Halfway House, the St Helena and the China Hall were all loud with beery bonhomie, but Arthur passed them all, his route along Halfpenny Hatch Lane lit only by the moon which had now risen above the horizon, and the whitish miasma that hung about the frost-crusted grasses along the path. From time to time he met another traveller. A lone woman shrank back as he loomed from the darkness, her bundle of laundry clutched to her chest, her face white and panicked until his low, 'Good evening ma'am,' reassured her that he meant no ill. A man already the worse for drink stumbled and almost fell against Arthur's substantial shoulder. At first it looked as though he would make something of it—blame Arthur for their collision. But Arthur set him on his feet with a friendly, 'Mind how you go, mate,' and the man continued on his faltering way.

At length Arthur left the wasteland behind him and the marsh regained some of its beauty. The night air whispered with the rustle of grasses and the trickle of water, muffled beneath its icy skin. Bats swooped above him and frogs leapt from the path. Ahead of him a friendly light shone out, and he quickened his footsteps.

A row of pleasant cottages clustered together close to the place known as Cuckold's Point, a view of the river to their rear, well-stocked gardens to the fore, and it was to one of these that Arthur Harlish bent his steps. The middle cottage of three had a blue front door on either side of which a tiny window showed the bright glow of a lamp. Arthur passed between beds of shivering daffodils and optimistic tulips, his legs brushing against new-furled sage and mint and thyme. He knocked perfunctorily and went indoors.

The door opened directly onto a room that was a reception hall, a parlour and also—as would shortly be seen—a dining room. Everything was of exemplary neatness and cleanliness, from the burnished brass of the fire fender to the densely worked tapestry of the thoroughly-brushed and plumped cushions. A high-backed settle and a chair of a lower—but more comfortable-looking—caste sat before the brightly burning fire. Ornamentation of a seafaring kind was abundant: a brass compass, a nautical clock, a staunchly-strapped sailor's chest, framed charts of far-flung straits, exotic shells, a stuffed macaw and a set of elaborate crystal ships' decanters. The smell of beeswax melded with the waft of fresh herbs that Arthur brought in with him, and mingled with the sharp tang of the river that pervaded the area, but all were overwhelmed by the rich aroma of stew. A heavy brocade curtain, richly decorated with multitudinous coloured silk threads, hung across an opening to a further chamber and, at his entrance, the curtain billowed, denoting some alacritous activity beyond. Wooden panelling—highly polished—over the other wall of the room concealed a small door. Only its being just then ajar gave away its presence at all, and through the narrow gap the smell of supper drifted. Arthur paused on the threshold to remove his boots and to hang his jacket on a peg, before making his way through the door and up a narrow stair.

'Good evening Mrs Quince. Good evening Pansy,' he called as he did so. 'I shall be down again directly.'

A few moments in his chamber was all the time Arthur needed to wash his hands and face and to put on a pair of hand-worked slippers but by then the parlour had been transformed into a dining room. The settle had been pushed back to make room for a small folding table. On the table was a white table cloth set with cutlery and plates and a glass of ale.

Before he had thoroughly seated himself or tasted the beer, Mrs Quince was before him with a deep tureen.

Mrs Quince was the lady of the house, the widow-woman to whom Arthur had earlier referred. Her husband had been the captain of a river boat, trading goods and passengers up and down the Thames. Whatever stories of seafaring adventure and distant shores the various mementoes of the room suggested, they had not been Captain Quince's. He had never travelled beyond East Tilbury in pursuance of his trade and had died a relatively young man. For the twenty or so years since his demise Mrs Quince had supported herself by accommodating lodgers in her cottage—usually sailors—and it was to these guests that her collection of maritime accoutrements could be attributed.

That Mrs Quince had been, *in her youth*, a lady of remarkable beauty, was unarguable. Popular opinion in Rotherhithe reported it so and Mrs Quince herself was far from contradicting what her neighbours were so adamantly certain of. Indeed, if anything, she rather thought that their protestations did not go quite far enough, for to say that she had been a beauty in her youth almost suggested that her youth was a thing now ended. What's more it did not, in her opinion, give sufficient recognition to the significant degree of her *current* beauty. It may be that her eyes were not as sharp as they had once been, or that the brilliance of her little square of looking glass had become somewhat tarnished, but where others now saw hair that was greying and thin, to Mrs Quince it was as thick and lustrous as it had ever been. Her skin, which an unkind observer might have described as mottled was, to her, as peach-like as could be. A very dull-eyed person may have discerned a little hairiness about the chin and upper lip, or mistaken a natural beauty-spot for a wart, and someone with no knowledge of the matter could have described the perfect plumpness of Mrs Quince's figure as fat, but Mrs Quince could be compassionate about their errors, telling herself that swine could not help their nature and she would certainly not waste her pearls before them.

Part and parcel of Mrs Quince's charming appearance was an ineffable elegance of manner and an unswerving pretention to being a lady. Whichever hand had been at work polishing and scrubbing during the day, beating carpets and brushing cushions, carrying coals, making stew and providing all the homely comforts that had greeted Arthur on his return from work, there could be no misapprehension of that hand belonging to Mrs Quince. She, it was to be inferred, spent her day at ladylike pursuits whilst a hired drudge did the donkeywork. The drudge in the case was Pansy, a slip of girl, small-boned and big-eyed, timid and altogether understanding of her place. She now appeared closely behind her mistress, carrying another tureen, of vegetables this time, and a jug of gravy on a tray. The tray seemed too large and heavy even without its burden to be supported on a frame that was so insubstantial. Arthur thought Pansy looked like a corn doll in an oversized pinafore. It was natural, therefore, as soon as Pansy appeared, that Arthur should rise and relieve her of her load, but he could not do that without offending the other lady although she was more than equal to the load she bore. So he found himself in the role of gallant, assisting both women, arranging the dishes, settling his hostess into her chair, helping her to the food and then heaping as much as he thought he could get away with onto Pansy's plate. It was not to be expected that Pansy would eat her supper in the dining room and accordingly she took her plate back to the nether regions of the cottage to be consumed in private.

During the meal Arthur attempted to interest Mrs Quince in the business of his day, describing the visit of Mr Talbot to the dock, the load of timber too warped to be of use that he had not suffered to be unloaded from its cart, and his designs for the ship's galley. He wished that there were another gentleman lodger to assist him in the carrying of the conversation at supper. The vacancy in Mrs Quince's second bedroom was the sole drawback of his lodgings. The house boasted only two bedrooms and he had been given his pick of them, choosing the front one for its view over the marsh. Mrs Quince slept in the chamber beyond the brocade curtain. This region, he had been strictly informed, was private, beyond the scope of his occupation. Pansy, he presumed, slept in some cubbyhole in the scullery. Another gentleman lodger would have been a blessing, for of course Mrs Quince's interest in his work, not to mention her understanding of it, was not profound, and before long, as usual, he found the conversation turned to matters of a domestic nature more calculated to be of interest to a lady, and his opinion sought on a matter of local precedence.

It appeared that, some twelve months previously, before Arthur's arrival at Cuckold's Point, a group of neighbours had gone to town together for supper and to the play. Mrs Quince had been of the party, along with her neighbours to the left—a widower, Mr Pink, and his daughter Petunia— and also to the right—a bargeman, Bill Bannock, his wife Joan and their sons Dick and Walt. The outing had been an enormous success but also a considerable expense and it had been suggested that as delightful as it would be to repeat the excursion, pecuniary practicalities precluded it. Their enthusiasm for the play had been so marked, however, that they had determined to meet together thereafter on a regular basis for the purpose of play-reading.

Mr Pink figured largely in Mrs Quince's discourse. It had been at Mr Pink's suggestion that the theatre trip had been convened. Mr Pink had secured the tickets and Mr Pink had reserved a table where they might have supper afterwards. Mr Pink had been most assiduous in squiring Mrs Quince, paying her the most elegant compliments. Mr Pink was a deputy assistant clerk in a City bank, a very learned man, the proud owner of a set of Shakespearian folios which—with all the generosity to be expected of such a paragon—had been offered for the use and enjoyment of the company. It was impossible for Arthur not to infer some particular attachment to Mr Pink on the part of his landlady.

In comparison with Mr Pink the rest of the party received only passing allusion. The Bannock men were 'reasonably' literate, though admittedly eager to improve their fluency and especially enthusiastic about the battle scenes of the history plays, the gorier the better. Mrs Bannock 'of course' was utterly unequal to the speaking of any parts, being but an indifferent reader, but she took great delight in listening to the others. Miss Pink had been most uncooperative at first, pretending shyness and throwing every kind of obstacle between her father and Mrs Quince, but had yielded at last to his particular urging and agreed to take part.

And so, the previous summer, the troupe had assembled some five or six times, reading *Hamlet* and *A Midsummer Night's Dream*, sharing the parts amongst them and passing Mr Pink's folio from hand to hand. In general 'naturally,' Mr Pink had taken the male leads and, in deference to her beauty and general superiority, Mrs Quince had been accorded the premier female roles. The Bannocks had swept up the remaining soldiers, courtiers and gentlemen between them, Miss Pink bobbing in and out in supporting female roles: maids, ladies in waiting, fairies and so forth. Miss Pink, once brought round to the thing, had proved herself to be a natural actor—Mrs Quince was prepared to admit as much; her rendition of Ophelia had left no dry eye.

Now the winter was all but past, it was intended by all parties that the play-readings would resume. *Romeo and Juliet* had been suggested as their first foray and here, it seemed, was the difficulty.

'Mr Bannock has proposed Miss Pink for the leading female role,' Mrs Quince said, her expression a picture of affronted pride. 'She is, perhaps,' simpering, 'a *little* younger than me. But, oh, Mr Harlish, if you could but *see* her. No one could call her a beauty. It is impossible to conceive of her winning the heart of a young nobleman. She is quite a spinster, I do assure you, whereas I …' casting her eyes downward in specious modesty. '*She* has not the air of a girl who could love to an extreme …'

'And yet you said her Ophelia was rather strong,' murmured Arthur. 'Forgive me, I am not well-versed in the Bard, but was not Ophelia in love with Hamlet?'

'Oh no!' Mrs Quince cried. 'Ophelia was mad. Her wits were addled. I grant you Miss Pink carried *that* off to perfection.'

'Not mad for love?'

'Mad for *want* of love,' Mrs Quince said. 'Exactly Miss Pink's situation. No wonder she excelled in the role. But do you not think, Mr Harlish,' with a very complacent look, 'that we should look *elsewhere* for our Juliet?'

'Elsewhere?' Arthur prevaricated.

Mrs Quince twirled her finger in a wisp of greasy hair that had escaped her cap. 'Yes, elsewhere. Juliet is innocent, but she is *passionate*, and *determined*, and then, in the end, so very *tragic* … Only a woman who has *lived* and yet who is in the springtime of her life, could do justice to the role.'

'I always find her insipid,' Arthur lied. 'She is not the kind of girl who would move me. Do you not think the nurse a far more robust character?'

'The *nurse?*' Mrs Quince almost shrieked, 'but she is a frump! An old woman! A fright! One of the Bannock boys will play her very well, I should think.'

'I can see it is quite a conundrum,' Arthur said, judiciously. 'I am sorry I cannot advise.'

Pansy appeared and began to stack their dishes.

'Do you participate in the play-readings, Pansy?' Arthur asked her, standing up to hold the tray.

'Oh no, sir,' Pansy said, shaking her head.

'But you can read?'

Pansy nodded the affirmative. 'And Mrs Quince lets me listen, if my work is done, to aid my heddication.'

Arthur smothered a smile. 'Indeed? And which play did you like the best?'

'The one in the forest, sir. I liked it when the fairy queen fell in love with the donkey.'

'Humph,' sniffed Mrs Quince, who had played the part of Titania. 'A very silly development.'

'Was not Juliet about fourteen years of age?' Arthur asked, a mischievous light in his eye. 'Pansy cannot be more than that. Perhaps *she* should play Juliet?' Before Mrs Quince could remonstrate he went on, 'After all, Mrs Quince, no one but you could carry off the ladies Capulet and Montague.'

Mrs Quince gave a coy smile and Arthur took the opportunity to carry the tray through to the scullery. When he returned the table was gone and the settle back before the fire.

'You work magic the moment my back is turned,' Arthur declared. 'But Mr Talbot gave me a cigar, earlier, and as the night is fine I will walk up and down the lane for an hour whilst I smoke it, if you will excuse me.' He took his jacket from its peg. 'Can I fetch you anything?'

Mrs Quince gave an artificial cough and placed a hand on her chest. 'Perhaps a medicinal tot of gin,' she murmured, 'but only if you go so far as the St Helena. The spirit at the China Hall is not fit to be drunk.'

Arthur nodded, slipped his feet back into his boots, and stepped out into the chill night.

5

The night in Yorkshire was deeply dark, and the cauldron in which the house—Tall Chimneys—sat was doubly so. Legend said that a giant's footprint had caused it, but new science had produced a different theory. The wearing away of water underground and the collapse of a prehistoric cavern had made a hollow, a combe in the moor. Trees now crowded around and down its steeply shelving sides, and the house, on the sunken plateau of its floor, wallowed in thick blackness. Moonlight passed quickly over its disc of sky and only the chill pinprick of starlight pierced, with a faint silver phosphorescence, the all-encompassing shroud of night.

All the windows were dark; no candle remained alight. The fire in the hallway was a heap of dull red embers. The dog, set to guard the house, lay stretched out across the enormous stone hearth, and thumped its tail on the wide, polished boards as she passed by.

Georgina pulled back the bolt on the front door, and stepped out into the blanketing gloom. Her feet knew the step, the gravel, the lichen-encrusted planters and the line where the sweep of drive met the apron of lawn and herbaceous border. That day, with her mother, she had knelt and worked over the flower beds, clearing weeds from around the clumps of daffodils and cutting back woody stems from last year's perennials. It was not a ladylike employment but, both here in Yorkshire and at their house in Wiltshire, Jocelyn Willow would allow no servant to labour at what she herself would not attempt, and Georgina had been brought up to perform tasks that no other girl of her birth would dream of doing. But this was to change. Georgina had been told that, in her cousin George's house, she must not take the tea tray from the maid, offer to fetch the water for her bath or tend her own fire. On no account must she dispose of her own night-soil. A personal maid, she had been told, might be assigned to her, to put on and take off her clothes, to wash her body and dress her hair. *This*, however, she was determined would not be. If necessary she would bar her door.

Tonight, she wore no veil. The pall of night was sufficient covering, even for her. She pulled it around herself like a comforting cloak. The breath of breeze on the bare skin of her face was thrilling, almost naughty. Her hair, loose around her shoulders, was immediately caught up by the eddying wind. It lifted and coiled like Medusa's snakes as she walked with soundless steps across the gravel and onto the spongey lawn. There was no dew, and she left no trail behind her.

The old fountain was no more than a shadow in the dim. She felt, rather than saw it, the surface of its water a black mirror reflecting night sky. She passed it by and entered the woodland, her feet following a path her eyes could not see, but which she knew in her memory; she had walked it since she *could* walk, knew every over-hanging bough, every protruding root, every mossy boulder as she climbed. There was no wind in the woods, and yet the trees sighed and creaked, swaying to some midnight rhythm even she could not discern. She knew she was not alone; night-time creatures were everywhere, burrowing, hunting, scurrying. The trees were alive, almost sentient, like drowsing dryads—but, crucially, she was not watched, not seen, not measured or assessed, compared or judged. It was, to her, the most exquisite freedom. In the deepest part of the wood she raised her arms above her head and tilted her face to the canopy, bathing herself in the unfettered freedom of the night.

The path took her steeply up the slope, over runnels of water and long-fallen trees, through secret glades where, in her childhood, she had played with Arthur and his brothers and sisters, and with the Burleighs' children. What adventures they had had! How happy she had been! Accepted, unself-conscious, with no sense that the world outside could be anything other than *this* was: delightful, benign, safe. But then her papa had died, and, perhaps brought on by this shocking trauma, her courses had come. She had felt her body, her appearance and its effect on other people, begin to change. Even polite people looked askance at her; others—the ruder ones—stared agape. Thrown more into her mother's company she had assimilated some unspoken but palpable sense that *out there*—beyond this enchanted circle of woodland and moor—where people thronged cheek-by-jowl, where there was commerce and communal interaction, in *society*, there was danger.

At last the path came to a place just before the lodge gates. The little gatehouse stood sentinel, a hexagonal building. It was just two rooms, one above the other, where all the Harlish children had been born and ate and slept, tumbled together like puppies in a pen. There were only two at home now. Betsy did all the work that her mother was supposed to do in maintaining the big house. Sally was too fat and too rheumatic to do much more than sit on a chair in any patch of sunshine she could find. Betsy's brother Frank worked alongside their father as groundsman and gamekeeper. Georgina had argued with all her might that the Harlishes should decamp to Tall Chimneys, where there was plenty of room, and where they would be better placed to cater for a tenant, should cousin George find one. She—Georgina—would take up residence in the gatehouse for the duration of her mother's travels. How she would relish it—the solitude, the thick walls and stout door between herself and the ravening world. But no. She had been told she must go to London.

London! Surely, the very lions' den!

All in the gatehouse were asleep at this hour, and Georgina passed between the gates and went out onto the moor.

The moon had not yet set. Here, out of the shadow of the combe, it cast a silver haze over the moor, colouring the heather, the meandering pathways, the boggy pools and ancient boulders in shades of pewter, pearl, charcoal and chalk. Georgina brought her shawl up and wrapped it around her hair and face. Not for disguise—the night was her friend, the moon a poker-faced companion, blessedly impassive—but for warmth. The wind whispered through the dense, low foliage, chill and sharp; it was still only March. A hard frost, even snow, was quite likely. Many a time she had walked the moor the whole night long, and seen no one at all. But once she had come upon a poacher setting snares. His face, below his pulled-down hat and above his high-wrapped muffler, had gone as white as a sheet as she, swathed like this in a diaphanous shawl, had passed him without a word, drifting above the close-cropped turf like a spectre. She knew that in the village there were rumours of a ghost. They made her smile, and she *could* smile, beneath her veil. Behind its shield, within its canopy, she was safe; no one could penetrate the stronghold of her thoughts.

Two miles across the moor was a stone pillar. Eroded by the wind, whatever lettering it had ever borne had been scoured away. Georgina's mother had taken her there many times, especially after Barnaby Willow's death. It held special memories for her, and sometimes it had seemed to Georgina that her mother hoped for some apparition, a ghost indeed, a shadow of her father's spirit, to appear. Georgina reached the spot and leaned against the stone. The night and the moor were vast, a whispering sea of running water and rippling verdure beneath an endless arc of sky. A barn owl swooped over the stone, close enough for her to feel the pulse of air from its wing. Oh, how she would miss this solitude, this peace. The shrunken version of it she created for herself beneath her shroud was a poor reproduction, but it was all she had. She had been forced to it, since that day in Salisbury.

It had been a few weeks after her papa had died. Georgina had been thirteen years old. There had been some legal business to be done with a man of law and she and her mother had travelled to Salisbury where he kept his chambers. Mr and Mrs Burleigh had been with them but even so

Jocelyn had been filled with apprehension on the journey, clutching Georgina to her and insisting upon having the blinds of the carriage drawn down. Ordinarily they never went to large towns or cities. In Georgina's understanding this was an adventure, but a perilous one.

Georgina was in her monthly bleeding, the second, much heavier and more uncomfortable than the first. Mrs Burleigh had given her willow bark tea to drink, but the jolting of the carriage on the pot-holed road, the hard seat and the bulky rags between her legs had exacerbated her pains and by the time they arrived in Salisbury she had been feeling wretched.

It had been a market day, the streets and pavements teeming with people and livestock. In addition there was to be a hanging but this was not a matter known to the Willows as their carriage pulled up outside the lawyer's building. The groom, with some little difficulty amid the thronging crowds, got the door of the carriage open and the step lowered. The horses were disturbed by the clamour and by a herd of cows that was just then being driven down the street. The other groom attempted to steady them but descending from the carriage was no easy matter.

Mr Burleigh handed his wife and Mrs Willow down and conducted them through the jostling crowds, across the pavement and into the building. Georgina, doubled up with cramps and feeling sick and faint, would have followed close behind but stumbled as she stepped down from the carriage. The groom had gone round to the other side of the vehicle to ward off the cattle, and it seemed likely that Georgina would lie against the carriage, almost in the gutter, unless someone came to her aid. The people passing by began to slow their steps, seeing her half-crumpled, her head in her hands. Perhaps they suspected her of being inebriated; on market days it was common to see men and women intoxicated before noon as the taverns opened very early. It was possible they imagined she had been run down by the carriage, their ghoulish appetites—already stoked by the execution soon to take place—whetted. One or two by-standers nudged each other and nodded in her direction.

A woman in a shapeless bonnet gave a disapproving shake of her head. A leering fellow made a rude remark. Georgina, mortified beyond words but unable to rise, shrank closer to the carriage. Then someone—a lowly clerk, by his clothing, not more than seventeen or eighteen years of age—stepped forward and raised her up. She lifted her head to say some word of thanks and to ask him to help her to the door but his expression, as she lifted her face, made her words dry in her throat.

At first he wore the look of a man who has publicly done his duty; a smug, complacent expression with, perhaps also, the expectation of some reward. He had cast a glance over his shoulder as he grasped Georgina's arm to make sure that everyone saw *he* had been the one to assist her. But when he looked back at her face his countenance took on a look of awed bewilderment, almost of disbelief. His eyes grew wide. His mouth hung open. His gaze raked her face. She could not fully read what he saw there but it seemed to be a sort of appalled desire, a greedy reverence. Slowly, he licked his lips and swallowed, the bulge of his Adam's apple moving the fabric of his dirty stock. He kept her hand in his and in fact tightened his grasp on it. His hand felt hot, damp and unpleasant. His frank appraisal went on and on. Then he smiled. His teeth were bad, crooked and yellow, and his breath was sour.

'Look at you,' he said.

'What do you mean,' she faltered out. 'What are you looking at?'

His grin broadened and his eye took on a distinctly prurient light. 'I'm looking at *you*,' he said.

Behind him the crowd was growing restive, feeling that there was nothing to see and that they had better continue on their way.

The clerk, perhaps sensing that his moment was passing, stepped to one side so that they could see the prize he had lifted from the road. He pulled her onto the pavement and into the circle of people.

'Look,' he said. 'Just look what I found.'

Now everyone was looking, their faces a medley of impressions from compassion to amusement, from ogling to scorn, but all examining her in blunt, shameless detail. Georgina looked back at them utterly aghast, trapped, humiliated and afraid. The man who had made the lewd remark stepped forward to extended a filthy finger to her cheek.

'Push off,' said the clerk. 'I saw her first.'

'What a beauty,' a woman at the front of the crowd cackled, and everyone laughed.

There had been movement somewhere up the street. The cry went up, 'The prisoner!' and the crowd surged forward. Georgina, still clasped in the grip of the clerk, was helplessly swept along with them, the press of sweaty bodies and filthy, farmy clothes on every side.

'Where are we going? No! You must take me back,' she cried out, struggling, but his hold on her was vice-like and, like her, he was powerless against the mob.

The street opened up into a square where the hanging was to be. The gallows were in place, the officials lined up on a rough platform that had been erected outside the courthouse.

At the point where the street opened up the press of the people suddenly lessened as they spilled out left and right and straight forward into the area. The clerk took this opportunity to push Georgina up against the rough stone of one of the buildings. He pinioned her there with his body. His face was revoltingly close to hers. She could smell his breath, feel the heat of him as he pressed himself against her.

'You must let me go,' she said, squirming to free herself. But her efforts seemed to inflame him even further. His eyes—very pale blue—took on a light of sick compulsion. His mouth hung open and she could see his tongue. He leaned forward and fixed his mouth on to hers, smearing his tongue over her lips. His lower body moved rhythmically. His clammy hands were on her bodice. Georgina stiffened, her eyes widened in horror. Past his head she could see the condemned man on the gallows, his head in the noose. He looked like an ordinary kind of man, a farm worker perhaps or a market trader. His clothes were very ragged. His face was bleeding. Somewhere in the square a drum beat rose in a crescendo. The sound reverberated around the quadrangle of buildings so that the one behind her seemed to vibrate with it and she, too thrummed with its beat. Then, suddenly, it ceased. The man on the gallows disappeared through a trap door. The clerk convulsed, removed his mouth from hers and rested his head on her shoulder for a moment. It was an oddly confiding, intimate moment. The silence in the square was absolute for the length of two or three seconds. Then the crowd erupted in frenzied celebration.

Mr Burleigh burst round the corner, his dark face suffused and glistening with sweat. He spied her, wrenched the clerk away and sent him sprawling into the gutter. He placed his arm around her shoulder and led her away.

That had been the first incident. But there had been others. A stranger who had happened to see her as she hurried along the village street had been so distracted that he had stopped in the track of a farmer's cart, and almost been mown down. An itinerant preacher at the market cross pointed an indicting finger at her as she passed behind his ragged assembly of congregants and accused her of bearing the devil's mark. A band of gypsies arrived and set up camp in some of Chanbury's woodland. Normally her mama would have permitted this so long as they did no damage and poached only what they needed for their sustenance. But the young men of the troop began to haunt the Chanbury grounds, to lie in wait for Georgina as she went about her daily chores. They leered and whistled at her and one of them tried to detain her in the orchard. Mr Burleigh had sent them away. Georgina's mother had said, 'It is you, Georgina. You attract notice. It will not do.'

After that, she had covered her face.

6

April came, and with it, Agnes Trimble's new gowns. They came, not boxed and beribboned as Lady Jane's did, borne by a wigged footman, but simply packaged in brown paper and delivered to the rear entrance of the house in Grosvenor Square. Miss Trimble could not, however, have taken more pleasure in their careful unwrapping and examination if they had come to her atop a stack of royal cushions and accompanied by a fanfare of trumpets. She had the parcels conveyed to her rooms by one of the under footmen, closed the door and slowly, reverently, unwrapped the layers of tissue and gauze.

Her room was small, in the part of the house where the nursery and schoolroom were located, overlooking the back of the house. The stables and ancillary buildings made for no very attractive view, but she made no complaint and, indeed, after so many years, she would not have liked a change even if one had been offered. She had a fire if the maids could stir themselves to light one. If not, she was not above lighting her own; she knew where the coals and kindling were kept and her ambivalent status in the house meant that it was not a trespass to venture into the below-stairs regions. She had a comfortable fireside chair, a washstand

and press. The window was draughty but she had commandeered the schoolroom curtains when that chamber had ceased to be required and they were thick. Her bed was narrow but amply supplied with covers, many of which she had worked herself from scraps of wool and material rejected by Lady Jane.

There was a small sitting room adjacent, gloomy and ill-furnished, that she had adopted as her own since no one else used it. Sometimes, when the Talbots were from home, Agnes would invite the housekeeper or the superannuated nanny who remained as a pensioner of Mr Talbot's goodwill, to drink tea with her in this locale. Here, also, there was a fireplace, but she rarely kindled a fire in the grate. *Two* fires, for her own use, would be too much luxury. She had two chairs, a tea table, a bookcase and a lamp. She kept her own china in a cabinet. This, and the books, were all that remained of her father's belongings, the only things that she could really call her own.

In former days the Talbot children had sought her out in this little retreat, bringing storybooks for her to read to them, lessons to be learned by rote, rent clothing to be mended, tears over a scraped knee or sibling unkindness. Occasionally they had brought less welcome gifts. Bobby, the oldest child and always prone to mischief, had delighted in scaring her with spiders and frogs and had once hidden in her closet to make ghostly moaning noises once she had snuffed her candle.

She missed those days—the days of real usefulness—when the house had rung with the children's shouts and laughter and when, with them, she had peered through the banisters to watch the Talbots' guests arrive for dinners and balls.

'Why do you not go down and dance?' Robyn had asked her once.

'Oh,' she had replied, with a teary eye, 'I am not wanted dear. Look how many fine ladies there are. And in any case, I have not a grand enough dress.'

Now, she looked at her new dresses as they lay across her bed. Naturally they were not grand, nowhere near the opulence of Lady Jane's gowns.

She would not presume to such distinction; it was not for the likes of her to equal the splendour of *real* ladies. At the same time, she was not an employee and a little spark of pride in her forbade the notion that she might be mistaken for a housekeeper or a governess. In choosing the fabric and style of her gowns she had attempted to create the semblance of a genteel, thoroughly respectable nobody. Also, there had been questions of longevity and practicality, for there was no knowing how many years might elapse before another gesture of such generosity might be forthcoming from Lady Jane. With this in mind she had urged—but been denied—designs that ignored current fashion, for those gigot sleeves and floor-length skirts that were *now* in vogue might mark a dress out as hopelessly outmoded in just a few years[xxii]. Always, at the front of her mind, was the need to be self-effacing. She had a strong anxiety that if she made too much noise or in some other way drew too much attention to herself Mr Talbot and Lady Jane might notice her, and wonder why they needed her. She really did not know, in the event of such a calamitous possibility, what she would do. For without the hospitality and protection of the Talbots, she was utterly friendless. Her father's legacy amounted to not much more than twenty pounds a year, barely enough to keep her in necessaries, let alone enough to pay for the humblest lodging. No wonder that this unprecedented gesture of Lady Jane's—for Agnes believed Lady Jane to be the author of this munificence—gave Agnes Trimble such pleasure.

Pleasure, gratitude and relief vied for supremacy in her breast as she surveyed the frocks before her. The material was brocade, but it was unfigured. The colours were sombre and matronly; a brown the shade of burnt butter and a dove grey. The sleeves, though in the fashionable style, were not as full as many ladies favoured. The necks were high, the bosoms ruched with vertical pin-tucks, the skirts full but not so full as to be unwieldy. With the dresses had come a selection of chemises, a corset and two new petticoats, stockings, some boots and a dozen beautiful lawn handkerchiefs. There were also three collars, one of lace and two of linen, which could be attached to either dress. Lady Jane's generosity quite overwhelmed her and she stood for a few moments in awe and a kind of stupefied thankfulness. Bonnets, she had been told, were also to be forthcoming from Madame Planché, one of the premier milliners in London.

Later, Miss Trimble descended the staircase for dinner. It was not often that the Talbots dined at home and even then it was rare for them to have no company. But this evening, dinner had been ordered for three. Even so, Miss Trimble had not been able to deny herself the pleasure of one of her new gowns, affixing the fine lace collar with hands that almost shook. The stiffness of her new petticoat gave a thrill that was palpable. It rustled as she moved. The sweep of the skirts across the stair carpets made her feel giddy.

On the landing outside the first floor drawing room stood Mr Talbot. He almost seemed to be waiting for her. She could give no other explanation for his being there.

'Miss Trimble,' he cried, standing back in an attitude of amazement and admiration. 'What transformation is this?'

Miss Trimble blushed, and pressed a hand to her ruched bosom. 'How kind you are sir,' she gushed, 'and how kind is Lady Jane. There never was such kindness, I am sure. I am overwhelmed. I am sure I do not know … I cannot say half so much as I would wish …'

Mr Talbot offered her his arm and with a gesture of gentle admonition from the other hand, brought her stuttering thanks to a halt. 'It was overdue,' he said in a low voice, and then, more loudly, 'and our very great pleasure, for we have no other friend of whom we are so fond or to whom we owe so much.'

He led her to the drawing room and pressed her into a chair—a good chair, a central chair just the perfect distance from the fire, illuminated but not dazzled by lamplight, and with a table conveniently near where, soon, he placed a glass of Madeira. Of all the seats in the room it was the one most obviously reserved for Lady Jane, but of that lady there was no sign.

'I am glad to have this opportunity to converse with you,' Mr Talbot said, taking the chair closest to her. Clearly, he had something very particular to say and Agnes almost suspected him of delaying the appearance of his wife so that he might have the opportunity to do so. It was a matter of a confidential nature, she surmised—a matter, if not private, then delicate. Of course, in her intimate intercourse with Lady Jane, Agnes was privy to things that it was tacitly understood were to remain beyond the cognisance of her husband. But she had never been taken into Mr Talbot's confidence before, and even as she settled her hands in her lap to give him her whole attention, she experienced a frisson of anxiety: what would Lady Jane say? Lady Jane had a way of winkling out secrets and Miss Trimble had no facility with concealment; her blush, her faltering voice, her shrinking eye would all betray her.

Perhaps Mr Talbot discerned her anxiety, for he pre-ambled his subject with, 'It is known, I think, throughout the household now, that my cousin Jocelyn's daughter is to make her home with us for the duration of her mother's wedding tour. Lady Jane has been so kind as to invite her, and I understand that apartments are being prepared for her.'

'Oh yes, indeed,' Miss Trimble said, for there could be no breach of Lady Jane's confidence to say as much. 'Rooms adjacent to Miss Robyn's are being refurbished. The young lady is to have new window and bed hangings and the Turkey carpet from the music room has been removed there, for it has in it just the shade of …'

But Mr Talbot forestalled further description. 'Indeed. That is very satisfactory. I'm sure she will be very comfortable. And if, as I hope, Robyn can be persuaded to come home, I think the girls will like to be in close proximity. But Robyn seems to think that if she can return to England at all it will not be until the summer. There's an exhibition in June, it seems, and, in short, I rather believe that it will fall to you to bear Miss Willow company. I hope I do not presume on your good nature to expect that you will be willing to befriend her?'

'To me?' Miss Trimble said, half in wonderment and pleasure that she should be entrusted with such a task, but her pleasure tempered by an equal measure of unease. Would Lady Jane consent to spare her? Might there not be provoked a little jealousy? A chill draught of resentment? For Lady Jane did like to have Agnes at her beck and call, ready to go at a moment's notice to the park, or to a gallery or to a shop, to run errands or deliver cards. And how—even if Lady Jane were prepared to relinquish her first claim—was Agnes to entertain a young lady, who would certainly *not* wish to spend her time as *she* did, in a kind of limbo—quietly sewing, reading or just *waiting*, sometimes for hours— until she should be required.

'It is a matter of a little delicacy,' Mr Talbot went on. 'I do not scruple to confide in *you*, Miss Trimble for, as I said before, we have no truer or more trusted friend in the world. Forgive me,' he broke off, as though distracted, 'there were to have been *two* new gowns, I believe?'

'Oh yes sir, there are,' Agnes assured him. 'This, and another, dove grey. And *three* collars.'

'That's good,' he said, nodding. 'I must say that shade was well-chosen. Chestnut, would you call it? Most becoming.'

Miss Trimble almost shivered with delight. 'Dark caramel, I think Madame Le Favre said, but I think you have it better.' She stroked the stuff of her gown with a reverent hand. 'Chestnut.'

'I hope you also chose a new pelisse[xxiii]. I think the one you generally wear will not suit at all.'

Agnes blanched, for her pelisse was very old, not very warm and, now she thought of it, of a shade of green that would suit neither of her new gowns. 'Lady Jane was *so* very generous,' she murmured, but with an apologetic air that made clear that Lady Jane's generosity had not extended to a new pelisse.

'But you were to have *new*,' Mr Talbot almost shouted, rising from his seat, adding, in a voice so low she could barely catch his words, 'I was quite specific.'

It suddenly dawned on Miss Trimble that if Lady Jane had been the instrument of the new wardrobe she had not in fact been the instigator of it. It did not take great penetration for her to apprehend that the delivery of the new dresses today, and the advent of Mr Talbot's confidential dialogue, might not be a coincidence.

'You mentioned a matter of a little delicacy?' she prompted.

'Oh yes,' Mr Talbot said, returning to his seat. 'Thank you. You remind me of my purpose. Miss Willow has lived a retired life and it is her own desire, and her mama's, that she should continue to do so. Even though she is to be in London, and it is the season, Miss Willow is not to be brought out, in the fullest sense. Apart from anything else I gather she is of a somewhat delicate sensibility, very shy, self-conscious about her appearance. And so, as much as I am sure Lady Jane would delight in Miss Willow's company, and as charming as it would be to introduce her into society, unfortunately it is a pleasure that must be denied.'

'I take it there is no …' Miss Trimble ventured, imagining the kinds of disfigurement that might prompt a girl to be so ill at ease.

'Georgina's mama has unhappy memories of her own experiences on what she calls the marriage market and she would not have Georgina subjected to it. That is all. However, there is no reason why the young lady should not be encouraged to enjoy *some* of the delights of London. The galleries, the parks, perhaps the theatre, so long as it is accomplished with discretion. None of that will be possible without a chaperone and it's here that I appeal to your kindness. I shall put one of the carriages at your disposal and, if you will allow me, I will provide you with funds.'

The vista of a Spring of enjoyable outings and charming company opened itself in Miss Trimble's mind's eye. A carriage at her disposal, and funds to spend! A young companion eager to be shown the sights! But almost before the scene had quite coalesced, the tread of exasperated feet on the stair and the sound of Lady Jane's carping complaint against some maid dissolved it. Mr Talbot set his jaw. It was clear that he was not quite ready for his wife's appearance.

Miss Trimble had only time to whisper, 'Of course, if Lady Jane can spare me, I shall be delighted. And you may trust me. I shall guard the young lady as though she were my own,' before the lady of the house swept into the room.

Miss Trimble leapt from her seat as though it were on fire, but she did not sacrifice her Madeira, which she carried off to a part of the room more suited to her station.

'Oh *there* you are, Agnes,' Lady Jane said. 'I sent to your room only to be informed that you had already come down. See what a mess the girl has made of my hair? I declare I despair of her! But never mind, it is mended now, as well as it can be. I see you have decided to give one of your new dresses an outing. You did not think the grey more suitable? But it does not matter. Dining at home scarcely warrants getting dressed at all. I almost determined on having a tray sent up to my room. If only you could have given me more notice, George, I could have invited some company. How dull we shall be!'

She waved away a footman with a tray of drinks and surveyed her image in a large mirror that hung over the fireplace. For a woman who had deemed dressing hardly worthwhile she had nonetheless gone to a good deal of trouble. Her gown was voluminous, highly figured, off the shoulder and plunging at the bosom. She wore a rope of gems at her throat. Her hair was parted at both sides, the centre section highly piled and decorated with gems, the rest curled into elaborate ringlets that fell over her ears.

'You are never dull, my dear,' Mr Talbot said chivalrously. 'If you do not wish for an aperitif, let us go down to dinner.' He proffered his arm and his wife took it. Miss Trimble fell into step behind them. 'Miss Trimble has been so kind as to offer to chaperone Georgina,' Mr Talbot said. 'I am so glad, for I would not have you in the least discommoded.'

'That is a relief,' opined Lady Jane, surprising them both, 'for I should not in the least know how to explain her, so rusticated as she must be. Her connexion to you is so very tenuous, and she has no family by which her rank may be inferred. Upon my word, the whole business is so very obscure. Such a veil is drawn over it. One almost doubts of it being quite respectable.'

'There is no question as to Miss Willow's entirely respectable standing,' Mr Talbot said through clenched teeth. 'Her father was a gentleman with a property in Wiltshire. Her mother is my distant cousin …'

'Yes, yes, through the Gilchrists of Spalding. So you tell me. But you may as well claim she is a descendant of Robin Hood! Of St George! Since there is no one to confirm or gainsay it.'

'*I* confirm it,' Mr Talbot said, 'and that is the end of the matter.'

7

The marriage of Jocelyn Willow and Mr Frederick Stockbridge was to take place at the end of April, and George Talbot travelled to Wiltshire in order to attend the bride down the aisle and to carry Georgina back to London with him. He was a frequent traveller around the country and Lady Jane did not at all object to it. She had a large circle of acquaintance; women who shared her delight in intrigue; whose principal entertainment was denigrating ladies not in their circle or, if they were in that sphere, at least not within earshot. She disliked balls in general because they provided few opportunities for the kinds of conversation she preferred—the confidential kind, uncovering misdeeds and scandal—and she was not a natural dancer. Of course she understood that there were some balls it would be injudicious to cut and it happened that whilst George was away in Salisbury just such an occasion was to be held.

The duchess of Sutherland[xxiv] had newly taken possession of Stafford House[xxv], and although the renovations were far from complete she had been unable to deny herself the pleasure of displaying what had been achieved so far by holding a ball. To refuse such an invitation would be tantamount to social suicide and Lady Jane had no intention of committing such an act, quite apart from the fact that she was very eager to see the renovations for herself. On the other hand it was tiresome to attend a ball without a husband. She had not *quite* the nerve to arrive unaccompanied, and, in any case, an escort of some kind was useful for the securing of seats at supper, the arrangement of the carriage and so forth. In this situation Miss Trimble could be of no possible use to her, more of a hindrance than a help; likely to be overcome by heat, trip over her frock or be trampled to death in the polka.

At first Lady Jane had determined to send a note to her sister, Lady Nancy. Nancy's husband, Colonel Wittering, would certainly not attend the ball; he was all but paralysed, slumped in a wheeled chair, his pain only just made bearable by more brandy than was good for him. But his continued connexion with his regiment meant that he could always command the service of a brother officer and it was not at all unusual for Lady Nancy to attend balls—also dinners, the theatre and promenades in the park—squired by quite a handsome colonel by the name of Cockerill. It seemed not unlikely to Lady Jane that where one affable colonel could be procured, so might two, and she had been on the point of dictating a note of enquiry to that effect when a message from her friend Baroness Charlton had been brought in.

It might perhaps be stretching the notion a little too far to refer to Lady Jane and Baroness Charlton as friends. Certainly, they spent a good deal of time in one another's company, and were as complimentary as could be on the topic of one another's gowns, soft furnishings, dinners and children. Neither would hear a word said against the other and yet there was, between them, a fierce rivalry and their acquaintance was barbed. Baroness Charlton had been nobody at all—a plain Miss Toft. The best that could have been claimed for her was that she was a gentleman's daughter, but that gentleman had happened to be a neighbour and friend of Lady Jane's father and so the two girls had necessarily been acquainted. Adelaide Toft's first gambit in superseding Lady Jane had been to marry a baron. To marry *anyone* could arguably have been enough to place her above even the daughter of an earl, if that daughter was unmarried, but to secure the hand of a baron had certainly been a coup. Years had passed during which it had seemed that Lady Jane would never find a match, and Baroness Charlton had lost no opportunity to patronise and condescend, even going so far as to introduce a succession of young men—by turns ugly, effete, barbarous, simpering and dissipated—who 'might do.'

Lady Jane's marriage—at last—had over-topped the baroness, however. A baron was, after all, the very lowest rank of nobleman, and Baron Charlton's title was the most august thing about him. His fortune and property were trifling, his person unremarkable, his mind and manner particularly middling. Mr Talbot, in comparison, was momentous; handsome, personable and very, very rich.

Having married earlier, Adelaide Charlton had naturally preceded Lady Jane in the production of children. This, again, she had claimed as a victory, though the first child had died and the second was sickly. The third, however, a daughter, had thrived and grown up to shoulder the entirety of her parents' hopes, for she had been provided with no younger siblings. The barony would pass to her brother and, since he was frail and prone to illness, would in all probability die out thereafter. But of Gertrude Charlton great things were expected. It seemed cruel to point out—although Lady Jane did find occasion to mention it as often as possible—that, at twenty years of age, the time for Gertrude to shine was surely come, and yet that lustre, that dazzling debut, had so far failed to materialise.

Lady Jane's own children were as yet too young to enter into the nuptial fray. She held them in reserve until they could be sufficiently primed, aimed and fired. She might well have deployed her stepchildren in a vanguard manoeuvre but what she perceived as the disadvantage of their quasi-Indian heritage, and her resentment against them that they would supersede their step-siblings, had caused her to treat them very much as reserves. In any case, Robyn showed not the least inclination to marry and was even older than Gertrude, so there was little to be gained against the baroness by bringing her into play.

The note from the baroness came two days before the ball, on the morning that George had set out towards Salisbury. Lady Jane opened it in her private sitting room. A footman stood in readiness to take any reply to the messenger, who waited on the pavement. Miss Trimble's pen remained poised above her paper to commence the note to Lady Nancy. Lady Jane enjoyed making people wait and so settled herself into her chair and adjusted the lamp before sliding her nail slowly under the seal of the paper.

My dear Lady Jane, I do so hope that Mr Talbot commenced his journey this morning without mishap or delay. For myself, I am sure I have no cause for concern, such a regular and experienced traveller as Mr Talbot is! Upon my word! He seems never to be at home! Of course one cannot help but be a little troubled about the dangers of travel, when one hears of robbers, riots and insurrection, not to mention the possibility of being overturned! My earnest hope is that your husband attains his destination without accident or incident and I have almost no doubt at all of this being so.

I presume you have received your invitation to the Sutherlands' ball. I am sure you have little appetite for it, with your husband away. However I appeal to your good nature, if you can find it in yourself, to assist me. Gertrude is naturally eager to attend, indeed Lord Pokerham has already secured the first two dances, but we have been asked to chaperone in addition a young woman lately come to us from Shropshire, a younger daughter of the earl of Shrewsbury. For this reason, since you have no daughter of your own to chaperone, would you be so kind as to make one of our party? Even I, with my great experience of these things, hardly feel equal to the supervision of two young debutantes.

Come and dine with us beforehand. Would you mind if we used your carriage? Ours will hardly accommodate us all.

Yours etc

Adelaide

Ah! thought Lady Jane. There, at last, was the real reason for the baroness' invitation, the sly minx; she would much rather arrive at Stafford House in the Talbots' splendid carriage than the Charltons', which was vastly inferior. Lady Jane skimmed over the note again. She thought that for someone ostensibly eager to assuage her fears for her husband, the baroness listed a plethora of accidents that might befall. The notion that Lady Jane might decline to attend the ball at all was laughable, and was there not a certain double entendre in that reference to her 'good nature'? She bridled particularly at the jibe about her lack of a daughter to exhibit. Let the baroness just wait until Beatrice was of age! But the baroness' company was certainly to be preferred to Lady Nancy's, and an opportunity to observe at close hand what kind of exhibition Gertrude might make of herself was not to be passed up. Moreover, Lady Jane had heard from other sources that the Shrewsburys' daughter was an ungovernable hussy that no one could handle; she had been passed from family to family for the past six months. It would be well that she should marry and doubtless that was Lady Shewsbury's intention in sending her amongst the premier houses of the country, for a troublesome daughter becomes less bothersome when she becomes a wife. A ball, especially a private ball such as the one Lady Stafford was to hold, was the ideal venue for noble young people to meet and fraternise. One could be assured of the quality of guests at a grand house; there was no danger that a young woman might interact with someone below her station. Respectability was guaranteed whilst, under cover of the music and in the guise of the dance, young people could talk and even touch in ways not permitted elsewhere. In short, a ball was a marriage mart unequalled in any other area of society, and if a mother wanted her daughter to form an attachment she could not do better than send her to as many as possible. How many balls had she herself endured, she considered, in attempting to find some suitable match for Robyn! But it had been to no avail, a humiliation that the baroness had often alluded to. Well, thought Lady Jane, now the baroness would see that it was no easy feat.

This last matter decided her, and she instructed the footman that she would write a reply.

8

The dinner before the ball was as dinners always were at Charlton House, which is to say, the soup was cold, the cold hors d'oeuvres somewhat warm, the fish bony and the meat tough. The baron had been detained and the footman was left to carve and serve, a task he undertook with palpable annoyance, not very ably assisted by an under footman who was scarcely more than a boy, no doubt brought in at the last minute, hustled into a spare livery and told on no account to wipe his nose on the back of his hand. Lady Jane behaved as charmingly as possible throughout, whilst the baroness threw looks like daggers at her husband's empty seat and upbraided the servants for every slip and mishap.

'I cannot think what could have kept the baron,' said Adelaide Charlton attempting to garner some prestige from her husband's rudeness. 'It must be a matter of great moment at the House. I do not quite recall the subject of today's debate.' She turned a specious smile on her friend. 'How glad *you* must be, Lady Jane, that Mr Talbot is not in parliament.'

'He has no political ambition,' Lady Jane replied. 'If I recall his words accurately he describes politicians as self-serving sycophants ill-qualified for any other occupation. I will admit that his business occupies more time than politics, but is *much* more rewarding and he, at least, never fears losing a vote.'

'Is Mr Talbot in business?' asked Lady Virginia, with ever-so-slight a curl of her lip.

Lady Jane inclined her head an iota of a degree to imply the affirmative before bending her gaze to the young woman who sat next to her at the table.

Lady Virginia Shrewsbury was of a diminutive stature, not much more than five foot, and so Lady Jane was able to look down on her in every way. The girl was of a rather pleasing plumpness, pretty, with a good complexion and dark blue eyes, and hair a lovely shade of golden blonde. Her features were regular, her teeth good, and all taken together she presented a comely picture. She was a very confident, forward young lady, almost pert, not at all dismayed by finding herself in yet another strange household. There was a light of mischief in her eye and a coquettish set to her head and her laugh was of a particularly infectious burbling type. It was easy to imagine her creating the kind of rumpus that had been reported in Brighton and elsewhere.

Beside Virginia Shrewsbury, Gertrude Charlton bore no flattering comparison. She was tall and cadaverously thin, with a sharp beak of a nose and eyes of a disconcerting paleness. Her lips were drawn over slightly protuberant teeth, her chin almost lost in the long column of her neck. Gertrude was a nice girl—there was no gainsaying that—and was doing her best to make their guest at home.

'Mr Talbot has many ships, Virginia. He brings ever so many things from India and the Indies and from America. I daresay this very table cloth was brought by him,' she gushed.

'I doubt it,' her mother remarked. 'It is fine Irish linen and has been in your father's family for generations.'

'Oh,' Gertrude looked for a moment abashed, but forged on. 'Not the table cloth, then. But he had medicine for Ernest brought from India. A sort of plant[xxvi]. Nanny crushes the leaves to make tea, or sometimes they are smouldered to infuse the air. He finds it most efficacious. Mr Talbot is a kind man, Virginia. I like him very much.'

The sickly son—Ernest—had been left in the country where the air was less disagreeable, even if thick with the aroma of burning hemp, so the four ladies were without any gentleman at dinner. Consequently the talk could be of a more confidential tone—as it often is, between women— than it would have been. The necessary requisites for a lady's reticule took up the soup and the hors d'oeuvres. There appeared to be a good deal that a lady could not do without: a fan, a coin purse, a *vinaigrette*[xxvii], a needle and thread, spare ribbon, a *perfume étuis*[xxviii], a pencil and a handkerchief.

'Mama, you will have to take charge of my reticule,' said Gertrude. 'I shall never manage to dance with it hanging from my arm.'

'I rather doubt we will not need one of the grooms,' suggested Lady Virginia with a mischievous smile. 'After all, our chaperones will have their own things to manage; in addition to our wraps and all their own essential things they will need their spectacles and pills for dyspepsia.'

'Mrs Orme carries an ear trumpet!' Gertrude replied, smothering a giggle.

'Girls,' said the baroness, 'let us not be silly. But of course we will take charge of your belongings.'

'I shall keep hold of my own, if you do not mind,' Lady Virginia said. 'In such a crowd as there is likely to be, we may become separated.'

'*That* I shall certainly not allow,' said Lady Jane. 'What is the purpose of a chaperone if she is to be so easily shaken off?'

'Gentlemen do sweep one along so,' Lady Virginia murmured. 'In Brighton it was quite usual to begin at the Assembly and to end on the sands. They have entertainments there, you know. Jugglers and men on stilts …'

'I have been to Brighton many times,' said Lady Jane, 'and I can assure you that no juggler, be he ever so agile, ever managed to draw *me* from the path of propriety.'

'No,' agreed Lady Virginia, casting her eyes downwards, 'I do not suppose so.'

Then Lady Jane said, as though she had no more than a passing interest in the subject, 'So Lady Virginia, you have been the guest of the dowager Duchess Staveley, I think? How is she? I have not seen her in town this season.'

'No,' the young woman agreed. 'She does not like to come to town but she purports to like the company of young people. My step-mama hoped I might be of some use to her, and that the country air of her estate in Derbyshire would be beneficial for me. I am sorry that, in both, my step-mama was disappointed.'

'Staveley Court is rather remote, is it not?' Lady Jane asked. The beef had been served by this time and they all sawed at it fruitlessly with their knives.

'Very remote. There is not a farmhouse or a cottage within ten miles of the place. I rode a great deal, in company with one of the grooms. I can vouch for the area's utter desolation. One day we got disorientated in a thick mist that came down. My horse stumbled and sustained an injury. We had to shelter in a tumbledown byre and it was many hours before we were found.'

'The groom was dismissed, I understand,' the baroness said, 'and quite right too. What was he thinking of?'

'I wonder,' murmured Lady Jane ironically.

'Oh,' Lady Virginia put her head to one side and chewed distractedly, a little smile on her lips. 'I am not sure. But it was the duchess' opinion that I would be less in harm's way elsewhere.'

'You can be sure we will have no mishap of that kind here,' the baroness said firmly. 'The season is at its height, and there will be plenty to entertain you, but I shall not allow you to stray from my sight.'

'Thank you,' Lady Virginia replied, but with an expression that suggested the prospect was not a happy one. She laid down her knife and fork. 'Do forgive me. I find I am not very hungry.'

'Neither am I,' declared Gertrude, laying aside her own cutlery. 'I am too excited for the ball. Shall we go and dress, Virginia? Mama? May we be excused?'

Lady Jane and her hostess retired to the drawing room, a small room cluttered with Charlton family heirlooms—dull, frowning oil paintings, rusty weaponry, a moth-eaten tiger-skin rug and the baron's prized collection of snuff boxes.

'It is interesting, and coincidental, Adelaide, that you have been asked to take Lady Virginia under your wing at just this time,' said Lady Jane from her seat on a low, under-stuffed settee.

'Oh yes?'

'Yes, for I myself am to take custody of a young ward also. For myself, I am fully cognisant of the reasons why she is to come to us. Her mama— a widow—is to be re-married and it seems the girl cannot be left at home alone. But,' she leaned forward confidentially, and lowered her voice to a conspiratorial whisper, 'Lady Virginia? I must own, it seems somewhat odd to me that she should be put at your door. There is no relation between you, that I know of? And, forgive me if I am misinformed, but has she not, in addition to the dowager Duchess, also been the guest of Marchioness Kirkpatrick, Countess Norton-Fitzwarren and also the Viscountess Rillington?[xxix]'

'Yes,' said the baroness, not meeting her friend's eyes. 'Such a popular young woman. She is wanted everywhere!'

'But nowhere for very long, it seems,' Lady Jane observed dryly, sitting back. Clearly, a more direct approach was going to be required. 'Why cannot she go home?'

The baroness' eyes glittered. She was, of course, as eager to impart tittle-tattle as Lady Jane was to hear it. 'I gather there has been a little family friction,' she admitted. 'Her papa has lately remarried, you recall.'

'Virginia and the new Countess of Shrewsbury do not get on? How distressing.'

The baroness lowered her voice although there was not the smallest possibility of their being overheard. 'I think there was some entanglement with her ladyship's existing children from her first marriage, in particular her oldest son.'

'Oh,' Lady Jane said slowly, as though enjoying a particularly delicious sweetmeat. 'A romantic entanglement. But I wonder what the nature of the difficulty could be? If both are of age, and they are attached, why should they not be engaged? There is no blood tie to prevent it.'

'I cannot say,' said the baroness, again speaking very low. 'I do not know the nature of it, only that there *was* a strong objection and it was thought better that there be some separation for the time being. It is my understanding that the Shrewsburys will not be in town this year, for that reason.'

'Is that so? What a sacrifice! Surely the young marquis[xxx] will wish to be in town?'

'The marquis might, but his new step-brother will not, I have been assured, though he is a man in his majority and one would expect him to do as he pleased.'

'Poor girl,' Lady Jane mused. 'It seems harsh that *she* should be sent away whilst the interloping family remains at her family seat. How old is she?'

'She is not yet eighteen.'

'My ward is twenty-three.'

'And not yet married?' Adelaide cried, aghast. 'Is there something wrong with her?'

Lady Jane shrugged. 'I can gather but little from George. I know her mother has very radical ideas on other topics; it may be the girl is overly opinionated. But I am assured that she will be no inconvenience. She is not to go into society.'

'Not go into society? But she is out?'

'I do not think so.'

Adelaide shook her head. 'Depend upon it, Lady Jane, she must be ugly, or deformed, or simple,' she declared with a kind of relish. 'Lady Virginia may be a little wayward, but she is not dim-witted.'

'No indeed, and in fact she is rather pretty, is she not? How nice for Gertrude to have an attractive friend. Georgina Willow arrives on Sunday, so I will soon be able to see what's wrong with her.'

The baroness considered for a moment. 'Willow is not a name that is familiar to me. Where do they reside?'

'In Wiltshire, up to now. But I do not think they will continue there. The mother was a Gilchrist, but that, too, seems to be a connexion too obscure to be made out. Ah! Here are the young ladies. Is it time to have the carriage brought round?'

9

Stafford House was located in the vicinity of St James' Palace, a very superior district. The house was splendid, constructed from Bath stone, in a neo-classical style very much aping—or, some said, being aped by—Buckingham Palace, which was also, just then, undergoing thorough extension and refurbishment[xxxi]. Stafford House had a covered entrance for carriages topped by a magnificent colonnaded portico. The carriageway was busy with vehicles bringing guests, turning and going off again. Many people, tired of the delay, decanted themselves on the drive and wove through the horses to the door, but the Talbots' grooms knew their business and got the ladies safely under the canopy right to the steps, so the party arrived in style.

All was crush and chaos in the magnificent Grand Hall as ladies arranged their dresses and gentlemen hovered, ready to escort them upstairs. The staircase was grand indeed, a dramatic sweep, decorated in the rococo style with scrolling curves, plentiful gilding, sculpted mouldings and trompe-l'œil frescoes. The girls and their chaperones looked around them in awe as they rose to the *piano nobile*[xxxii] where their host and hostess awaited. From being rather torpid, Lady Virginia became extremely animated now the ball was at hand, and her excitement infected Gertrude.

'Oh, mama,' she said, as they mounted the staircase, 'I think I shall faint. I am sure I shall not remember the steps of the dances. I am sure to stumble or to turn wrong.'

'Your partner will guide you,' the baroness soothed. 'Put yourself in his hands.'

'I shall do likewise,' said Lady Virginia, dimpling her cheek, 'so long as my partner is to my liking.'

Lady Jane took the opportunity to survey the other guests, especially the women, her eye avid for any suggestion of indiscretion; over- or under-dressing, too few or too many jewels, the appearance of paint. 'Lady Poppleton is gaining weight,' she observed. 'She has only been married three months. It is too soon for any sign … unless … Look at General Siddick! His bride cannot be more than half his age, poor girl. How pale she looks! The Billing girls are over-trimmed, are they not? A want of taste, in my opinion, but their mama lets them get away with everything. There is Countess Finchley, with her beau, and she only a month out of mourning. They say he took a house not two miles from Finchley Court and was seen walking across every day. Poor old Finchley! His estate can hardly be settled as yet.'

At last they were announced, but only the briefest of sentences could be uttered with Lord and Lady Stafford before the two girls urged their party into the ballroom.

The ballroom was already busy, and Lady Jane and the baroness had some difficulty securing themselves seats in the periphery. Their charges were instructed to stay close by but Lady Virginia was almost immediately surrounded by gentlemen eager to engage her as a partner and she was good enough to pass those she could not oblige on to her friend. Lady Jane watched her charge closely, but apart from displaying an avid, almost expectant, interest in the other guests she said or did nothing that could require the least censure.

Lady Jane allowed her eye to skim the rest of the company. Really, she thought to herself, the season was devoid of remarkable beauty this year. None of the debutantes was particularly attractive—too fat or too thin, heavy-browed, freckled, wanting poise. Perhaps Lady Virginia *would* find herself a husband, for she was certainly the prettiest girl on view. The girls from previous seasons, like Gertrude, were marked as passed-over, left behind from the year of their own *entrées*. What man would want what had been dismissed by others before him? As always there were more ladies than gentlemen. It was assumed that more men would arrive later, from clubs and private dinners. The politeness of those who had arrived promptly counted against them; they were too eager, too *desperate*.

Around the periphery of the ballroom chaperones and sharp-eyed mamas inspected the marriageable men and unspoken-for girls like cooks at a market, looking for something worth taking from the unpromising goods on display. But in truth all the company was eclipsed by the splendour of their surroundings. The ballroom was magnificent—high-ceilinged, richly decorated with frescoes, chandeliers aglitter with gas lighting. Elegant curtains, beautifully embroidered and fringed with tassels, framed each long window. The parquet floor had been polished until it shone like a mirror.

Lord Pokerham, Gertrude's first partner, soon presented himself, but he did so with a great deal of hesitancy and with many a glance over his shoulder to where his august mama stood sternly observing him. He bowed stiffly and mumbled some rehearsed compliment about the beauty of Gertrude's dress before standing by to take her to the set when the first dance should be announced. She took little notice of him, however, and it was left to the baroness to occupy him with conversation whilst the girls filled their cards and craned their necks to see above the crowd.

The baroness introduced the viscount to her companion as 'the son of my dear friend, Countess Sotherton,' and Lady Jane inspected him narrowly. She could hardly smother her smile, for the young man was as tall, angular and chinless as his dance partner, with prematurely thinning hair, buck teeth and a high, reedy voice. After the initial obligatory greetings he had little to say, so Lady Jane suggested he make himself useful by arranging their seats for supper.

'Of course,' he said, and lurched off in search of a waiter.

'An excellent suggestion,' said the baroness, 'for then, of course, he will be able to take Gertrude in.'

'I am sure it is what he desires above all things,' Lady Jane replied. 'You are hopeful of a match?'

'*Very* hopeful,' her friend confirmed. 'The countess and I are of one mind on the matter. He is not perhaps of the most prepossessing appearance and he is somewhat shy, but Gertrude does not require to be dazzled by good looks, and a gentle-mannered person such as he will be better for her than a dominant personality. For the countess' part, she is anxious to secure a match outside the usual circle, for there have been, in their family, some alliances that have been a little near.'

'Near?'

'Well, the earl is her cousin on both sides, and that isn't the only example in their family tree.'

'I see. How extraordinary.'

'But not uncommon amongst the higher echelons. The countess has a number of daughters. It seems not unlikely to me that one of them might attach themselves to Ernest, if we can only establish the connexion through Gertrude.'

'Is that so?'

'Oh yes,' the baroness replied very complacently. 'We noble families do prefer to marry amongst ourselves if we can.'

Lady Jane winced at the jibe, but parried it with, 'The Sothertons certainly seem to. Oh look. The set is forming.'

'Yes indeed,' said the baroness, 'and here comes Lord Pokerham to claim Gertrude. She looks well tonight does she not? That colour suits her I think. Madame Le Favre procured the silk especially. It is not every girl who can carry such a colour.'

'I should think not.' Gertrude's dress, though fine silk, was yellowish green, the colour of an over-ripe olive. 'How would you describe it?'

'I think Madame Le Favre called it *opaque couche*[xxxiii].'

'It is singular.'

Having reserved their seats by the draping of wraps the ladies took a turn around the room, greeting acquaintance and ready to decline any invitations to dance, should they be forthcoming, which they were not. Lady Jane spied her sister, half-way down the set, partnered by Colonel Cockerill, and they exchanged nods, but no more.

At the end of the room, hard by a French window, stood Amory Balfour. He stood alone, looking over the heads of the crowd, making no attempt to converse and seeming in no hurry to select a dance partner. He looked extremely handsome, his coat expertly tailored, his waistcoat rich with silken embroidery.

'Good evening Lady Jane,' he bent himself sufficiently to say. 'I hope I find you well. Is your husband here?'

'No, he is from home at present. I am here with Baroness Charlton. I do not think you have been introduced. Baroness, this is Mr Balfour, a business associate of Mr Talbot.'

Mr Balfour bowed. 'Charmed,' he said and then, looking over to where Gertrude and Lady Virginia were stationed in the set, added, 'I presume one of those young ladies is the cousin Mr Talbot mentioned?'

'Oh no,' Lady Jane said. '*She* is not to come for two or three days. And I do not believe she will be seen at such an occasion as this. My understanding is that she is rustic, and not fitted for society.'

'My mistake, ma'am,' said Mr Balfour. He bowed again, and moved away.

'What a disagreeable man,' shouted Baroness Charlton above the hubbub of music and conversation. 'I have never seen such an arrogant air. He makes no attempt to dance. Such rudeness! And, I do not know why it is, but I cannot bring myself to like such a man. One wonders … can he be …? Well, he cannot be quite like *us.*'

'I know what you mean,' Lady Jane agreed, 'but Mr Talbot likes him. He has dined with us and I found him unexceptionable.'

At last Baron Charlton found them. He was profuse, but a little slurred, in his apologies for having missed dinner. He was a rotundly built man with heavy jowls and greying hair scraped across a balding dome. His eyes were bleary and his demeanour unnaturally expansive although his conversation—as always—was truncated, delivered in clauses, more like military communiqués than discourse.

'Matters at the House,' he explained to Lady Jane, waving an arm in a gesture meant to suggest concerns of global moment beyond her ken. 'Interminable debate. Bishop of Bath spoke for two hours. Impossible to get away.' Turning to his wife he became lugubrious. 'Dear Adelaide,' he said, taking her hand. 'How charming you look.'

'Matters at the House?' she hissed, snatching her hand away. 'Matters at the club, more likely. Really, Archibald. I'm ashamed of you. Why come at all if you must come like this?'

'Came as quick as I could,' he said sulkily. 'Wanted to see Gertrude. Where is she? Did she save her old papa a dance?' He looked vaguely over his shoulder. 'Brought a few fellows with me. Where have they got to? I knew Sutherland wouldn't mind. Excellent fellow. Must introduce them.'

'Fellows from the House?' enquired Lady Jane with a smirk.

'Oh no, fellows from the …' the baron began, before seeing her trap. 'Ah! See what you did there! Clever of you Lady Jane. Ah ha! Yes! Very quick.'

The set ended and the girls were brought back, and just at that moment they were joined by the baron's friends. Five or six gentlemen shambled into their purlieu in states as poor or worse than the baron. They were flushed with wine, their dress askew. Their noisy repartee and unruly behaviour drew the attention of everyone in the vicinity.

'Shocking,' said one matron.

'I wonder they were admitted,' said another.

Lady Virginia, flushed anyway from the exertions of the dance, glowed even more brilliantly at this augmentation to their party.

'I say,' hooted one of the cohort, a tall man with blond hair, a hooked nose and a monocle, 'what splendid young ladies. Do introduce us, Charlton. Who's the pretty little one? She's the pick of the pair. The other looks …'

It was clear that a derogatory comment was on the tip of his tongue. Gertrude blushed, and took a step away from them, towards her mama, but Lady Virginia looked eagerly at the new-comers, quite basking in their admiration even if it had come at her friend's expense.

'That's Lady Virginia Shrewsbury,' the baroness said quickly, but in an acid tone. 'I do not think I have had the honour of being introduced to *you*, sir.'

'That's Lord Perry,' the baron said. 'Splendid fellow.'

'Lady Virginia?' said Lord Perry, screwing his monocle more firmly into place. 'Isn't she the one who got caught *in flagrante* in Brighton?'

At this Lady Virginia did have the decency to look abashed, but Perry's companion, a younger, rather ruggedly-built man, said, 'I say, Perry. *That's* no way to speak of a lady,' and her shame was erased in a dazzling smile.

'This is Johnny Rex,' said the baron. 'New in town. Never met the fellow before but Perry says he's sound.'

Rex seized Lady Virginia. 'May I have the pleasure? Perry, you can take the other.'

Lady Virginia, nothing loath, followed her partner to the set.

'Something of a booby prize,' Lord Perry muttered, but took Gertrude's arm.

'I'm engaged to dance this with Captain Brimming,' protested Gertrude, fending off Lord Perry.

'Oh, he won't mind,' said Lord Perry, grasping her more firmly and pulling her onto the floor where the next set was forming.

Captain Brimming clearly *did* mind. He stalked away in a very offended manner. Lord Pokerham, who had been promised the next dance by Virginia, scuttled back to his mama. The baron and the rest of his party retreated to the card room and were not seen again.

The baroness could only look on in horror as her charges were pushed and manhandled in the Scotch reel. Gertrude, dishevelled and dizzy from being whirled at great velocity by her partner, looked as unhappy as possible. Lady Virginia was less discomposed, seeming indeed to be rather enjoying the rough-and-tumble energy of Mr Rex's performance. She threw herself into the dance, and into her partner's arms, as they spun down the set.

'We must intervene, Adelaide,' said Lady Jane. 'The girls are being made a spectacle.'

'But *how?*' wailed the baroness, rummaging in her reticule for her vinaigrette. 'Oh! I think I shall swoon.'

'Nonsense,' said Lady Jane, but pressing her back onto one of the chairs. 'Sit here. I will find you some wine, and see what can be done for the girls.'

She bustled away, pushing through the crowds, and in her search for a waiter came across her sister Lady Nancy, and Colonel Cockerill. She spoke a word to him, and gestured towards Gertrude and Virginia.

Gertrude's hair had become disarranged and her dress was torn but mercifully nobody was taking particular notice of her; Virginia and Rex were quite the focal point of every eye–a shocking aberration of proper deportment as they leapt and laughed in gay abandon.

By the time Lady Jane returned to the baroness with a glass of wine, Lord Perry and Mr Rex had been removed from the set by four bewigged footmen, and their places taken by two officers of Colonel Cockerill's acquaintance. One of them was Captain Brimming, who seemed mollified to have ended the set with Gertrude, even if he had not begun it. He was a pleasant looking fellow, not handsome, but with kind grey eyes and a shock of sandy-coloured hair. Gertrude had quickly recovered her composure, her expression all relief and gratitude.

'A timely rescue, sir,' said the baroness, somewhat stiffly in the circumstances, when the captain returned Gertrude to her side.

'Oh yes,' gushed Gertrude. 'Thank you so much Captain.'

'My great pleasure ma'am,' said the captain with an elegant bow. His friend had melted into the crowd. 'Supper will be served after the next set, I believe. May I escort Miss Charlton?'

Gertrude seemed to welcome this offer but her mother said, 'You may escort Lady Virginia. Miss Charlton is engaged to sup with Lord Pokerham.'

Captain Brimming looked disappointed, but bowed gracefully to Lady Virginia. 'Honoured,' he murmured.

Lady Virginia replied with a smile that did not reach her eyes.

'Gertrude, dear,' said the baroness, 'let us go and find an antechamber where we might repair your coiffeur and see what can be done about your frock. The hem is down at the back. Thank heavens I have a needle and thread in my reticule. Lady Virginia, I think you should sit the next dance out. You look rather flushed.'

'Yes ma'am,' said the young woman ungraciously, dropping into her seat with sullen pique.

The baroness and her daughter disappeared into the crush, leaving Lady Jane and her charge alone.

'You do not wish to be taken into supper by the captain?' Lady Jane enquired above the noise of the ballroom

'I do not see why my partner had to be removed. He was vastly entertaining company, I must say. I said he could call on me tomorrow.'

'That was precipitate of you. We do not know his situation.'

'No,' Lady Virginia said, but in a tone which suggested that this was not quite true. 'But he is an acquaintance of the baron. Surely *that* suffices?'

'Not necessarily. I heard the baron say he has only just met the man. He could be anyone.'

Lady Virginia turned a defiant face. 'I do not care,' she said.

'You *should* care. Your behaviour in the dance was outrageous. People were aghast to see you disporting in such an unseemly manner. Really, young lady, you must learn to be a better judge of character. Those gentlemen were inebriated and behaved very rudely. It was quite wrong to allow their behaviour to be the guide of your own.'

'The baroness *said* that we should trust ourselves to our partners,' Lady Virginia retorted.

'She assumed you would be dancing with gentlemen.'

'Mr Rex *is* a gentleman!'

'I hardly think so, after that exhibition. You must apologise to Lord Pokerham. You were to have danced with him, were you not?'

Lady Virginia folded her arms and looked insolent. 'Why should I apologise? It was not my fault that Mr Rex would not be refused. Indeed,' she added wistfully, 'I rather like a man who brooks no refusal. I like a man who knows his own mind and will not be turned from it.'

'You made no effort to refuse him! If you will not apologise on your own account you should do so for Miss Charlton. Lord Pokerham is her particular friend.'

'Oh, she doesn't care about *him*,' Lady Virginia countered. 'It's the captain she likes. But he's only a second son and will get little, so the baroness has vetoed the match.'

'Is that so?' mused Lady Jane, storing away this information. 'Because he is not titled?'

'Because he has no money.'

'Ah. With whom were you to have danced this next?'

Lady Virginia consulted her card. 'A Mr Binsley. I know his sister slightly. Their father is Sir Gabriel Binsley.'

'I am acquainted with the Binsleys. Their country estate neighbours ours. I shall make your excuses. Indeed, I am quite of the mind that we shall go home after supper, for I believe Gertrude to have suffered a great deal at the hands of Lord Perry before the captain came to her aid, and *your* behaviour has left much to be desired.'

Lady Virginia turned an anxious face to her and for the first time Lady Jane believed her words to be heartfelt. 'Oh do not, Lady Jane,' she implored. 'I am not at all tired and am quite ready to stand up with Mr Binsley as soon as he presents himself. What, after all, is the point of a ball if it is not to allow ladies and gentlemen to meet one another? The dance floor is a market, as surely as the auction ring, isn't it?'

'You have a rather commercial view of it, Lady Virginia,' Lady Jane mused, but she could not disagree.

'So do let me dance again,' Lady Virginia urged. 'Afterwards, I promise you, I will go in to supper with Captain Brimming and be as charming as you like. I ... I am sorry that I misbehaved before.'

Lady Jane considered, but then relented. 'Very well. If you are quite recovered from the reel, and if you will behave in a decorous manner, you may dance the next set.'

10

It could be that Lady Stafford had been over-generous with her invitations, or that a host of people—like Baron Charlton's friends—had gained admittance without invitations. Whichever it was, the ballroom and then the supper room were choked with guests. Ladies were crushed up against one another. Waiters bearing trays could hardly penetrate the crowds. Gentlemen, made jocular with wine formed a scrum around the buffet. There were insufficient places at table, forcing people to collect food from the buffet and eat it standing, squashed into window alcoves or out on the galleried landing. The buffet was soon devastated, delicate pastries strewn asunder, the poached salmons reduced to their skeletal remains. The carving knife had disappeared and a Hussar drew his sword to tackle the cold roast. He did it partly in jest but a nervy lady screamed, causing panic. Although the orchestra had laid down their instruments the hubbub of conversation was almost deafening. The air was filled with noise, the heat was intense and a young woman fainted.

Lord Pokerham's waiter had not failed in his duty, however, and the viscount handed Gertrude and her party to a place at the bottom of one of the long tables where a slightly open window gave welcome fresh air.

Captain Brimming managed to get himself between Gertrude and Lady Virginia leaving Lord Pokerham to content himself with a place on the opposite side with the baroness and Lady Jane. Their waiter did his best to serve them with the choicest of what was available and procured in addition a bottle of champagne.

Lady Jane found she was surprisingly hungry, and applied herself to her plate before being at leisure to observe, 'I do not see our hostess. I have not exchanged two sentences with her. One would not wish to neglect one's duty.'

'She is in another room,' Lord Pokerham replied. 'There was a separate supper laid out for the Staffords and some few selected guests. Mama is there. I was invited also, of course, but I would rather be here with Miss Charlton.'

'That's very gallant of you,' the baroness said, throwing Gertrude a significant look.

'Yes,' Gertrude said, but thinly. 'Thank you Lord Pokerham.'

Lady Jane sniffed. 'It is not gratifying to find one has been passed over,' she said. 'I am sure, if you girls had not been in such a hurry, we might have been invited to sup with the Staffords. But there was not time for the duchess to mention it before you hurried us away.'

'I think this is preferable,' said Gertrude, beaming, as Captain Brimming filled her glass.

Lady Virginia, who had found Mr Binsley on her other side, was clearly of Gertrude's opinion; she was wreathed in smiles, her head bent close to her neighbour as he whispered some joke.

'I think this is a bear-pit,' Lady Jane carped. 'I never was more crushed in my life. I am sure you girls find the dancing is impeded by the crowds, do you not?'

But neither Gertrude nor Lady Virginia would accede to any such notion; both declared the ball to be excellent in every way.

'And it is my opinion,' said Lady Virginia, 'that we have yet to enjoy the best of it.'

After supper both young ladies expressed a desire for air. Their wraps were brought and Lord Pokerham and Captain Brimming were permitted to take them through one of the sets of tall, glazed doors to a veranda that looked out over the gardens of Stafford House. It extended almost the whole length of the house, past the supper room and the ballroom, supported below by dozens of ornately carved stone columns. Braziers burned along its length.

'At least they cannot get into the gardens from there,' the baroness said, fanning herself. 'Who knows what dangers may lurk in the shaded walks?'

'I would not put it past Lady Virginia to climb over the parapet and shimmy down one of the columns,' Lady Jane observed. 'She is certainly a very spirited young woman. She did not seem in the least discomposed by that incident earlier.'

'No,' her friend agreed. 'She seems to court adventure.'

'I think she has invited Mr Rex to call on her.'

The baroness rolled her eyes. 'Oh dear. Well, that cannot be permitted.'

'Of course not. But the captain seems a very amiable fellow. He is known to Colonel Cockerill. That must be a recommendation.'

But the baroness shook her head. 'I am afraid that, too, is a connexion that must be discouraged. He has nothing to offer.'

The ladies had returned to their seats in the ballroom, which was now quieter, the majority of guests still attempting to garner something from the wilted salads and pooling blancmanges in the supper room, and many more having indeed found their way downstairs to the gardens. The orchestra lounged on the dais, waiting until it should be time to take up their instruments once more. A few waiters collected discarded glasses.

'Upon my word,' said Lady Jane, 'I am beginning to be very pleased that Georgina Willow will require no entrée, for it would exhaust me to be forced to attend occasions like this every evening.'

The guests began to reassemble and the orchestra reconvened themselves on the dais. The girls returned refreshed from their time out of doors.

'Such fun,' Lady Virginia declared. 'The gardens below us were full of people promenading. We could see it all! I think the whole of society must be here! One man walked around the parapet of the fountain but fell in at the last. A lady got her skirt caught on a rose bush ...'

'Did you find it amusing Gertrude, dear?' asked the baroness, interrupting Lady Virginia's flow. 'Was Lord Pokerham attentive?'

'Yes,' Gertrude replied. 'Attentive, but not very loquacious. I do not think he spoke two sentences in all the time we were on the veranda.'

'He is not talkative, as others are,' said her mother, casting a glance at where Lady Virginia rummaged in her reticule. 'Is something amiss, Lady Virginia?'

'I cannot find my handkerchief. I had it outside. Let me run back. I may have dropped it.'

'Do not be long,' called Lady Jane. 'The set is forming.'

Just then the Duke and Duchess of Stafford were seen to be approaching, touring the ballroom in order to converse with their guests. The usual pleasantries were exchanged, Lady Jane and the baroness expressing themselves as delighted to have been invited, and declaring the ball to be the occasion of the season so far. The duke spoke at length about the mouldings on the ballroom ceiling and the particular difficulties of incorporating so much gas lighting. The duchess divulged that the curtains had cost so many hundreds of pounds that she had quite lost count of them. Gertrude went off to the set with a small, rotund colonel a head shorter than she was as the host and hostess moved off, but Lady Jane's attention was then taken by the countess of

Sotherton who came across the room so that she and the baroness could congratulate themselves on the success of the evening so far.

'I do believe Pokerham is on the point of proposal,' the countess confided. 'He was surprised at the strength of his objection to Lord Perry's interference.'

'As unpleasant as that incident *was* for poor Gertrude,' the baroness put in, 'I cannot think but that it did the viscount's suit a great deal of good. For to be so roughly handled by one man cannot but reflect on the gentleness and decorum of another.'

'I hope,' said the countess rather stiffly, 'that neither Pokerham's person nor his suit needs much to recommend it. He is rather superior to anything else that might offer, I think.'

'Oh indeed he *is*,' the baroness gushed. 'Archibald and I never thought to look so high when we contemplated the kind of gentle-tempered man who might suit our delicate flower.'

'Pokerham *is* gentle-tempered,' said the countess, mollified, 'but I will go so far as to say that he is not at his best in a ballroom. He prefers the quiet of home; a library is his ideal milieu. I think, when you visit us at Sotherton—which I hope you *will* do, when things are settled—you will see quite a different side to him. Is Gertrude a great reader?'

'Not a *great* reader, thus far,' the baroness prevaricated, 'but then our library is poor at Charlton. She has not had the opportunity.'

The countess seemed satisfied, and presently returned to her party. Lady Jane turned her attention to Lady Binsley, her neighbour at Ecklington, who just then passed by.

'Oh Lady Binsley,' said Lady Jane. 'How delightful to see you. It is not often that you come up to town, I think?'

Lady Binsley agreed to this observation. 'We would not have been here, but that Sir Gabriel has an exhibition of his paintings. He is an artist, you know, quite well received.'

'Yes, of course,' said Lady Jane, who now recalled a number of daubings on the walls of Binsley Park that had been attributed to its owner. 'What a happy coincidence then. We supped with your son. A delightful young man.'

'Thank you. But he is headstrong, like his uncle Edward. You may not know, but Gabriel's elder brother was killed in a riding accident. That was many years ago now, just after Mr Talbot and his father went to India.'

Lady Jane, spying an opportunity, said, 'George does not often speak of that time. You knew his mama, I presume? She was a Gilchrist, I think, from Spalding? I suppose she often had her people at Ecklington, especially after the late Mr Talbot went abroad.'

Lady Binsley narrowed one eye. 'I am not sure I quite recall,' she said. 'Why do you ask?'

'No reason in the world,' said Lady Jane airily. 'It is only that we are to have a distant relative of that line to stay with us. Miss Willow. Her mama is connected via the Gilchrists. Jocelyn. Perhaps you recall her?'

Lady Binsley pretended to consider. That she was pretending was patently obvious to Lady Jane; Lady Binsley had no facility for subterfuge.

'No,' said Lady Binsley with a regretful smile. 'I am sorry I do not recall. Excuse me, I must find Lysander.'

Lady Jane watched her go, her determination to fathom the web of intrigue that surrounded Jocelyn Willow and her daughter not one whit reduced.

It was only at this point that Lady Jane realised Lady Virginia had not returned to them.

'Where can she have got to?' Lady Jane said, looking at the dancers to see if she could spy her charge. 'I suppose it is possible that she went straight into the set.'

'Not with her wrap,' cried the baroness. 'Look! It is missing, and I recall she still had it about her shoulders when she went in search of her handkerchief.'

'Oh, the minx,' said Lady Jane. 'She has given us the slip after all. You remain here, Adelaide. We cannot leave Gertrude unchaperoned. I shall go in search of Lady Virginia.'

The long veranda was peopled by several groups of guests, but Lady Virginia was not amongst them. Lady Jane walked the length of it twice but her quarry was not to be seen. On her second tour she spied Mr Balfour, who stood sentinel by one of the glazed doors, half in and half out of the ballroom.

'May I assist you with anything, Lady Jane?' he enquired.

'Oh, Mr Balfour.' Lady Jane hesitated, for it would be beneficial to have an aide in her search. The gardens, for example, would be beyond her scope. She cast an eye over the balustrade at the smooth, extensive lawn below, and the shadowed gravel walks beyond. Even though the dancing had recommenced, the outdoor precincts of Stafford House were still thronged with people sauntering about and she would not put it past Lady Virginia to have gone down there to join acquaintances. But it was difficult to admit to having lost her charge. Her own reputation would be damaged. Lady Virginia's of course—unless there was a very convincing explanation for her disappearance—was lost beyond saving. If only Baron Charlton were less incompetent, or her own George were here. He was not a man to desert his wife at a ball, and he had that ability to organise others in a way that was efficient but discreet. If he had been here, Lady Jane was persuaded, he would enlist the help of his friend, so she quickly explained to Mr Balfour the nature of her difficulty.

'If you would be so good as to search outdoors,' she suggested, but he was already half way through the doors to the main stairway.

For her part, Lady Jane made a careful tour of the ballroom and the supper room. This latter venue was deserted now, with only the waiters clearing away debris of the repast. The galleried landing was busy but mainly with gentlemen who spilled from the cardroom. They smoked cigars and discussed their horses. She visited the anteroom provided for the ladies to relieve themselves, but found only a young woman in tears perched on a stool before a large mirror, her consoling mama, and a disconsolate maid whose job it was to empty the pots. All this time Lady Jane's concern was mounting—and her anger also, for had not Lady Virginia been strictly instructed to remain close at hand? What could the girl be thinking, to disappear without explanation? Did she not know she was already so far compromised that any further shadow of impropriety would cripple her?

The baroness remained at their place in the ballroom, her eye constantly upon Gertrude, who now danced with one of the Sothertons' younger sons, a callow boy pale with fatigue and anxiety. The baroness' smile was fixed; she would allow no trace of alarm to darken her features. Nobody must know, until the very last hope was gone, that there was anything amiss. Lady Jane caught her friend's eye and gave the slightest possible shake of her head to indicate that she had had no success in her quest. She toured the ballroom again, the veranda, the supper room and even put her head into the cardroom. Ladies were permitted, but generally the only ones who frequented the tables were older dowagers with impregnable reputations or those already so close to the edge of the pale that a little *more* indecorum could hardly hurt. There was no sign of Lady Virginia, however, and her attempts to arrest the eye of the baron failed, so she withdrew.

She was at a loss. Other than raising the general alarm, she could not think how to proceed, for the girl had now been missing the best part of an hour. She leaned on the finely carved balustrade of the gallery to steel herself for the task.

Coming up the stair below her was Mr Balfour, and on his arm was Lady Virginia.

The girl seemed unhurt, although her hair was disarranged and her dress hem muddy. The lace at the yoke of her gown was torn. She made no apology for her absence, standing defiantly whilst Mr Balfour, with utter discretion, murmured a few words of explanation.

'She was in the gardens,' he said. 'There was some fellow with her but he ran off as I made my approach. So far as I know there were no witnesses so all could still be well.'

'I cannot sufficiently express my thanks, Mr Balfour,' said Lady Jane.

'I am honoured to have been of service,' the gentleman replied. 'I made so bold as to order your carriage. I was certain you would wish to go home.'

'Indeed we shall,' Lady Jane agreed. 'Certainly this young lady shall not show her face in the ballroom again. I rather doubt of its being welcome anywhere, after this.'

Mr Balfour bowed and withdrew.

Lady Jane turned to where the young woman stood, mutinous and sullen. 'Lady Virginia,' she said, 'I take it you make no accusation? You were not accosted? You have not been … harmed?'

'No,' came the reply. 'Not in the slightest. I have nothing to say on the subject at all. It was nothing. That gentleman had no right to interfere.'

'He *had*, since he came at my behest to find you,' Lady Jane snapped. 'You can have no notion of the seriousness of what has occurred here. You must at least name your … the man who was with you. The Baron must confront him.'

'I will not name him.'

'Hoity-toity madam! He must be made to engage himself to you, unless he be already married,' Lady Jane hissed. 'I take it he is not?'

But Lady Virginia clamped her lips tightly shut, and would say no more.

11

The wedding of Jocelyn Willow and Frederick Stockbridge was a quiet but very elegant affair. Although there was a parish church at Chanbury Jocelyn had chosen to be married in Salisbury. Her first husband was buried in the graveyard of Chanbury church and she could not bring herself to pass his mouldering remains in her bridal finery.

Arthur Harlish had been granted a day's holiday in order to attend the marriage of his benefactress. His journey to Salisbury had been arduous, spent on top of the mail coach in weather that, though mercifully dry, had been cold. He had travelled overnight from Holborn to Reading, had time only for a quick breakfast before embarking again towards Salisbury. Once arrived he had walked away from the city, hoping to find a farmhouse where he could stay more cheaply than at an inn, and had been lucky to find one where, moreover, the kindly farmer had agreed to drive him back to Salisbury the following morning, where there was to be a market.

The guests were few; in addition to Arthur there were the Burleighs and one or two of the Willows' tenant farmers, and Jocelyn's cousin George Talbot. The groom had no family living apart from his adopted son, who was stationed on Gibraltar. The groom brought an old comrade from his time in the Marines, a Colonel Black, but no one else.

The bride was attended to church by her cousin and her daughter. When the ceremony was complete she lifted her veil and the groom kissed her. Georgina's veil remained in place, concealing the tears that poured unchecked down her cheeks.

The day being exceptionally fine the carriages were sent back to the inn and the party walked the short distance across the cathedral precincts, where they were to part ways.

Arthur would not have missed the opportunity of paying his respects to his family's great friend, nor of having some few moments' conversation with Georgina. He was not surprised to see that she concealed her face; his mother had prepared him for that. Her demeanour, though, was so different from the carefree child he remembered. Although she stood amongst the guests she somehow remained apart from them, holding herself aloof. At last he made bold and went to walk by her side.

'I am very happy to see you, Miss Willow,' he said, although conscious of the irony of his words for, in truth, her could not see her at all.

'And I you,' Georgina replied, in a soft tone. 'You are well? Tell me about your new life in London. It has a particular significance for me you know. I too am to live there for a time.'

There was, in her voice, such a heaviness of misgiving that he did his best to throw a positive light over things. He spoke of his lodgings with Mrs Quince, making gentle fun of her pretentions to beauty and gentility. He described the spirited play-readings which had lately recommenced every Sunday afternoon and the long walks with which he occupied his Sundays that he might not become embroiled in them. He walked for miles, he told her, along cobbled streets and across large, airy parks and also out into the countryside beyond Rotherhithe to Bostall Heath and Falconwood. He explained his work with enthusiasm, using his hands as he spoke, an energetic light in his eye.

'Are you lonely, Arthur?' she asked him, and the question surprised him—so personal, when he had been speaking in generalities. 'You have mentioned no friend or companion with whom you spend your leisure hours.' For herself, without her mama, he inferred, she expected to be very lonely indeed.

'I am rarely alone. It is not like in Yorkshire, where the moor stretches to the horizon and no human soul is to be seen. In London, you are never more than a few hundred yards from anyone and often you are so crushed in that people press on you on every side. The City streets are like that, and The Strand, which is the theatre district. I have been there at night and it is thronged just like it is day.' He thought for a moment before adding, 'Sometimes, I crave solitude. And silence. There is no silence in London.'

He could tell that he had conjured Yorkshire vividly to her mind. In spite of the impenetrable stuff of her veil he sensed a relaxation in her restraint.

'There was not often complete silence there,' she murmured. 'The wind and the trees were an almost constant soundscape. But there are times, especially at night, when the wind fades and the trees hold their breath.'

'Ah, yes,' he sighed.

They shared the remembrance of it for a moment, and then she said, 'Being alone is not the same as being lonely, Arthur,' and he felt gently chided, for he had not answered her question.

'No, it is not.'

'I do not know when I shall be able to go back to Yorkshire,' she told him, when a few more moments had elapsed. 'Not this year, certainly. To tell the truth, I do not know what this year will hold for me. Everything is to be new.' Her head turned toward where her mama stood with her new husband. Arthur thought Mrs Willow—or Mrs Stockbridge, as he must now remember to call her—looked happy in a way she had not done since Barnaby Willow's death. He wondered if Georgina begrudged it. For *her*, it had come at a cost.

'New is not always bad,' he said.

They had come out of the cathedral precincts and into a busy thoroughfare where traders passed to and fro between the market, the inns and the stables. People of every degree were there, heavy-laden carts trundled up the street, children running amongst them. A man drove a pig before him with a stick. A woman carried a basket of chickens. Arthur could see nothing that might discompose his companion and yet he felt her hesitate.

He took her arm. 'Does something trouble you?'

'Yes,' she said. 'A long time ago, something happened here.'

Arthur and Georgina arrived at the inn and, as they waited for the carriages to be loaded, she went on haltingly—omitting the vulgar details—to describe the incident involving the clerk.

'An uncouth fellow,' he said. 'I hope Mr Burleigh clipped his ear.'

'I do not know,' said Georgina, with an air of testy incredulity, and he surmised that his response had not satisfied her, that she felt he had failed to grasp the full awfulness of the experience, and how it had affected things since. 'But why, Arthur,' she burst out in a sudden fit of passion, 'why did he look at me? What did he see?'

Arthur took her hand in his. 'Why,' he said, shaking his head a little, and trying to see through the layers of her coverings, 'I cannot say. In general I believe that young ladies like to be looked at, and young men are drawn to do so. I do not excuse *him*, that clerk. He was excessively rude. But it may be that he just thought that you were …'

'Do not say something *kind*,' she broke in, snatching her hand away. 'Do not say anything *polite*. Our friendship goes back too far for falsehoods between us.'

'It may not be a falsehood,' Arthur replied. He touched the stuff of her veil. 'How can I tell?'

It was time for the bridal couple to depart, and Jocelyn took her daughter to one side.

Arthur heard Mrs Stockbridge say, 'Trust your cousin George,' as she enveloped her daughter in a fierce embrace, 'and believe me when I say that all I have taught you in the past has been false. There is *nothing* to fear, my dear girl. Nothing. Nothing at all. Do not hide yourself away, Georgina. Promise me you will try.'

He saw Georgina nod and heard a muffled, 'I will try,' from beneath her mantle.

Perhaps she would try, he thought, but he was not confident she would succeed.

12

As Lady Jane thought over the events of the ball, she could not do so with any degree of satisfaction. She had been appointed to watch over Lady Virginia and so she must take the blame for the lapse that had resulted. She could not trust her friend the baroness to keep this dereliction of duty to herself; on the contrary the baroness would be all too eager to point the finger of blame. News of this kind—disagreeable, embarrassing news—did permeate with astonishing velocity amongst the *ton*. She was certain that even at that very moment, the people promenading in the parks would have no other subject on their lips. Sure enough, as the day wore on, she received a number of notes from those who purported to be her friends, enquiring with specious concern after her health, anxious to know why she had left the Staffords' ball so suddenly, eager to ascertain if anything untoward had occurred.

'No reply. No reply,' she said again and again, waving the footman away. To Miss Trimble she said, 'Ghouls! How they feed on other people's misfortune. Oh, but I wish the baroness would send me word. I am *avid* to know what Lady Virginia has had to say for herself.'

In due course the baroness did send a sequence of notes to her friend, reporting that Lady Virginia continued in her determination not to name her companion in the gloom of Stafford House's gardens though both the baron and the baroness had used every means to coax the name from between her recalcitrant lips. Even Gertrude had tried, but failed so, until the matter could be referred to the earl, there was no more to be done. '*It may very well be*,' said the baroness, '*that the earl will require some account from you, as you were more nearly involved than I.*' This observation confirmed Lady Jane in her suspicion that the blame for the incident was to be laid firmly at her door. A subsequent note revealed that both Captain Brimming and the reprobate Rex had called at Charlton House but been refused admittance. A third brought the triumphant intelligence that Lord Pokerham, also, had called and that *he* had been received, and, after a tortured half hour of awkward silences and inane observations about the weather—inferred by Lady Jane but not absolutely described by the baroness—had brought himself to a proposal. Gertrude had accepted, of course. Lady Jane wondered whether she had done so in a rush of affection, or in duty to her parents, or simply to put an end to the ordeal. No doubt they had clashed teeth in what might have been intended as a kiss, and the matter had been settled.

'Perhaps she will come to care for him,' Lady Jane said to Miss Trimble when she had précised the contents of the final note.

'Oh yes, I do hope so,' said Agnes. 'Are you acquainted with the Sothertons at all?'

'I met the countess last night. She did not particularly impress me. She has a pronounced squint and one never does know which eye to fix. Notwithstanding, the baroness has *her* eye on one of the daughters for her son, Ernest.'

'I thought him an invalid.'

'He *is*. But that may be an advantage. The Sothertons are so congenital it would be best to avoid progeny. With him enfeebled and her inbred it could hardly make for healthy off-spring.'

'I suppose not. But then ...' Agnes hesitated, '... what would be the point? For marriage was first ordained for the procreation of children, was it not?'

'Indeed. Perhaps the Sothertons' ancestors should have thought of that before they married each other.'

They were disturbed in their conversation by a knock, and a servant brought forth a card on a silver tray.

'Mr Balfour presents his compliments, and wishes to know if you are at home,' he said.

Lady Jane took the card gingerly by one corner. 'No,' she said. 'I am too tired to receive callers today, and I have Miss Willow's rooms to arrange.'

The man bowed and withdrew.

Agnes Trimble said, 'That is the gentleman who assisted you last evening?'

'Yes. It was quite right of him to call, but he is taciturn by nature and I could not face entertaining him on my own, even for a quarter of an hour.' It did not occur to her that, with Miss Trimble in attendance, she would not have been on her own, but Agnes was the last person to remind her.

Instead she said, 'I hope you do not mind, but thinking to alleviate you of the burden of it, I have overseen matters for Miss Willow. I think you will find all in readiness.'

In fact, as the time for their guest's arrival had drawn near, Miss Trimble had found herself more and more excited at the prospect of a young person to befriend, to advise and to escort. She had made careful preparations in the rooms that were to be given over to the young woman's use, providing additions from other parts of the house that she felt would not be missed; a footstool, for example, which had never been used, a redundant folding screen and a writing desk that master Bobby—being abroad—could have no present use for. She had assisted with the hanging of the new curtains and supervised the making of the bed. She entered the suite every day, to ensure that a fire was lit and the rooms were aired. 'I think … that is, I *hope* that you will find nothing wanting,' she concluded.

'I am sure that *anything* we provide will be superior to what she has known up to this,' said Lady Jane, who had an idea that country properties were furnished in a rudimentary way to begin with, and that Mrs Willow's very odd ideas could only have contributed to the spartan surroundings at Chanbury.

'Yes ma'am,' said Miss Trimble.

'I have decided that, for the first few days, we will keep to the house,' Lady Jane declared, stretching her feet out to the fire. 'We cannot know what roughness of manner we might have to deal with, what ignorance, what want of elegance. Her table manners, for all we know …'

'Quite right, ma'am. We should prepare ourselves. But,' Agnes hazarded, 'it seems to me probable that Mr Talbot's cousin is to the greater degree a lady.'

'Does it?' replied Lady Jane in dudgeon. 'It does not seem at all probable to me. How can she be, when she has lived in obscurity, has never, that I know of, shown her face in town, consorts with servants quite as though they were equals and in all things has shrouded herself in mystery and anonymity? A lady has nothing to hide. A lady need not shrink from society. A lady is not ashamed of her antecedents.'

'No ma'am,' said Miss Trimble quietly, bending over her work. There was silence between them for a few moments, but then she ventured, 'I am sure that is why Mr Talbot intends me to take the burden of Miss Willow's supervision. He would not have you to the least degree inconvenienced, and whilst you would find an unrefined young person very trying, it would be nothing to me. I have not your superior taste. *My* feelings are not so nice. Would you like me to ring for some tea?'

Lady Jane waved a hand in vague assent, but she made no other response. In truth her feelings about her imminent guest were confused, and the closer the day came to her arrival the more bemired Lady Jane felt.

Mrs Willow—or Mrs Stockbridge, as she must now be called—had declined to know Lady Jane. Here was a personal snub it was impossible to overlook or to forgive, and although the daughter could not be held responsible for the mother's offensiveness neither could she quite, in Lady Jane's mind, be absolved from it. She had met Mrs Stockbridge's rebuff in like manner, by declining to know her. This made Georgina Willow a stranger, and a stranger beneath one's roof was never comfortable.

There could be no contradicting the fact that Mrs Stockbridge was singular, eccentric and perverse; she was *strange*. Lady Jane felt an inherent abhorrence of the mother that must extend to an instinctive shrinking also from the girl. There could be no honour in the acquaintance of either—indeed quite the reverse; there could only be humiliation and social discredit. Her expectation was for something distasteful, even something disgusting, in the girl's person or manners. She must be coarse, a baggage or a simpleton. She might be degenerate or hysterical. No other explanation offered itself for the injunction that she was to be kept out of society. Lady Jane flinched from the association as she would from a leper's touch.

Then there was that old, unresolved suspicion that there was, in her husband's enigmatic connexion with his cousin and her daughter, something dubious, something secretive. Why could he not explain it? Why did it provoke in him such a strong and immediate defensiveness? What was there in it that he had to protect? Lady Jane resented it and she resented the women who called it forth in Mr Talbot. Considered in this light it seemed an outrageous imposition that she should even be asked to *meet* Miss Willow, let alone to shelter her. It was not much less than an abomination.

But Lady Jane's inquisitive streak could not look away from it. She burned to penetrate whatever mystery was being concealed from her. In this respect the arrival of Georgina Willow was welcome, for surely *she* would let slip some hint, some clue, of what Mr Talbot was so very eager to conceal.

Last of all in the alembic of Lady Jane's ruminations was the teaspoonful of vitriol that would revel in anything shameful, primitive or vulgar that might attach itself to her husband. As wealthy and well-respected as he might be *now*, there was no gainsaying that his father's people had been chancers. What if his mother's family also had doubtful roots? If Lady Jane were to unearth something salacious, nobody need know. Indeed, she would be the last person to broadcast such news. But it would be pleasing to hold it over him. Several advantages could accrue, not the least being the benefits her own children might gain. For if there *were* something dubious in the Gilchrist connection her own nobility would allay it in a way that George's first wife could not.

13

Sunday came, and the hour of Georgina Willow's arrival drew near. Lady Jane, who had not even got dressed the previous day, was up early and clothed in her finest array, but whether to impress or to intimidate her guest, she could not say. Still there warred within her a sense of outrage that this person should be foisted upon her, a mistrust as to the young woman's respectability and a needling, insatiable curiosity.

The day was very fine. A dancing hoard of daffodils in the park opposite seemed gathered in celebration of the Talbots' guest. Fresh-unfurled leaves quivered in anticipation. Birds hopped excitedly from branch to branch, seemingly eager to secure for themselves the best view.

Lady Jane had commanded additional flowers for the hall and drawing room; extravagant displays of hot-house lilies, roses and freesia filled vases and urns, their perfume rising to the lofty ceilings. She could not say, as she inspected the florists' work, whether she wished to overwhelm her guest with sheer abundance, stun her with heady aromas or simply provide for her own self something substantial she could hide behind. She walked from the salon to the drawing room, the hall to the dining room, from Georgina's room to the salon, inspecting everything with critical minuteness. Nothing must be amiss—no speck of dust, no drape out of place, no bruised petal—that could earn Miss Willow's disapproval. But she chided herself, for what did it matter to *her* what some chit of a country girl thought? She would not have the young woman believe for a single second that any particular preparations had been made for her arrival; she was not important enough to warrant the least alteration in the Talbots' usual domestic arrangements. Lady Jane told herself that the extra flowers and the delicacies ordered for dinner were coincidental to Miss Willow's arrival amongst them.

The young woman's luggage had come the previous afternoon. Miss Trimble had overseen its unpacking and storage. Nothing definitive could be deduced. The cut of the gowns was good, the quality excellent, the number sufficient. Their owner could be presumed to be a woman of average height and build. Lady Jane, who had herself clandestinely gone into the guest room and inspected the things, did not know whether to be relieved or disappointed.

It was not to be supposed that Mr Talbot's carriage could be seen in Grosvenor Square before two o'clock. The waiting was agony, Lady Jane's curiosity both morbid and avid. Poor Miss Trimble caught the brunt of her patroness' mood; she was criticised for talking too much, and then too little, for dinting the cushions of the sofa, for looking out of the window too often but then, when a carriage was heard approaching, not often enough. At last they determined that a turn in the park would be beneficial. Accordingly they ventured out for an hour or two, taking Dickie the aged spaniel with them, greeting acquaintance who, like them, were on foot, or who rode by in open carriages. Families returning from church, parties of ladies and gentlemen taking the air, marriageable young women eager to be seen, children playing at the lakeside; the great and the good were on show. Nothing was said to Lady Jane on the subject of the Staffords' ball; there was no caustic jibe, no direct affront, but she was aware of words whispered behind hands, of sly glances and muttered details.

'They may gossip,' she said to Miss Trimble in a grim tone, 'but upon my word Lady Virginia's misadventure will be as nothing when they learn of the abomination to come. I declare I do not know how I am to live down the shame of it.'

'We do not know,' suggested Miss Trimble, 'that there is anything absolutely shameful about Miss Willow. She may be an ordinary, unremarkable young person, quite harmless.'

'Then why has she been *hidden*?' hissed Lady Jane.

At first they sauntered beneath the trees and along the gravelled carriageways, but the further away they got from Grosvenor Square the more anxious Lady Jane became. She feared being from home when her husband and the young woman should arrive. *That* would give her guest the upper hand. It would permit Mr Talbot to set quite the wrong note. For if the girl *were* crude and countrified there could be nothing to be gained by showing her the library and the music room. She should not be allowed to pollute the salon or the long drawing room and the gallery would be wasted on her. No, in *that* case she should be hustled along the servants' corridor and taken to her room by the back stairs. The old schoolroom, Nanny's parlour and Miss Trimble's rooms should be the extent of her curtilage and the sooner she could be transported to the greater obscurity of Ecklington the better. These considerations made Lady Jane hurry her steps back in the direction of Grosvenor Square, and the walk that was to have occupied an empty couple of hours ended up taking less than one.

It brought them to the corner of the square just as Mr Talbot's carriage drew up before the house. The door opened and a posse of servants poured out, some to help with the luggage, others to assist the passengers down, some to stand in a phalanx of welcome quite as though Miss Willow were a bride or royalty. Lady Jane and Miss Trimble, hurrying along but impeded by the lame and lazy dog, could only look on in horror as Mr Talbot handed down a woman swathed from neck to foot in a velvet cloak, her head and face hidden behind a thick veil. His determined air of geniality was striking—his smile somewhat fixed—but his manner was most assiduous, gentle, his touch very tender as he took his guest up the shallow steps and into the house.

His wife and Miss Trimble—both out of breath and overheated—arrived on the steps and at the door just as it was closed behind the new-comers. Lady Jane rapped sharply. The sounds of greeting and of welcome within drifted out to them, possibly drowning out the sound of her increasingly frantic knocking.

'Oh Agnes,' wailed Lady Jane, turning on her friend a look that was both irritated and importunate, 'You must make them admit us. This is intolerable. They have shut us out.' Then, irritation mastering her sense of desperation, added, 'Look what you have done! You have made us late. I did not wish to walk so far. This calamity is *your* doing.'

She turned to the door again and hammered on it. Dickie, hot and tired and ready for his nap, gave a bark that was surprisingly commanding. One or other of these things at last caught the attention of the people within. The door was opened and Lady Jane half stepped and half fell through it.

The servants assembled within recognised at once their mistress' state of high dudgeon, and quickly betook themselves to their duties apart from two, a footman who was divesting Mr Talbot of his coat and hat and a maid who hovered at the foot of the stairs ready to be of use to the lady. After the brightness of the day outside the hall was temporarily dim in Lady Jane's eyes. She could but indistinctly make out the towering arrangement of flowers, the hall stand, the loitering servants and her husband shrugging out of his greatcoat.

'There you are,' he said, with a genial smile. 'You have arrived at the perfect moment, for we have just alighted from the carriage.'

'I saw you,' Lady Jane said between dry, rasping breaths, 'from the corner. Miss Trimble and I have been taking the air.'

'Delightful,' her husband said, 'but I trust you have not over-exerted yourself my dear. You look exhausted.'

Somewhere in the gloom—behind the flowers, behind the hall stand, in the shadow of the dining room door—Miss Willow must be lurking, unless she had already been conveyed to her room. Lady Jane looked around her with a kind of wildness, her heart beating in her breast, her breath coming in short gasps. She was suddenly overwhelmed with heat. The scent of the flowers was cloyingly sweet. It stuck in her throat. She wrestled with the fastening of her pelisse.

Mr Talbot gave her a speaking smile, his eyes trying to convey some plea she could not comprehend. She watched his gaze slide significantly to where the maid waited. There was an expectant silence. In her distraction, Lady Jane did not know how to fill it.

Behind her, Miss Trimble gave the slightest possible cough. Lady Jane forced herself to look across the hall to where the stairs rose to the first floor landing. She blinked moisture from her eyes. There, at the foot of the stairs, behind the maid and in the shadow of the tumbling flower arrangement, stood the young woman. Her cloak had been removed and handed to the waiting servant, but her hat and veil remained in place. Her dress was grey, her hat a colourless creation, her veil a sheer, impenetrable black.

'My dear,' said Mr Talbot, taking his wife gently by the elbow and guiding her across the marble floor towards their guest. 'let me introduce Miss Willow. As you see we are just arrived. We have not yet taken off our things.'

She allowed herself to be steered by him but almost reluctantly, as though he led her to some doom, some dreadful apparition. He must have felt her apprehension because he pressed her hand with his. Or it may be that he wished to communicate something—caution, forbearance—she did not know.

Miss Willow, still no more than a column of shadow in the dim, folded herself into a curtsey before holding out a hesitant hand. Lady Jane looked at it. It was small, and trembled slightly. They stood thus in a kind of tableau for a few seconds, not speaking. Lady Jane's regard scanned the fabric of Miss Willow's veil, which was sheer and dark, maddeningly obscure. At last, as Miss Willow's hand remained extended and as Lady Jane did not take it, George himself laid hold of it so that he stood between the two women, making the connection they themselves seemed unable to form.

'And this other lady is Miss Trimble,' said Mr Talbot, bringing Agnes into the montage. 'She is the lady I have told you about.'

Perhaps Miss Willow smiled. It was impossible to tell. Miss Trimble certainly did, exuding all the welcome and reassurance her little frame could muster. She opened her mouth to make some greeting, but Lady Jane, seizing the initiative, said, 'You will remove your veil, I hope. There can be no necessity for it *here*. Why do you hide behind it at all? Come, let us see you.'

'My dear,' Mr Talbot murmured, 'let us not insist on that quite yet. Miss Willow is shy. Give her time.'

Indeed he had found her most introverted, in respect of her appearance. In conversation, she had been restrained, though not impolite. She had not removed her veil for the whole of the journey from Salisbury and, at the inn at Reading, had requested to dine alone in her room. In vain had he offered a private dining chamber for the two of them, and tried to assuage her fears. 'We are cousins,' he had said, 'and you are to be my guest. You have nothing whatever to fear from me.'

'From you, no,' she had conceded. 'But what if someone *else* were to see me?'

'What if they do?' he had laughed, but kindly. 'Look around the room.' They were just then in the reception hall of the inn. The place was busy with travellers just arrived and securing rooms, people ordering dinner, servants carrying trunks. 'What a variety of faces there are,' George had remarked. 'See the fellow with the bulbous nose? And that lady has no front teeth. The groom in yellow livery has been in a fight; he has a black eye. The innkeeper's wife is fat, is she not? I myself have a scar, here,' he lifted his hair so that she could see it. 'We all of us have our imperfections, my dear. And yet no one is staring, no one takes the least notice. Why should you be any different? What a dull world it would be if we all looked alike!'

'Some calamity will ensue if I am seen,' she had replied, and he had heard the tears in her voice.

'I know your mother had spent many years believing so,' he had said. 'But she believes so no longer. Any danger, if there were any, is passed. It is like waking from a nightmare. It seemed so real, the threat so imminent. But in the morning, it is gone.'

'You do not *know*,' she had replied, her voice full of doubt. She had raised her hand to where her veil fell in front of her face. 'You have not seen.'

'I do not need to see your face to know there can be nothing in it which could cause the kind of disaster you fear,' he had said although, of course, he could not know what the veil concealed. 'No calamity will touch you whilst I am near,' he had said, reaching out and taking her hand in his. 'Trust me, my dear.'

'I will try,' she had whispered. 'I will try, in time.'

Now, Lady Jane retorted, 'Time? For what? This is not shyness, it is artifice! She is *coy*. But I'll not be prevaricated with. As we *are* to meet, let us do so face-to-face.'

Miss Willow's struggle was clear to see. She stiffened. Her hands clenched themselves, and from behind the veil there came a small mew of distress. But, at last, she reached behind her head and removed a pin. She did so hesitantly, as though her arms were heavy. Her hands faltered with the fastening—dithering, putting off the moment of revelation. Then, at last, with a sigh, she lifted her bonnet and veil away.

Whatever Lady Jane had expected, whatever she had feared, it was not what confronted her. It was her turn to stiffen. Then, in a violent, instinctive action she recoiled, cannoning into Miss Trimble and treading on Dickie's foot. His yelp—of pain, of surprise, of affront—drowned out Lady Jane's shriek but it contained all the same feeling. Her face, ashen, turned to where her husband stood beside Miss Willow. George smiled, but uncertainly. He wanted to look at Georgina but with a supreme effort, in deference to her sensibility, kept his eyes on his wife. *She* met his every awful expectation, his every dread of cruelty and affronted pride. His face displayed disappointment, but not surprise. The young woman flinched, her trepidation of doom amply satisfied by Lady Jane's revulsion. Lady Jane looked again, from George to Georgina, at their hair—dark, thick and curling—at their eyes—the same dark pools. In concert—in their shared distress—they turned towards one another, and it was as though one person reflected in a looking glass made two.

Lady Jane screamed. Suddenly, suddenly, the truth bore down on her. She was deluged with it, like a drench of ice cold water, a shock that would have knocked her off her feet if George had not, by some instinct, reached for her arm. It was appalling, quite as appalling as every phantasmagorical imagining that had plagued her for weeks. It was crass, too dreadful to contemplate but yet impossible to ignore. Here, at last, was the revelation of George's secret, the truth of his 'cousin' Jocelyn and this girl. Not some distant relative, not a tenuous blood connexion but very flesh of his flesh and blood of his blood. Georgina Willow could be none other than George Talbot's daughter.

14

There was movement—swift and undignified—a flurry of manhandling, shoving and jostling and somewhere within that a sharp, stinging slap. Lady Jane and George found themselves behind a mercifully closed door in the small sitting room that was attached to Lady Jane's own bedroom. Neither quite knew how they had come there other than they had been propelled by a tidal wave of raw, angry emotion.

Lady Jane, although commanded to sit, found herself rigidly unable to comply. Her arms were clamped to her sides, her hands clenched. Beneath the skirts of her dress her knees pressed themselves together but even so she was conscious of paroxysms of uncontrollable tremors that seized her limbs and made her heart beat very quickly. This assault, and whatever deception her husband urged upon her, must be fought, and she held herself together in this adamantine determination. Only her tongue would not be stilled. Her mouth emitted torrents of words, of accusation and complaint.

George, unlike his wife, seemed unable to be still. He paced restlessly across the room—which was not large—circumnavigating again and again a sofa and a tea table and Lady Jane, who stood like a pillar between the two. He stopped for a moment to pour some liquor from a decanter, but could not stand still long enough to drink it before he was off again, his hands now in his pockets, now in his hair, his agitation apparent in every gesture and barked retort.

'How *could* you?' Lady Jane said again and again, her voice in a crescendo. 'How could you bring that creature here, beneath our own roof, to taunt and shame me? She is your own child! How can you deny it? And you seek to foist her in my nest like a cuckoo. Oh, you traitor! You miscreant! I'll not have it. I'll not have it, do you hear?'

'She is not my child,' George roared, partly to be heard above her shrieks but also in expiation of his fury. 'You are wrong. You wrong her and you wrong me by your charge. I was at sea when she was conceived.'

'Not your child?' his wife screamed. 'She is the *image* of you! A blind man would see it! Everyone will see it!'

'No one is to see her,' George enunciated, as though speaking to a dim-wit.

Lady Jane, incensed and offended, drew herself up. 'And now I see why! No wonder she was to be kept hidden. Not go out into society? Of course she cannot go into society. She ought not to have been brought from whatever obscurity you have kept her in. Indeed, she ought to have been drowned at birth. Oh! That you should attempt to smuggle her here. Such false pretences as you have employed!'

'That is not the reason, Jane,' he said, appealing—but hopelessly—to her better sense. 'It is Georgina's own desire to be obscure. She is shy. More than that, she is deeply afraid. It is no wonder that Jocelyn declines to expose her to the cattle-market that is London. You know what it is like! Georgina is innocent—wholly unspoilt. A girl like her will be torn limb from limb!'

The name of George's cousin was like a dagger plunged into an already fatal wound. 'Do not mention that woman's name in my hearing,' Lady Jane hissed, her voice very low and vehement. 'I will never have her name spoken again. She is an adulteress! A harlot! I despise her. She is a disgrace to her sex.'

'Silence, woman,' her husband thundered. 'I will have no word said against her.' The urge to raise his hand to his wife again was almost insuperable, and in order to suppress it he clasped his hands together in an attitude that gave him an air of supplication.

Lady Jane might, perhaps, have inferred from his unconscious gesture some element of the torment of soul her husband suffered, but she was beyond such nuance. 'Of course not! Your precious 'cousin' Jocelyn,' she sniped nastily. 'And you expect me to believe there is nothing between you?'

'Nothing of the kind you suggest.'

'Oh George,' screeched Lady Jane, 'how can you tell me such lies? Do you think so little of me that you will perjure yourself in this way? The chit is even named for you!'

'I thought you a woman of better sense,' he replied bitterly, loosing his hands and tearing at his hair with them. 'I do not know where this ridiculous notion can have come from. You cannot have seen Georgina for more than a few seconds. I hardly saw her at all! I presume you believe you saw a slight resemblance, a mere *family* resemblance …'

'There can be no family resemblance where there is no blood tie!' Lady Jane crowed. 'By your own account, she is related to you only by marriage. So how do you explain it? There can be only one explanation.'

George was temporarily floored, caught in a net of his own devising. To cover his confusion and give him time to think, he returned to his untouched drink and took a sip. 'I cannot account for it,' he said at last. 'I am not so minutely cognisant of the Gilchrist family tree. I presume that like many a noble family—like your own, for instance—they were in the habit of marrying their near relations. My mother must have been connected to her first husband by blood.'

120

It was a wafer thin elucidation but Lady Jane, with the Sothertons so near the front of her mind, could not absolutely discount it as a possibility.

Seeing her consider his proposition, even as unlikely as it was, George quickly took himself onto surer ground. 'It is my contention that you were predisposed not to like the girl, and a passing similarity was all you needed to leap to this ridiculous and wholly unfounded conclusion. But then, for you to express it, before her, before the servants! Oh Jane, such indiscretion! Have you no self-control? No. You see scandal and intrigue in every commonplace thing. You are bemired in it and can think and speak of nothing else and so you conjure it into being here. This is your fevered imagination, Jane, and your jealousy. That is all.'

'I deny it,' Lady Jane bellowed. 'She must leave. I will not have her here.'

'She will *not*,' George returned, speaking into her face. 'Whatever sin you believe me capable of, whatever iniquity you impute to her mother, Miss Willow is innocent. She is our guest and she will be shown due courtesy. You may dine in your chamber if you prefer not to see her. You may go and stay with one of your sisters. I do not care. But Miss Willow remains here.'

Lady Jane gasped, and against all her determination not to show her husband a sliver of compliance or to relent in the smallest degree, tears sprang into her eyes. 'You would send me from the house?' she croaked.

He came to rest at last, across the sofa that divided them. 'No, of course not,' he said. 'I offer it as a suggestion for your greater comfort. If it is so hateful for you to have Georgina here, you may go elsewhere. Perhaps a little time to reflect will bring you to your senses, for you certainly seem to have lost them.'

Pain now added itself to Lady Jane's ire. It wounded her, that he would side with his shameful by-blow in preference to his lawful wife. 'Am I to understand,' she stammered out, 'that, between us, you choose *her*?'

He looked at her hopelessly. 'If you force me to it,' he said slowly. 'I cannot send her away. She has no one in the world but me. But us. Even if your vicious calumny were true, I could not put her on the streets. Oh! But it is *not* true, Jane,' he urged, summoning every ounce of patience and of persuasiveness. 'Let us not pursue this. Let us not hurt each other with these matters.' He reached for her hand and there was a moment when the episode might have been ended in tears and forgiveness. But she snatched her hand from his grasp.

'Let us, do you mean,' she said coldly, 'continue in the charade we have practiced in the past?'

'Let us simply acknowledge the truth of the matter,' he said as reasonably as he could.

'That is what I am trying to do.'

George set his teeth. 'She is not what you think. It is impossible in every way.' He spoke severely, his manner very authoritative, but the note of desperation in his voice was not quite gone.

She tried to read his expression, but he would not meet her eye. His regard wavered, slid away from hers, and she was reminded again of the sense of dissimulation she always had when he mentioned Jocelyn Willow. She did not believe him. She called up what last thread of dignity remained to her. 'I will not be displaced by your illegitimate child,' she said. 'I shall continue to do my duty, even though you have so palpably failed in yours. The ignominy of this shall come to your door, George, not mine. Be it on your own head.'

'Oh Jane,' he cried out in despair, 'you must desist in this miscomprehension. It cannot be so. Why will you not see?'

But she was unmoveable. 'You will not trust me with the truth,' she said coldly. 'Therefore I must construct my own using what understanding I have. There has always been a shiftiness about you in relation to your supposed cousin. I know there is something you will not tell me. Miss Willow is your duplicate. Your legitimate children are not more like you than she is. As to dates and times, it is too long ago for anything to be proven. Therefore my conclusion is that in your youth you were your cousin's lover, and Georgina Willow is the result. Of course you may argue that you were unmarried at the time, or that your first wife was the victim of your deception, and not I. That is irrelevant. You have been deceitful and dishonourable.'

It was George's turn to feel injured. There was nothing she could have said to hurt him more. The truth could be so simply told and perhaps, then, all would be well. He licked his lips, which were dry, and opened his mouth to speak. Her face was haughty, her cheek livid on the side where he had slapped her. He took a breath and raised his eyes to meet hers. But what he saw there stopped his voice. The rest of her face was impassive, carefully neutral, but she had in her eye an acquisitive light, a febrile, greedy glimmer that reminded him of her insatiable appetite for gossip. No. He could not tell her what, after all, was Jocelyn's secret and not his.

He turned from her and took up the glass he had filled earlier, throwing the rest of its contents down his throat. He put the glass down and strode towards the door, seizing the handle and wrenching it open.

'You are wrong,' he threw out, but in a low voice that would not carry beyond the room, 'wrong and ridiculous and obstinate.'

He did not mean to slam the door but his utter despair at his wife's irrational wilfulness over-mastered his intention, and the sound of it reverberated throughout the house.

Left alone, Lady Jane sank at last to the sofa, and covered her face with her hands.

15

Georgina, clutching her veil to her face, was escorted to her chambers by the petite lady who had been introduced as Miss Trimble. She was kind, clearly wanting very much to be comforting, talking incessantly of the appointments of the room, the carpet which had been fetched from the music room, the arrangement of the clothes in the drawers and the press. If she hoped that her ceaseless chat would drown out the shrieking indictments and apoplectic wailings that emanated from Lady Jane's apartments, however, she must have been disappointed. *Those,* even when unintelligible, were embarrassingly audible, though several closed doors interposed themselves between the rooms. When they were intelligible, they were excruciating.

Georgina had long schooled herself to dread dramatic consequences to the disclosure of her face, but she had not expected them to be violent. The sudden torrent of loud imprecation that had erupted from her hostess had been shocking enough, but the addition of flailing arms raining blows upon poor Cousin George had turned shock into fright. Georgina had flinched as though she herself were the object of Lady Jane's anger, finding herself in the arms of Miss Trimble. The sound of one resounding slap finding its target had made the high ceiling echo and set the crystal chandelier jangling in discordant chimes. Who had dealt it, Georgina did not know, but Lady Jane's tirade had, for a few shocked moments, ceased. In that hiatus the lady of the house had been bundled past them, half-carried up the staircase by her husband. Then Georgina had been gently turned and brought up to her room.

Miss Trimble continued to fuss around the room, opening and then closing the casement, poking at a fire that already burned with too much heat for the day but she could not hide her dismay, when she at last turned to face Miss Willow, and saw the hat and veil had been restored.

The older lady mastered her feelings, however, and pulled the bell for tea. 'For I am sure, my dear,' she said, bringing her avalanche of words at last to a terminus, 'that you are quite desperate for a cup. I know *I* am. Such an energetic walk home that we had. I think poor Dickie is all but done in. Are you fond of dogs?'

The inanity of this line of conversation, in other circumstances, might have been amusing, but as it was Georgina clung to it as a shipwrecked person might cling to a barrel. 'Oh yes, very,' she said. 'We have a number of them at home. One is a particular favourite. The rural dean's poodle got at Mrs Burleigh's spaniel, and the result … a litter of strange, woolly little creatures! Mrs Burleigh allowed me to keep one. Oh! Poor Moppet, how I miss her.' Then she dissolved into tears.

'There now,' Miss Trimble crooned, crossing the room to urge Georgina into one of the chairs. 'You have had a very trying few days. I am sure the wedding was a strain. How could it not be? When you are to part from your dear mama? And then the journey here. Such a distance! And now this … most awkward of welcomes. I declare I do not know what to make of it.' She went nimbly to where she had stored Georgina's handkerchiefs, and lifted one from the drawer. 'Here you are my dear. Blow your nose and dry your eyes. Tea will be here directly I am sure.' She stood behind the chair and stroked Georgina's shoulder through the stuff of the veil, murmuring comforts until the paroxysm of sobs subsided.

It was ridiculous for either of them to pretend that the encounter with Lady Jane had been of no moment and Georgina said, 'Why was Lady Jane so angry? I do not understand. I wanted so much to make a friend of her.'

Miss Trimble hesitated, for she would not for the world wish to say anything derogatory about her patroness. On the other hand Lady Jane's behaviour had been extraordinary and some explanation must be made for it.

'I think perhaps she was not quite prepared for …'

'For my appearance?' Georgina concluded for her. 'Yes.' She nodded sadly. 'But now she is making the vilest accusations of poor Cousin George. What is the use of pretending we can't hear her? I do not know how she can even imagine such a thing.'

'She is over-wrought,' said Miss Trimble, 'and over-tired. There was a ball on Friday evening. She chaperoned a young lady and there was an incident …' All the details of Lady Virginia's misdemeanours came pouring forth but it was obvious that Georgina was taking no notice. She remained fixed in the fireside chair. Agnes could not see her face, but her attitude suggested that she was staring into the flames. Her handkerchief was balled into her hand; she had stopped crying at least.

A knock at the door announced the tea tray and Miss Trimble took it from the maid and set it down on a low table, talking all the while. The argument in another part of the house sawed on, Lady Jane's high-pitched voice punctuated by Mr Talbot's angry interjections, until there was the sharp percussion of a slamming door, followed by silence. Miss Trimble's flow of verbiage had been a brave but forlorn attempt to distract from—if possible to drown out—the terrible exchange occurring elsewhere in the house. Now it exhausted itself. She took her tea cup and drained it as though it were a life-giving elixir.

In part she was a little exultant, for this tender young flower was to be her own protégé, and all the pleasure she had imagined in escorting her was now increased, for whilst she had been prepared for a dull-witted, a sullen or a naughty girl, did not Miss Willow seem to be an extremely personable young lady? Agnes' view in the hallway had been blocked by Lady Jane, and in the furore the young woman had hidden her face. She did not know the cause of Miss Willow's inhibition—unless it be to conceal the likeness Lady Jane had so vehemently objected to—but on the whole she assumed some blemish or disfigurement that had caused an acute self-consciousness. If things had been otherwise there might have been a danger that Lady Jane would appropriate Miss Willow to herself, leaving Agnes out in the cold. But her aversion to their guest would seem to preclude that possibility. An intimate friend on an equal footing, even if so much younger, was such a delightful prospect!

On the other hand, Lady Jane could not be discounted altogether. She was capricious. She would not like to be abandoned in favour of anyone, even—especially—a person so objectionable to her as Miss Willow. Lady Jane would require careful handling.

The silence in the house was now portentous, brooding, the aftermath of the row percolating like a sour smell through the rooms and along the landings. Miss Trimble could imagine the servants cowering in the below-stairs regions, arguing amongst themselves as to who should go to their mistress for her directions, as the dressing hour was now almost upon them. She knew that *she* ought to go to her, although she dreaded doing so.

'There now,' said Miss Trimble, 'It has gone quiet. I am sure Mr Talbot has set things straight. Do drink your tea. Will you not … might it not be easier if …?' But Miss Willow brought her cup inside her veil to drink, and Agnes left her question in abeyance.

'I hope so,' said Georgina. 'Lady Jane must see it is ridiculous. She must be *made* to see it. Quite apart from the stain she casts on my mama, can she not see how she sullies her own husband? I never saw such a display of histrionics. Is she often thus?'

'Do not be troubled,' Agnes said, sidestepping the question. 'It was quite understood that you were to have little to do with Lady Jane *anyway*. I am to have the great pleasure of accompanying you. There are galleries, and the park. We are to have our own carriage and I am to be supplied with a purse of money. Perhaps, if we are *very* discreet, we might even venture to the theatre.'

'Oh, yes,' Georgina said in a heavy voice. 'Of course, we must be discreet.'

'For no other reason,' Miss Trimble assured her, sensing she had pressed a bruise, 'than that your mama has requested discretion, and you seem …. forgive me … you seem very reserved. But rest assured, I understand discretion better than anyone. As I have been circumstanced … you might say it has been my life's work, to be invisible.'

'And mine,' Georgina said with a sigh. Some impulse propelled her to her feet, and she paced the room for a few moments before bursting out, 'But I do not know how I can remain in the house of a woman who believes such wickedness. Oh this is a poor beginning indeed, very poor, and I am heartily sorry for it.'

Alarmed, Miss Trimble put down her cup. 'Not remain? But where else could you go?'

'I do not know,' Georgina almost cried. 'I know no one in town, and yet, how can I remain?'

'For that very reason!' Miss Trimble replied, rising too. 'You have nowhere else to go! And believe me, my dear, in a few hours, or tomorrow, all this will seem like a bad dream.'

That much, Agnes thought, was probably true, for Lady Jane was subject to moods that, though dour whilst they lasted, passed over relatively quickly.

'I do not know,' said Georgina very despondently. 'I do not understand it.' She stood at the window, but saw nothing of the park that basked in the spring afternoon sunshine.

Although it must have been patently obvious to everyone in the house—even in the square—what misapprehension had taken place, Miss

Trimble attempted an elucidation of it. 'Mr Talbot has always claimed that his connexion with your mama is a very distant one,' she said, coming to stand behind Georgina.

'And so it is.'

'Indeed. But then, you see, it appears, from Lady Jane's reaction, that there is quite a striking resemblance between you and him.' Agnes turned and looked at Miss Willow. The gauze of her shroud fell sheer to her waist, and no suggestion of the person within it could be discerned.

'I do not see it.'

'Of course not, for we don't see ourselves as others see us. Even in the mirror …'

'I hardly ever look in the mirror.'

'Well there you are! But it is quite natural that there should be *some* similarities between people who are connected, however distantly. It is unaccountable to me that Lady Jane had not expected it. I can assure you that you need have no anxiety. Lady Jane might be most vociferous, but Mr Talbot is master in this house.' That much, she felt, it would be true to say. Lady Jane herself had often owned it, albeit with a resentful, regretful air.

Miss Trimble watched carefully to see if her words had allayed Miss Willow's unease. She thought she saw a slight relaxation in her stance. She laid her hand on Georgina's arm. 'Do not think of leaving us,' she said, her tone very earnest. 'However grim things seem *here*, to be out *there*, without a friend, would be worse. And I cannot tell you, my dear, how I have looked forward to your coming. Do not deny me the great pleasure of your company. I wish so much for us to be friends.'

What could anyone say to such a plea? Georgina returned the pressure of Miss Trimble's hand. 'I promise,' she said, 'at any rate, to do nothing precipitously. And as to our being friends, I feel *that* will be so, wherever I am.'

'Thank you my dear,' said Miss Trimble, then ventured, 'That being so, will you not trust me so far as to remove your veil? I am a very plain person, you can see. I have no beauty and I do not look for it in others. I may flatter myself, but I think I am not so superficial as to set any store by physical appearance.'

Georgina turned away. 'You must understand,' she said at last, 'that I have spent my life avoiding exposure. I do not even know why! Except that Mama said it was necessary. It has become a habit with me. I … I have the sense that people cannot be trusted.' Her voice, as she spoke, showed her great struggle, the conflict at her heart. 'But Mama has gone away,' she went on, almost to herself, 'into the wide world where we have never, before, allowed ourselves to venture. And she packed no veils.'

'Perhaps she feels the danger is passed?' suggested Miss Trimble.

'Perhaps,' replied Miss Willow. 'Yes, perhaps. But then, *she* knew what the danger was. How shall I recognise it if I encounter it?'

'I presume she trusted your cousin to guide you, as she now trusts her new husband. Your cousin, in his turn, has entrusted me, my dear.'

Miss Willow seemed to ponder, but at last, when she turned back to face Miss Trimble her drooped shoulders, the hopeless spread of her out-stretched hands, showed that her attempt to make some sense of her situation had been defeated. 'It is not so easy,' she said, 'to put off something one has been accustomed to for so long.'

'I understand,' said Agnes. 'If you will permit me, I will help you try.'

Miss Trimble left the room and bent her steps to Lady Jane's apartments, but she did so in great trepidation, and it took some courage for her to lift her hand and knock.

Georgina remained alone, and as she *was* alone, she flung back her face-covering. She turned from the window and looked around the chamber. It was large, very nicely appointed, and she saw—in a vase of flowers on a bureau, in an assortment of books on a side table and in a beautifully embroidered cushion on a low chair—that thoughtful preparations had been made for her comfort. It seemed likely to her now that these had been provided by Miss Trimble, for Lady Jane did not seem at all the kind of woman to have taken such a personal interest, or to have had such kindness. Indeed she seemed to be a volatile creature, subject to the most peculiar fancies, and Georgina considered the long weeks that stretched before her as the guest of such a woman with dismay and trepidation.

But then it occurred to her that it was not entirely true to say that she had no acquaintance in town. There was Arthur Harlish. He had been at the wedding, and seemed to be still the good friend she had always known him to be. But she had neglected to ask him to call upon her, or to find out his address.

She could barely contemplate how the excruciating awkwardness of her situation in the Talbots' house could be borne, but it comforted her to know that Arthur was near. *How* near, she did not know, for she had no conception of the size or geography of London.

On an impulse she decided that she would go out of the house to walk in the park she could see from her windows. The room was too hot and she felt suffocated for lack of air. The best part of two days spent in a carriage made her yearn for exercise. She had been rudely treated by her hostess and it was insupportable that she should be locked away as though *she* had done something wrong. So much freedom she had relinquished at her mother's behest, and she had come almost to love her captivity. But her entire liberty she would never give up, especially to a woman such as Lady Jane Talbot seemed to be. Georgina pulled down her veil and found a shawl in one of the drawers. Then she opened her bedroom door and passed through it.

The landing, stairs and hallway were empty except for the old dog, which lay in a patch of sunshine and thumped its tail as she passed by. The door was not locked, and she went out into the square.

16

Mr Talbot—ever genial—had arranged for Arthur to be conveyed back part of the way to town with Colonel Black, who had room in his carriage and could take him as far as Twickenham, where he would be able to pick up the regular coach. Black had been an affable enough companion and had regaled Arthur with many a tale of derring-do from his time with Mr Stockbridge in the Marines, but Arthur had spent a good deal of the journey dozing in the corner of the carriage. They had changed horses twice, eating hasty meals whilst the new ones were put to, the colonel kindly covering the expense of Arthur's dinner before they set off again to drive through the night. But the regular coach had been delayed by a lamed horse and it was past noon when Arthur arrived back in town.

He could have taken an omnibus but he decided to save his sixpence and walk. The day was fine and he needed to stretch his legs. He crossed the river at Waterloo and walked east along Southwark Street. His small valise was light, containing only his spare shirt and shaving tackle. His only frock-coat had had to serve for travel and the wedding, but he hoped that its rather stained appearance would have gone unnoticed in the finery of all the other guests.

He was familiar with the London streets now. At first they had daunted him, bustling with traffic and with people whose cockney speech had been all but incomprehensible. But in gradual explorations he had become master of the geography and his time amongst the stevedores and shipwrights at the docks had made the local speech intelligible. It was Sunday, so the usual business of the streets was absent; no stalls or hawkers, no errand-boys or washer-women. Couples were out strolling, enjoying their Sunday rest, and although the mean streets and shadowed by-ways did not seem to Arthur to be a pleasant or refreshing locale, he supposed that for those used to the hard labour of the docks or the smell of tanneries and glue-works, they were fresh and peaceful enough.

Before long he came out onto Jamaica Road, which would take him past Surrey Docks and towards what he surprised himself by thinking of as 'home.' It was as far as possible, in every way, from the cramped little gatehouse where he had been born and brought up. Mrs Quince, for all her eccentricities, kept a clean and tidy house, strict hours and every appurtenance of gentility she could muster. Mrs Harlish had never been celebrated for her housekeeping and a jolly chaos had usually reigned, with meals served as-and-when, or sometimes not at all. The two landscapes were as dissimilar as possible. Many a time, taking a last turn up and down the lane outside Mrs Quince's cottage before going to bed, Arthur had tried to imagine the smell of the moor, the sound of the owls hunting in the woods, the rush of clean, fresh wind against his skin, but utterly failed. The marsh around the house was of a completely different ilk—salty, sour-smelling, sometimes almost noxious. The birds were water fowl, squawking and complaining as they passed in chevrons overhead, squabbling over fish-heads and whatever other jetsam the river tide brought to the muddy banks. At night only choruses of frogs disturbed the tangy air. He *had* been lonely, although he would not have admitted as much to Georgina. *Very* lonely. His time—too brief—with the Burleighs had brought it home to him and now as he walked across the marsh he found his heart was heavy.

The ground either side of Halfpenny Hatch Lane was strewn with rubbish. The ramshackle encampments of workers were spreading ever wider as more people came to dig out Mr Brunel's tunnel. Grubby children waded about in the greasy little streams, stirring up the stinking mud. Women emptied their slops wherever they felt like it and insects swarmed in clouds over the rotting peelings and boiled bones. Around the public houses men and women caroused, their week's wages spent on beer and cheap gin. The meanness of it sickened him.

But he was tired, he told himself. The journey, the lack of sleep, the wedding and the trip home again had exhausted him. Some tea, a good wash, a hearty supper and a proper night's sleep would put him right.

As he approached the little cottage, however, it was obvious that none of these things would be readily available. Even as he passed through the gate and between the borders of cornflowers and bluebells he could hear a commotion from within the blue-doored cottage; laughter, some hushing and then the voice of Mr Pink declaiming:

> *O! She doth teach the torches to burn bright.*
> *It seems she hangs upon the cheek of night*
> *Like a rich jewel in an Ethiope's ear;*
> *Beauty too rich for use, for earth too dear!*[xxxiv]

Arthur allowed himself a small smile, for a man built less in the likeness of Romeo than Mr Pink it would be hard to imagine; he was small in stature but large of girth, with a round, ruddy face and sparse, greying hair. There was no doubt though, that he was a man of a passionate nature. No wonder Mrs Quince wanted him for her beau. He gave the rest of Romeo's speech with great puissance, quite emulating a man smitten by love, at last concluding in a voice charged with passion, *'I ne'er saw true beauty until this night.'* The ardent nature of Mr Pink's delivery did not disappoint the ladies within, who gave an audible sigh, and Arthur took this opportunity to go indoors.

The troupe was gathered around the fireplace in Mrs Quince's drawing room. The fire was not lit, the day being warm from the spring sunshine that poured in through the window, but a small spirit stove on a side table hissed and popped beneath a cast iron saucepan and the air was filled with the aroma of punch. Bill Bannock had his own secret recipe for this concoction, and it was clear that he had been dispensing it with a liberal hand, for all the play-readers were pink-cheeked and Dick and Walt wore expressions of addled satiety. There being insufficient seats, the two young men were propped against the wooden panelling and against each other, and it was likely that if either of these supports had been removed they would have slumped to the ground. Mrs Quince and Miss Pink sat side by side on the settle. Mrs Bannock reclined in the easy chair in a somnolent posture. Mr Pink occupied the hearth rug and had the folio in his hand. Pansy crouched in the doorway that led to the scullery, her legs folded beneath her, her expression very rapt, even her pale complexion a little flushed.

Arthur's entrance galvanised them all and there was wholesale moving of seats, offering of punch, taking of his frock-coat, greetings, hand-shaking and effusive welcome. Dick and Walter Bannock pitched themselves from their buttress and ricocheted off the settle quite as though thrown about on the deck of a ship at sea. They slapped Arthur heartily on the back as they passed and came to rest by the window, narrowly avoiding the upset of Mrs Quince's stuffed macaw. Arthur's valise disappeared from his hand and a glass of punch was placed in it. Mrs Bannock offered him her seat, making an ineffectual attempt to raise herself from it, which he of course declined. In vain did he attempt to let them know that he wished to go to his room, to wash his hands and face, to change his shirt, to lie down and rest, to do anything but disturb their theatricals and certainly not to be encompassed within them. But they would hear none of it, and before he knew it he was seated on one of the dining chairs and had the folio in his hand.

'You must be Lord Capulet,' Mrs Quince told him. 'Dick is to be Tybalt and of course his brother must be Mercutio so that they can fight it out in Act three. Mr Bannock has been reading Lord Capulet up to this but he will not mind giving it over to you.'

'Oh no,' said Arthur, pushing the folio away. 'I would not dream of taking Mr Bannock's role. And recall, I will be out of the house for your next reading.'

'I hope not,' said Miss Pink, who had not spoken up to this point. 'We are in sore need of more gentlemen for our play.'

She had a soft, musical voice. Arthur looked at her properly for the first time. Before this he had seen her only briefly. Her commodious pelisse and a closed bonnet had kept her person and her features hidden. She, like her father and like Arthur himself, left home early each day to travel to her occupation, but that morning twilight was no time to converse and they had made do with a polite nod. What time Miss Pink returned home in the evenings Arthur did not know. In his late evening perambulations up and down the lane, or as far as the St Helena for Mrs Quince's medicinal tot of gin, he had never seen her and, now he thought about it, the lights of the neighbouring cottage had usually been extinguished by that time. Now the evenings were lighter as Arthur returned from the docks, Mr Pink was not infrequently to be seen in his garden, turning over the soil and tending his vegetable seedlings, but Arthur did not recall ever seeing Miss Pink in that locale. It seemed curious to him that, although such close neighbours, he and the lady were strangers.

Mrs Quince had given him to understand that Miss Pink was an old maid, without claim to beauty, but this was far from the case. She was perhaps a year or two closer to thirty than he was, but her face was pleasant to look at, not lined or wrinkled to any degree, her fair hair was neatly arranged, her eyes grey and very kind. Her mode of speech was rather genteel—genuinely so, unlike Mrs Quince's affected pretention— and conveyed to Arthur immediately that she must spend time with people more refined than the inhabitants of Cuckold's Point. She gave him an encouraging smile. 'My father has been carrying more parts than he can manage. And I know Mr Bannock is particularly desirous of attempting the role of friar Lawrence, which is a substantial part, you know.'

Arthur had a hazy remembrance of the play and could not positively agree that this was the case, but her entreaty, and the warm glow of Mr Bannock's grog that had now permeated to his empty stomach, and the eager encouragement of the other members of the company made him relent, and he took up the folio.

'I fink[xxxv] I 'ave a few lines before you,' Dick Bannock said, lurching from where he had come to rest in the window alcove. He leaned over Arthur's shoulder to fix the place, drew a deep breath and bellowed, '*Vis, by 'is voice, should be a Mon'ague!*'[xxxvi]

They read the scene to the end, Arthur finding that, after all, other than a brief altercation with Tybalt he had little to do. In the distribution of the female parts Mrs Quince had clearly won her point. She read the part of Juliet, and very coyly, concentrating the full power of her charm and beauty on Mr Pink as she said, '*Saints have hands that pilgrims' hands do touch, And palm to palm is holy palmers' kiss.*' She managed in the final word, to pucker her lips and almost demonstrate the action. Mr Pink blushed to the colour of his name, and Arthur saw Miss Pink close her eyes in a brief expression of exasperation. It was no surprise that, as soon as the scene was concluded, Mr Pink bid the company farewell, gathering up his folio and his daughter and taking himself home. Mrs Quince mastered her disappointment and urged the Bannocks to remain, mentioning supper, which caused Pansy to pale and scurry back into the scullery, presumably to see how the supper she had prepared for three could be stretched to four more. There being no more punch, however, the Bannocks made their excuses and left, stumblingly, into the late afternoon.

'What a very enjoyable and edifying afternoon,' Mrs Quince declared. 'I am so gratified that you agreed to participate. You will have seen what dire need we have of competent readers. Mr Pink, of course, is superlatively good. Oh!' with a sigh, her hand pressed to her bosom, 'do you not think he has the voice of a nightingale? And I flatter myself that I have some little facility …' She cast her eyes downwards, and Arthur bowed his assent.

'Miss Pink is not at all as I had pictured her,' he ventured. 'What is her occupation?'

'Oh,' Mrs Quince sniffed, 'she is in the millinery.[xxxvii] She says she works in a great house in Hanover Square but I forget the name of it now. By all accounts she has risen in the profession and now supervises several girls in the first-light.'[xxxviii]

'I wonder why she has never married,' mused Arthur.

'She is devoted to her father. Many a lady hereabouts fancied their chances with him,' Mrs Quince informed him, 'but Miss Pink would not let them near.' She spoke bitterly, and Arthur inferred that Miss Pink stood between Mrs Quince and the object of her intention. 'He is in the City, you know, a clerk in a bank. In my opinion it is a sin for him to remain unmarried. What comfort he could offer a lady, if she were worthy of him. The pity is that so *few* hereabouts would be worthy.' She sighed, and looked longingly at the place on the hearthrug where Mr Pink had stood.

Arthur's stomach rumbled and he stood up. 'I must go upstairs to wash and change. Will dinner be served soon?'

'Oh yes,' Mrs Quince said, shaking herself from her reverie. 'Pansy has made a pie. It will be ready when you come down. Leave your coat and your boots. Pansy will brush them up for you.'

As usual, in the time it took Arthur to change his clothes and splash his face with water, the drawing room was turned into a dining room and a beautiful pie sat upon the table, its crust brown and glossy, the aroma of its inner treasures filling the room and making Arthur's mouth water. As they ate he attempted to interest Mrs Quince in his travels to Salisbury, the wedding finery, the welcome he had received from the Burleighs, and of his journey back with Colonel Black. 'Miss Willow is coming to stay in town with my employer, Mr Talbot,' he concluded. 'I hope I shall see her, although we made no arrangement.'

'No doubt she hopes to follow her mother down the aisle as quickly as possible,' Mrs Quince said, a cynical light in her eye. 'Do you have hopes in that direction?'

'Not at all,' laughed Arthur.

'Is she a comely girl?'

'I cannot tell you. As a child she was pretty enough, I think …'

'You men,' scoffed Mrs Quince. 'You never notice these things.'

'Perhaps not,' replied Arthur, but he thought it was an accusation he could refute. He had noticed Miss Pink. 'To me, she is simply Georgina. I have known her since she was a baby. But nowadays she hides her face away.'

This greatly interested Mrs Quince. '*Does* she, indeed? How curious. Poor thing. Perhaps she has pox scars? I have known some women disfigured by pustules. There has been no accident, that you know of?'

Arthur shook his head. 'No.'

Mrs Quince sighed. 'Anything like that would be a tragedy, but then, great beauty *can* be a curse, in its way.' She raised a hand to her face and drew a finger lingeringly from raddled brow to sagging jaw. 'Many suitors are too much in awe to approach. Ah, yes,' she concluded, with a theatrical sigh, 'the beautiful woman is destined to a life of loneliness.'

17

In his anger and dismay, George Talbot left the house in Grosvenor Square without any clear idea of a destination. He would not call forth the carriage again; the horses and grooms had done enough for one day. And he hardly had the patience to wait until his usual mount could be saddled and brought around.

The day had been fine but now, as the April afternoon wore on, the temperature had dropped. A brisk wind had sprung up. He had neglected to put on his top-coat and even his hat, flinging himself down the stairs and out of the door, propelled by incendiary ire against his wife, disappointment and quandary. Lady Jane had shamed him with her accusations, her hysterical behaviour, her strident, appalling indictments. Poor Georgina! What kind of start was *this* for her sojourn amongst them? What must she be thinking, what suffering, in these unfamiliar surroundings? Thank goodness for Miss Trimble who, he hoped, would take the poor young woman in hand, and somehow smooth over this terrible beginning.

George walked quickly away from the square, along Grosvenor Street, heading west towards Hyde Park. He had no mind to meet anyone, could not have borne to so much as pass the time of day with any acquaintance, should he meet one. But at this hour the park would be deserted, for the dinner hour approached and all respectable people would be at home, dressing. He felt he could safely enter the park, so he did so, ignoring the myriad pathways that criss-crossed the grass, striding instead over the turf, passing swathes of faded daffodils, walking beneath trees just come into leaf and one or two breaking out into blossom. They were lovely, but his temper was so stoked that he hardly saw them.

The wind was chill and he walked very briskly, swinging his arms so as to keep warm and also in an attempt to expiate his anger. He did not recall ever having been so angry, even with his wife. How could she be so obtuse? Why would she not see sense? Obstinate, irrational woman! She had struck him, flailing at him with her hands, with Miss Trimble and the servants and Georgina looking on in awed, appalled silence. But then he recalled that he had struck her too, a sharp slap to shock her into silence. He was ashamed at that, but how else could he have stopped her tirade of vile allegations? How else could he have stopped her from putting the most vicious ideas into the heads of the servants and of Georgina herself? How else could he have stopped her from stumbling upon the truth?

He crossed Serpentine Road and circumnavigated the bottom of the Serpentine itself. Its edges were muddy, trodden no doubt by nannies and their charges. All his children had liked to come here when they were young. Once, he and Rafe had flown a kite. Hadn't Bobby lost a sailing boat? How he had cried, his distress out of all proportion to the loss. But that was Bobby to a tee; he did get so zealously attached to things. Oh! How George missed him! As though conjured by his recollection, he could see a semi-submerged vessel amongst some reeds, its sails limp, its mast broken, some other child's prized possession gone too far out of reach to be saved.

In the remembrance of his children, and in the sad spectacle of the toy boat, he found his anger had ebbed away. He stood on the bank of the lake, his shoulders drooped, his hands loose at his sides, the very image of dejection and misery. He missed all of his children. It was two years since Bobby had gone on his tour. When he came back he would be a man, twenty one years of age, the same age George himself had been when he married Bibi. In two years Rafe, now seventeen, would follow in Bobby's footsteps. The girls would marry, he supposed, and be lost to him forever. Well, perhaps Robyn would not, but she was her own woman. Beatrice was her mother's child—prideful and sly—and would grow into a facsimile of Lady Jane. Either way, his own four children were slipping from his grasp, as the string of the boat had, from the childish fist that had held it, and he had been increasingly aware, these past few years, of feeling bereft. Was that why he had asked Jocelyn to send Georgina to him? Was that why he wanted to establish a connexion with her, to garner to himself the loose, unsuspected thread of family association?

There were reasons why he could not own Jocelyn as more than very distant kin. She could not come to town, even after all these years, in case she might be recognised and all her carefully woven veil of misdirection be pulled away. But he had thought Georgina would be safe enough if he could keep her from society's eye. He had forgotten, of course, that his wife was a society woman, that the thirst for scandal, for gossip, the insatiable need to tear each other to shreds that he so despised in the *ton* was represented—was nurtured—in the very bosom of Lady Jane. He had forgotten—or, more accurately, he had chosen to forget—Lady Jane's needling curiosity about Jocelyn.

He walked on, wandering aimlessly, taking no notice of his direction or of the scene about him, deeply lost in his thoughts. Yes, he admitted to himself, there *was* something that had been missing in his life that he had hoped Georgina would restore. It had begun in 1813 when he had been informed of his sister's death, and been augmented the following year at the loss of his dear Bibi. Guilt and grief had eaten away at him. His remarriage had not cured it, success in business had not distracted from it. It had been selfish of him to put Georgina at risk in an attempt to assuage it, and he had not known *then* of her peculiar sensibility.

He had been selfish in other ways too. Lady Jane's specific allegation earlier might have been without foundation but he was by no means guiltless. She had accused him of faithlessness and he could not gainsay it. He had taken comfort where it had offered itself and lately that had been at Pear Tree Cottage. He supposed, now, that to properly protect Georgina, to be able to look his wife unswervingly in the eye, that association must be given up. He would do it for Georgina's sake, but he feared that no sacrifice on his part would prevent his wife from spreading rumours about their guest. Why, even now, she was probably at her desk penning a note to Baroness Charlton or another of her cronies, hinting, suggesting, remarking in all apparent innocence of the *extraordinary* likeness between Miss Willow and himself. She would not scruple to besmirch his reputation. He hardly cared about that for himself, although of course it would do his children no good. But it would only take one of her correspondents to recall the name Willow, or the name of his sister, for the connexion to be made. It was unlikely but it was not impossible. And there would be Georgina, helplessly trapped in the lions' den her mother had been so desperate to keep her from, the object of unfair censure, stained by the sin of another.

He found himself beneath a spreading oak tree. Evening was coming—it must by then have been about five o'clock—and the patch beneath the tree was shadowed, a gloomier hue of the shade that was enveloping the whole park. He could see the water of the lake below him, steely grey and stirred to little waves by the breeze, but no light sparkled from it; the sun was wreathed in thick cloud.

From the corner of his eye he saw something stir—a tall dark pillar, hidden, like him, in the shadow beneath a large tree. The figure stood a little way off, hesitating to approach and yet not—seeing his palpable anguish—going away. George stepped out from the canopy of the tree.

'Mr Balfour.'

Balfour—for it was he—removed his hat and bowed before coming closer.

'I did not wish to disturb you,' he said. 'I could see you were deep in thought, and yet I felt … forgive me … but I felt it was not right to leave you. I have been following you at a distance for this last half an hour.'

George looked around him. He had no recollection of coming to the spot and he did not think he recognised the place. 'I have been walking aimlessly,' he admitted.

'And you came out in a hurry, I deduce,' said Balfour. 'You are cold. Please take my cloak.' Before George could accept or decline this invitation Balfour had swept off his outer garment and thrown it around his shoulders. It was wonderfully warm and it was only then that George realised how chilled he had been.

'You have dined?' Balfour enquired.

'No,' said George. 'I have had nothing since breakfast at the inn in Reading.'

'Ah yes,' said Balfour. He held his hand out in a gesture that suggested that their walk from here should be in the same direction, and together, and George found himself falling into step. 'You went to collect your cousin. Lady Jane told me that she was looked for today.'

'*Did* she?' George almost hooted. 'Well, as much as she might have been 'looked for' I am sorry to say that my poor little cousin has not been very graciously welcomed.'

The two men strolled over the grass until they came to one of the gravelled pathways, which they then followed. Still George had no absolute understanding of their whereabouts or their destination. Every time they came to a junction, though, Mr Balfour, without seeming to lead or dictate, did exactly that.

'I am sorry to hear it,' said Balfour coolly. 'The young lady is objectionable?'

'By no means. That is, as regards her person, I cannot tell you … But Lady Jane objects to her.'

'I see. She is disenchanted with young ladies in general perhaps. She told you of the drama at the Staffords' ball?'

'She told me nothing. There was no opportunity. We had hardly taken off our travelling clothes before she erupted in … I can hardly describe it … an unreasonable assault.'

'It was a most distressing occurrence for Lady Jane. I am sure she is still upset by it. I'm no gossip so I shall not relate the details. I would not have said as much as I have if I had not felt sure that she would have related the whole to you with her own lips.'

'It may have some bearing on the matter,' said George, although privately, he doubted it.

They walked on in silence for a few moments, in no hurry, Balfour seemingly intent on their surroundings, two gentlemen taking the air. And yet George could sense that his companion had some strategy, some design, as they distinctly took one path rather than another. He suddenly felt embarrassed, to have been discovered hatless and coatless, in distress, in a place and at an hour where no respectable person would be found.

'You will wonder what on earth I am doing here,' George said at last with an awkward laugh.

'No more than you might wonder what I am,' Balfour replied mildly. 'But, in point of fact, I have drawn my conclusion. You have argued with Lady Jane and came out of the house suddenly.'

'Yes,' agreed George. 'That sums it up. Lady Jane …'

'You owe me no explanation,' Mr Balfour interrupted. 'It is none of my business.'

'No,' George said, and shut his lips. But a strong desire to share his troubles, to confide in a friend, overcame him. His conundrum was not so very terrible, not shameful; it was simply another person's secret that he was honour-bound to keep. 'And yet,' he burst out, 'I feel I would like to give you one. It is … not very easy to explain. Miss Willow is a distant cousin.'

'Yes,' said Balfour. 'You said as much when we discussed it at the club.'

'Yes. But, Lady Jane suspects a much nearer connexion. Her suspicions are wholly unfounded and yet there is, in the connexion, something that, if known, could cause a third party harm. In telling you this I confess more than I have done to Lady Jane.'

Mr Balfour ruminated for a moment before saying, 'It satisfies me. Would it not satisfy her?'

'Oh no,' George shook his head sadly. 'She would need to know every detail and then, once she knew it, she would transmit it far and wide. The secret would be out.'

'I see,' said Balfour, nodding sagely. 'Well, you know your own wife best, I think.'

'*You* know her pretty well now, Balfour. You know at least that she has harangued me from my own home.'

Balfour shrugged. 'I am not married,' he observed. 'I know very little of ladies and nothing at all of ladies who are married. Much, I conjecture, goes on behind closed doors that is not admitted to in public.'

'You conjecture correctly, in my case at least,' said George. 'But I think badly of myself. I have left Miss Willow defenceless.'

'If I must give an opinion I agree with you that the young lady is the principle concern. From what I understand she is not at fault and should not be made to suffer for the misconceptions of others.'

'You are right,' George said, stopping abruptly and looking around them. 'I ought to go home. In any event I have detained *you* long enough. Surely, you ought to be at dinner.'

Balfour shook his head. 'You find me quite at your disposal. In point of fact I often come to the park at this hour. I prefer it when the crowds are gone. I walk at night also, along the streets, when I can have them to myself.' He began to walk again and George had no option but to follow.

'You like solitude?'

'I like not to be the object of curiosity. It does not matter how successful I am, or how much money I make, how finely I dress or with whom I associate; a man with a black skin who is not carrying a tray or driving a horse is stared at.'

'My dear fellow,' said George, turning to face his friend, 'I am sorry that is the case.'

'It is not your fault.'

'But I ought to do more to counteract it. My first wife was of Indian extraction. She experienced the same discrimination. When I was in India, though the only white face amongst a sea of brown ones, I never felt singled out. Bigotry only afflicts white people.'

'White people have taught themselves to believe they are superior. It is a lesson they must unlearn, but that will not happen overnight. It has taken them hundreds of years to acquire.' Mr Balfour seemed philosophical rather than angry or offended. He pointed ahead of them. 'See. My carriage is waiting at the South Gate[xxxix]. I hope you will allow me to convey you back to Grosvenor Square?'

George looked around him and this time he saw that they had come nearly all the way across the park, towards Kensington Palace. Evening was almost upon them. He shrugged off Mr Balfour's coat and handed it back to its owner.

'You're very kind. But there is somewhere else I must go first. I will find a cab. I must not trouble you further.'

Mr Balfour waved George's words away. 'It would be my pleasure, and not the least trouble. Where would you like to go?'

They had come to the gate now. Mr Balfour's carriage waited at the side of the road, his man already had the door open. George looked up and down the street but there was no cab to be seen in either direction. The only person in view was the lamp-lighter, making his way down the road. Everything appeared in shades of grey–the pewter street and the lowering sky, the onward steal of night. Without Balfour's overcoat George began to feel cold again, and, as he hesitated, a shower of rain began to fall.

'Get in, Talbot, and give the address to my man,' Balfour urged. 'There is no point in getting soaked as well as starved.'

George did as he was bid, giving the driver an address in Chelsea.

'If you will give me leave,' said Balfour, as the carriage moved off, 'I will go home via Grosvenor Square. It is an atrocious hour to call but I shall risk Lady Jane's wrath in the hope of ascertaining for myself that all is well. If it is not, you can be sure of my assistance, and my discretion.'

George held out his hand towards Balfour, who, in the deep gloom of the carriage, was no more than a shadow in the seat across from him. 'Balfour, I thank you,' he said.

18

All was not well.

It was full evening when Mr Balfour arrived at Grosvenor Square. The house was in a hue and cry, every lamp lit, the front door open to the air and the rain, the square and the park at its heart filled with Talbot servants running hither and thither carrying lanterns and calling Miss Willow's name. The windows of houses on either side were filled with inquisitive faces but so far no neighbour had come forth to make enquiry or to offer aid.

Miss Trimble stood in a state of extreme discomposure on the shallow steps that led to the front door. Her hair, usually tightly bound, had partially escaped and was plastered to her head by the rain. Her shawl, hastily wrapped around her spare frame, had slipped from her shoulder and trailed on the floor into the wet. She paced up and down the steps, maintaining a wittering diatribe of concern and anxiety, sometimes berating, sometimes exonerating herself, but always bewailing the catastrophe that had befallen.

Mr Balfour's carriage drew up at the door and its owner was on the pavement before his man could descend to assist, heedless of the rain, which now fell persistently.

Miss Trimble's expression had brightened momentarily at the possibility that Miss Willow might be inside the carriage that had drawn up, but now fell again.

'Oh sir,' she said, wringing her hands, 'I hoped you might have found her.'

'Ma'am,' said Balfour, sweeping off his hat. 'Permit me, in the circumstances, to introduce myself. I am Amory Balfour. I am just come from Mr Talbot. Be assured that I am in his confidence. Tell me, what has occurred here?' He waved his arm towards the precincts of the park. 'Has someone gone missing? Has some worse atrocity taken place?'

Miss Trimble, recalling Mr Balfour's name and the assistance he had provided to Lady Jane at the ball, almost wept with relief at his coming but controlled herself enough to say, 'Yes, sir, Miss Willow is missing. Not worse, although, who knows, perhaps … by now … Oh sir. I cannot bear to think of it. Where is Mr Talbot? Lady Jane thinks … Oh! It is too dreadful to even speak the words. She believes they have run off together. It seems there is no wickedness that she would *not* believe him capable of. Her mind leaps from one unspeakable thing to another. I almost think she has gone mad! But *I* do not share her opinion. I think she has gone astray. Miss Willow, I mean of course. Oh dear, forgive me. I am making no sense …' She gathered herself with an effort of will and said, 'Miss Willow was not in her room when I went there. I had been gone some time, much longer than I wished, but Lady Jane … However, be that as it may, Miss Willow was not there and no one in the house had seen her. But the lamp-man said he had seen a young lady in the park half an hour before and so I have asked them to search it. But, if she is not found there … Oh! I do not know what I shall do.' She turned on Mr Balfour a face of misery and perturbation. 'And,' she concluded, as though this last was the most calamitous detail of all, 'she has had no dinner. None of us has. Lady Jane gave no instruction and Cook did not know what to do.'

'How long have they been searching?' Balfour asked. 'When did the lamp-lighter see her?'

Miss Trimble considered. 'They have been searching for an hour. Perhaps more. But the lamp-lighter saw her half an hour before that, he says.'

In the park the bushes thrashed as men pushed through them, and spring flowers were trampled underfoot, but there was no sign of the missing woman.

'It is not a large park,' Balfour said. 'If she were there she would have been found by now, even if she were lying insensible. Instruct your men to spread out, and to search the streets hereabouts. Tell them to be methodical. I will go east along Brook Street as far as Bond street, and then back to the square via Grosvenor Street. Send some north, up Duke Street to Oxford Street, and back via North Audley Street. Others south …'

'Yes, yes,' said Miss Trimble. She understood at once Mr Balfour's plan. The area of London in which Grosvenor Square was located was built as a series of squares, with buildings intersected by crossing streets. Some of the blocks were themselves bisected by alleys and groves, giving access to the house backs, stables and kitchens. A systematic search should be able to cover them all, in spite of the dark and the rain that fell in sharp showers.

'What does the young lady look like?' asked Balfour, speaking above the gusts of wind and the splattering of the rain. His face was beaded with raindrops, his tight-curled hair aglitter with raindrop jewels.

Miss Trimble hesitated. 'She will be veiled,' she said. 'Beneath the veil I have not seen. But I doubt she will reveal herself. Her dress is grey. I pray she has some kind of shawl or wrap. Her pelisse is in the hallway still. Oh that she should have strayed on such a night as this! She promised me she would do nothing desperate, and so I must console myself by believing that she is simply lost. Lost! And on such a night as this!' Miss Trimble looked in terror at the enfolding night and dreary rain, as though seeing midnight necromancy and biblical deluge, although it was by that time only something after seven of the clock and the rain was by no means a torrent. 'I wish Mr Talbot were here,' she said, almost to herself.

'He shall be fetched,' said Balfour.

Miss Trimble crossed the street and entered the park in order to locate Mr Talbot's butler, Mr Gerrard, who had taken charge of the search. Mr Balfour spoke a word to his groom before setting off on foot in the direction he had indicated. The groom remounted the carriage, it turned and set off back in the direction from which it had come.

The rest of the search party gathered itself on the pavement in front of the house, divided into groups of three and four and then set off towards the various points of the compass, leaving Miss Trimble alone on the step.

Lady Jane had been, by turns, inconsolable, irrational, enraged, hysterical and maudlin. She would take neither tea nor spirits, nor send any instruction to the cook. She had gone into her dressing room and begun pulling gowns and underclothes from the press, intent upon leaving the house upon the instant, but had then collapsed onto her bed in a paroxysm of moans and inarticulate weeping. Miss Trimble had tried every remedy, from smelling salts to laudanum, but Lady Jane refused each one. She would not listen to reason or to her duty and declined to have the doctor or her sister sent for. Miss Trimble herself had been roundly abused for desertion, sent away and called back. At last, from sheer exhaustion, Lady Jane had fallen asleep and Miss Trimble had been able to creep from the room.

The disturbance that had shaken the house on the discovery that Georgina was not in her room, nor anywhere within, had aroused Lady Jane once more, and she had embarked on a further tirade of wild accusations before fixing on the idea that the young woman and her

152

husband had absconded together. She saw no contradiction between this and her earlier assertions and would not listen to the reasonable suggestion that both could not be true.

At last Miss Trimble had caused the family doctor to be sent for, and he was at that moment in Lady Jane's chamber administering a therapy for hysteria.

Now that the men had dispersed, the square seemed desolate and eerily quiet, and Miss Trimble stepped back into the doorway where there was a pool of light. She could have shut the door and waited in one of the ground floor rooms but her anxiety over poor Miss Willow and a hesitation to become embroiled again in Lady Jane's crisis made her remain on the threshold. Minutes passed—five, ten, fifteen. The party that had gone west, towards the park via Upper Brook Street and back again via Upper Grosvenor Street returned first. They had searched carefully, they said, not neglecting King Street Mews, Blackbourne's Mews and Park Street. They were wet and cold, and not very enthusiastic about continuing, but Miss Trimble, summoning an unusual authority, sent them off again to look in the northwest quadrant encompassing Green Street and North Row.

Mr Balfour, searching alone, could not cover so much territory at such speed. He walked quickly along the deserted streets, looking in every doorway and diverting down the alleys that branched off into stable yards on either side. He was beset by misgiving for, even if he were to find the lady, the likelihood of her being willing to put herself into his care seemed remote. He was a stranger, a dark stranger, and no doubt she would be disorientated, distressed, wet and woebegone. That she had suffered an ordeal was manifest from what Talbot had told him, and this coming hard on the heels of parting with her mother. In searching alone he was suddenly aware that he had placed himself at something of a disadvantage; he might be mistaken for a villain and had been, before. Even if he could persuade the young woman to trust him there might be others who would impute to him nefarious designs. He thought his best scheme, should he come upon her, was to knock at the door of the nearest respectable-looking house and beg the lady, if there was one, to take Miss Willow in until he could return with the person he had met on the step of Talbot's house and who he assumed to be Lady Jane's housekeeper. He did not fear meeting a footpad. He was armed with his sword-stick[xl] and could use it. Should any assault be in train when he came upon Miss Willow he would not hesitate to defend her to the death if required. With these grim thoughts he proceeded to quarter the roads either side of Brook Street, but crossed South Molton Street and came out upon Bond Street without having overtaken the missing girl.

Bond Street was a location given over to prestigious and fashionable retailers, tailors, jewellers and other commercial premises. It being Sunday these were all shut up, but the road itself was a busy thoroughfare, connecting areas to the north and west with Piccadilly and the Strand. It was much busier than the streets Balfour had searched so far and instinct told him that a respectable young woman alone would have shied from it. Hackney carriages plied their trade along the road and there were people of all degree walking. Amongst these were some women; matrons in their Sunday best, and also some who were unmistakably women of ill-repute. They loitered in doorways or ambled in twos, arm in arm. But none was veiled and Balfour flattered himself that he would know a young lady of respectable family and gentle up-bringing from one of these poor creatures. He had turned right, determining to walk along Bond Street until it should intersect with Grosvenor Street. The rain continued, not heavy now but of that fine, drenching type, and he wiped his hand over his face to clear moisture from his brows and thick eyelashes.

About three quarters of the way down Bond Street he passed a tiny opening, wide enough only for a man to pass, which he vaguely knew to be Lancaster Court because he had at some time in the past had occasion to send a man there to collect some goods. He hesitated at the opening. There were no lights, the way was dark and very narrow. He imagined only refuse, malodorous piles of indeterminate leavings, hazardous pot-holes, perhaps a chained dog. Surely no young lady would have ventured here? He was about to pass on when the smallest sound—a foot moving on the cobbles, an in-drawn breath, a muffled cry—caught his attention.

'Miss Willow,' he said, as loudly but in as unthreatening a way as he could. 'I am a friend, sent by Mr Talbot. Are you there?'

He listened again. All seemed quiet. Perhaps he had mistaken, or perhaps he had heard only one of the street women plying her trade with a casual customer. Were the two of them now frozen in the midst of their business, pressed into the deepest shadow of the mean little by-way? He swept the image away.

'Miss Willow,' he said again, 'if you are there, and cannot speak, make some sound. Clap your hands. Do something. Let me help you. Do not be afraid.'

He began to edge into the alley, feeling the damp brick with one hand, and reaching into an inner recess of his cloak with the other, to bring forth his sword-stick. The sound of his own feet on the slick stones was maddeningly loud, no matter how carefully, how quietly, he placed them down. He began to speak, inconsequently, as he inched further and further into the black throat of the passage. 'I know you have come from Reading today, and before that, Wiltshire I believe. You must be tired. And the lady at the house says you have not dined. I have not dined either. Let us hope there will be something prepared for us when we get back.'

Again, he was arrested by some sound, the smallest possible noise. It could have been a bird stirring in its roost, a mouse amongst the filth, it could have been his own cloak brushing against the wall. He wished he had a light and cursed himself for not bringing away one of the lanterns that the men from the house had been using. He had not even a match about him. He looked back. The entrance to the alleyway was now some half dozen yards back. The gas lights of the streets were bright but did not reach into the alley. In front of him it was impenetrably dark. He opened his eyes wide but could make nothing out; no building, no gateway, no obstacle. He imagined high walls on either side of him, behind which the yards of houses and the storage places of the various shops were located. He took another step, his sword-stick—still sheathed—held before him, his other hand on the wall.

'This is not a happy introduction to your stay in London,' he observed. 'Your cousin George is most anxious about you. He will wish to make amends. There are very pleasant places to visit and I am sure he will wish to show you them all. Everywhere is better than *this*, indeed. If he does not, I shall do myself the honour of escorting you.'

His foot touched something. He half recoiled, thinking it a bundle of rags, or something worse. He reached down and touched silk, a shawl, he thought, and the gauze of a fine veil. The body beneath his hands stirred, and made a small mew.

'Miss Willow,' he said, squatting beside the form, which was curled up against the wall, very wet, no doubt very wretched, 'is that you?'

The slightest nod—she was not capable of more, he deduced.

He removed his cloak and draped it over her, trying as he did so to arrange her hat and veil and shawl as best he was able for the sake of her modesty. But the way was narrow and in her swoon to the ground she must have dislodged matters and, in the utter darkness, and being a man unfamiliar with feminine accessories, he could not be sure he had been successful.

'Will you trust yourself to me?' he whispered. 'Put your arms about my neck and I will lift you up.'

It seemed an effort. She was barely conscious, only half hearing him, but she lifted her arms and clasped her hands behind his neck, and he lifted her up.

She must have fainted away altogether as he carried her home. She spoke no word, and rested her head against his shoulder. Her garments, as he had feared, were disarranged, her shawl trailing behind, her bonnet askew, but her veil remained over her face.

Mr Balfour walked briskly, his eyes steadfastly on the way ahead, but the weight of the young lady in his arms, her trusting head and clinging arms, filled his heart to overflowing.

19

Cold, wet, exhausted and famished—but nothing worse. This was the diagnosis of the doctor who attended Miss Willow. She was stripped of her wet clothing and put to bed, fed hot soup and then left to sleep, which she did for twenty four hours. Miss Trimble was in constant attendance, urging gruel, bread-and-milk, weak tea and dry toast at intervals when her patient was lucid, reading or sewing quietly beneath the shaded lamp when she was not. She kept the window curtains closed, the bed curtains also, but there were times when her care required her to look upon her patient. She did so askance, the least to discompose the woman in the bed, her eyes everywhere but on the young woman's face. She tried to sweeten the cup of Georgina's discomfort by an endless flow of chatter: the weather, the news from court, Dickie's paw, which had been discovered to be infected, some little altercation between Cook and the housekeeper over the proper quantity of oysters required for a pie. Nevertheless it was impossible for her not to see Georgina, to see her face, and what she saw filled her old heart with a peculiar compassion and a kind of awe. But she would make no mention of it. *That*, she knew, would be to knock down all the delicate foundation of trust she was laying; she would not remark upon the very thing Miss Willow was most painfully sensible of.

Throughout Miss Trimble's ministrations Georgina lay very still on the pillows and kept her eyes fixed on the canopy of the bed. But she wore no veil.

A very few days, however, saw the young woman restored. It may be that having survived the embarrassment of being looked upon by Miss Trimble and finding, in the older woman's demeanour, no mortifying response, she was encouraged. She was young and healthy. Although shy of her appearance and clearly labouring under tribulations of the mind she was not physiologically fragile and on the third day she rose from the bed, washed and dressed herself and brushed off the set-back as nothing more than over-excitement at the wedding, a long journey and a poor sense of direction.

She said she recalled nothing of her escapade beyond a kind voice speaking to her in the darkness and being lifted up in strong arms. What wretchedness of feeling, what distracted thoughts must have bent her footsteps from the relative safety of the park to the dark and disorientation of Mayfair was only to be speculated upon, but a fear of reviving the impact of her hostess' excess of spleen made everyone feel that it was a speculation best left in abeyance.

For the first week Mr Balfour called daily, bringing flowers and invitations—to dine, to his box at Drury Lane, to picnics and to galleries. All were refused, but gently. Miss Willow he did not see at all. She saw no callers, he was informed, but thanked him most profusely for his kind attentions.

Lady Jane also kept to her bed, and—not to be outdone—for much longer than Georgina. She was in truth exhausted by the physical exigencies both of her hysterical outburst and the treatments that had followed it. The doctor visited daily to administer massage therapy and magnetism.[xli] It was at his decree that Lady Jane remained within the precincts of her private apartments but it suited that lady to stay out of sight. She refused absolutely to look upon her guest, to encounter her or to have any kind of intercourse with her. Some shame at her uncontrolled outburst made her reluctant to see anyone but Agnes or her own maid. She harboured a continuing, brooding conviction that she had been severely wronged by her husband, wounded and dishonoured by him. She was not at all moved from her belief that he had shamelessly brought in, beneath her nose, his illegitimate child. She chose to nurture her resentment against him and her young guest in private until she should have some proof that would direct her future course. In the meantime she adopted the role of martyr: haughty, sullen, long-suffering, silent.

Mr Talbot, of course, could not be barred from the room and he visited her daily, sat and read to her, held her hand and did all in his power to show his constancy and conciliation. He spoke of generalities, not referring to what had occurred but rather of the future; a house in Brighton, improvements at Ecklington, the progress of his ship. She replied in monosyllables, expressing neither interest nor opinion, glad when, at last, he got up and went away.

She was perhaps not more glad than *he* was, when their awkward hour should have passed. A sulky wife is never a pleasant companion. A wife who has believed—and continues to believe—dishonourable things of him is apt to stir a man's ire. But when he has given up, for her sake, an association which had vastly comforted him and *still* does not get the credit of it, then he begins to feel like a fool. George's interview at Pear Tree Cottage had been tearful and heart-breaking. He was genuinely attached to the lady there and he was sad that he could no longer have recourse to the comforts and charms of her company. But so it must be, he had convinced himself. To be innocent of one charge he must be innocent of all.

When he left his wife's rooms he made straight for Miss Willow's, and between the two of them there developed a cousinly friendship of the most cordial kind. *She* was not surly, *she* was not silent. She was interested in his business, in his ships, in his schemes for Ecklington. To be sure, she retained her veil but, indoors, it was of a lighter kind and he felt assured that he was, by small degrees, gaining her trust. There were times when, the candle being angled just so, or the light falling through a window at a certain degree, he felt he could have glimpsed her features through the stuff of her gauze, but he made no effort to do so. He would not hurry her.

To save her blushes he dined at his club—often with Mr Balfour—leaving Miss Willow and Miss Trimble to a quiet meal in a small breakfast room rarely used before. Cook prepared a buffet from which they could help themselves, negating the need for a footman. When George returned he found the ladies sewing or reading or playing cards, and it pleased him to join them. Sometimes Georgina would play the pianoforte, which she did rather well, and it was with reluctance that, at the close of the evening, he made his way to Lady Jane's chambers to bid her goodnight.

On one of these occasions he was waylaid by Miss Trimble.

'I hope you do not mind my mentioning it sir, but I think that Miss Willow is ready to go out. She has mentioned it to me and I think she has recovered sufficiently for there to be no danger in it for her. And, I wondered sir, if you would not think it a presumption, whether a visit to Madame Planché might not be in order.' Madame Planché was Lady Jane's milliner. 'She could perhaps devise some closed bonnet[xlii] ...'

'Madame Planché,' cried George warmly. 'Of course. I must say, Miss Trimble, I am delighted that you have won Miss Willow's confidence. She seems, with you, quite easy.'

'She *is*, sir,' said Agnes, blushing with pleasure. 'We have become very good friends.'

'And,' George stepped closer and lowered his voice, 'tell me, Miss Trimble. Beneath the veil ...?'

But Miss Trimble shook her head. 'As to that, sir, I feel I should remain silent. I must not trespass on the confidence Georgina has placed on me.'

'No,' George said. 'You are very good.'

20

In point of fact Miss Willow absolutely declined a visit to the milliners. Miss Trimble's gentle suggestion—that a closed bonnet, with a *very* deep brim, might do just as well as a veil, but with the added advantage of allowing Georgina to *see*, properly, rather than through a gauze—was well-intended no doubt, but Georgina was not ready for such disclosure. To her surprise, however, she found she would very much enjoy some fresh air and exercise. Her first week at Cousin George's house had had the most alarming start. She had not expected to be ill, and her strategies for the avoidance of exposure had all come to nought in the necessity for her to be nursed. But Miss Trimble's kindness—and, importantly, the absence of Lady Jane—had made her feel emboldened. Apart from Lady Jane the house held no threat and was pleasant enough, but she longed to be out of doors. Perhaps, after all, she might be able to partake of some of the delights of London without undue publicity.

The weather at that period was kind and George took her to the park, to walk along the river, out for rides in his carriage. No mention was made of her face-covering which, out of doors, was thick, impenetrable crêpe. She knew that her friends did not approve of it and that they hoped in time she would have sufficient confidence in them and in herself to remove it. But there was no question that they would insist. Their forbearance was exactly what she needed, not to enable her to persist in her shying-away, but to gather the strength to emerge from it. She felt that in all probability she *would* be safe with Cousin George. Allowing him to see her would only be a small step on from allowing Miss Trimble to do so. But then, outdoors, there was the crowd, the strangers, the grooms and waiters. These she could not rely on.

Several enjoyable days were spent in George Talbot's *barouche landau*^{xliii} exploring the less-frequented parts of the town and on one of these occasions they encountered Amory Balfour.

That day, because of a sudden cloud-burst, they had resorted to Angerstein's gallery^{xliv}. It was a small place, crowded by others who had sought escape from the rain. Georgina's shrouded form was viewed with curiosity by many but she had found that it was a sufficient impediment to prevent unwanted approaches. They assumed, she supposed, a deep and unshakable mourning. It made her, curiously, both visible *and* invisible. The garment itself was notable but the person beneath was rendered almost non-existent, particularly if she remained silent, which she usually did. Georgina ignored the curious glances and outright stares. She could, if she had wished, have returned the stares, pulled a face, winked or leered or stuck out her tongue. *That* was another strangely satisfactory quality of the veil; beneath it there was an odd, contradictory freedom.

Georgina had been desirous of seeing the pictures but had not anticipated how congested the small rooms would be. In addition—she had to admit it—it was frustratingly difficult to *see* the canvasses; the light was poor in any case and her veil made it seem as though she viewed them through a dirty window. Nevertheless she kept her attention on them until she was aware of Mr Talbot saying to her, 'Oh, Georgina, here is your knight, Amory Balfour.'

Mr Balfour stepped boldly through the crowd. Such was his general air of authority and importance that people fell back to allow him through.

Those nearby were clearly intrigued; *two* unusual figures in such a small space! They watched with avid interest. Balfour took not the smallest notice of the spectators. He bowed. As usual with him it was a stiff, formal bow. Prompted by its decorum George made as though to conduct an introduction in the stilted, conventional way, but Balfour stopped him with a gesture. *That*, he knew, would attract too much attention and reveal too much about Miss Willow.

Relieved, Georgina held out her hand. 'I am very glad to see you Mr Balfour.'

She spoke low, and Balfour bent to hear her. His gaze fixed on the place where he guessed Georgina's eyes to be, as though no intervening voile were between them. 'I am most happy to come across you,' he said, also in a confidential tone. 'I hope I do not startle you?' Normally he would not have said so much, would indeed have considered such a question demeaning, but he felt Miss Willow's particular sensibility.

The on-lookers, understanding that nothing would be heard of the conversation, turned back to the artworks.

Georgina shook her head. 'Not at all! Why should I be startled?'

'Oh,' he made a vague gesture at his face. 'Some people find the colour of my skin an impediment. You, of course, that night, had no apprehension of it. If you *had*, indeed …'

'It would have made no difference,' Georgina concluded for him. 'My parents' dearest friend, Mr Burleigh, hales from the Caribbean. Even if I could have seen you that night, my instinct would have been to trust you, as I trust him.'

'Ah, Miss Willow,' said Amory, smiling with pleasure—surprising himself, indeed, with the amount of pleasure her words gave him—'you could have said no more flattering thing.'

Much had Mr Balfour thought about Miss Willow in the days since their first encounter. She had not spoken to him on that occasion and of course he had not seen her face, but he felt that some connection had been made between them. *His* heart, certainly, had been quickened. He could not explain why but he, a confirmed bachelor, had been conscious of a new throb of awareness, a new lightness about his soul. He only knew that she was at the source of it. George Talbot's sharing with him, over several dinners, the young lady's extraordinary shyness, her gradual progress, had only increased his interest. That she wore a veil even indoors intrigued him. It was not unusual for ladies to disguise themselves in that way when out in public. Veils were expected of women in mourning. Many a love affair and many a discreet visit to a doctor were achieved under the cover of a thick veil. With some women it was merely an affectation, with some—the scarred, the toothless, the knocked-about by brutal husbands—it was a necessity. It did not seem to him likely that any of these motives could explain Miss Willow's behaviour.

'Won't you join us, Balfour?' said George now, as they loitered in the gallery. 'We are just going to view the Beaumont collection.'

'I should not wish to impose,' he said.

Georgina felt his diffidence, his peculiar discretion, and she remembered his kindness on the night of her distress. 'You do not impose, sir,' she said, and when Mr Balfour offered his arm, she took it.

Mr Talbot and Miss Trimble, falling into step behind them, exchanged a significant look.

Thereafter Mr Balfour was often of their party although, like George, from time to time business precluded it. When not attended by the gentlemen Agnes and Georgina walked in the various parks or drank tea in out-of-the-way little shops that Agnes found. Georgina enjoyed the older woman's company but there was not the thrill, the sense of wide-flung possibility that existed when Talbot and Balfour were present. In spite of herself, Georgina found that the wider world, the world she had been denied, held many attractions, many interests. From beneath her veil she enjoyed the opportunity to watch others. People—strangers— had acquired, in her imagination, an unspecific but nevertheless fearsome quality. But now she found aspects of them that were reassuringly ordinary, sometimes even humorous. She found they all had their quirks, their inhibitions, their flaws and also their virtues. She saw kindness as well as cruelty, tenderness as well as brutality. Of course she saw only the commonplace folk; Miss Trimble was careful to keep away from those locations where the well-to-do of society congregated.

It may be that she associated Mr Balfour in her mind with Mr Burleigh but Georgina felt easy in Amory's company. He rambled alongside her, helped her over stiles, settled the rug over her skirts as she took her place in the barouche. Sometimes he rode with them in the carriage but more often he rode his horse alongside them. He was a fine horseman and looked very handsome on his large, black mount. Often he spoke few words, seeming to enjoy the scenery, the exercise, without the need to fill the air with inconsequential talk. Georgina was not used to the kinds of formal but meaningless conversations that were usual amongst the ton; she did not talk for the sake of talking. When she did talk—prompted by his gentle enquiries—she spoke to him of her parents, of Yorkshire and of her friends the Burleighs. She told him of the things that mattered to her. In his turn he described to her the discrimination he had suffered at school as the only black face amongst an entire roll-call of white, the number of times he had been mistaken for a groom, a delivery boy, a thief.

In this he could not have chosen a topic more likely to excite her extraordinary sympathy. 'We are judged by our appearance,' she said. 'It is why I wear this veil. I wonder you have never remarked upon it! Perhaps you *have*, privately.'

Of course he *had*, but he would rather have died than have admitted as much. At the same time he had found that, as time went on, it mattered to him less and less. He said, 'I hope I am not so shallow as to judge anyone by their appearance. Character is so much more important, and lasts longer! The most beautiful woman, the handsomest man, will not *always* be so.'

'But an ugly person will always be ugly,' she put in.

'Ugly is as ugly does,' he replied. 'Blind men have to evaluate people by other means than sight—by their character, by their attitude to others, by their opinions and beliefs, the tone of their voice and their mode of expression. Since you render me effectively blind, Miss Willow, by your veil, so I have had to make my appraisal of you.'

'*Do* you so,' she replied, laughing. 'And how do you find me? But perhaps I ought not to ask.'

'No indeed, for flattery is invidious and I know you would abhor it. But then, if I tell you the truth, perhaps you will take it for flattery.'

'I might be offended!'

'No,' he demurred, 'I do not think so. But you have me at a disadvantage.'

'How so?'

He raised his hand and plucked at the skin of his cheek. 'My veil is as real as yours, in some ways. It forms a barrier that the world struggles to see through. But I cannot veil my eyes. You will be able to see if you wound me. But I will not know if I hurt your feelings and I would not do so, not for all the world. I will confess this much to you, Miss Willow. I would like to see your eyes. The eyes are the window to the soul, they say[xlv].'

They were walking on Hampstead Heath. George and Miss Trimble were some way behind them. The wind was fresh, but warm, and scented with flowers. Georgina turned to face him, and the stuff of her veil blew back so that it moulded to the contours of her face. He could almost make it out; high, sculpted cheek bones, a Grecian nose. He searched the voile for her eyes. For a moment he almost thought she would pull back her veil and let him see her face.

But she turned again and said with a note of sadness, 'You give me much food for thought. Do you really think of your skin as a veil?'

Amory quashed a sigh of disappointment and they walked on together towards a stand of trees. At last he said, 'In that it predisposes people to think a certain way of me, yes. If you wore a black veil, it would be assumed that you were in mourning. If you wore a white one, you would be perceived as a bride. My skin makes some people—ill-informed, obtuse, bigoted people—believe I am only half human, that I have not the feelings of white men, that I can endure more hardship, am uneducable, pre-disposed to criminality, have a base nature …'

'Stop,' cried Georgina, and he was in some way gratified to hear the anguish in her voice, 'I will hear no more. It is as I suspected; the world is a terrible place. People are cruel.'

They came to a little knoll of trees and Georgina sank down on a fallen log.

'If I may speak one word more on the subject,' Amory said, 'it is this. The world is not terrible and people are not cruel, in general. Some of them are ignorant. I pity them their bias but it does not impinge on me. I am myself, the best iteration of myself that I can be. That is the only authenticity that really matters, I think. I will not let them encroach on it. They shall not embitter me, or wound me, or stand in my way.'

'Such courage,' Georgina murmured, so low that he hardly caught the words.

21

Miss Trimble, in befriending Georgina, in being looked up to by her, was happy. In the house, whilst Lady Jane was indisposed, it was understood that Miss Trimble was de facto mistress. Her orders, her requests and directions—although respectfully and gently given—were all acted on without quibble. Miss Trimble thrived. To be out of the house, away from Lady Jane, to ride in the carriage and be treated to the courteous attentions of Mr Talbot made for a holiday indeed, and all her hopes of Miss Willow's advent were more than amply fulfilled.

Miss Trimble had been timid with George in the past, shrinking and subservient, but now she enjoyed his confidence. She flattered herself that Mr Talbot found she was by no means an irksome addendum to their party. It was only now that this great change had come that she realised how burdensome the weight of Lady Jane's oppressive companionship had been to her all these years. What alteration a little fresh air, a little amusement, a dish of tea at a wayside inn, a posy of flowers from a gypsy woman, could bring!

On the other hand she remained anxious about Lady Jane who, left at home alone whilst the rest of them gallivanted, could only be storing up resentments and punishments that would be visited on Miss Trimble at some later date. Of course Lady Jane was angry and affronted, and bitterly did she rail against Miss Trimble for her dereliction without at all acceding to Agnes' offer to stay at home to bear her company.

'By no means,' Lady Jane said with a haughty sneer from amongst the ruffles of her silken dressing gown, 'would *I* presume to teach *you* your principles. If you feel it quite right to consort with adulterers, and to besmirch yourself by association with tainted women, I am the last person to stand in your way.'

'I am sure there has been no wrong-doing, Lady Jane,' Agnes replied very humbly. 'And I cannot very well refuse Mr Talbot.'

'It seems that nobody can,' Lady Jane said tartly.

'I'm sure he would be delighted if you would consent to be of the party, my lady. We *all* would,' offered Agnes, hoping that her insincerity would not show.

'With Miss Willow? Never!' the suggestion was flung back violently, along with a glass of Madeira that Lady Jane had been drinking at the time.

The doctor, called to treat the resulting relapse in Lady Jane's condition, recommended that either she, or Miss Willow, should be removed from the house. 'The proximity of the young lady seems to exacerbate her ladyship's malaise,' he opined.

Agnes had no doubt that the doctor was correct, but the prescription brought a dilemma for her. She thought it more than likely that Mr Talbot would take Miss Willow away. They had spoken of it, indeed. Derbyshire had been mentioned as being particularly convenient for some business that must be attended in Sheffield. The Lake District, though much further, had not been ruled out. Of course, she—Agnes—would very much wish to accompany Miss Willow and Mr Talbot on such a tour. She thought it hardly likely that they would venture on it without a female companion for Georgina, and who better than the trusted Agnes? But it was inconceivable to her that Lady Jane would consent to it; her need—in her own estimation if in no one else's—was the greater. And what if, against all probability, Lady Jane did consent to it? What was to prevent her finding that in fact Agnes Trimble was not indispensable—was not really even necessary—at all?

The three of them—Mr Talbot, Miss Willow and Miss Trimble— discussed the situation in low tones over their tea one evening. The peculiar delicacy of Miss Trimble's situation, though not absolutely mentioned, was a strong concern. Mr Talbot and Miss Willow were concerned about it, much to Agnes' gratification. To Agnes there was a delicious thrill in *conspiring*—she thought of it in such terms—so confidentially with the master of the house. That she was looked-to, consulted, included in the discussion made her almost heady. If she had reflected she would have upbraided herself, for of course Lady Jane was a great friend and everything was due to her. But in the exhilaration of the moment, with the kettle boiling over the spirit stove, the second best china at her disposal, the plate of Mr Talbot's favourite cakes ready to be brought forth from beneath their cover, she did not reflect.

Miss Willow also seemed to take an almost childish delight in the slightly clandestine nature of their talk. It was as though the three of them, a little band of comrades, were in league against an enemy. Naturally, no one spoke of Lady Jane in that way. *Her* best interests—what *she* would most prefer and what would be most beneficial to *her* health—was their primary concern. But there was no disputing that, as well, they all did very much relish the idea of a tour in the north *together*, without her.

'The house in Brighton will not be at my disposal until June,' Mr Talbot said, taking his tea from Miss Trimble's hand. 'And, unfortunately, Lady Jane dislikes Ecklington, though she would be *very* well cared for there.'

'She would need a companion wherever she went,' Miss Trimble said, helping Georgina to one of the cakes. 'She dislikes her own company and she is used to having someone to write her cards and so on.'

'I might call upon Lady Nancy,' said George. 'She might have some solution to offer.'

'Did you not mention that your daughter Robyn might come home?' Miss Willow enquired. That evening she wore the lightest of her veils. It gratified George beyond his ability to express, that she should be so improved in confidence. The veil—a fine, flimsy piece—was sheened and lustrous, reflecting light in such a way as to prevent Georgina's features being visible, but it was a decided improvement on the thick crêpe of her outdoor apparel.

'Oh yes, I do hope so. But if she does, she will come with us. She will not be left here with Lady Jane. Our other daughter, Beatrice, will not return from school until July.'

'You might consult with Baroness Charlton,' Miss Trimble ventured. 'There was some mention of a visit to the Sothertons. Should Lady Jane be sufficiently recovered, an invitation there might appeal. She would not take me to such a place as that in any case.'

'My dear Miss Trimble,' said George triumphantly. 'An excellent notion! I think we can be sure that an invitation from the countess would effect a miraculous improvement on Lady Jane! Ah!' He put down his empty cup. 'I shall begin to make our arrangements. But tomorrow, my dear, I hope you have no engagements?'

Miss Willow looked up from her embroidery. 'I believe I am at your disposal,' she said with what he took to be a smile.

'That is very good. I shall take you to the Surrey docks that you might see my new ship. What do you think to the idea? Will it amuse you? The men have their half day on Saturday afternoons so the place will be deserted—no smiths, carpenters, stevedores or jacks to discompose you. What do you say?'

'I should like it very much,' said Georgina warmly.

'And I have asked your friend Mr Harlish to meet us there. I hope you will be pleased to see him?'

'Indeed I shall. And … Mr Balfour? Will he join us?'

'Ah no,' replied George. 'He is from town for the next few days I believe. Business must be carried on, you know! Business must be carried on. But he is to come here this evening in person to say his farewells. Ah! I think I hear the door. That will be him.'

Sure enough, in a few moments, Mr Balfour was shown into the drawing room. His expression—normally severe—melted at the sight of Miss Willow, whose figure and gown showed to particular advantage and who had incorporated the fixings of her veil into the arrangement of her hair. He had not seen her hair before. It was thick and dark, very lustrous. With difficulty he drew his eyes from her. 'How cosy you all are here,' he exclaimed, declining the tea that Miss Trimble offered him. 'But it is a very fine night; mild and windless. The moon is full. What do you say to a turn about the square?'

They all assented to the idea. Miss Trimble fetched the ladies' shawls and they proceeded down the stairs and out into the square. They walked once around its perimeter, passing the quiet houses, their footsteps the only noise in the empty quadrangle. The park, at its heart, was almost as bright as day, the moon pouring a pearly light over the trees and flower beds, rendering them in a silver sheen. Mr Talbot and Miss Trimble continued to discuss, in lowered tones, the possibility of an invitation for Lady Jane to Sotherton. 'I think she would be sure to accept,' said Miss Trimble. 'She would not like the baroness to have the advantage of her.'

A little in front of them, Georgina said, 'I understand you are to go away, Mr Balfour.'

'Yes,' he said. 'I have business in the west country. An important matter. Several associates have trusted me to conduct the affair.'

'I will miss your companionship,' Georgina said. She meant it. She saw through his superlatively haughty mien; he was one of the kindest men she had ever known.

He pressed her hand, which lay on his arm. 'It is such a very bright moon,' he said. 'I think there can be no impropriety in us venturing into the park. Do you? It will not bring back for you recollections of a disagreeable kind?'

'Oh no,' she replied. 'I hardly recall that evening. I was distressed. Lady Jane had been so … And of course I had eaten nothing since breakfast. Then again, at home and in Yorkshire, I often walk at night, as you do. I must have supposed I could do so with equal impunity here.'

'London is not like the countryside.'

'No, indeed.'

They crossed over the paving stones of the wide roadway and entered the park. George and Agnes bent their steps in the same direction. The gravel of the pathways shone with an eerie luminescence. The stands of tulips and other spring flowers glowed with dew. The pool at the centre of the gardens reflected the full moon back as a mirror, its bland, impassive face staring up at the sky.

'How delightful,' sighed Miss Willow, breathing in the night-scented air.

'All we need now is a nightingale,' said Balfour.

At a little distance the tread of the others' steps could be heard on the pathway, the murmur of their voices in conversation.

'I have been thinking of what you said to me on Hampstead Heath,' said Georgina slowly.

Balfour inclined his head so that it was close to hers. 'I said many things, I think.'

'Yes. You spoke of your sense of personal integrity, that it was sufficient for you. That you did not need the approval of others, nor fear their censure. I will confess to you Mr Balfour that I envy you. I wish I had that confidence. I wish I could be sure that people would not fall on me, or shrink from me, but only *see* me. Myself, I mean. My inner self.'

'I wish I could promise you that they would,' he murmured. 'But I cannot. Unfortunately, some people are superficial. They cannot help it. Our confidence must be of sufficient substance that we can at least endure it. To be indifferent is enough. But if possible we must forgive it. I will answer your confession with one of my own. I do not forgive those who look down on me. I despise them. One day I hope to find forgiveness in my heart.'

Georgina looked down at the polished surface of the water, where the moon's face floated. 'Your heart is full of courage,' she said sadly. 'Mine is full of fear.'

Gently, Balfour took her arms and turned her towards him. 'I would give you all my courage,' he said thickly, 'in exchange.' His eyes burned, deep pools of passion, as he fixed her with his gaze.

She lifted her head to him. The moon poured over the fine stuff of her veil and lit ebony fires in the filaments of her hair. The park, all around them, held its breath. In an agony of slowness she lifted her arms and pulled away her veil.

Georgina knew very well what she had feared, but the moments passed and the spectre of her imaginings did not rise in Amory's face; he did not flinch. He did not startle. He showed no sign of rapture, neither did his eye burn with avaricious fire. The sight of her seemed to cause no alteration in him. His face, like the disc of moon in the pool beside her, remained impassive.

After a moment she turned from him, allowing her veil to fall over her face, and walked back towards the house.

22

That night sleep did not come to Georgina. Long after Miss Trimble had bidden her goodnight and she had extinguished her candle, Georgina lay awake staring at the canopy of the bed. Moonlight poured in through her window. She had left the curtains parted, that it might do so; the cold, soulless moon, its indifference a reminder of Amory Balfour's face. Her mama was right, she was perverse. He had seen her and not been revolted. Neither had he displayed the greedy, consuming rapaciousness of the clerk in Salisbury, and other men since then. And yet she was not satisfied. What *had* she wanted?

Presently she got up and walked to the window, looking out across the roadway to the deserted park. The moon had gone down but she could still see the fountain by the light of some miasma it had left behind it in the air. The gas lights, in comparison, threw a poor, weakly light. She almost expected to see Amory's dark, imposing silhouette where she had left him, turned to stone by the curse of her visage. But the place was empty and, as she watched, its shining brilliance dimmed to ordinary shadow and gloom.

She crossed the room to the chest of drawers and pulled open the top one. It contained all her veils. She rifled through the fabrics, feeling their weight, their embellishments, knowing them all by their heft and slither. For so long she had felt safe within their folds, protected, rendered almost invisible. But the past few days she had begun to feel them as an impediment, a barricade. Inside their shelter had begun to feel claustrophobic. At times she had struggled to breathe. She had caught herself being annoyed, that they obscured her vision of things she wanted to look at properly.

She pushed them back into the drawer and closed it, crossing to the fireplace where she poked a little life into the dull embers.

The question remained unanswered. What had she wanted? She did not know.

She stared into the coals and conjured all her fears, her childhood hauntings and her mother's vivid but non-specific admonitions, the absolute need for discretion, for reticence, for quiet obscurity. They must not be 'recognised'. Nobody must know 'who they were'.

Why not? She wondered for the thousandth time. Who were *they*? Who was *she*? This, she felt, was at the heart of her fixation. Flesh and blood she was, skin and hair, bone and sinew. That manifestation of her had given her cause for apprehension. The unaccountable effect it had on other people had been humiliating, frightening. She distrusted it—almost hated it—and had hidden it away. But there was something more, something deeper; this question of identity—who, *beneath* the outer carapace, she really was. That there was some mystery, some dubious history, was obvious. Until she uncovered it, she did not think she would ever be able to have that personal authenticity that she so envied in Amory Balfour.

Her mother would not tell her. Perhaps George Talbot would?

23

The following day the weather turned dull and drear, threatening rain. The closed carriage was brought out for the trip to Surrey Docks. Beneath her veil Georgina was wan and hollow-eyed for lack of sleep. But her determination of the night before had not wavered and she looked for an opportunity to speak to her cousin George alone. It felt momentous to her, a turning-point, and she feared what he might tell her. But she thought that without the truth she could not carry on.

George was in high spirits. He had written a letter to Baroness Charlton, describing but not explaining his wife's recent ill health and requesting, in confidence, the assistance of her old friend. Knowing the baroness, he was certain that an appeal to her *confidential* aid would have her running to Grosvenor Square. He did not think that his wife would be so indiscreet as to level accusations against him, or that she would hint at scandal in relation to Georgina Willow. No. She would place herself at the centre of the matter; she was exhausted, in want of diversion, much put-upon, very desirous of a change of scene. Baroness Charlton would do the rest.

In addition, George was always energised by a trip to the docks. His ship was a thing of pride and joy to him. He was sure that Georgina would prove herself a most appreciative audience. The upper decks were in place, the captain's quarters and galley in situ, the gargantuan engine in readiness. There was much he could show her.

The ship was a goliath, standing above the dock, balanced between its stanchions and towering over the workshops and offices as a Gulliver over Lilliput. Georgina looked up at it and was almost cowed. She had never seen such an enormous vessel: so self-assured, so majestic, so brave.

Arthur was already on board as their carriage drew up, but hurried down the companionway to greet them and assist them aboard.

Georgina remained subdued, asking few questions as she drifted, swathed in her impenetrable black mantle, along the decks and through the narrow passages of the ship. She tried to shake herself from her reverie for Arthur's sake, but in truth her mind was on other things.

Happily, Arthur had enough enthusiasm for both of them. Even though he spent five-and-a-half days out of seven on the ship it was still a thing of beauty and ingenuity to him. He showed the ladies the decks and the hold, the cargo bays, the heads[xlvi] and crew quarters, the lifting gear and navigational equipment. He showed them the telegraphic device that Mr Talbot had insisted on installing because he was so certain that before long, telegraphic messaging between continents would be possible.[xlvii] They surveyed the captain's quarters, where the fineness of the carpentry, the provision of book shelves and china cabinets made Miss Trimble declare she believed she could be quite comfortable on board a ship.

'And what will you do, Mr Harlish, when you have completed the building of this ship?' Miss Trimble asked when the tour was finished.

Arthur held out his hands. 'That will be up to Mr Talbot. I hope I will be permitted to go on her sea-trials. Every ship must be tested, you know, put through her paces. The crew must become accustomed to her. I should like to see how she performs.'

'Mr Harlish knows every rivet and seam in this vessel,' said George, slapping the young man on the back.

'You will not sign up as a sailor?' said Georgina. It was almost the first time she had spoken. Her voice trembled.

'I do not know,' Arthur prevaricated. He did not wish to distress Georgina but the question of his future was one that he would like to settle. 'I could be a ship's engineer, I think, if Mr Talbot had no further use for me.'

'No further use for you?' George laughed. 'As soon as this ship is commissioned, you will be starting anew. I shall have a fleet of steam ships plying their trade between here and the Indies, Africa, the Americas—and you, Mr Harlish, will design and construct each one.'

Arthur glowed with pleasure. 'I shall not disappoint you, sir,' he said.

'You shall rise, Arthur,' said George. 'I am not greedy and the profits of this venture will accrue to you in time. You shall own a house, a carriage. You will take a wife, perhaps.' He waggled his eyebrows. 'And other men will doff their hats to you. Do you like my vision of your future?'

'Very much, sir,' Arthur managed to stammer out. He had not dreamed of such success.

'And what is more,' said George, 'you shall have the naming of our ship. What do you say to that?'

Arthur could hardly say anything, so overwhelmed was he.

'Mama will be very happy,' said Georgina fumbling for her handkerchief. 'She will be proud of you. And you must write to your parents, Arthur, and tell them of your success.' George's kindness to Arthur threatened to break into smithereens the fragility that had dogged her all day. Surely, she thought, he would be kind also to *her*?

They made their way back to where the carriage was waiting for them, and Arthur helped the ladies inside.

'Come with us,' George said. 'I should like to see your lodgings, if I may. At the very least we can save you from a drenching in the shower of rain I see coming our way.'

Arthur had hardly the presence of mind to give the direction to the groom before he climbed into the carriage. But as the horses turned and went out of the dock he said, 'As to the naming of the ship, sir. What do you say to *The Georgina*?'

'Oh! Arthur,' said Georgina, breaking down in earnest.

'Yes indeed. An excellent notion,' cried George.

'Oh, my dear,' said Miss Trimble, reaching for Georgina's hand, 'does that not make you feel very proud? Your namesake shall go out into the world.' The unspoken words 'even if you do not' hung in the air between them.

The Talbot carriage made its way along the narrow and littered pathways of Rotherhithe marshes, passing the tunnel-workers' makeshift encampments, piles of spoil, lines of ragged washing and the public houses—thronged, even so early in the day, by men and women of low degree.

'Dear me, Arthur,' said George doubtfully. 'This does not look very salubrious. You walk this way every day, do you?'

'Yes sir,' said Arthur. 'Occasionally there are ruffians, people the worse for drink. But on the whole the people are harmless—only poor, wretched and hungry. In any case, I think I pose a fairly substantial figure. It would be a foolish man who would think to make sport with me.'

The marshes did not display their most advantageous face to the passengers in the carriage. Recent rain had turned the pools and runnels turgid. The grass was limp, scuffed and flattened by the passing of many feet. The carriageway itself was very poor, potholed and sullied by the woebegone ponies and cadaverous cows who were allowed to roam. The horses made their tortuous way along Halfpenny Hatch Lane, the carriage swaying alarmingly. Thin children and rough-looking women stood barefoot in the mud as the carriage passed by.

'You were right,' murmured Georgina, looking out of the window at the sorry-looking scene. 'It is nothing like Yorkshire.'

Arthur's thoughts turned to Mrs Quince. He was not sure what reception they would get from her. He had not for a moment considered the possibility that Mr Talbot might wish to visit Cuckold's Point, and so he had not warned his hostess of it.

'I ought to speak to my landlady,' he said, as the carriage neared the row of cottages. 'It may not be quite convenient to her to receive visitors at this hour.'

'We will not stay above five minutes,' said George. 'But I should like to see the place. I wish to be sure that you are comfortably accommodated. If I am not reassured, we shall look for somewhere else. Somewhere in a more respectable location.' He looked askance at the forlorn landscape around them.

'Mrs Quince is eminently respectable sir,' Arthur felt he had to say. 'If anything, she considers herself rather above her situation. Her house is very well maintained. If I may say so without slighting my mother, Mrs Quince is a better housewife than *she* is.'

Georgina managed a faint smile. Sally Harlish's fecklessness was a subject of despair to Annie Burleigh and Jocelyn Willow.

'I think Miss Willow is in need of a cup of tea, if Mrs Quince can spare us one,' said Miss Trimble. 'She is tired today.'

'I *am* tired,' said Georgina. In truth she was exhausted and depressed.

'Let me see,' said Arthur, getting down from the carriage almost before it had drawn to a halt. 'Give me a few moments, if you will.'

Of course Mrs Quince was delighted and honoured by her visitors. She hoped the entire neighbourhood would witness the grand carriage, the elegantly dressed ladies and the handsome *rich* gentleman who made their way up her garden path and entered through her door. As always, everything was in a neat and tidy state in her drawing room, the fire lit, the fire-irons polished, the carpet beaten and, as luck would have it, the kettle but just now come to the boil. She had Pansy bring out the best china, which had never in Arthur's remembrance been allowed from the confines of its cabinet before. Tea was made, a fruitcake spirited from some secret repository in Mrs Quince's own private apartment. Miss Willow was seated in the comfortable chair by the fire, Miss Trimble and Mr Talbot urged onto the settle. Arthur brought forth a dining chair for Mrs Quince and he perched on the window ledge hard by the stuffed macaw.

From the moment of her guests' entrance into the parlour Mrs Quince was overcome by an excess of genteel pretention. She gathered up all her ladylike affectations for their delectation, primarily by a liberal scattering of the letter h. 'I am so very *honoured*,' she said regally, 'by your visit and by your *haquaintance*. I have long wished to be *hintroduced* to Mr Harlish's very good friends.'

'The pleasure is all ours,' said Miss Trimble. 'What a very commodious room you have here ma'am. What an interesting array of artefacts. Your husband was a seafaring man, I apprehend?'

'Oh no, ma'am. He was a river captain. These things all came as gifts from my gentlemen lodgers. It is such a pity that you did not happen by on a Sunday. Then I could have *hentertained* you with some high culture and theatricals. My neighbours come in, on a Sunday, to read Shakespeare. Perhaps, Mr Harlish, you might go next door to see if Mr and Miss Pink are at home? They should be sorry to miss the *hopportunity* to meet the ladies and gentleman, I should think.'

'Miss Pink?' echoed Miss Trimble. 'That cannot be the same Miss Pink who is employed by Madame Planché, the milliner? Oh I do hope so. She is an excellent creature.'

'Yes indeed,' assented Mrs Quince. 'It is my understanding that she is well thought of there. And Mr Pink is a chief clerk in a bank.' In this she promoted Mr Pink some two or three rungs, but no one dared to contradict her. 'You see,' she concluded complacently, 'we are a very superior neighbourhood.'

'I am well acquainted with Mr Pink,' said George. 'He handles my business at the bank. What a coincidence!'

'Miss Willow is somewhat fatigued,' said Arthur. 'Perhaps she does not wish for more company.'

'I do not mind,' said Georgina faintly.

'I shall accompany you,' said Miss Trimble, who had reasons of her own to speak privately with Miss Pink.

'And I, indeed,' said George. 'Mr Pink has often spoken to me of his garden. I should be glad to see it, since we are here.'

They all left the room leaving Mrs Quince and her mysterious, swathed visitor behind. Mrs Quince was very perplexed by the lady who retained her veil even indoors and sat, like a column of obsidian, enveloped from head to waist in darkest crêpe. She managed, by some deft and practiced means, to convey her cup to her lips within its confines. What horrors the veil might conceal Mrs Quince could only imagine. She raised a hand to her own face—lovely in her own mind—and was thankful for it.

'You must forgive me, ma'am,' said Georgina from beneath her covering, her voice very dull. 'It must seem very rude of me to hide my face from you.'

'Not at all,' cried Mrs Quince. 'No one knows better than I do how *himpertinent* some people can be. It is not my place to comment, but hereabouts I am known for a certain fairness of face.' She gave a self-deprecating little smile. 'Many is the time I have been stared at. I shall not deign to repeat the ribald comments what some people have been so rude as to make, nor the baseless *haspersions* what have been cast at me. I am sure you only try to protect yourself from similar *hassault*.'

Georgina looked, through the thick weft of her voile, at Mrs Quince. A less perfect exempla of physical beauty it would be hard to envision and yet, in her own eyes she was beautiful. 'You put me to shame, indeed Mrs Quince.'

'Oh my dear, there is no need for that,' said Mrs Quince, misunderstanding Georgina's remark. 'Beauty of face is not given to all and many indeed squander what *hallocation* they have. But I have always told myself; "Kitty," I have always said, "one day you might grow old and ugly. Your hair may fall out …"' fondling a greasy grey lock that had come down from her cap, '" … and your skin may lose its freshness and bloom …"' now stroking her raddled cheek, '" … but if that sorry day shall ever come, or if some tragic mishap should befall, I pray that you shall have the grace to bear it."'

'Yes,' said Georgina. 'That is what I hope for. Grace to bear it.'

'My poor dear,' said Mrs Quince, leaning forward. 'Are you very badly scarred?'

Suddenly the room was full of people. Mr Pink, rotund, flushed but full of ineffable gallantry, made his bow and introduced his daughter. Miss Pink, all compassion and gentleness, took a low stool close to Miss Willow and began to speak of Arthur. How long had Miss Willow been acquainted with him? Was he not a very fine and very clever young man? And an excellent reader of Shakespeare! Had Miss Willow ever heard him read aloud?

The ability of both the newcomers to ignore her thick drapings made Georgina shrivel with shame. They must have been warned, she thought, they must have been prepared. But how ridiculous, how *odd* they must think her. What kind of creature was she—an aberration, a crank—that she must be excused, explained!

All around her was merriment. Georgina sat in the midst of it, but it eddied around her as though she were an impervious rock in a lively sea. More tea was made and then a decanter of port brought forth. Coals were placed upon the fire although the room was already warm. Mr

Harlish and Miss Pink laughed together, their heads bent low over a folder of humorous drawings they had found on a shelf. Mr Pink paid flattering attentions to Miss Trimble, ignoring the daggers being flung at him by their hostess. Presently, Arthur proposed sending Pansy to an alehouse for victuals, and Mr Talbot said that if so, he would certainly pay for them.

The longer it went on the more ridiculous Georgina felt, swathed in her veil, separated from the company and not able to meet them eye-to-eye. Food, if it were indeed to be delivered, would pose a difficulty, for whilst she could drink from beneath her veil, she could not eat. Should she, then, abstain? What kind of rudeness would that be?

The effect of the humble but exquisite little parlour, the unpretentious company, the genuine laughter, made her feel more and more alien and at last she rose from her seat and walked to where her cousin sat near the door.

'Will you walk outside with me, Cousin George?' she asked. 'It grows warm in here, and there is something I would speak to you about.'

'By all means,' said George, rising, and reaching for her cloak where it had been hung on a hook.

They stepped out into Mrs Quince's narrow little garden, where early peas scrambled up nets and carrot seedlings raised their feathery heads.

'Mr Pink's allotment is behind the houses,' said George, leading her in that direction. 'And there is a good view of the river.'

They walked past the Pinks' cottage, which was the end one of the row, and into an area of garden. A path took them between well-hoed vegetable beds, past a glasshouse and through an orchard of fruit trees.

'Miss Trimble was taken with this,' George said. 'It made me remember that we have no garden at Grosvenor Square. It had never occurred to me before that she might enjoy the supervision of some plants and flowers. In truth, Georgina, before you came, I had not given any thought to Miss Trimble. She was a fixture. My wife's companion. But what a treasure she has turned out to be. You are fond of her, are you not?'

'Very fond,' said Georgina. 'And I very much hope that, if we do go to Derbyshire, she will be able to accompany us.'

'It is my avowed intent,' said George.

They had come through a wicket gate to a place that was half scrub, half shingle, the bank of the river Thames. Before them the river, having swung in an enormous meander, flowed south. The lowering sun was behind them and cast their shadows on the smooth, oily surface of the water. The outlines were distorted, exaggerated. Georgina looked at the outline of herself as it lay, undulating slightly, on the murky floe. It reminded her of the stone milepost on the moor—cold, obdurate, unreadable.

'I wanted to ask you, Cousin George,' she began, 'about my mother. About her past. She has never told me, though I have begged her often enough. Of papa she will speak, and of our friends the Burleighs. But of her childhood she will utter not one syllable.'

George opened his mouth to speak—to demur, she was sure—but she went on. 'No. I *must* know. And if not from you, then from whom? This much I have been able to ascertain. She has lived in fear of being recognised; as though, at some point, she was—or did—something reprehensible. I cannot think *what*. She is so *good*! But I gather there are those who would punish her in some way—expose her, destroy her—if she were to be discovered. I have been given to understand—indeed, it has been indoctrinated into me—that if she were recognised dire consequences would ensue. Now she tells me all danger has passed. So good for her. But I am left with this legacy …' She grasped the hem of her veil and held it out before her, and George almost thought she would pull it away. 'In my mind I believe that my appearance poses, or, at the least adds to, that danger. I cannot separate them—her dread and my appearance. And it is true that, in the past, my face has had the most unaccountable impact on people. But I am ready, Cousin George. I am ready to emerge if only I can know the truth.'

She was facing him now; even through the crêpe, he could see the light in her eyes. Her voice was charged with passion.

'Oh, my dear,' he said, taking her trembling hands in his. They were cold, and he chafed them with his own. 'It is not my secret to tell.'

'But you *must*,' she cried out. 'I have been sent to you so that I can escape this … this …' She loosed his hold on her and grasped her shroud again, '… this *prison*. That is what I feel it to be. More and more, each day. It used to shield me but now it is constricting. It is suffocating.' In her fever she began to wrench and pull at the fabric, to rend it with her nails. 'Oh! Let me *out*,' she moaned, beside herself with anguish, 'Let me *out*!'

George lifted his hands, ready to help her, to release her. The air was salt-tanged, fresh and invigorating. She would be better—be liberated— if she could feel it on her face.

But a shout from the orchard stayed his hand. One of the grooms pushed his way through the wicket gate. Behind him a mud-splattered rider held a message aloft.

'Mr Talbot, sir,' gasped the groom. 'This message is come for you. The rider has not stopped from Dover. He went to the house first, but not finding you there, he was directed to the docks. A watchman there had overheard this address, and so he has found us. It is come from France, he says.'

George took the letter from the rider and tore it open. The lines were few, but very disturbing. 'We must go at once,' he said, turning an ashen face towards Georgina. 'There cannot be a moment's delay.' He turned to the groom. 'Ready the horses. Fetch Miss Trimble.'

He had already begun to walk back towards the carriage, determined to do himself what he had urged others to perform, that the thing might be done more quickly.

'What has happened?' asked Georgina, panting as she hurried behind him. Is it Mama?'

'No,' he replied, and now his face was ghostly. 'It is Robyn. She is gravely ill.'

24

Amory Balfour's business had taken him to Bristol, where he was to negotiate with various parties for the purchase of a large area of land, comprising several parcels. The business had been complicated, with different owners having different ideas about the value of their land. Some, with other interests in the area, would benefit from the development envisioned by the purchasers. Others had much to lose by the deal for which the value of the land would scarcely compensate them.

Whilst in Bristol Balfour had put up at an inn. The accommodation there was good enough but not lavish. His room—though the best in the house—was small, and he had no private sitting room. After supper he had taken to walking the narrow streets of the town rather than to be subjected to the stares and resentment of the local drinkers at the inn. Before its abolition the slave trade had brought many thousands of wretched men and women through Bristol. Many Bristolians still thought of black people as merely cargo. The difficulties experienced in recent years by the docks[xlviii] and the loss of income from the trade in human flesh had left a taste of bitter resentment in the mouths of local people

One evening, about a week after he had parted from Georgina, Amory took his cloak and his sword-stick and set out in the direction of the docks. For all he knew his own parents might have come through there, packed into the hold of a ship, denied fresh air, their rations of food and water barely sustaining life. Although he had been adopted as an infant by Mr and Mrs Balfour, and had felt loved by them, his real mother and father had never been far from his mind from the time he had realised that the Balfours were not his natural parents.

He walked between the high, crowded buildings, avoiding the pools of ordure that had been thrown down or left by animals, waving away the invitations of prostitutes, side-stepping a dog that rushed at him to the length of his chain. The night was very dark. The gas lighting that illuminated the streets of Mayfair and Piccadilly had not come to Bristol. This quarter of the town was made up of business premises and workshops. The windows now were dark; all was locked up, the workers gone to their homes. There was no moon. His footsteps echoed on the cobbles as he walked. On the air he could smell the sharp tang of salt.

The tide was out. Hulking vessels lay on the mud of the riverbed, tilted on their hulls. In the darkness they looked like beached sea monsters—brooding, potentially dangerous, but marooned. The mud was dull, absorbing sound, a deep quag of slime and oozing silt.

Amory proceeded along the deserted quay, stepping over coiled ropes and large metal anchor points that had been set into the cobbles, avoiding stacked crates and a pyramid of barrels left ready to be loaded the following day.

Somewhere across the city a church bell tolled the hour. He stopped and got out his pocket watch. He could barely read the dial, turning it this way and that to catch a gleam of light, but finding none. The sky was a blanket of cloud. No star, no lamp, no brazier relieved the thick pall. The diamond in the ring on his little finger looked like a dull, dead pebble. The bell rang out ten times and then fell silent.

Amory turned to retrace his steps. As he did so he thought he heard the scuff of a foot on the ground, the gasp of a sharply drawn breath. He scanned the area but could see nothing. The crates and barrels were no more than darker shadows in the mine of the night. Then, off to the left, a cat yowled. Nevertheless, he took a firmer hold of his sword-stick.

He had reached the end of the quay and was turning towards the narrow alleyway that would take him back to the inn when he saw the dark silhouettes of three men before him. There was nothing at all to be gained and probably much to be lost by pretending he had not seen them, so he raised his hand to his hat and said, 'Good evening gentlemen. I wish you a pleasant walk.'

No reply came back to him. He continued to walk, directly towards the men, not hesitating in his pace. They spread out across his path.

Amory continued to walk, but his mind was a whirl of possibilities. He could turn and run. But, in the darkness he was sure to fall foul of the ropes and baskets that were stacked all along the quay. He did not think, even if he were to get that far, the quay would lead him to safety. Towards that end of the docks was a wasteland of marram grasses intersected by rivulets. The warehouses all along the quay were locked up tight. And of course he could not leap off the dock into the mud, which was treacherous and likely to swallow him whole. His only option was to walk boldly forward, but as he did so he grasped his sword-stick with his other hand and pulled the blade from its sheath.

'I hope you mean me no harm, gentlemen,' he said, keeping his voice loud and steady. 'I'm a peaceable man, just going back to my place of lodging.'

He was close enough now to see that the men were rough, hard-looking fellows. One wore a broken-brimmed hat pulled low over his eyes. Another's coat was bundled and bunched in the middle, probably tied round with string to keep it closed. The third was smaller than either of the others and of a lighter build. Amory speculated that he was a youth, brought along to make up the numbers. This third man stood to the left of the others and Amory made towards him, thinking that he would be the most likely to give way.

'Come now gentlemen,' Balfour said very reasonably. 'We are not going to have words, are we? Let me by, and I shall find you a shilling for some ale. What do you say?'

'A shilling, is it?' said one of the men contemptuously. 'I think it'll cost you more'n that.'

'A shilling each, perhaps,' said Amory, hoping he had so much loose change about him.

'We're not to be given small change by the likes of you,' spat the dumpy man. 'Your type shan't lord it over us, if we can help it.'

'My type?' asked Amory, but knowing full well the answer.

'You 'ave your place,' growled the first man, 'but it is not in the best room of an inn, and it is not buying up land, and it is not wearing boots you are barely fit to clean.'

'You don't like it, that I have a position in the world?' Balfour's tone was stony.

'Oh yes,' came back the reply. 'I like that you shall have a position in the world, so long as it is beneath my boot.'

'Or chained, like that dog up the alleyway,' amended his friend.

'Aye. That would do well enough.'

During this exchange the three men had edged closer to Balfour and he found himself all but hemmed in behind by a wall.

There was perhaps a foot or two of space between the wall's end and the youth, and Amory prepared himself to make a dash at it, get through and then take to his heels. But suddenly the men closed up, cutting off that means of escape. He came to a halt. He could smell the men: bad breath, grog, sweat and fish. 'Fishermen, are you?' he hazarded, but half-heartedly. He knew that they would not be charmed, nor bought, nor threatened from their intention. He brandished his weapon.

The man with the broken hat launched himself forward. Amory caught him a blow on his arm that he was almost sure would draw blood. The man recoiled for long enough for Amory to turn his attention to another. He lunged, but the fine blade buckled. The man must be wearing several thick layers beneath his coat. The youth threw himself onto Amory's back, knocking his hat to the ground and fastening his hands on Amory's throat. Amory threw his head back, and felt it connect with the gristle of the young man's nose. His assailant cried out and fell to the ground, his hand to his face. Then the thick-coated man was on him again, landing a broad-knuckled punch that split Amory's lip. The other man ran at him, shoulder-first, like a battering ram, pushing Amory backwards into the wall. Amory raised his blade again, slicing the man's face, before it was wrenched from his grip and he heard it clatter on the cobbles. He was pinioned by one and punched by the other, his own retaliatory blows sometimes connecting but more often not. He thought if he could stay on his feet he might withstand them, but then the youngster was on him again, and he sank to his knees.

He felt pain—on his face, in his gut, his privates—and tasted blood in his mouth. His ears were full of roaring, and he wished he could have looked into Georgina's eyes one more time.

25

It was not very long before Lady Jane felt that her decision to remain in the secluded eyrie of her private apartments had been a mistake. Although George visited every day, and Miss Trimble made every effort to comfort and distract her, Lady Jane could not but be aware that, elsewhere in the house, matters went on much as before—or even more pleasantly. She heard the carriage being brought around every day and heard reports, via her maid, of excursions to such delightful locations as Hampstead, Richmond and Windsor. It was infuriating to feel that she was not missed. That nobody *cared*. The pall of bitter resentment she had hoped to cast through the house, the sense of discomfort she had wished to inflict, appeared to be having no impact at all. Far from creeping around the landings in despair and misery, or from wringing their hands in abject shame, those who should be most afflicted were in fact gadding about town with gay unconcern!

What was more, a flurry of communications from Baroness Charlton and others of her intimate circle made Lady Jane aware that she had missed several entertainments that she would very much have liked to attend. She had missed them *not* because she was unwell but because, simply, she had not been invited.

The Shrewsburys were spreading reports of her shortcomings as a chaperone, as evidenced by the events at the Staffords' ball. Such carelessness, it was implied, could only reflect moral lassitude. Miss Robyn Talbot's singular lifestyle—living independently, abroad, unmarried, and *painting pictures*—was brought forward in evidence of Lady Jane's ineptitude as a society Mama. Mr Talbot's frequent travels away from home were seen as ample proofs of her wifely inadequacies. There was even, whispered very quietly, some mention of the little house in Chelsea.

It was scarcely any comfort to Lady Jane to hear from the baroness that Lady Virginia continued to give trouble. Young Mr Binsley called daily and had been assiduous in making advances of the most respectable kind. Sir Gabriel and Lady Binsley had indicated they had no objections to the match. But Lady Virginia had refused to entertain his proposals, and often it had been left to Gertrude to amuse the young man whilst Lady Virginia skulked in her room or slipped out alone. The reprobate Mr Rex continued to hold a most alarming fascination for her. Somehow or other—the baroness did not know how—they had been able to enter into communication and had arranged a number of assignations. The minx had been seen at Vauxhall with him, and in a box at the Theatre Royal, her only chaperone an old maid of doubtful pedigree who had snored her way through the play. In vain had the baroness confined her young charge to her room; she would always contrive to escape. The Shrewsburys had been appealed to: Lady Virginia must, for her own good, be removed to some other house. But it seemed that the duke and duchess had exhausted the goodwill of all their friends in relation to their wayward daughter; nobody would touch her with a bargepole.

It added to Lady Jane's sense of injustice that whilst the Charltons were clearly no better supervisors of Lady Virginia it was she—Lady Jane— who was blamed as the originator of the girl's misadventures. What was more, the forthcoming marriage of Gertrude Charlton to Lord

Pokerham riled. For all the young man's personal deficiencies, it was a very good match for Gertrude, much fêted amongst the *ton*, likely to become the most celebrated event of the season.

All these matters fermented in the crucible of Lady Jane's ire, but the two weeks she spent confined to her chambers allowed all the incandescence of her initial *chagrin* to cool into a glutinous residue of toxic umbrage. She lay in bed, or reclined on her *chaise longue*, fulminating and plotting her revenge.

The news of Robyn's illness did not particularly discompose her, but Mr Talbot's determination to go instantly to Paris opened up for Lady Jane a chink of possibility. With him out of the way Miss Willow would be undefended.

He was to depart very early the day after the message arrived and Lady Jane rose from her bed and joined him as he ate a hasty breakfast before dawn had quite broken over the rooftops of Grosvenor Square.

'I do not like to leave you, my dear,' he said as he drank his coffee. 'But the report of Robyn's condition is so very alarming.'

In fact he felt little reluctance to leave his wife, but was very averse to leaving Miss Willow behind under her sway.

'Of course you must go,' said Lady Jane. 'For myself, I feel much improved. I believe I shall go out today.'

'I am glad to hear it,' he said. 'I think it will be good for you, to engage in society once more, to be busy about all your usual concerns. As for things *here*,' he threw her a look that he hoped she would not misconstrue, 'I wish them to remain exactly as they are. No attempt must be made to upset things.'

Lady Jane lowered her eyes and made no reply.

George, feeling he could neither do or say more, wolfed down a sweet roll and took up his hat. 'Good bye, my dear. No, do not come down to the door. You might catch a chill.'

He kissed her cheek and went from the room, which was a small parlour on the first floor adjacent to his chambers where he often breakfasted informally when his business took him out early.

Lady Jane followed him to the door to watch him go, down the landing and out to the stair head. The door to Georgina's rooms opened as he passed. He, much surprised but not at all displeased—indeed, somewhat amazed—stopped in his tracks. He spoke a few words to the occupant—Lady Jane could not hear what—and held out his hand. Then, Miss Willow stepped out. She wore a loose wrap over her night attire. Her dark hair tumbled over her shoulders unconfined by cap or curl-papers. Her feet were bare. She wore no veil. George Talbot put down his valise and opened his arms. He embraced her very tenderly and she laid her head on his shoulder for a moment before releasing him. He nodded, bent to retrieve his bag and went on his way.

Miss Willow glanced up the landing and her eyes met Lady Jane's. The two women held each other's gaze for a few moments—unsmiling, unspeaking—until Georgina turned away and went back into her room.

Later that morning the Talbot carriage drew up at Charlton House and Lady Jane was shown into the fusty drawing room with the recommendation that she would have to wait but a few moments. The baroness was upstairs with Miss Charlton and the dressmaker, but would be down again very soon.

The drawing room was not unoccupied. A young man was already there, lounging against the fireplace and smoking a small cigar, but he threw this into the grate as soon as Lady Jane was announced.

'Mr Binsley, I think,' said Lady Jane, recognising the gentleman from the Staffords' ball.

'Good morning your ladyship,' replied Mr Binsley. 'I hope I find you well. This is a very shabby room, is it not? I believe I know every cobweb and dust mote in it. I could probably identify each one of the baron's snuff boxes blind folded, I have examined them so often. May I ring for some refreshment for you? The baron has a particularly fine sherry here. I have drunk many pints of it, waiting for Lady Virginia to condescend to come down to me, but she rarely favours me with an audience.'

'I am sorry to hear it,' said Lady Jane, seating herself on the least sagging and threadbare chair available. 'I wonder you persist. A young gentleman like you must not want for ladies more appreciative of your notice.'

Binsley sighed. 'Indeed,' he agreed. 'But there is something about Lady Virginia that has me in its thrall. I find I cannot put her from my mind. You were not at the dowager's dinner the other evening? We had dancing afterwards, and Lady Virginia did stand up with me twice. She cannot find me absolutely repulsive.'

'I have been unwell,' said Lady Jane. 'And, in addition, I have a young relative with me just now. She is proving most troublesome. I have come to commiserate with Baroness Charlton; we both have our crosses to bear.'

The sherry was brought, and Mr Binsley handed Lady Jane a glass.

'Is this the mysterious veiled lady?' he asked when the servant was gone. 'Everyone is talking of her. Tell me, is she most horribly disfigured?'

Lady Jane smiled. 'I see my husband's attempts at discretion have fallen short in more ways than one,' she said dryly. 'Where have they been seen?'

'At Hampstead I think, and in various parks. My sister tells me that Madame Planché has been inundated with requests for veils. They are to be quite the fashion.'

'Well there's a turnaround,' mused Lady Jane. 'In my day young ladies were anxious to be *seen*.'

'And so they still are,' Mr Binsley assured her, drinking off his sherry and pouring more. 'Only, *now*, seen in their veils. Do tell me about this young woman. I should so like to be the first to be able to reveal her identity. Shall you bring her to the baroness' ball?'

Lady Jane almost choked on her sherry. 'The baroness is to hold a ball?'

'Yes indeed, on Wednesday. Did you not know? It is to celebrate Miss Charlton's engagement. It will be almost the last ball of the season I should think. Will she come, the veiled lady? Who is she?'

'Her name is Willow,' said Lady Jane. 'She is but a very distant relation, on her mother's side …'

'Willow?' shouted Binsley. 'How curious. My mother was a Willow, before she married.'

'Was she?' said Lady Jane, affecting to be only mildly curious, but remembering with spleen that Lady Binsley had refuted any knowledge of the name on the night of the Staffords' ball. 'Yes indeed, that is curious. Were they a numerous family?'

'Many sisters, all married now. One of them—my aunt Caroline—resides with us. Poor thing, she is much broken in spirit and mentally eccentric. Her mind wanders. Normally she is not permitted to leave the country— she must be closely supervised—but she is in town at present, to have a tooth drawn.'

'How distressing. Whereabouts in the country did your mother's people reside? Spalding? Wiltshire?'

'Neither. My grandfather was rector at Binsley, which includes Ecklington you know. Mama has lived in that area all her life.'

'I had no notion of it,' said Lady Jane, wishing that she had spent more time at the Talbot's country seat. How much sooner the mystery of Jocelyn Willow might have been solved. It was obvious to her now that Jocelyn Gilchrist, daughter of some all but extinct, probably barely respectable Spalding family, had married one of the rector's male relations—a brother perhaps, or nephew; the very sullen, limping man whom Lady Jane had met at Eton. It stood to reason that the surviving Willows—God damn them for their duplicity—*must* know something of the obscure young woman who had allied herself to them. 'It is high time that I paid your mama a visit,' she observed. 'I feel I have neglected her acquaintance, considering we are such near neighbours. Is she at home today?'

'I do not think so. She spends a great deal of time at the gallery, where Papa's paintings are on show. Poor Aunt Caroline will be at home alone today, and her tooth drawn but yesterday.'

Lady Jane consulted the clock. 'I don't believe I can wait any longer for the baroness,' she said, rising. 'I have many calls to make today. If you do happen to see her, perhaps you will tell her that I am wholly recovered from my indisposition, and very ready to add my salutations to Miss Charlton and his lordship, should she deign to invite me.'

26

Lady Jane returned to the house in Grosvenor Square later that day in a daze of exaltation. A confused but ultimately illuminating hour had been spent in the small room allocated to Mrs Caroline Foley *née* Willow at the Berkley Square residence of Sir Gabriel and Lady Binsley. The nurse had been very surprised at anyone asking for her patient by name, but made no difficulty about showing Lady Jane into the chamber, or of leaving the 'old friends' to converse whilst she betook herself to the kitchen for some luncheon.

Caroline Foley was indeed a poor, broken woman. She lay marooned on a chaise covered by blankets, unable to rise without aid. What remained of her hair was white, but not much did remain. One side of her face was swollen as was to be expected, but the surgeon's work had left her with barely a tooth in her head. Her cheek on the other side and both her lips were caved in around her gums. She slurred and mumbled. Not much could be made out from what she said and of what *could*, little made any sense. Many years spent in a sanatorium had reduced her mind to an echoing cavern of ghosts. Her childhood days were vivid to her, however, and she had spoken of her upbringing at the rectory with some degree of lucidity. Her cousin Barnaby, in particular, was a shining light where much else was shadow and doubt. But what burned the brightest was her sense of betrayal at his loss. On that topic she had spoken articulately enough, and Lady Jane had come away satisfied.[xlix]

Miss Trimble and Miss Willow were out of the house when Lady Jane regained it, and she went immediately to Miss Willow's rooms. All was neat within; the bed made, the chamber pot scoured, the fire laid ready for lighting. The window sash had been raised and the gauzy curtain fluttered in the draught. Lady Jane lingered over her guest's few personal belongings—a hair brush, some hat pins, a small pot of lavender-scented salve—before crossing to the drawers and pulling out the veils that lay folded within. Crêpe, organza and lace, fine chiffon, they slithered out and coiled around her feet like a nest of roiling snakes. On an impulse she selected one and pulled it from the rest, draping it over her own head and face. The first sensation that assaulted her was the sudden and oppressive heat that accumulated within even so fine a canopy, which came she supposed from her own person. The second was the scent of Miss Willow, which lingered about the fabric. It was not at all unpleasant, but it was very personal. The sense of having broached Georgina's defences—part and parcel of having uncovered her secret— surged in Lady Jane's bosom. She would triumph! She looked out at the room through the drapes and folds of the mantle. Everything was dimmed, overlaid as though with a layer of dust, the brightness of the day outside the window, the gleam of the jewelled heads of the hat pins, the bright colours of the bed counterpane all muted to tones of sepia and grey. She searched her soul for an atom of compassion for the girl who had suffered this attenuation but found there only the brightly burning flame of her own rancour.

She pulled the veil from her head and stooped to gather up all its fellows before stalking from the room.

Miss Trimble and Miss Willow returned from their walk late in the afternoon. They were laughing as they came into the hall. Their outer clothing smelled of fresh air and a little of the spring shower that had fallen on them for a small part of their walk. For Lady Jane the contrast—to the stuffy drawing room of Charlton House and the sick chamber of the patient in Berkeley Square–not to mention the gloom and sourness of her own house—was stark. It added to her malice.

'And so you are returned,' she said, startling Agnes and Georgina in the process of removing their outer layers. 'I hardly expected you to be away so long. Tea was served an hour since.'

'Oh! Oh … yes,' stammered Agnes. 'We did not expect you to be downstairs my lady; otherwise we should not have dreamt of keeping you waiting.'

'I *did* wait. But in the end I drank my tea alone.'

'I am so very sorry,' fluttered Agnes. 'Had I but known …'

'You have been too much distracted of late, Agnes,' Lady Jane said, full of spleen. 'You have been neglecting your duties.' Leaving poor Agnes to wither at this indictment, Lady Jane turned a superlatively haughty eye to Miss Willow. 'Good afternoon, Miss Willow,' she said, through lips that were thin with disdain. 'I hope you are recovered from your misadventure.'

'I … I am, thank you ma'am,' replied Georgina. 'I hope you are recovered from your … your …' she groped for a suitable word, 'your indisposition,' she came up with at last. She remained near the coat-stand. She had already handed her pelisse to the footman who stood there, but made no move to remove any more of her outerwear.

Lady Jane waved an imperious arm. 'You will remove your veil,' she barked. 'Come, come. Give it to Baxter. As I think I have already told you, it is quite unnecessary within doors. Indeed, it is unnecessary *anywhere*.'

Georgina had only that day consented to an appointment being made for her at Madame Planché's millinery shop, where Miss Pink could assist in the selection of some bonnets. They would screen her face without covering it. But now, at Lady Jane's absolute command, she felt what little self-confidence she had garnered slip away.

She stepped a pace or two backwards and grasped the hem of her veil in her hand. 'I think, ma'am, it is not for you to determine my mode of dress,' she faltered.

'Indeed it is,' said Lady Jane, and she crossed the hall to where Georgina stood. 'I forbid you to wear a veil.' She took hold of the veil in her own steely grip. The fine fabric tautened between them. 'Take it off, I say. It is mere affectation in you, to hide your face away. Your only object can be to attract attention to yourself, to weave some air of specious mystery, and indeed you have succeeded. *Everyone* is speaking of 'the lady in the veil'.'

She could not have said anything more likely to discompose Georgina. 'I hope not,' she said faintly.

'We have been most discreet,' Agnes cried. 'I am sure ...'

But Lady Jane snapped off Miss Trimble's attempt at mitigation. 'Do you contradict me, ma'am? I have heard it this morning with my own ears. Everyone is *avid* to know the identity of the strange shrouded woman.'

'Then,' said Georgina, speaking very earnestly in the hope of appealing to some shred of compassion in her hostess, but feeling indeed extremely anxious, 'I really must not remove it. Public attention is the *last* thing I desire.'

'Fiddlesticks,' said Lady Jane. 'Why else would you behave in so conspicuous a manner? I daresay, without this ridiculous artifice, no one would have noticed you at all! Now take it off.'

'Cousin George has made no stipulation ...' Georgina tried, clutching the veil more tightly.

'But George is not here. You shall not disoblige me. I will tolerate no refusal.'

'I am very sorry,' said Georgina, taking another step away. 'I think I must.' But she could feel the veil's fastening being pulled away from its attachment on her bonnet by the tension of Lady Jane's firm hold.

Miss Trimble managed to attract the notice of Baxter, the footman, and indicated to him by a sharp sideways motion of her head that he should withdraw from the hallway. For herself, she took a step towards Georgina, knowing that even so small an indication of partiality in this matter could go against her.

And indeed Lady Jane cawed, 'Stay back, Agnes, unless you wish to know my displeasure. Miss Willow has enjoyed this masquerade long enough at my expense. She may have taken *you* in, and obviously George is fool enough to believe any tale of woe she might have fed him, but *I* am not so green.'

Lady Jane and Georgina stood, face to face, their white-knuckled hands on the veil.

'You will do as I say,' said Lady Jane very menacingly, in a voice that was almost a hiss, 'or I shall see to it that your mama's disgusting little secret is known far and wide.'

Georgina's gasp and sharp intake of breath was evidence enough of her shock. A tear fell from beneath the mantle and fell with a splat on the marble floor. She croaked out, 'Mama's ...?'

'Yes.' Lady Jane nodded. 'Today I had a most illuminating interview with ... let me see ... she must be your cousin once removed ... Caroline Willow. I must say I think you have been most deleterious in your duty to *her*, poor old thing. But not nearly so cruel as your mama was, twenty-odd years ago.'

'I do not know who you mean,' said Georgina faintly.

'It doesn't matter,' said Lady Jane. '*I* know everything. And unless you oblige me in a few particulars I shall be sure to see that everyone else is informed of the facts. Your mama will find every respectable door barred to her. Mr Stockbridge will rue the day he met her. I am sure she has not told him the truth.'

'I am sure she *has*,' cried Georgina, but in a kind of anguish, because she had not understood why *he* could be trusted with something that *she* could not.'

'Lady Jane,' Miss Trimble hazarded, 'are you quite certain that you are fully cognisant of the facts? And, you know, to make such a caution on Miss Willow, it seems hardly …'

'Do not tell me what *seems*,' Lady Jane bellowed. 'We have all been taken in by what *seems*. Now we will see what *is*.'

She redoubled her grip on the stuff of the veil and with a sharp, rending motion, tore it in two.

Georgina made a noise that was somewhere between a shriek and a groan, stepped back, but found she had come to the door. She could retreat no further. But in any case, what was the use? She steadied herself. Her every instinct was to cover her face with her hands but she fought it. She only needed one glance at Lady Jane's triumphant, knowing expression to be sure that the threat was by no means empty. She lifted her hands very slowly and removed the remnants of the material. 'I would have removed it, without your tearing it,' she said with stubborn defiance. Her eyes were pooled with tears and as she spoke another spilled over, but she held Lady Jane's gaze. 'For mama's sake, I would do anything.'

'I am glad we understand each other,' said Lady Jane. Her eyes raked Georgina's face. She bit back her smile of triumph and affected to scrutinise the young woman's appearance with a critical eye. 'Hmm,' she mused, 'no scars at all. *That* is what they are saying, you know. But I cannot see what you have been so coy about. You are well-looking enough, I suppose, though no special beauty. I dare say you will pass without particular remark at the ball.'

'The ball?' Georgina stammered, mashing the vestiges of her veil in her hands.

'Yes.' Lady Jane offered a false smile. 'My good friend Baroness Charlton is to hold a ball the day after tomorrow. They do not move in the best circle and in any case most of the important people will have left town by then. The best families tend to return to their country estates, you know, at this time of year; they tire of the season. But poor Adelaide has her daughter's engagement to mark and so she is to hold a ball. You will do me the great honour of accompanying me.'

Georgina shook her head, not so much as a denial but in a stupor of bewilderment, and so the tears fell in earnest. 'I … I have never been to a ball. I do not know the dances. I have no suitable dress.'

'Oh!' Lady Jane waved a dismissive arm, 'all that can be arranged. Madame Le Favre is coming here tomorrow. And Agnes knows the steps to all the dances, do you not, Agnes?'

'I used to,' admitted Miss Trimble, 'but that was many years ago.'

Lady Jane turned away and walked towards the stairs. It was impossible for her to suppress her jubilation any longer. 'Things have not changed, I assure you,' she said over her shoulder. 'I doubt anyone will ask Miss Willow, in any case.'

Once she had regained the privacy of her chamber Lady Jane took out her handkerchief and pressed it over her mouth to stifle the shriek of victory she had felt welling up in her from the moment she had unmasked Miss Willow. For the two weeks of her convalescence she had been troubled by a sense of having overlooked or forgotten something of great moment. It had been there at the instant of her first glimpse of Georgina, but the girl's undeniable and appalling resemblance to George—and, as she had thought then, the *only* explanation for it—had over-shadowed it. Since then it had hovered at the edge of her mind, like the echo of the memory of a voice saying something important but not quite distinguishable. Her brief view of the unveiled Georgina that morning had brought it back to her, brought it back in all the full vividness of its amazing potential. Her visit to Caroline Foley had been an unlooked for windfall, exonerating George but implicating Jocelyn, giving her just the leverage she needed to convey all the prospective profit of Georgina Willow to her own door.

And there was undoubtedly great profit to be made. *This* was the sense that had lingered at the periphery of Lady Jane's consciousness but which had been obscured by an onslaught of affronted anger. Now it shone clearly to her, and what glittered more radiantly than any other consideration was the prominence and acclaim that would accrue to herself. Let those society matrons cut her now! Let them gawp and flap like farmyard fowl as she led Miss Willow forth! 'Oh yes,' thought Lady Jane, as she fell to her knees in a paroxysm of triumph, half weeping with joy and satisfaction, 'Oh yes! Let them cut her now!'

27

Georgina found the three days that followed this encounter very strange. The shock of being so suddenly compelled to put off her veil could not be soon got over. It dismayed her excessively to have found, at the hands of Lady Jane, such unfeeling treatment. And to be threatened! With no attempt to pretend that the threat was anything other than a bullying tactic by which Lady Jane intended to have her own way! This was painful indeed.

Her first instinct was to be extracted from the awful prospect of the Charltons' ball and she scribbled a letter to her friends the Burleighs in the hope that they could receive it and make arrangements to retrieve her before the day of the ball came. She left the letter on the hall table and girded herself to endure Lady Jane's treatment until it should be answered.

It was exceedingly odd to Georgina to wear no veil. The sense of exposure was acute, and she was tempted to walk with her head bowed, to shrink and cower into shadows. She fought a continual, instinctive urge to hide her face. On the other hand, in her rational mind she had to admit that there was a certain sense of lightness, of freedom, such as she had not felt since her night-time perambulations on the moor in Yorkshire. She was conscious of a freshness to the air and about her skin, a greater freedom in movement. And everything, to her uncovered eye, was so vivid! Colours were startling, the fineness of detail quite staggering. In part she delighted in it, as a liberated person will delight in their release, but there was also a sharp stab of guilt when she thought of her mother, of all that she—Georgina—risked, *and* of all that she protected, for her sake. The conundrum of this troubled her greatly; she wrestled with it.

Second in the scale of perplexing things was the behaviour of Lady Jane. She acted as though she had made no threat, done no violence, but the threat and the violence palpably remained all the same—another paradox. Her manner was as charming as possible; the foregoing two weeks apparently forgotten as though they had never been. Georgina, stunned, could only meet her hostess' absolute reversal of conduct with astonished compliance. In truth she was most fearful, both of the ordeal to come and of the consequences of refusing to endure it. That Lady Jane was manipulative and cruel was manifest. That she had her own object in parading Georgina before the company at the Charltons' ball was also apparent—but *what* that object was, Georgina did not know.

The third, the least complex but perhaps the most difficult to bear, was the absence of Miss Trimble. She was separated from Miss Willow, kept busy elsewhere with the writing of cards, the running of errands, the management of Dickie and any number of other tasks that would divide her from her young friend.

In her stead, Lady Jane took up the mantle of Miss Willow's management. This was trying indeed to Georgina, but could by no means be avoided. It was clear that Lady Jane meant to monopolise every moment of Georgina's time and Georgina did not dare to challenge her. On the first morning Georgina was summoned to breakfast in Lady Jane's private sitting room where she was horrified to see her letter to the Burleighs torn up into shreds and scattered across the hearth. Lady Jane made no remark about it but once she was sure that Georgina had seen it, she called the maid and had it swept up and added to the coals. Then commenced a tour of the artworks and artefacts of the house and the collection of books in the library. Georgina, incensed about her letter but too afraid to challenge Lady Jane, forbore to say that she had already had this tour; it seemed impolitic to remind Lady Jane of her dereliction of duty at the time of Georgina's arrival. Later, Georgina was subjected to a lesson in etiquette, modes of address, the niceties of social intercourse. She was in need of none of this instruction but it pleased Lady Jane to give it all the same. Georgina was regaled with a history of the premier families—who should be courted, who avoided, who had disgraced their name, who promoted it by some great alliance—a roll-call of the great and the good, the horrible and the heinous of the English nobility.

She was forced again and again to walk the length of the long drawing room, her air and deportment corrected, her posture criticised.

'Hold your head up! Keep your eyes forward!' was the repeated cry.

In the afternoon they took tea, their conversation—stilted and artificial—ranging from books to music, from nature to architecture. Lady Jane had no interest in Georgina's opinions on any of these topics, but wished to establish her ability to converse on them if called upon to do so.

As promised, Madame Le Favre the dressmaker came, with two young apprentices who saw to the pinning and the tacking of several gowns which were to be added to Georgina's wardrobe. 'I shall need only one gown, shall I not?' Georgina protested. 'It is but one ball.'

But Lady Jane shook her head. 'Who knows what may occur thereafter? I think it not unlikely that one or two further invitations will ensue. We must be prepared.'

'I thought you said the season was all but over,' said Georgina.

'And so it is,' said Lady Jane smoothly. 'But not *absolutely* ended; there is a little enjoyment to be wrung from it yet.'

The two little seamstresses kept their heads down and their eyes averted as they went about their business, but Georgina saw them exchanging significant looks between themselves. Madame Le Favre made no scruple about examining Miss Willow very minutely, with a narrow, appraising eye. The dressmaker was a hard-faced, gimlet-eyed woman, but with slack lips, used to spreading gossip. Georgina's heart sank within her. She was certain that, before the day was done, a detailed description of her appearance would have been circulated. What terrible damage it might do to her mama she could not know. She *could* know, however, what carnage would ensue if Lady Jane did not get her way.

Georgina felt as though she had woken from a nightmare to find it real.

Georgina and Lady Jane dined in state, just the two of them in the lofty dining room, attended by a full complement of servants, so that Lady Jane could see for herself that Georgina's manners at table were unobjectionable. Where poor Miss Trimble ate her dinner Georgina did not know. She quailed under the censorious eye of her hostess, the barely-concealed curiosity of the staff, and could eat but little.

At the end of the first bizarre day, when Georgina was on the point of extinguishing her candle, a timid knock announced Miss Trimble. She was dressed for bed, her hair in papers, a threadbare grey wrap over her night dress. She crept into the room and closed the door very quietly.

'Oh, my dear,' she whispered, taking hold of Georgina's hands. 'How are you? I have been worried about you all day, but have had no opportunity to come to you. Lady Jane has kept me very busy doing nothing. Oh! I feel for you very acutely. Shall you bear it, do you think?'

Agnes' kindness made Georgina's eyes swim. 'I shall have to, for mama's sake,' she said. 'I do not know what Lady Jane has ascertained but she is certainly in possession of some information. I do not doubt that. Oh! I wish Cousin George were here! I wish mama had never gone away! I wish …' but she stopped short of wishing Mr Balfour might come. What, in any case, could *he* do?

'You are being very brave, my dear,' said Miss Trimble. 'I am proud of you, and, after all …' She lifted one tremulous hand to Georgina's cheek and pressed the other meaningfully on the place where the décolleté of Georgina's nightgown revealed a triangle of silky white skin, the seat, perhaps she thought, of the soul, '… after all, you have nothing to be ashamed of. You are pure and good, my dear.'

'Is there nothing that can be done?' asked Georgina, suppressing a wail. 'Can my cousin not be written to? Can Arthur not be sent for?'

Miss Trimble shook her head. 'I fear not,' she said. 'Nothing could be done in time, and I have been informed that her ladyship has ensured that no post leaves the house, but that she sees it first.'

'Oh! She is scheming!' Georgina hissed. 'What does she hope to achieve?'

Agnes shook her head, but thought she knew quite well what Lady Jane's object was.

On the second day Georgina was summoned to the long drawing room where a man had been brought to play the piano, and where Miss Trimble, supervised by Lady Jane, waited to teach her the steps of some of the more popular dances. In point of fact Georgina was familiar with many of these; she had danced, privately, with the Burleighs from time to time, and she and Lucas had often amused themselves by practicing steps that, for her part, she never expected to perform in public. The exercise would have been delightful–their occasional stumble, wrong turn and collision would have caused them both amusement—but Lady Jane's overbearing presence quashed any iota of enjoyment.

'We are not doing this for *fun*,' Lady Jane carked from her seat at one end of the room, when a smile made a momentary appearance on Georgina's face. 'I daresay the gentlemen will not notice,' she added. 'They, no doubt, will have their thoughts on other matters, but the ladies certainly will notice. Any small slip will have them on you like a pack of dogs.'

Georgina stopped in the midst of a *sauteuse*, causing Miss Trimble to tread on her toe. 'Are they really so cruel?' she asked with a stricken expression.

'Perhaps they will make allowances, since it is your debut,' replied Lady Jane. She motioned to the pianist that he should continue. 'Now, go back to the start. Begin again.'

That same afternoon, over tea, Lady Jane said, 'Is it right that I acquaint you with some details pertaining to our host and hostess. The baroness is an old school-fellow of mine. She was nobody at all until she married the baron. Of course, a baron is the very lowest degree of nobility. They hardly signify in the scheme of things, but naturally they feel some recognition is due. His property is entailed, but they have a son, Ernest. If he is at the ball—which I doubt—you need not pay him any attention. He is a sickly boy, not likely to live, let alone to marry. When he dies some canting clergyman will get the property, who is the baron's nephew.' Lady Jane smirked as she thought of this possibility, but then straightened her face to say, 'Baroness Charlton has quite a horror of it, as you can imagine. In point of fact the baron himself does not enjoy good health. He drinks far more than is good for him. Ah! But now,' with a regretful sigh, 'it will not matter. Gertrude is to marry Lord Pokerham, who has estates in Surrey and also in the midlands, and ten thousand a year. He will be the count of Sotherton when his father dies. They are sure to be able to find Adelaide a pretty little dower house for her dotage. I would have you pay particular notice of Lord Pokerham, Georgina. He is a man who could do you a great deal of good.'

Georgina frowned. 'I cannot see what good he could do me, your ladyship. I think it unlikely I shall ever see him after tomorrow night. He is to marry Miss Charlton. I cannot think it would be seemly to pay him any but the most distant notice.'

'That is not the way things work,' Lady Jane scoffed. 'An engagement is all very well, but it is not a marriage.'

Georgina looked at her aghast. 'You cannot mean …?'

'I mean nothing,' said Lady Jane, sipping her tea. 'But *if* he pays you any attention—and why should he?—do not slight him. He is shy, as you are. I think it not unlikely that he dreads the ball as much as you do! Oh yes, I think you will find you have much in common.'

Presently, Lady Jane went on, 'The Charltons have staying with them a young woman, Lady Virginia, one of the younger girls of the Duke of Shrewsbury. She is a flibbertigibbet. You should have nothing to do with her. Her own reputation is all but destroyed and any association you have with her will undoubtedly leave its stain.'

'I shall be careful to avoid her,' said Georgina.

'I think *that* will hardly be possible, since she is the Charltons' guest. However, I would have you make as stark a contrast as possible between her behaviour and your own.'

'I shall do nothing to embarrass you,' Georgina murmured.

'No,' Lady Jane gave an unctuous smile, 'I know you will not. For you have a great deal to lose.'

After tea Georgina retired to her chamber. Her conversation with Lady Jane had disturbed her more than somewhat, another puzzle to add to the pile she had already accumulated. It seemed that Georgina was not to sink to the depths of an acknowledged flirt but to encourage the attentions of an all-but-married man. How were both those to be achieved?

All in all Georgina was disgusted by Lady Jane. She had been as derogatory as possible about her so-called friends the Charltons, dismissive of their poor son, and almost seeming to wish for his death. It was clear that their daughter's success was a thorn in Lady Jane's side. How bitter she was! Her viciousness was without equal! Georgina despised her. But she feared her, too. There was no question but that Lady Jane would make good on her threat if Georgina gave her the least reason to do so.

She paced backwards and forwards in her chamber, her hands restless, her thoughts very disturbed with ideas of the darkest and most desperate kind.

The dressing bell was rung, and at the appointed hour Georgina went down to dine. Her eyes were swollen from crying, her face red and blotchy. Lady Jane scolded her severely and dismissed her. She went, without dinner, to bed.

28

On the third day—the day of the Charltons' ball—breakfast was interrupted by a visitor. A card was sent up, *'Madame Planché's compliments and apologies. She regrets she is unable to attend upon Lady Jane's guest today, but has sent her most trusted assistant, Miss Pink, in her stead.'*

Lady Jane studied the card quizzically. 'I did not ask Madame Planché to call,' she mused. 'What can this be about?'

Georgina was pale, her eyes shadowed. She had not slept, but she had at last managed to control her angst and this morning had appeared before Lady Jane in a more composed—a more resigned—attitude. 'I think,' she offered now, 'that Miss Trimble arranged it for me. We had been discussing the acquisition of some bonnets. In all the activity of the past few days, I expect Miss Trimble forgot to cancel the appointment.'

'Hmmm,' said Lady Jane, considering. 'Well, I suppose there can be no harm in her coming up. But I must say I think it neglectful of Madame Planché not to come herself. I don't know who she thinks I am, to be palmed off on an assistant.'

Miss Pink was shown into the room. By some instinct she could not quite understand, Georgina did all she could—without saying a word—to communicate to Miss Pink that their previous meeting at the house of Mrs Quince should not be mentioned. She need not have worried. Miss Pink would not have presumed on so slight and so brief an acquaintance. She indicated to the liveried boy she had brought with her that he should put down the hamper he carried and withdraw to a corner. She proceeded to bring out some sample bonnets, all of a design that would screen the wearer's face to all but those who were directly before her.

'We shall not need anything of that kind,' cried Lady Jane. 'Miss Willow's days of hiding herself away are quite over. Madame Planché has dispatched you for no reason.'

'Except,' Georgina put in, 'I have no bonnets at all that do not incorporate a veil. I shall need *something* …'

'But not these.' Lady Jane cast a withering eye over the assembled samples. Georgina cringed at her rudeness.

Miss Pink began to pack away her wares.

'How is the weather out of doors, Miss Pink?' Georgina asked, by way of compensating for Lady Jane's disgusting behaviour. 'Does it rain? I have not been out since Sunday.'

'It has rained a little,' Miss Pink replied carefully. 'Have you been unwell, miss?'

'We do not make small-talk with milliners,' said Lady Jane very sneeringly. 'Let her take her things and be gone.'

Georgina began to assist in wrapping up the ribbons and trimmings that Miss Pink had arranged prettily on the lid of her basket. As she laid them into the hamper she grasped Miss Pink's hand and squeezed it. An answering squeeze gave her to understand that Miss Pink saw that something was very much amiss.

'Since Miss Pink has been so good as to call,' Georgina tried, 'perhaps we might send her to Miss Trimble's chamber? *She* may like to consult with Miss Pink. Then her journey will not be quite wasted.'

'I do not think so,' said Lady Jane. 'Miss Trimble has but recently been furnished with new headgear. She is in want of nothing further.'

Miss Pink, however, gave the slightest possible nod before beckoning the boy forward.

In the afternoon Georgina's new gowns were delivered. This time Madame Le Favre personally saw to the last-minute tucks and tweaks, her lips bristling with pins. The gown was of crimson silk, richly figured, setting off Georgina's dark hair and pale complexion. It was scandalously low off the shoulder and at the bosom, with puffed sleeves cuffed above the elbow. A corset pulled her waist to a tiny size but everything else about the dress made her feel out-sized, conspicuous and exposed. Layers of starched petticoats held the skirts out so wide she doubted she would fit through the door. There was so much flesh on show that she could barely look herself in the mirror without blushing. Her skin crawled at the idea of being so entirely on show. The colour of the gown was so bright. There was no possibility of remaining in a shadow, or blending into the décor, both of which things she had wildly thought might be achieved.

'I would prefer something more modest,' she said, turning a beleaguered face to the seamstress. 'Some lace at the bosom, a shawl ...'

'Nonsense,' hissed Madame Le Favre through her pins. 'This gown will be the envy of every girl in London. Every eye will be on you. The other young ladies will muster in their insipid pastel shades and their demure little muslins and wonder why they have turned out at all.'

'But I do not *wish* ...'

'Let us not be ungrateful,' Lady Jane interposed, for, of course, she had insisted upon being present. 'I have had the Talbot rubies brought from the bank. My own maid shall have the arrangement of your hair. We must make *something* of you, you know, unpromising though you are.' She exchanged a look with Madame Le Favre—a secret, complicit smile—and Georgina's heart sank.

'You wish to humiliate me,' Georgina said. '*That* is your object.'

'I wish to *save* you from the ignominy your mother has condemned you to. Somebody must, indeed, if you are not to be consigned—like her—to a lifetime of obscurity and shame.'

'My mother has done nothing wrong,' Georgina flung out, but with more of loyalty than of certainty.

Lady Jane and Georgina dined early. Again, the dining room was set, the servants all deployed. Again, Miss Trimble was absent. The room was chill, the food unappetising, and Georgina struggled to eat more than a few mouthfuls. There was a lump of anxiety and distress in her throat that she could not swallow down. The closer her ordeal came the more she dreaded it. Her inner core quailed, pulpy and unreliable. She had clung on to some slim shred of hope that *something* might occur, even at the eleventh hour, to save her from the trial that was before her. Her cousin George might return and immediately veto the entire scheme. Her mama may be found not to have gone abroad at all. Mr Balfour … But no. Of him she had no hope. Had he not seen her face and, through it, seen *her*? Had he not recognised the *flaw* in her that necessitated concealment? Now everyone would see it. There was no help for it. And what could not be helped must be endured.

After dinner the ladies retired to bathe and dress. The maid came and Georgina was helped into her clothes. Her hair was dressed, piled high at the back, braided through with ropes of seed pearls and studded with rubies. Small curls were laid across her forehead and allowed to fall into ringlets in front of her ears. A tendril or two was teased out that it might emphasise the length and slenderness of her neck. A heavy rope of rubies—brought from India by the old Mr Talbot, the maid said—was placed around her neck, a matching bracelet clasped to her arm over her long, silk glove. The maid knelt to place a pair of low-heeled red silk slippers onto her feet.

It was done. Georgina looked at herself in the long glass, appalled at what she saw: a sacrifice, a condemned woman. Her eyes glittered with tears she dared not shed. Her mouth was a maw. A shriek of dismay pressed itself into her throat.

Below, the front door of the house began to reverberate with a series of imperious knocks. Hope swelled in Georgina's breast. Perhaps, after all …

From the hallway a man's voice could be heard—very authoritative, most determined to be heard. Another voice rose to meet it—Gerrard, the butler—equally dogged in his resolution not to admit the caller. Words were bandied. Georgina could not hear what was said but that there was an altercation was indisputable. She went to her door, as though to open it.

'I do not think you should go down,' advised the maid.

'I want to know who is come,' Georgina said, laying hold of the door handle. 'It may be that someone has called for me. A friend. A messenger.'

'The mistress has ordered that no one should be admitted,' said the girl, tidying away her hair-dressing accoutrements with efficient hands. 'For these three days past, that has been our orders.'

Georgina was seized with anger. 'So, there may have been callers?' she said. 'People wishing to see me? And they have been denied?'

The maid paled, realising that she had said too much. 'I could not say, as to that, miss.'

Georgina ran to her window. The day was gone. Twilight had stolen upon Grosvenor Square whilst she had been prepared for sacrifice on the altar of Lady Jane's malevolent agenda. The lamp-man was making his way around the square. She could not see the door or the portico from her window. She wrestled with the sash but it would not rise beyond a few inches. If she cried out through it she would not be heard.

Below, the voices rose to a climax. Then the door was slammed. She strained to see the figure who would leave the house. A man. Tall. Broad-shouldered. She got only the briefest glimpse. Then he was gone. Georgina's heart sank.

The maid went away and she was left alone. Georgina went about the room and extinguished all the lamps so that she could not see her reflection in the mirror. Darkness was the only invisibility left to her. Only the firelight illuminated the space in an eerie shade of purgatory. Georgina, in her crimson gown, with the dark fire of rubies at her throat and in her hair, indeed felt as though she had arrived in hell, but with a strong sense that in truth, the full horror of the inferno was still to come. She sat down on the chair by the hearth, and waited for the torture to begin.

The clock on the mantelpiece ticked the inexorable minutes away. A coal fell in the grate. The heat and darkness and her own emotional exhaustion overtook her, and she fell into a kind of swoon.

Presently, a noise in the corner of the room brought her back to a sort of consciousness. In the shadows she made out a dark figure. Or was it the drape of the curtain? She sat up. 'Who is that?' she asked, squinting into the gloom. 'Is that you Agnes?'

'No,' said a familiar voice. 'It is I. It is Arthur.'

Then he stepped from the dimness and came forward. He still wore his greatcoat. His hair was tousled and a little damp from the fine rain that had begun to fall outside, but not very damp. In truth, he had been standing rapt, gazing at Georgina for some moments, rehearsing the words of Romeo in his mind.

> O! She doth teach the torches to burn bright.
> It seems she hangs upon the cheek of night
> Like a rich jewel in an Ethiope's ear;
> Beauty too rich for use, for earth too dear.

'How did you get in?' asked Georgina, reaching forward to take his hands.

'With a great deal of difficulty,' Arthur said, shaking off his reverie. 'The man at the door would not entertain me at all. I had to go to the back. Thankfully, I came across the groom that drove us on Saturday. He remembered me, and came in to find Miss Trimble. *She* brought me up here, and waits at the end of the landing in case her ladyship comes near. But Miss Willow, what has happened? Miss Pink sent me a message. She is sure you are in difficulty.'

'Oh Arthur,' cried Georgina. 'I *am*. Everything is in pieces. Lady Jane has found out something about Mama. I have always known there is a secret, some reason why we must always be obscure. I have always thought that it is because of me.' She lifted a hand to her face. 'Some fault or flaw in the way I look. But I do not know what it is. But now … now I do not know. Lady Jane says there is a terrible disgrace in Mama's past and if I do not comply, she will reveal it to the world. Oh Arthur! What am I to do? Just *look* what they have done to me?' She indicated her hair, her face, her person. 'Indeed, indeed, I am a wretched creature.'

Arthur knelt down on the carpet. He took hold of her hands. 'Miss Willow,' he began, but then checked himself. 'Georgina,' he tried again. 'Do not distress yourself. You are not without friends. I will take you away if you wish. I have Mr Bannock's little wherry standing by and Dick and Walt will row you down river to Cuckold's Point. Her ladyship will have no suspicion of where you might be. I am sure Miss Trimble would not reveal it. I will have word sent to the Burleighs and they shall come for you. But I must in fairness say this: I do not know what information Lady Jane has but I do fear there is *something* in your mother's history. So I will not tell you that Lady Jane's threat is an empty one. I *can* take you away, but there may be consequences.'

Georgina nodded. 'Yes,' she said. 'This is what has tortured me. I have thought of running away, of locking my door. I have thought … Oh Arthur … I have thought of doing myself some damage. But then I think of Mama. I *must* do this, to save her. I cannot come away with you, Arthur, although I wish with all my heart that I could.'

He looked at her dress. 'You would have had to change your dress,' he said, with an attempt at lightness. 'I could not very well have bundled you across London and into a wherry in *that*.'

She looked down at herself. 'No,' she agreed. 'It is very ridiculous, I know.'

'It is the fashion, I suppose,' said Arthur. He remained on his knees before her. He hesitated, pressing his lips together, clearly wondering whether to speak what was on his mind. At last he said, 'Georgina. There is something about your appearance that marks you out. For any other woman to be as thoroughly unconscious of it as you are would be suspected as artifice, pure affectation.'

'That is what her ladyship says.'

Arthur waved this aside. 'She has no understanding, but I do not blame her. No one could conceive it—it could not have come about—if it were not for the extraordinary circumstances of your upbringing. It is the result of your mother's absolute insistence that you live a sequestered life. A sister in a closed order has had more exposure than you have to the world, Georgina!

'Yes,' Georgina murmured. 'Mama said she had put me into a kind of prison.'

'And so she has. But Georgina, let me tell you what you clearly do not know yourself. You are beautiful. You are strikingly, incredibly beautiful.' He shook his head, at a loss for the words. 'You must forgive me,' he stumbled on. 'I could explain the internal workings of a steam engine; for *that* I have language aplenty. But for beauty, I have not the vocabulary. I can only say that I have never seen a more beautiful woman than you are now. I doubt any man alive has. No wonder men stop and stare at you. No wonder other women look at you in envy. No one, having seen you, would ever forget you. *That*, I am sure, was your mother's fear.'

Georgina regarded him with an expression of doubt, but not of disbelief. It would explain so much. But why had she never been told? She was conscious of a sharp stab of anger—that this secret had been kept from her—and also of humiliation—that she herself had not discerned it.

'I have no idea of flattering your ego,' said Arthur, rising now. 'I tell you simply so that you can arm yourself with it.' Below, in the hall, the longcase clock began to strike the hour. Soon the carriage would be brought round and Georgina would be summoned forth. 'Let it be a kind of shield to you—a veil, if you like. When you are out this evening, and people stare at you, *that* is why. They do not find fault. They are not revolted. They are *amazed*. And, whatever is in your mother's past, whatever she has sought to hide, it is not apparent in *you*.'

29

Charlton House was not at all a convenient house for a ball, and so the baroness had hired Almack's Assembly Rooms[li] for the celebration of her daughter's engagement. For all Lady Jane had claimed that the season was almost over, a good many carriages crowded King Street, and the Talbot carriage went round several times before her ladyship was satisfied that—the majority of guests being inside—she could make her arrival with the utmost impact.

The carriage drew up and the footman lowered the step. First her ladyship, and then Georgina stepped down.

Georgina moved as though she were in a strange, dislocated dream. After Arthur's departure she had drunk off a glass of strong wine. The glow of it in her stomach and the light-headedness that had come almost straight after had aided her in enduring her ordeal so far—the slow descent of the stair, the rank of goggling servants, a teary-eyed Miss Trimble—but Arthur's words had been of more assistance still. She was bemused by them, but she did not suspect him. She thought Arthur incapable of telling an untruth.

Lady Jane offered her arm as they descended the carriage. Georgina ignored it, communicating as powerfully as she could, without actually speaking, that she needed no help and would not in any case have taken any from her ladyship. She struggled to maintain her state of adamantine calm and held her head very erect.

The building had an entrance straight from the pavement. The ladies went in, and up the stairs to the ballroom. Georgina mounted as though ascending the scaffold. The crowd of guests that would normally be waiting to greet their hosts had disappeared. Lady Jane and Georgina reached the top landing meeting nobody.

The noise that emanated from the ballroom was almost deafening. Conversation, the shrieks of ladies, the guffaws of men, a small dog yapping, the scrape of instruments tuning up, the clink of glass as punch and champagne were served. All these clamoured together, jangling and jarring in Georgina's ears. Carried on the billow of sound was a hot waft of imperfectly washed bodies, sour breath and candle smoke. Georgina swallowed down a ball of bile. The rubies felt heavy on her neck, a leash, a restraint.

Somebody at the top of the stairs—a footman perhaps—removed her cloak. He may as well have removed all of her clothes. She felt as naked as a babe.

The master of ceremonies inclined his head to Lady Jane, and she gave him their names. Lady Jane drew Georgina into the archway of the portal as an artist places the subject of his painting centre-frame.

Georgina stared into the abyss. Her dazed eyes surveyed the room and it seemed to her to be so full that two more people would overwhelm it; the walls would bulge, the floor collapse. She could not see for the life of her how dancing could possibly take place unless half the guests were to be trampled.

Hundreds of candles burned from sconces. The air was thick with their smoke and heat. She could see it, a pall above the heads of the ladies and gentlemen. It added an oppressive layer, augmenting still further her sense that the room was a drum about to burst.

She allowed her eyes to rake the crowd. She would not permit herself to acknowledge whose face she sought. There *were* black faces, but topped by wigs and supported by livery, carrying trays and tending candles. One struggled to quiet the yapping dog that writhed and snarled in his arms.

Madame Le Favre had been quite right. Amongst the marriageable young women there was a proliferation of pale colours in muslin, silk and tulle, dresses as nearly bridal as made no difference. Only the girl who *was* nearly a bride—Georgina recognised Gertrude Charlton from her taut expression and from the blinking discomfort of the young man who stood beside her—wore a dress of a darker hue. Gertrude glanced over to the door and their eyes met. Gertrude's face crumpled as though punctured. For all the supposed happiness of the hour her expression upon seeing Georgina betrayed only the misery of inadequacy and failure. Georgina felt the accusation of it, and dropped her eyes.

The voice of the master of ceremonies rang out, unbelievably loud, quite overpowering the other cacophonous noises in the room.

'Lady Jane Talbot,' he cried, 'and Miss Georgina Willow.'

There was an immediate hush. Even the orchestra ceased their sawing and plucking. All eyes turned to them. Georgina girded herself. The fingers that clutched her little reticule were white and bloodless. She fixed her eyes on the cornice at the far end of the room. It was elaborate with bunches of fruit and posies of flowers, much gilded. Above it, across the ceiling, cherubs gambolled in an Arcadian scene, fauns and dryads cavorted beneath trees. She wished with all her might that she could be transported there, but she felt Lady Jane urging her forward, and she stepped into the room.

A sort of corridor had opened before them. Lady Jane's supreme satisfaction in the moment seemed to physically inflate her; Georgina could feel her expanding. They ran the gauntlet side by side, but the older woman's complacency took up most of the space. Georgina found herself forced too close to the awe-struck on-lookers and so more able to gauge their reactions. She heard gasps and sighs and words whispered behind fans. A man smacked his lips and said, 'I *say*,' in a most vulgar tone. A woman murmured, 'It is the veiled lady,' and the rumour was taken up, passed on, so that even those at the back of the room with no view at all repeated it, and craned and jostled to get a glimpse.

At last they came to the place where the baron and baroness stood with their daughter and prospective son-in-law.

Lady Jane, her voice as cutting as a shard of glass, said, 'Adelaide, my dear. I'm so sorry to have been tardy. May I present my ward, Miss Georgina Willow.'

Georgina curtseyed, straightened and felt her hand touched. With difficulty she raised her eyes.

'Most welcome,' barked out the baron, his eyes—already mazed from too much punch—very wide and ogling, a drop of spittle in the corner of his mouth. 'Upon my word. Well, well. Miss Willow, is it? Upon my word.'

At last he dragged his eyes from Georgina and turned to his daughter, as though needing her assistance to free himself from his trance. 'Gertrude, my dear. Gertrude …'

'Yes Father.' She pried Georgina's hand from where the baron still clasped it. 'I am delighted to make your acquaintance,' she repeated for the hundredth time that evening, but probably with less sincerity.

'Thank you,' Georgina mouthed. 'And I yours. You must forgive me for the intrusion. I know I have no right …'

'That's quite all right, Miss Willow,' said Lord Pokerham, some vestige of manliness rising up into his character. 'Come, let me introduce you to my mother and father.'

Lady Jane and the baroness faced each other. 'Lady Jane,' said the baroness, without quite knowing how she was going to complete her remark. The fact was that she had not invited Lady Jane to the ball, on the pretext of the letter she had received from Mr Talbot—surely, Lady Jane was still too ill to accept any invitation—but really because Lady Jane's credit amongst the *ton* was so low. But now, here she was; she could not very well be ejected. And she had brought with her such a creature! A sensation indeed. Baroness Charlton allowed her eyes to survey her guests' faces. Every one betrayed rapt amazement. This would not be soon forgotten. And whilst it was irksome in the extreme that her own possession of Lady Virginia *and* Gertrude's coup with the Sothertons should be over-topped by this gambit of Lady Jane's, still, *some* of the glory of it would come to the Charltons' door. In all likelihood, because of this young woman's extraordinary debut, this would be proclaimed the ball of the season! The baroness returned her attention to Lady Jane who, all smiling condescension and specious sweetness, stood before her. 'I am so glad you are well again,' she said, returning her ladyship's honey ounce for ounce.

'Thank you,' simpered Lady Jane, but she would not stay to bandy further words. She pursued Georgina, determined not to be separated from the girl; *everyone* must know it was Lady Jane Talbot who had brought this trophy amongst them.

The Sotherton contingent was encamped a little further into the room, their woebegone expressions betraying their increasing doubts as to the suitability of the Charlton match for their boy. Almack's rooms, though large and well appointed, were not the venue they would have chosen. A public assembly room was not at all the same as a private ballroom. If only the Charltons had a larger house! But no, Charlton House was cramped and notoriously fusty. Quite unsuitable. And heaven only knew what horrors their country house would prove to hold! And the Charltons' friends! The baroness had been indiscriminate with her guest list. The room was too crowded and with people of inferior degree. The baron had invited a number of fellows from his club, many of whom were not at all what they ought to have been. The punch had been mixed too strongly and even so early in the evening there was a ribald tone that the countess found quite offensive. But what was this? Who did Pokerham have on his arm? The countess elbowed her second son, Lord

Tonge. The youth stood up from where he had been lounging against a pillar. The dowager countess adjusted her *pince nez*. The count gave a horsey snort. '*Much* more the thing,' he drawled.

Reports about Georgina surged around the room like an in-coming tide. 'A pretty little estate in Wiltshire,' was passed ear to ear, and 'six or seven thousand a year,' and 'the last of the Gilchrists; *very* good blood, you know. The line goes back to William the Conqueror.'

Georgina was squired around the room, first on one arm and then on another, her hand pressed—sometimes kissed—and introduced to people whose names and faces she instantly forgot. She gave herself up to it, her body limply unresisting whilst her will scrabbled for a purchase on some high eyrie. Let the evening, the people, do with her person what they would—as Arthur had told her, it was a shield she could hide behind. So long as her mind remained untouched. Lady Jane followed behind, as though attached by some cord—possessive, controlling—speaking for her, her voice unctuously smug. Yes, apparently, Miss Willow was *passionately* fond of music, *very* eager to dance, enjoyed riding above *all* things, *delighted* in the play, would be at home to callers every Thursday and Saturday from ten.

Faces loomed into her field of vision. Old men's faces fat, flushed, greasy. One ran a thick tongue over his lips. Another drooped his eyelid in a lascivious wink. She watched a third run a finger around the inside of his stock, as though finding it suddenly too tight. Young men's faces, their eyes wide and staring, their mouths flapping, their ability to string a coherent sentence apparently gone. Some of them managed to splutter out an invitation to dance, and she found herself offering a dance card that she did not know she held. She saw matrons' faces—narrowly appraising, taking in her hair, her figure, her jewels—and girls' faces, narrow-eyed, peevish, their lips sewn into purses.

The tide of rumour about her had swollen to a flood. The tidy estate in Wiltshire was now hers outright—her poor brother utterly disinherited—and was so vast it occupied half of neighbouring Dorset. It had been added to by several hundred acres of grouse moor in Scotland

and a palazzo on the shores of Lake Como. Her six or seven thousand had doubled of its own volition. The Gilchrists were discovered to have some distant claim to the throne. Carried along on this fantastical floe, like awkward flotsam, was the tricky matter: who *exactly* were her parents? And what was their connection to the Talbots?

At last the orchestra struck up the first dance, and she was led to the set. Her partner—an older man with a small beard and a large stomach—manhandled her through the dance. He was a widower, he told her, with three young daughters at home. Did she like children? His mother resided with him. Did she think that *in general* an aged mother was an impediment to a successful marriage? It was clear that he found the exigencies of both the dance *and* of conversation rather trying; he wheezed, and his brow poured sweat. She made vague replies, and was glad when the dance was ended and he took her back to Lady Jane.

She was handed punch. She drank it, and her next partner claimed her. It was Lord Tonge, a more callow version of Lord Pokerham, his cheeks peppered with pustules, his protuberant eyes set too far apart in his head. He danced with no co-ordination, his thin limbs subject to sudden unpredictable flings and jerks, like a puppet. He poked her quite badly in the side and stood on her toes innumerable times. But at least he did not speak, seeming to have lost that faculty. He fixed her, throughout, with eyes that never blinked or wavered—transfixed, as though by a spell.

There was a short interval during which various young ladies approached; eager, they said, to make Miss Willow's acquaintance. Had she been in town very long? Why had they not seen her at the play? At Vauxhall Gardens? Was it true—leaning near, and speaking confidentially—that she was the woman they had seen in the impenetrable veil? Was she in mourning, and, if so, how did she explain this sudden emergence?

There was no requirement for Georgina to make an answer. The girls themselves offered all her replies. 'No,' said one, a ginger-haired girl with pale blue eyes, 'the veiled lady is in hiding from an ill-intentioned Prussian Prince.' 'On the contrary,' said another, a portly girl with becoming dimples, 'she has been horribly scarred as a child by a careless nurse-maid.' 'You have been misinformed,' a third girl said. 'The veiled woman is well known to be a spurned mistress seeking revenge upon her lover.'

'You are all quite wrong,' said a fourth girl, and at her words the other three shrank away. 'The lady in the veil simply wishes to be left alone. Am I right?' She held out her hand. 'Good evening. I am Lady Virginia Shrewsbury. I expect you have been told to keep away from me.'

'She certainly *has*,' said Lady Jane, stepping forward. 'I am most surprised to see you here this evening Lady Virginia. It was my understanding that you were *persona non grata*.'

'I heard the same about *you*,' said Lady Virginia with a mischievous grin. She turned back to Georgina. 'Do say you will take supper at our table, Miss Willow. I assure you we will be the most amusing company.' She glanced over her shoulder to where a cohort of gentlemen, including Lord Perry and the infamous Mr Rex, lounged against a wall, their flushed faces all turned in her direction.

'Miss Willow's supper arrangements have not been fixed,' said Lady Jane. 'Good evening to you, Lady Virginia.'

Georgina found herself led to another part of the room. The heat was over-powering; she longed for some fresh air, some cool water to splash on her face. But there was to be no respite. She was touched, pushed, jostled. Faces were thrust towards her only to be pushed aside and replaced. She was gawked at, like an exhibit at a circus of curiosities. It was insupportable, but it *must* be borne. Invitations were pressed upon her. Would she dine? Would she ride in a *barouche landau*? Would she join a party in a box at the theatre? Lady Jane answered for her; she would be delighted, and would be at home to callers on Thursdays and Saturdays from ten.

It transpired that Georgina was engaged to dance every set. She danced with tall men and with short, fat men and thin; with louche, lecherous men who took liberties and with others almost too petrified by her to do anything but walk woodenly through the steps.

All the time the noise in the room buffeted from wall to wall. She heard snatches of conversation, the shriek of instruments, the barking of the infernal dog, which ought to have been removed but which its doting owner could not do without. The women's voices tinkled like so many discordant bells, and the men's gravelled and grated like shovels in a mine.

From time to time she looked about her—for aid, for some sign that the tribulation would soon end, for a sympathetic eye that was not coloured by spite or lust or strangulated thrall—but saw only strangers and strangeness. She danced, she stood, she danced again; the faces blurred into a sweaty homogeneity.

30

The last dance before supper was announced. Somebody took her hand.

'Would you *like* to dance, Miss Willow,' asked a deep, velvet voice, 'or would you rather take a little air?'

She looked up. The man was tall, about her own age, with straight dark hair and kind, brown eyes. He was handsome, his skin the colour of burned honey. A small smile played about his mouth.

'I am sorry,' she said, struggling to emerge from the mindless state she had been inhabiting. 'I do not think I know your name.'

'Do you not?' he said, raising an eyebrow. 'And yet, we have met before.'

'Forgive me.' She looked at him properly, discarding the consciously clouded vision she had employed all evening. 'No,' she said at last. 'I am sorry, I do not recall.'

'Never mind,' said the gentleman, tucking her hand into his elbow and leading her through a doorway she had not noticed before. She glanced over her shoulder. Lady Jane would not like her to go out of sight. But her ladyship was engaged in an animated conversation with a uniformed gentleman with a monocle. Georgina hesitated on the threshold. The doorway led into a smaller chamber, perhaps used for cards on other occasions but now set out with supper tables. It was brightly lit. Waiters moved between the tables polishing cutlery and distributing wine glasses.

'Do not be alarmed,' her escort assured her, seeming to read her reservations. 'Lady Jane knows me. And she knows you are with me. Here is a window open, you see. Is not the fresh air very pleasant? I think it a great shame that there is no veranda here at Almack's, nor any gardens. But there are none and so this will have to suffice. With whom do you take supper, Miss Willow?'

'I hardly know,' she said, breathing great draughts of the air. 'Lady Jane has taken all that in hand.'

'I do not doubt it,' her companion said with a rueful grin. 'She has a habit of doing that. I understand this is your first ball. How are you enjoying it?'

Georgina said, 'I am *enduring* it. I am sorry. That sounds ungrateful, but it was not my choice to come.'

'I quite understand. Her ladyship has pressed the obligation on to you.'

'Yes, she has.' Georgina felt it safe to admit as much. 'I find the room very hot, and the people not at all courteous, except you. And there was a young lady earlier, Lady Virginia Shrewsbury, *she* seemed genuinely kind. But Lady Jane does not approve of her.'

'No. Won't you sit down?' The gentleman indicated a window seat and when Georgina had lowered herself onto it he spread his coat-tails and perched beside her. 'I have only been back on English soil a few hours,' he told her, 'but even in that short time I have discovered that Lady Jane is not well-regarded at present. Lady Virginia gave her the slip at a ball much like this one. Of course the impropriety was all Lady Virginia's, but the blame has been laid at Lady Jane's door. I suspect you are her means of climbing back into favour.'

'I wonder how she thinks I can do that?' mused Georgina. She was cooler now, and calmer. She took a closer look at her friend. His suit was very fine, his stock tied high and tight and fastened with a jewelled pin, his waistcoat beautifully embroidered. She raised her eyes to find his on her face, his expression somewhere between sardonic and sympathetic.

'Do you *really* wonder that, Miss Willow?' he asked, narrowing one eye.

'Yes indeed,' she protested. 'I have no acquaintance in town. Who will listen to *me*?'

'I do not think Lady Jane hopes they will *listen* to you.'

'No,' she shook her head and dropped her gaze. 'She only wants them to look at me, whatever good *that* may do.'

He sighed. 'I think you may find it will do a good deal.' He motioned to one of the waiters, and soon two glasses of champagne were brought to them. He raised his to her, then put it to his lips. She scrutinised his face again. He allowed her to do so, an amused look in his eye. She thought there was something … But it eluded her.

'You still have not told me your name,' she said.

He smiled. 'No. I have not. I think I shall withhold it. That will stand me in better stead than all those other men who told you their names, only for you to forget them again.'

She laughed then, the first time she had done so for days. 'You are right,' she said.

'Ah, Miss Willow,' said the stranger, regarding her warmly, 'you should laugh more often. Your expression all evening has reminded me of a fox at bay, the moment it is cornered and it turns to face the hounds. Although all is lost, it wonders if it has just enough wile and strength to evade them. Have you ever seen such a thing?'

'No, but I have seen an old dog who is about to be shot. My mother's friend Mr Burleigh had to do it, for the dog was in dreadful pain. The look in its eyes—though they were clouded and half blind—it knew what was coming and yet there remained some iota of trust.'

'Yes. I'm sure it was the same—terror, but attached to the faintest tendril of hope.'

Georgina nodded. It was exactly what she had felt: utter powerlessness, utter fear, but, somewhere at her core, a sense that she might, just survive.

The man drained his glass and stood up. 'My time is almost done,' he said. 'The dance will conclude, and then I must return you to Lady Jane.'

Georgina stood and took his arm. 'I have enjoyed this quarter hour better than any I have lived through for the past three days,' she said. 'I hope it is not indecorous to say as much.'

'Not at all,' he said, with a wide smile. 'And in return I shall say that I have enjoyed this quarter hour better than any I have lived through for the past three years.'

'Oh,' cried Georgina, who had thought her own recent trials very hard. 'You mentioned you have been abroad. Have you been in a foreign war, or imprisoned? Or ill?'

'No indeed,' he replied, as they walked slowly back to the ballroom. 'I have been doing the things that young men *do* abroad. I have seen ruins, gazed at paintings, climbed mountains, swum in lakes, danced with ladies, drunk with men …'

'But it has not made you happy?'

'No. It has made me homesick and lonely.' They had come back to the door of the ballroom. The dance was very energetic, the heat almost unendurable, sweat pouring from the musicians as they worked at their instruments. Lady Jane raised her hand and began to make her way across the room. 'However,' the gentleman turned and faced her, and raised her hands to his lips, 'now I am home, and I am glad of it. And I feel, Miss Willow, that I shall never be lonely again.'

Lady Jane was beside her, and the gentleman was gone, melted into the throng.

'It is supper time,' Lady Jane said. 'We are to sup with the Sothertons. Lord Tonge is to take you in.'

'Very well,' said Georgina. 'But, Lady Jane, who was that gentleman I was with just now?'

'Him?' Lady Jane sniffed. 'Did you not recognise him? That is my stepson, Robert Talbot.'

31

The Sothertons and Charltons took supper in an alcove, removed from the hoi-polloi by a small screen. The addition of the two latecomers had not been anticipated and too many chairs had been squashed around the table. Georgina found herself wedged between Lord Pokerham and Lord Tonge—a place of some honour considering she had not even been invited to the ball and had never met either of them before. It pleased Lady Jane, however. She sat between Baron Charlton and the dowager countess and exuded waves of self-satisfaction.

Lord Tonge made several attempts to engage Georgina in conversation but none of them got beyond, 'And so, M …M … Miss W… W… Willow,' in spite of the gimlet glances and occasional kicks to the ankle administered by his mama. Lord Pokerham did better, but his remarks were of a general kind that did not need much in the way of reply. His high, reedy voice reminded Georgina of a flute, or a particularly lugubrious bird. She nodded and smiled through his several observations about the weather and wished he would not neglect his other neighbour. Miss Charlton looked as unhappy as possible, said nothing, and stared miserably at her plate. At last, whilst Lord Pokerham occupied his overbite with a chicken wing, Georgina leaned behind him to say, 'Miss Charlton. I have not offered you my congratulations. When is the wedding to take place?'

Gertrude turned swimming eyes towards her. 'We are not sure …' she mouthed, but the next word, which could have been 'when' but was more likely to be 'if' was lost, as Gertrude dissolved into tears.

Then Lord Pokerham turned towards his betrothed and they exchanged looks of sympathetic wretchedness; perhaps the only thing they had in common. He took her hand from where it lay in her lap, and patted it. 'There, there,' he said quietly and, Georgina thought, very tenderly.

'The *day* is not absolutely fixed,' said the baroness shrilly, from where she was marooned between the count and the countess, 'but matters are well in hand. We think, probably, in June.'

'There are several details not yet settled,' the countess observed. She looked significantly at her son, before turning her gaze to Georgina. 'There is many a slip twixt cup and lip, as the saying goes.'

'I do hope not,' grumbled Baron Charlton, calculating in his head the moneys laid out so far.

'No indeed,' his wife concurred. 'I assure you, there will be no reneging on *our* side, and I am sure his lordship is too honourable to give back word.'

'There will be no dishonour in an insuperable legal impediment,' the count offered, 'however much our son wishes to marry your daughter.'

'Or, indeed, how little,' Lady Jane murmured.

The count went on. 'I do not mind telling you that our man of law is most unhappy about some of the terms offered.'

'I do not know what more I can proffer,' blustered the baron. 'I am bled white as it is.'

'Oh Archibald,' scolded his wife, 'let us not speak of such vulgarities. This is to be a celebration.' She raised her glass to the unhappy couple: 'To Jeremiah and Gertrude,' she cried.

After supper Georgina found herself in an anteroom set aside for the necessaries of the ladies, and mercifully, just for a few moments, freed from Lady Jane. Gertrude Charlton sat in a low chair before a mirror, staring disconsolately at her reflection whilst a maid pressed a cloth soaked in rosewater to her cheeks and forehead.

'I am so sorry to have upset you with my question,' said Georgina. 'I apprehend … forgive me if I am wrong … but I apprehend that the match between yourself and Lord Pokerham is not of your choosing.'

'It is of neither of our choosing,' Gertrude burst out. 'His mama and mine concocted it and what can we do but comply?'

'He seems a very sweet young man, and attached to you,' Georgina offered.

'He *is* sweet,' Gertrude conceded.

'But Gertrude loves another,' said Lady Virginia, joining them. 'Oh, what wretched creatures we are! Gertrude is to marry a man she does not love. I am prevented from marrying the man I love and you, Miss Willow … Well. None of us knows what secrets *you* harbour, so very enigmatic as you are. What a stir you have made, *quite* as Lady Jane intended, I am sure.'

'I am here absolutely at her behest,' Georgina agreed. 'I am her creature.'

'For sure we are all in the same leaky boat,' said Lady Virginia, 'beset by monsters on every side. What are we to do?' She turned a winning smile on the maid. 'Why don't you go and find us a bottle of champagne, and four glasses,' she said. 'You may tell the maître 'd that Miss Charlton requires refreshment. I shall see you are not the loser by it.'

The maid scuttled from the room.

'Why four glasses?' asked Gertrude dully.

'The maid shall have her share,' Lady Virginia said. 'I am sure she is as miserable as we are, kept from her beau, or pawed by some awful waiter. All women have their crosses to bear, Gertrude.'

'*Are* you attached to another gentleman, Miss Charlton?' Georgina asked. 'Does Lord Pokerham know?'

'Oh yes,' said Gertrude with a heavy sigh. 'We have been very frank with one another. He quite understands that I had already given my heart to Captain Brimming; but the captain has no money, only his army pay, so it is quite impossible. For Lord Pokerham's part, he *must* marry someone to whom he is not related at all. The Sothertons are too congenital. But a girl with no noble connections could not be tolerated. And so I am to do for him. He *had* made up his mind to it, but now … I think, Miss Willow, upon seeing you …'

'But I have no noble connection,' Georgina assured her.

'That might be overlooked, in your case,' Gertrude mumbled.

'But Gertrude,' said Lady Virginia, 'why would that upset you? It seems to me that a very little encouragement from Miss Willow might solve all your difficulties. Your engagement could be broken off. What would you care? If it freed you to marry Captain Brimming? *He* would not object to a girl who had been jilted by another. Indeed, he might be the only man who would not!'

'But so much has been made of it,' wailed Gertrude. 'The *ton* expects our marriage, and mama would be mortified.'

'We endure a great deal for the sake of our mamas,' Georgina agreed.

'My mama is dead,' said Lady Virginia. 'I have a new one, but I assure you I will endure nothing for her sake. It is she who keeps me from my beau. Oh, here is our champagne. Thank you. Here. You may take your glass and drink it somewhere else. I will find you if another lady comes in.'

The ladies drank their champagne, and very quickly did they find it restored their spirits.

'Your step-mama does not keep you very effectively from your lover, does she, Lady Virginia?' said Gertrude slyly.

'No! We have devised means to see each other from time to time.'

'How so?' asked Georgina.

'He has come to town disguised, much as you did. He is not to come into his property until he is five and twenty. Until that time his uncle has the supervision of his estate and his mother rules him with a rod of iron. His mother is my papa's new wife. They say we are too much brother and sister to be married, but they are wrong. There is not a drop of shared blood between us. In reality I believe they hope to find better matches for both of us. But we are quite determined and we bide our time. He will come of age at Christmas and then we shall do as we please. In the meantime he goes about as Mr Rex.'

'I see. So, when it comes to it, you will marry whether your parents agree to it or not?'

'We will. Is it not all a jape? How we laugh about it! His income is not large—only five thousand a year. But I could be happy with less, so long as it is with him.'

'So I feel, about Captain Brimming,' said Gertrude. She raised enquiring eyes to Georgina. '*Would* you be kind to Pokerham, Miss Willow?'

Georgina shook her head. 'I would not be unkind to anyone. But I will not encourage the attentions of a gentleman for whom I have no feelings, and in any case …'

'Ah!' divined Lady Virginia. 'Miss Willow has a secret lover.'

'No, indeed,' said Georgina, blushing.

'Miss Willow!' It was Lady Jane, flushed and anxious. 'You have been an unconscionable time in here! Ah, and now I see why. Did I not tell you to avoid Lady Virginia's company?'

'You did,' said Georgina, rising. 'But I could not very well abandon Miss Charlton when she was in need of succour.'

'You should all return to the ballroom,' said Lady Jane, herding them like a flock of ducklings before her. 'The dancing is due to recommence. Who are you to dance with next, Miss Willow?'

'I have no idea your ladyship.'

'Let me see your card. Oh! It is Lord Pokerham. How satisfactory.'

'Once more into the lions' den,' murmured Lady Virginia, as they went back into the ballroom, 'for *you*, at least Miss Willow. There are girls in here who would cheerfully tear you limb from limb, I do assure you, and men who would do much worse.'

The weight of her tribulations landed heavily once more on Georgina's shoulders. 'I am aware of it,' she said. 'I wish it were not so.'

But she felt, as she girded herself to her ordeal, that she could perhaps bear it a little more bravely now.

32

The excessive strength of the punch and the wholesale consumption of wine and champagne over supper had further debauched an occasion that had not been very refined to begin with. Ladies as well as gentlemen had been made raucous, their shrieks and bellows rising ungoverned to pollute the Arcadian innocence of the ceiling friezes. Several matrons dozed in their chairs as their charges cavorted on the dance floor and allowed themselves to be fondled in dark corners and behind the curtains. The dog, mercifully, also slept. By what means he had been subdued was not clear. He slumbered on the lap of his keeper, snoring loudly, his tongue protruding from between his teeth.

Men staggered from one partner to another, or sometimes switched in the midst of the dance, blearily unsure as to which girl they had begun the figure with. They blundered into waiters, scattering glassware across the scene and spilling wine, making the floor treacherous.

The heat was oppressive. Sweat poured off the dancers, streaking the paint of women who would have sworn on the bible that they never used such artifice. Someone threw open a window, only to find that the draught sent showers of hot wax onto the naked shoulders of the ladies.

The window was fastened shut, the heat redoubled. The orchestra played as though in a frenzy and the guests danced on.

Lady Jane surveyed the scene with supreme satisfaction. What a shambles it all was! How utterly vulgar and disgusting! What a failure Baroness Charlton had made of things! The baron had withdrawn to the cardroom and would not be seen again. The schism that had opened up between the Sothertons and the Charltons over supper seemed to be widening with every moment. The two factions had taken up positions on opposite sides of the room, and threw glowering looks at each other. It would not surprise Lady Jane one iota to find that, by morning, the engagement had been called off. The behaviour of the guests was as unseemly as possible. Baroness Charlton must be ashamed of them. Oh! It could not be more delightful! The ballroom was a carnage of broken glass and spilled wine, but over and above all sailed the beautiful, the exquisite Miss Willow, like an angel strayed into purgatory. Even as Lady Jane looked on, she could see that Georgina drew every eye. Men danced with other girls, yet looked at *her*. Gentlemen along the peripheries of the room hung on her every supple movement. Ladies—admiring, envious—followed her with their gaze.

Just now Georgina danced with Lord Pokerham. That he was captivated by her was quite clear; *she* had called forth from him some manly bearing and self-confidence that Gertrude Charlton had utterly failed to summon. He stood erect with Miss Willow in his arms, guiding her adroitly through the battlefield of the floor. What an unexpected bonus, Lady Jane thought to herself, to add to the triumphs of the evening.

Her desire had been, foremost, to restore her own reputation amongst the ton. She would not be snubbed! She had her own daughter's entrée to think about and could allow no shadow of her failure with Lady Virginia to taint it. Miss Willow had more than amply compensated for Lady Virginia's fall from grace. Who would remember *that* small interlude after *this* triumph? Miss Willow was in every way a superior girl to Lady Virginia. Already Lady Jane had been inundated with enquiries, invitations, promises to call. There was no doubt at all that Miss Willow was a sensation.

Second in her intention had been to expose her enemy, Jocelyn Stockbridge. Lady Jane herself would not have divulged the information Caroline Foley had imparted, but she trusted to the *ton*, presented with Miss Willow, to unearth it in time. She did not care if Georgina, having been so elevated, should then be knocked back down to lie in her mother's disgrace. Lady Jane would claim to have been as taken in as all the rest! However foul the stain of Jocelyn's sin, whoever it might taint, Lady Jane would not be touched. Her hatred against Jocelyn Stockbridge burned very hot. The woman was disgraced! How dare she embroil George in her shame by claiming kinship when she ought to have dissevered herself absolutely from him and from every respectable person? How dare she besmirch George—and by association, Lady Jane and her children—with her dirty little secret? How dare she foist her by-blown child onto the very hearth of the Talbot home? There was, in Lady Jane's mind, no contradiction between *this* heinous sin and her former charge—Jocelyn's determined aloofness—for of course her ladyship saw things very much in the light of her own resentment, and conveniently forgot that Jocelyn had buried herself in the country as quietly and discreetly as possible for the past twenty years.

Last of all in Lady Jane's motivation had been a desire to disobey and disoblige her husband. Although she now understood him to be innocent of the accusation she had made against him, she did not think him wholly without blame. He had as good as sent her from the house. He had taken Miss Willow's part against her. Most of all, he had denied her the truth—which he surely knew. Well here was the consequence of *that*. She would teach him to keep secrets from *her*.

In all these considerations, the exposure of Miss Willow to society—and the worst of it, at that—had seemed to Lady Jane the perfect revenge. She could not have been more satisfied with the success of her scheme.

Most regretfully did Lord Pokerham bring Georgina back to her chaperone. 'I hope I may call on you,' he fluted. 'It would be my honour.'

'Of course you will bring Miss Charlton,' said Georgina. 'I should like to know her better.'

'If you like,' said Pokerham doubtfully.

'With or without her, my lord, you are welcome,' said Lady Jane.

Georgina's next—and final—partner made his approach. Lord Perry screwed his monocle firmly into place and regarded Georgina through its lens with an owlish eye. 'I believe the next dance is mine,' he said, 'and long have you kept me waiting for it, Miss Willow.'

'I have not determined the number of sets, my lord,' replied Georgina.

'This is to be the last of them,' said Lord Perry. 'You have certainly saved the best to last. Come now, let us form up.'

But then another gentleman made his approach, a captain of militia, rather burly, small, but not on that account to be taken advantage of by a monocled lord. 'You will excuse me sir,' he said very sharply. '*I* am engaged to dance this last with Miss Willow.' He turned to Lady Jane, who held Georgina's dance card. 'I am Captain Parry. You will see my name, ma'am.'

Lady Jane squinted at the card. 'The writing is so poor,' she said. 'I cannot say.'

'It is Perry,' said Lord Perry, very tetchily. 'I wrote it myself.'

'In point of fact I rather doubt that,' said Lady Jane, who had closely supervised Georgina's dance card and would not have permitted Lord Perry to get his name upon it. 'I think you took advantage of the similarity in your names to trespass on this gentleman's prerogative.'

'Outrageous, ungentlemanly behaviour,' blustered the captain. 'I have only remained at this fiasco in order to claim my dance with Miss Willow, and now you attempt to steal her from me.'

Lord Perry retained his grip on Georgina's arm. She suspected him of being more than half inebriated. His eyes—even his good eye—were bleary. By preference she would have danced with the captain, who though rather bullish, did seem to be sober.

'I am very sorry, gentlemen, but I cannot dance with you both,' she said.

'No indeed, and being his superior by birth, and possession being nine tenths of the law, I claim precedence,' said Lord Perry, yanking Georgina forward.

'Sir, you are too violent,' Georgina protested. But Lord Perry was much stronger than he looked, and very determined. He half-dragged her towards the head of the set.

'And we must not take the premier place,' argued Georgina. 'That is for Lord Pokerham and Miss Charlton.'

'They will not mind,' hooted Lord Perry. 'You are quite the most superior girl in the room. Even Pokerham will admit that, I think. Indeed, you are the most superior girl in London, and I must have my turn at you.'

'Sir,' said Georgina, most affronted, and pulling away from him, 'I am not an object to be used.'

'Five minutes in a darkened room with me and you will find you like it very well,' crowed Perry. 'Here. Now take your place and we shall show them a thing or two, I think.'

But the captain was not at all to be trespassed upon. He had marched behind Lord Perry and Georgina and as Perry swivelled on his heel in preparation for the set he found Captain Parry before him.

The captain, high in dudgeon if low in stature, barked, 'Sir. I will not be supplanted. I am engaged to dance this set with Miss Willow and I must insist upon that honour.'

'Go to the devil,' snorted Lord Perry, and shoved the little captain away. Captain Parry stumbled, slipped on the wet floor and fell hard.

A trickle of blood oozed from the captain's head and added itself to the mess of wine and winking glass shards on the ground. A lady screamed. A number of the captain's brother militiamen surged forward to lay hold of Lord Perry. Other gentlemen, not at all involved in the affray but feeling themselves insulted, retaliated. The brawl that erupted was fierce, but not very violent, the majority of blows missing their mark. It was, however, the end of the ball. The orchestra seized their instruments and scrambled from the stage.

A soft voice behind Georgina said, 'Come away, Miss Willow. Your carriage is being brought round for you. See, I have your cloak.'

She looked up to find Robert Talbot at her elbow.

33

Robert Talbot had met his father at the bedside of his sister Robyn. Both men had been summoned in the same way, by a letter announcing her sudden and serious illness. Robert had received his in Monte Carlo, where he had been briefly staying on his way back home. He had been tired to death of his Grand Tour, very desirous of being back on English soil, glad of any excuse to expedite his journey, although his sister's condition gave him cause for grave concern.

The hot little garret apartment Robyn insisted upon occupying had been the scene of their reunion—father with son and daughter, brother with sister—and very affecting it had been. The three of them had a strong bond that George's other children, though dear, could never break into. Robert and Robyn—being twins—had, in any case, a special affinity. Although the circumstances were not happy ones they had all felt the quickening of their mutual affection, and on George's part this was not decreased by his recent unhappiness with Lady Jane.

Robyn had indeed been very ill, with a high fever, but cholera—the scourge of the city—had not been suspected and by the time her father and brother arrived she was in fact through the worst of the affliction.

George had engaged the services of a nurse, and provided everything that could possibly be of any use as well as a great many things that could be of no use at all but which he felt might cheer the patient's spirits. Once this had been achieved, the room tidied and aired, the sheets changed and the patient put into fresh nightclothes, refreshments brought in and the three Talbots as comfortable as ripe cheese and rough wine could make them, George had told as much as he was able of Georgina.

'I remember her very well from our visits to the house in Yorkshire,' said Robert, balancing his chair on its two back legs. 'She was an adventurous child, always climbing trees. Lady Jane was appalled, when I told her. I am sure she has been predisposed not to like Georgina since then.'

'Very likely,' said George. 'She dislikes anything in the least indecorous.'

'She dislikes it, as it relates to *her*,' Robert amended. 'In others, she likes it well enough. It feeds her thirst for scandal.'

George could only nod; it was but too true.

'Bobby,' croaked Robyn from her pillows. 'Have mercy on my poor chair. You will break it and then it will only be good for firewood.'

Now Robert was a man, he disliked to be called by his childhood name, but allowed it from his sister. He looked down at the chair. It was scuffed at the legs, and splodged with paint. 'It is only really good for firewood now, Robyn. But since it pleases you to live like an impoverished old blue-stocking, I shall desist.'

'It seems strange that Georgina should *now* be so very retiring,' Robyn went on, settling her head more comfortably on the pillow, 'when, as you say Bobby, she was a brave little girl. Does she wear a veil all the time?'

'I'm afraid so,' said their father. 'Georgina has been imbued with some misapprehension that her mother's desire for anonymity is her fault; that there is, in Georgina's own appearance, something that will cause her mother harm.'

'And why does Georgina's mother desire anonymity?' enquired Robert.

'Ah! *That* is a secret I am not at liberty to divulge. She had her reasons, but in my opinion she took the thing too far. Be that as it may, once Jocelyn made the connection she tried to get Georgina to lay aside her veil, but she would not. Since she has been in town, I have encouraged her to emerge, and so has Miss Trimble.'

'Dear Miss Trimble,' said Robyn with a sigh. 'I wish she were here. She is the *best* nurse.'

'Indeed she has been invaluable, and I have reason to believe there is good progress. On the morning of my departure Miss Willow allowed me to see her face.'

'Did she?' said Robert, leaning forward. 'And was it dreadful?'

'It was astonishing,' said George. He leaned back and laced his fingers behind his head, conjuring back into his mind's eye the image of Georgina. 'Simply astonishing. I have never seen anything like it in all my life, in all my travels …' He shook his head. 'I do not think I have the words to describe it.'

'So ugly, do you mean? The poor thing,' said Robyn.

'Not at all ugly,' said her father. 'Quite the reverse.'

'Beautiful?' said Robert.

'Exquisite. Heavenly. Helen of Troy could not have been more sublime.'

'Intriguing,' said Robyn. 'I wonder if she would allow me to paint her.'

'It does not sound as though we will ever be allowed to *see* her,' said Robert, 'although I own I would very much like to.'

'I am very worried about her,' said George. 'I had to leave her entirely at Lady Jane's mercy. I did stipulate as emphatically as I felt was safe that Lady Jane was to maintain the *status quo* so far as Georgina was concerned, by which of course I meant that she was not to be compromised to any degree—not compelled to remove her veil, not forced into society—but I fear, the moment my back is turned …'

'What about your friend Mr Balfour? Could he be called upon to watch over Miss Willow?' Robert helped himself to the last of the wine.

'I think he would have been only too pleased. But unfortunately he was called away on business a day or so before I left. I have no idea if he is even back in town.'

The three of them sat in silence for a while. Robyn closed her eyes and was soon asleep. From below, in the streets of Montmartre, came the sounds of the end of the Parisian day: booksellers packing away their wares, shops drawing down their shutters. George and his son exchanged glances and rose silently from their seats. They bent and kissed Robyn, then crept from the room.

The evening was warm and rich with the scents of honeysuckle and garlic. The uneven pavements and old stone walls exuded the heat they had absorbed during the day.

'Let us repair to our hotels, bathe and change, and then dine,' said George.

'Yes sir. And then let us speak more of Miss Georgina Willow,' Robert replied.

George had been happy to spend the evening with his son. Bobby—Robert, as he now preferred—had been a difficult child, subject to strong obsessions, very passionate. George was rather surprised that Robert had not returned from his tour engaged—or even married—to some foreign heiress. But close enquiry revealed nothing of that nature. All Robert wished to discuss, was Georgina Willow. The upshot of their conversation over dinner was that Robert should quit Paris early the following day and return to London, where he could watch over Miss Willow until Robyn should be recovered enough either to be brought home by her father, or left in Paris. And very glad Robert was, as he accompanied the ladies back to Grosvenor Square in the Talbot carriage, that he had done so.

There had seemed no point in making a scene with Lady Jane whilst at the ball, or of carrying Miss Willow off. *That*, he had been sure, would only add to Georgina's abject embarrassment. That she had been embarrassed, uncomfortable and humiliated had been evident to see. Robert had watched her arrival at the ball—her inspiring features fixed, her excellent head held very high, her hands white-knuckled with tension—and marvelled at her fortitude. But he had marvelled more at her beauty. Truly, he had thought to himself, she was an Adonia[lii], a flawless exempla of classical loveliness. Her skin was like warm marble; the urge to reach out and touch it was almost irresistible. Her features were in ideal proportion—large, soft eyes; a wide, passionate mouth; sculpted cheek bones and a smooth, alabaster brow. Her form was as perfectly wrought as by a master sculptor's hand. She moved like a prima ballerina—such elegance and grace. She was a goddess! An angel! She seemed to exude radiance in the same way that the streets of Montmartre had exuded heat. He felt himself illuminated by it, roused as he had not been by the antiquities of Egypt, the panorama of the Alps, the art of Italy. He had watched her—indeed he had not been able to take his eyes from her—subject herself to the stares of the crowd, the sweaty attentions of the gentlemen, the envious glares of the women. Everything, in comparison to her, was coarse and vulgar, ordinary and trivial. She, in comparison to everything else, was superb. He did not blame the gawkers and gogglers; who could help but admire Miss Willow? But his understanding was shot through with a powerful stab of jealousy. How dare they? It was all he could do to prevent himself from striding towards her and sweeping her from the room. He did not know what could have induced her to undergo such an ordeal, but he was sure—from Lady Jane's superlatively smug air—that his step-mother congratulated herself on having engineered it.

'My father will be astonished, madam,' he said, as the carriage rumbled over the cobbles, 'that his express direction has been so manifestly cast aside. He assured *me* that Miss Willow was to be kept out of society.'

'Your father has been very good to me,' said Georgina faintly.

'Miss Willow obliged me by accompanying me to the ball,' said Lady Jane. 'It did not seem much to ask, under the circumstances.'

'Under *what* circumstances, madam?' enquired Robert.

'The circumstances of her being my guest,' said Lady Jane. 'She will oblige me further by being at home to some few callers tomorrow morning.'

'I should think Miss Willow will be too tired to see anyone,' declared Robert. It is almost three o'clock now. If I were her, I would sleep until noon.'

'Nevertheless,' said Lady Jane, 'she will oblige me.'

Robert turned to where Georgina sat beside him. In the dimness of the carriage she looked white and woebegone, although still very beautiful. Her fragility almost enhanced her flawlessness. She regarded him with round, limpid eyes. 'I do not mind, Mr Talbot,' she said in a low voice. 'I will do as her ladyship requests.'

'There now,' crowed Lady Jane, 'you see? She is a good girl.'

Robert continued to gaze at Miss Willow. Every so often the carriage passed one of the gas lamps on the roadside and the interior was bathed in light. It illuminated the girl at his side with a particular hue—warm and golden—and set the rubies at her neck on fire. In her fatigue she had leaned against him. He felt the weight of her against his arm. The confluence of their bodies seemed to transfer some of her essence into him. It intoxicated him like fine wine.

'I have never seen the Talbot jewels look so fine,' he murmured.

'They must go back to the vault tomorrow,' said Lady Jane. 'I have never cared for them since I discovered your mother wore them. But you will not have seen *that*.'

'No,' said Robert, narrowing his eyes. 'I was never so lucky to see her at all. Would that she had lived. Would that she were still alive today.'

'Oh, but then—' began Lady Jane.

'Precisely.'

They reached Grosvenor Square and the step was lowered. Robert half carried Georgina from the carriage to the hallway, but left her there in the charge of Miss Trimble and a maid.

'You do not stay here?' enquired Lady Jane.

'No ma'am,' he replied. He bowed stiffly, and left the house.

He had no intention of staying at the house in Grosvenor Square, although it was both his home and his birth right. He had engaged a room at his club, the Oriental,[liii] and would remain in it until his father returned from Paris. He walked in the direction of Hanover Square, through the empty, glistening streets. In the park across the square, the first bird began to sing, He found his heart very light within him.

'I must be in love,' he said aloud.

34

Amory Balfour had been so severely maimed by the three cut-throats that the night watchman who found him in the early hours of the morning took him for a corpse. Once he had found a weak mist of breath from the swollen, bloodied lips, and a faint, fluttering pulse behind the crusted lacerations of the arm the watchman identified Mr Balfour as a runaway.[liv] Everything of value had been removed by the thieves; Amory's pocket-book, watch, ring, boots, coat and waistcoat had all been stolen. What little remained of his attire was muddied and torn; in truth he did not look at all like a gentleman. He had been beaten to a pulp; his eye all but blinded, his jaw displaced, his face and arms cut about for sheer devilment by the thugs who had been surprised to find that a black man's blood flowed as red and freely as any white man's would.

At first the watchman had been horrified by the man, who presented as mangled and lacerated a figure as any it had been his misfortune to see in his long career patrolling the docks. He was minded to walk away. Perhaps, by the time he returned, the victim would be dead, and—so appalling were the injuries—it seemed to the watchman that death would be a kindness. Once the poor man was dead it would be very little trouble—although highly illegal[lv]—to send for a certain doctor who was known to pay handsomely for corpses. It would be less trouble still—but also less remunerative—to roll the body over the edge of the dock. The tide, by this time, was in. The dead man would float downstream and become someone else's problem. But then a groan and a flicker of consciousness recalled the watchman to his duty, and a boy was sent to fetch a magistrate.[lvi]

For a week Mr Balfour lay insensible in a squalid bed in a dark and dank room, cared for in a negligent way by Mrs Pitbull—nurse, midwife and gin drinker. She dressed his wounds with rags larded with some evil-smelling salve of her own devising, and fed him some thin and greasy soup. She sold what remained of his clothing except for his under-garments. The profit from this, added to the allowance left by the magistrate for the man's care, provided three penn'orth of gin from a local tavern every day of her patient's incapacity. Under this slip-shod regime Balfour's wounds became infected, and a fever added itself to the catalogue of lacerations, bruises, contusions and swellings that constituted his woeful condition.

At the end of the week Mr Balfour's man-servant at last discovered his whereabouts, and the patient was transferred back to the inn which, although not in itself very luxurious was at least clean and well-aired and where a less gin-soaked nurse took over his care. A doctor was summoned, but by that time Mr Balfour's wounds were so badly infected that they could not be stitched. The fever caused Mr Balfour to have bouts of delirium and at times he had to be strapped down for fear that he would do himself or someone in the room a mischief. Maggots were applied to eat away the putrefying flesh and the lacerations were left to heal themselves as they might. As regards his arms and shoulders this did not matter very much, but the scars to Mr Balfour's handsome black face were a shocking ruination of raised, pink weals and puckering.

Some three weeks after his attack, his business having been concluded by the means of letters and the services of a local man of law, Mr Balfour left Bristol and went to his country residence, which was in the county of Oxfordshire.

Henley Court held many happy memories for Amory. It had been the home of his childhood and youth, and his most vivid memories of his parents were to be found in its neat, formal gardens and oak-panelled reception rooms. His business in London gave him fewer opportunities to visit than he would have liked, but recently he had been conscious of a desire to spend a great deal more time there, perhaps to cease his habitual resistance to matrimony and to establish his own family within its brick-and-cobble walls.

But his return there after his assault and illness was anything but happy. He found his usual vigour had all but deserted him; he was tired and listless, and found pleasure in none of the things that, formerly, had pleased him. Although he had never been a vain man, the view of his ravaged face in the mirror was disgusting to him. He, who had become inured to insolent stares, curious appraisal and the thoughtless bigotry of the ignorant without at all allowing these things to dent his pride, was suddenly self-conscious. He saw even his own servants looking at him askance. The children of the village regarded him with open horror. On his first Sunday at church the clergyman's sister—a woman not known for having a faint heart or a sensitive disposition—had to stifle a scream when he emerged from his pew.

Balfour had been told by his doctor that in time his scars would fade, but that they would never disappear. His left cheek and forehead would always be laced by thick, pink welts. The sight in his injured eye would become less cloudy but the puckering of the lid would be permanent. It might well be that there would always be some discomfort in the jaw, and the callous around the break might very well produce irregularity to the symmetry of his face. The wanton infliction of cuts, the frenzy of the kicks and blows he had received, would leave him disfigured for life.

The healing of Balfour's invisible hurts was harder to predict, perhaps because he himself did not acknowledge the severity of them. Of course his pride was bruised, although how he thought he could have held his own against three determined brigands was hard to fathom. His fear as they had overwhelmed him had been very real, and quite understandable. But for a man who had congratulated himself on his resilience, who had honed himself to be unassailable, the memory of his fear was very troubling. The ordeal revisited him in the night, bathing him in sweat and rousing him, yelling, from sleep. Hurt pride and the recurring trauma of the assault were bad enough, but what plagued Amory most was the incandescence of his fury. He was consumed by anger at his assailants, and at the sheer prejudice of men that could make the colour of his skin a cause for their contempt. Had they not abused him, spoken of his 'type' and likened him to a dog? He brimmed over with wrath, railing against unfairness, but somewhere deep beneath his anger at the world there was a caustic, unrelenting self-castigation—that he was different, that he was so easy and automatic a target for the world's unthinking disdain; that no power on earth—no wealth, no success, no education, no philanthropy, no refinement of manner, no 'Englishness' of speech, or habit or of style—could supersede the colour of his skin.

June, now, had arrived. The countryside burgeoned with wild-flowers and the crops in the fields grew lustily. Woodlands were alive with birdsong, and local society—replenished by other families returned for the summer—was busy with balls, dinners and house parties. Ordinarily Balfour would have been included in a good many of the summer's entertainments, and might, himself, have hosted a dinner or two. But this year he felt no inclination for the frivolous drives, picnics and outings with which country society frittered away their days. He would not expose himself to the curious scrutiny of his neighbours; their intrusive enquiries would only infuriate him, reminding him of his failure to defend himself against his assailants, scratching away his emotional scabs and leaving him weak and bleeding once more. As much as the matrimonial gambits of society mamas had irked him in the past, as much as he had disliked the flirting eyes and coquetry of young ladies desperate enough to consider *him* as a potential husband, their pity would be worse. He could be no kind of company; his bleak despair and ever-surfacing ire subjected him to black moods and sharp retorts.

He gave instruction to his servants that he was not at home to any callers, would accept no invitations, was not by any means to be intruded upon. He had the gates of Henley Court closed and locked.

For two weeks more he wallowed in his self-pity, drinking more brandy than was good for him, keeping the shutters of the rooms tightly closed, hurling insults and priceless ornaments at the housekeeper if she tried to open a window or remove the accumulation of dirty glasses and over-flowing ashtrays he had scattered about him.

But then a letter came. It was a business letter, detailing the movement of stock, the impact of policy on the markets, the transfer of some deeds, nothing that interested him for a moment until he came to the last paragraph: *We owe thanks to a curious quarter that I have been able to settle these matters. Your friend Talbot's ward, Miss Willow, caused sufficient of a sensation to keep many men in town who would otherwise have departed; their signatures to the various deeds were therefore easy to come by.*

The idea of Miss Willow—out in society, presumably free of her veil—galvanised Amory as nothing else had been able to do. He rose from his couch and called for his valet.

35

June was an exceptionally fine month. London's parks and gardens bloomed but no amount of dry weather, no exuberance of floral display, could prevent the London season from fading. One town house after another was shut up as families departed for their country residences, the natural consequence of the parliamentary session winding to its close. But the house in Grosvenor Square remained resolutely open. Callers were received, dinners and musical soirées held, the paving stones in front of the house were a constant melee of carriages and horses. Delivery boys rapped on the door almost hourly, bringing cards, flowers and invitations for Miss Willow. The below-stairs staff began to despair of their summer respite. The house in Brighton, taken for the Talbots, remained empty.

Mr Talbot lingered in Paris, his daughter occupying his time and care. Lady Jane encouraged his continuance abroad. He could, she told him, devote his time in no better way. For herself, she would endure his absence as best she could.

In truth, Lady Jane positively revelled in her unfettered management of affairs in Grosvenor Square. She was suddenly popular! She had never enjoyed such renown, had never been so courted by ladies of the first circle. She was welcomed on equal terms by duchesses and marchionesses and they declared to her, with no hint of irony, that they could not understand why they had been denied the great honour of her acquaintance before. They came, of course—with their sons in tow—for Miss Willow's company, but Lady Jane glossed over that. *She* had launched Miss Willow, *she* was the chaperone of the season's sensation and it was only through *her* that these pushy mamas and lovelorn lotharios could access the object of their desire. She stood, as bold and impregnable as the Archangel Michael at the gates of paradise, and none could pass except through her.

Once they had penetrated to the holy of holies they found Miss Georgina Willow at home. She sat upon a settee surrounded by a veritable jungle of hot-house flowers. She poured tea, smiled and nodded whilst the stately mamas eyed her, prognosticating on her likely capacity for childbearing and telling themselves how becomingly their family jewels would lie against her white and elegant neck. The young men, for the most part, stared open-mouthed at the vision of loveliness offered up for them; the sweetest and juiciest of fruit, ripe for the plucking if they would but dare to reach out their hands. Some *did* dare, most bullishly, by means of invitations to theatre boxes and rides in a *barouche landau*. They boasted of their prowess on horseback and their vigour on the sports field. They regaled her with their family annals—distinguished action in battle, peculiar intimacy with monarchs, exploration of wildernesses, tigers and elephants slaughtered wholesale—without seeming to notice that Miss Willow's face betrayed no astonishment at their ancestors' derring-do but only a fixed, polite, but disengaged interest.

Some did *not* dare, but only looked on in a kind of hopeless, mawkish trance, stuttering out responses to Miss Willow's occasional enquiry, unable positively to say if they took milk in their tea, preferred cake or bread and butter. These, we can be sure, received a severe dressing down from their mothers. Could they not have made more of an effort? But in fact Miss Willow found these inept young men more tolerable than their boastful brothers, and *much* more bearable than the third sort of young man who managed to negotiate the bastion of Lady Jane. This last cohort were the lasciviously forward, the sexually charged, who regarded her with ill-concealed lustfulness, their eyes bloodshot and bulging, their lips perpetually parched. She did not like the greediness in their eyes, their hot, moist hands.

She was glad that Robert Talbot made himself a frequent participant in the at-homes. Lady Jane might resent his presence but she could not very well turn him out. He lounged in a chair or pretended to peruse a book whilst the matriarchs put Miss Willow through her paces; but when the young noblemen were too raffish, or sought to speak privately to her, then he roused himself to interfere on her behalf.

If left to herself Georgina would not have agreed to a furtherance of acquaintance with any of these young men. She was bored by the boastful, annoyed by the abject and repelled by the rakish. Not one of them saw *her*, the reality of her that was beneath the flawless skin, behind the limpid eyes. But of course she was not left to herself; Lady Jane must have her pound of flesh, and so Georgina was escorted to dinners and at-homes, and driven in the parks. She was *shown*, she was *paraded*, she was *exhibited*. She felt that she was a curiosity in a museum and that Lady Jane was her curator, a conjurer without whom Miss Willow could by no means be produced.

Poor Miss Trimble could never be included in these outings; she was utterly relegated. How much more an agreeable companion would she have been than the odiously self-important Lady Jane! Georgina did not know if she did not dislike her keeper even more than the ogling spectators to whom she must be displayed. But she bore it, for her mama's sake, and fielded the intrusive questions as to her antecedents, and replied vaguely about the whereabouts of Chanbury Park, and did all she could to keep hidden what her interrogators so manifestly wished to lay bare.

The emotional toll of these trials was considerable. Her face—so newly exposed to the world—felt raw, and it was hard to meet the eyes of her callers without a blush. She fought to keep her head up. Her hands, of their own volition, would creep to her temple to make a visor. More than once she was asked if she had a headache, if she shielded her eyes from the light, if she felt quite well. Lady Jane would scowl across the room at her, and Georgina would clasp her hands together in her lap and steel herself to being looked at. It would have been more bearable if the young men had shown themselves capable of conversation, but they seemed to have read no book, viewed no art, seen no play upon which they would discourse with any degree of enthusiasm. Their conversation was all of each other, envious or derisive, petty or malicious. The hours in the salon were like time spent in a desert—dry and draining, her skin flailed, her eyes gritty and inflamed. Lady Jane was the relentless sun, her guests like sand—invasive, intruding. It was bliss, when the day's exposure was done, for Georgina to retreat to the quiet shade of her room. Sometimes she would pull open the drawer where her veils had been kept. But, of course, it was empty. At night she burrowed beneath the sheets, but in the morning she rose, and washed, and dressed herself as though for a part in a play.

Thankfully, by some unfathomable means, Robert Talbot contrived to inveigle himself wherever Georgina was bidden. She would look down the dining table and find him there regarding her with a steady gaze, an amused eyebrow raised in greeting. She would lift her glasses at the opera to find him in an opposite box, a smile on his lips. She would glance behind her from her seat in the carriage and find him, a new horseman in her entourage.

It reassured her, to have him nearby.

36

It took no little ingenuity on Robert's part to source for himself
information as to Miss Willow's engagements on any particular day.
Invitations to dine at the tables where Miss Willow was to appear were
not easy to come by and many a society matron did he have to flatter in
order to secure himself a seat. A *barouche landau* might take any route and
be difficult to catch up with. The palms of grooms must be liberally
greased and Georgina's suitors stood many drinks that Robert could be
sure to be in the right park at the right hour. Many were the ploys that he
was forced to employ, but his chief aide in his campaign was Miss
Trimble. On re-entering the house in Grosvenor Square he had lost no
time in seeking out Agnes' little sitting room; many hours the two of
them had sat there, sharing intelligence that they might, in their own
words, 'save' Miss Willow from the machinations of Lady Jane, the
dribbling love-making of the infatuated admirers and the interrogations
of the *ton*.

Robert did not in the least mind it and, as time went on, he found it
more and more of an imperative. What had begun as an amusing and
enjoyable game took on, in his mind, an interest and importance that was

almost a fixation. His unerring goal was to place himself in Georgina's way, to be always on hand. He found that there was, in all of London, nowhere he would rather be than at her side. And then, to interfere in the plans of the other swains was also most satisfactory; not just for the devilment of it—although this did please his mischievous streak—but in pursuit of his own quite serious quest for Miss Willow's hand.

There was no doubt in his mind that he was very much in love with her. He felt that he had loved her from the first moment of seeing her. Her image—supremely beautiful, proud, brave, but also disarmingly vulnerable—haunted his waking and his sleeping hours. His feelings were very far from brotherly, but it pleased him to present himself in that proprietary light before his rivals. As a close relative he could claim all kinds of privilege that they could not. With him, she needed no chaperone. He could quite justifiably stand up for her, intercede for her, act as her champion and protector. Which other man could do so, with her father dead, her brother, her stepfather and her cousin George all abroad? He relished the role of hero. Wrapping Georgina's cloak around her at the Charltons' ball, carrying her off from the mayhem, helping her into the carriage—these things had fed a heroic flame and caused it to combust into an inferno. He very much hoped that Georgina saw him in the light of it. Its brightly burning core assuaged the stabbing sense of abject jealousy that overcame him when he considered the other suitors who clamoured for her attention. He despised them all, considering them, to a man, fops and puppies, brutes and rogues. There was not one who was worthy of Miss Willow's notice, let alone her hand.

Of course he saw what Lady Jane was about. She would have Georgina married to the richest, most eligible man in England, regardless of his personal qualities or character, regardless of any incompatibility of mind. Lady Jane would not be particular as to affection, so long as there was prestige for herself as having made the match; and in some ways, Robert suspected, the more miserable Georgina was made by the marriage the more his stepmother would congratulate herself upon it. But he would not permit Lady Jane to have her way. He himself, after all, was no inconsiderable catch for any young lady. Perhaps his grandfather

Talbot—the Robert for whom he had been named—had been not quite a gentleman, but no one could say that of his father. His maternal grandfather had been a Nawab[lvii] and from both sides of his family he stood to inherit an exceedingly large fortune. He flattered himself he was not ugly—many young ladies, on his tour, had been kind enough to confirm his own opinion—and he was quite certain that, given time, he would be able to win Miss Willow's heart and hand.

For all these reasons it gave Robert enormous gratification to be able to take Miss Willow away from Lady Jane. The occasions were rare, for Georgina's social calendar was fraught with engagements of every sort, and Lady Jane was by no means to be left out of them. But from time to time, when he found that no calls were to be made that day and that Georgina was at liberty to do what she liked, Robert lost no time in having the carriage put to and Miss Trimble in readiness.

He found that what Georgina liked, on these days, was to get right away from town, to go to places where she would not be seen, claimed or importuned. She did not say so in as many words but he could easily imagine that she desired to be where there were no love-sick sighs, no bawdy innuendo, no messengers bringing cloying love letters and awful poetry. That she was in receipt of such cringingly dreadful missives he knew from Miss Trimble. Now that Georgina was free of the veil she hoped that she would come to appreciate the benefits of being unfettered, but he was sensitive enough to realise that the shock of it, to her, would not be inconsiderable. For himself, he loved to see her turn her face to the sun, to see her eyes light up at a particularly impressive vista. Naturally, he liked to look upon her without any impedimentary shroud.

He had her driven north to Highgate or east towards Woolwich, places where there was countryside, quaint villages but no crowds, where, frankly, he could enjoy having her all to himself. He rationed himself to the odd brief glance at her, avoided overt flirtation, offered no compliments beyond what was usual, and kept his conversation light. Instead he tended to engage Miss Trimble in talk, reminding her of his mischief as a child, recalling her aid in times of sickness, her help with his schoolwork. Miss Trimble was only too happy to dwell on these memories and so Miss Willow was left to her own thoughts, her own uncomplicated enjoyment of the day.

On one of these excursions they found themselves returning to Mayfair via Rotherhithe. They had been out along the river, enjoying the tang of the air, the squabble of seabirds, the sight of wherries plying their way up and down the broad Thames. Georgina's cheeks were rosy with fresh air and sun. The breeze had teased her hair from its combs and it riffled pleasingly against her neck. She had removed her gloves, and Robert fought the urge to reach out and take one of her hands in his.

Miss Trimble dozed on the opposite seat, exhausted by the air and perhaps made somewhat soporific by the chilled wine they had drunk with their picnic.

'The season will soon be finished,' said Robert. 'Indeed, it is quite unusual for it to go on as long as it has, but I understand the House has much business to conclude. Shall you accompany Lady Jane to Brighton?'

Georgina shrugged. 'I cannot say. Until your father returns I will do as she determines, I suppose.'

'Brighton is very agreeable, they say.'

'Is it not just as London is, but with the addition of sea bathing?'

Robert laughed. 'I suppose so. Much of society here simply moves itself there.'

'I wonder they can stand it,' said Georgina. 'Do they not get heartily tired of each other? For myself, I would rather go somewhere quiet. Society has exhausted me and I have only endured a month of it.'

'For the most part, society loves to hate itself. My stepmother is never happier than when she is in spleen at some dowager's mis-doings. And then, of course, there are the scandals. Where the *ton* is, there is tittle-tattle. Life in the country, to her, is very boring. I think it was my father's plan that you should go to Ecklington. That, I think, would be quiet enough for you. But it would be far too quiet for Lady Jane. She dislikes it.'

'Then I suppose I shall not see it. But in point of fact, your father spoke of taking me north, to Derbyshire, or even to the Lakes.' She sighed. 'Perhaps we might have gone to Yorkshire, to Tall Chimneys. I should have liked that very much.'

'You feel at home there?'

'Oh yes.' She turned bright, animated eyes towards him. 'Yorkshire is home, even more than Chanbury is. In Yorkshire I can be completely myself.' Her face, as she spoke, was so illuminated that Robert felt himself almost irradiated by it. He looked away in confusion.

'I have kept my father apprised of Lady Jane's machinations,' he said, fiddling with the cuff of his shirt. 'He is very angry. But he cannot leave Robyn at present.'

Georgina said, 'What can he do, that you cannot? It is too late to do anything. She played her cards very cleverly. What is done cannot be undone and now I must wait to see what consequences ensue.'

Mastering himself, Robert said, 'It is possible there will be no consequences. No unpleasant ones, anyway. Have you hated *all* of it?'

Georgina considered. 'Not all, perhaps—except the sense of being a curiosity, to be stared at and preyed upon, has been very trying.'

Robert shifted on his seat, not sure how to broach his next topic. 'You have been thrust into society very rudely,' he said slowly. 'It is no surprise that you have found the experience to be somewhat traumatic. But will you wish, I wonder, to go back *absolutely* to your old mode of living, when your mother returns home?'

She threw him a narrow look. 'Do you mean, shall I go back to wearing a veil?'

'I hope not *that*,' he replied with a slight frown. 'But I gather you lived a very retired life. You did not go into society at all, even locally. I do hope that you will not revert to *such* a sequestered existence. I hope I can persuade you that society, company, *friendship* can be delightful. In short, Miss Willow,' and now he did, very tentatively, take possession of her small, white hand, 'I offer you *my* particular and very warm friendship in the hope that … the hope that …'

He fixed her with a look that he prayed would communicate to her all he hoped for.

She met his gaze very steadily, and did not remove her hand from his. Indeed, she laid her other hand on top of their knotted fingers and applied a gentle pressure. 'I know you are my friend, Robert,' she said, smiling. 'I know you have been my guardian angel these last weeks. You have made it bearable—you and Miss Trimble between you. I do not think I knew until quite recently how very lonely I have been. I feared intimacy. But now I do not. So, in answer to your question: no, I do not think I shall return to my former life. I hope, when Mama comes home and she and Mr Stockbridge find somewhere to settle, that we will see you often.'

She released his hand and sat back in the carriage, surveying again the landscape as they travelled through it. Robert struggled for purchase. How to build on what had just passed between them? How to press his suit without repeating the hackneyed wooing of Georgina's other paramours? He was sure she must be sick to death of receiving proposals. And what could he say, what form of words could he use, that would not join all the other worn-out phrases and stale protestations in the echo chamber of her mind?

Whilst he pondered, Georgina said, 'Are we not in Rotherhithe? I recognise these marshes. Arthur's lodgings are nearby. Oh, do let us call. I long to see him.'

Robert agreed, though reluctantly. He recalled Arthur Harlish and seemed to think he had been a pleasant enough fellow, but he did not wish to share Miss Willow at that point or—if he could help it—ever.

37

It took some little time for Georgina's knock at the blue cottage door to be answered. Pansy, the little maid-of-all-work, at last opened the door to them. Her eyes were like saucers upon beholding the party on the doorstep, particularly at the radiance of the young lady who, of course, she had not seen unveiled on her last visit.

But yes, she was able to stammer out, Mr Harlish was at home, although not within; he was in fact 'out the back' in Mr Pink's garden where, the day being fine—and it being Sunday—the play-reading had removed. She offered to show the ladies and gentleman through, but then baulked, for they would by necessity have to pass through the scullery and Pansy did not think Mrs Quince would be amenable to them seeing her pots and pans and washboard, no matter *how* scrubbed and shining they might be. Accordingly she directed them around the side of the houses and then herself rushed through the scullery, down the kitchen steps and through the gap in the hedge so that she might warn Mrs Quince that her elegant guests had returned.

Arthur was very happy to see Georgina—not the least because her arrival had spared the company from Romeo's affecting speech on the discovery of Juliet's supposed corpse. Mrs Quince, as Juliet, had, for the sake of verisimilitude, lain herself on a blanket on the grass in an attitude of peaceful repose, the more to provoke in her Romeo an agony of dismay and mourning. Mr Pink—reading the role of Romeo—had been disconcerted by this ploy. He was not sure his arthritic knees would allow him to kneel beside the corpse with any degree of manly dignity. Arthur had been more struck by the comedy in the scene than the tragedy. By no stretch of his imagination could he see a young and lovely girl in the person of his elderly and ugly landlady, or a lovelorn gentleman of Verona in the portly and embarrassed Mr Pink.

Thankfully, at the arrival of the guests, the play was given over, tea called for and seats found. Mrs Quince scrambled up from her blanket with astonishing alacrity and, upon seeing Miss Willow and being given to understand that this was the same lady who, before, had been hidden beneath a thick mantle, enfolded her in a sisterly embrace.

'Of course, my dear,' she said, stroking Georgina's flawless cheek with a horny finger. 'Now I understand, and who better? We are fellow sufferers indeed, both cursed by a cruel hand. Oh! What a cross we have to bear! Such beauty as ours is not often inflicted. But I flatter myself I have a *very* few years more *hexperience* than you so I will make so bold as to *hoffer* some small nuggets of *hadvice*. Hold your head up, my dear, and do not let their envy sour you. Not *all* men are ill-intentioned and not *all* women are spiteful. No, though many, *many* are.' She smiled, baring brownish teeth, allowing time for the great balm of her comradely succour to have its effect.

Georgina returned her smile and at last Mrs Quince released her, saying, 'Let us sit together and combine our radiance. It does not do for such as we to stand in competition. Sit by me, my dear, and Pansy shall pour you some tea.'

Georgina could only comply. She and Mrs Quince sat side by side, like Athena and Hera[lviii]. Arthur sat close to Georgina, but not as close as Mr Robert Talbot, who appropriated for himself the seat immediately adjacent. Consequently, Georgina and Arthur could only converse through him. It would not have been seemly to refer to their last meeting—in Georgina's bedroom—so Arthur contented himself by saying, 'I am so very happy to *see* you, Georgina. That is, Miss Willow. I hope you have been quite well and … not discomposed at all?'

Georgina assured him that she had been quite well, and not too much discomposed, once she had accustomed herself to her new situation.

'The ball. Was it very awful?'

'Yes,' she admitted, 'it was. But then I made acquaintance with two young ladies who I liked very much. So it was not *all* awful.'

'I hope it was not only young ladies whose acquaintance ameliorated the ordeal,' said Robert. 'You met *me* at the ball.'

'We have all known each other from childhood, if it comes to that,' said Arthur. 'I expect Miss Willow had simply forgotten all about you.'

'No indeed, Arthur, I had not,' cried Georgina. 'But I had thought Mr Talbot abroad. I did not expect to see him at the ball, or anywhere else.'

'Well,' said Arthur, standing up and brushing cake crumbs from his lapels, 'at least, that evening, you found you had a friend to turn to if you had need.'

'I did, Arthur,' said Georgina, fully understanding that it was his own friendship to which he referred.

'I think I can *always* be relied upon to look after Miss Willow's wellbeing,' said Robert darkly. 'I can assure you she is rarely out of my sight.'

'Happy fellow,' said Arthur. 'But there are some of us who care about her even when they cannot see her. Pray excuse me. I will walk with Miss Pink, I think.'

The Bannock men perched awkwardly on their chairs and ogled the young lady. Walter spilt his tea and Dick held a piece of cake suspended in front of his mouth. Bill wrung his hands, chafed at his shirt collar and from time to time flapped his mouth in a fruitless attempt to utter even a half-articulate sentence. At last Mrs Bannock, ashamed of them all, sent them home. 'I am most terrible sorry,' said Mrs Bannock as she took her leave. 'I shall box their ears when I get home.'

'Do not concern yourself,' crowed Mrs Quince. 'I have known for a long time that your menfolk are *henamoured* of me. They will master it, I am sure. Good day to you Mrs Bannock. Good day.'

Rather less pleasing to Mrs Quince than the admiration she believed she had provoked in the Bannocks was the flattering attention Mr Pink gave to Miss Trimble. The lady of Cuckold's Point liked to think of her neighbour's affections as very much her own, but for the interference of his daughter. To see him, puffed up like a turkey cock, doing the honours of his flower garden and vegetable patch quite as though it had been laid out by Capability Brown, was offensive in the extreme.

She sniffed and enquired in a stage whisper, 'Who is that wizened little woman who accompanies you, Miss Willow? I have quite forgot her name.'

'That is Miss Trimble, my dear friend,' said Georgina.

'Miss, is it? Yes, I would have supposed her to be unmarried, and of too great an age now to contemplate wedlock, I suppose. But she will make no progress with Mr Pink. His heart is all my own, would his daughter take herself out of our way.'

'Miss Trimble would have no thought of such a thing,' declared Georgina, although, looking at Agnes' flushed complexion and bright eyes, she doubted her own words. She watched Mr Pink and Miss Trimble and, beyond them, Arthur and Miss Pink, who strolled, arm in arm along the pebbly bank of the river. How easy it seemed to be, for them, to form an attachment. There seemed no awkwardness, no stuttering, stumbling attempts at gallantry—neither any ribald insinuation. Oh! How she longed for straight-forward, uncomplicated conversation! The kind of intercourse that had been possible when her face had been hidden from view. The kind of intercourse she had enjoyed with Mr Balfour; but where he was now, she had no idea.

38

For Miss Trimble, the visit to Cuckold's Point was a highlight in an otherwise lonely few weeks. Apart from the occasional summons from Robert Talbot, she had been excluded from all the activity of the house. She was hardly required by Lady Jane, and was prevented as far as possible by all the jealous machinations of that lady from seeing Miss Willow. The joy of the springtime outings in the *barouche landau* with Mr George Talbot and Miss Willow were a distant memory. Agnes occupied herself as best she could in reading to Nanny and helping the housekeeper with the household mending, and spent the rest of the time fretting about how Georgina might be faring as she was swept along in the current of Lady Jane's despicable plan.

But, in this desert of uselessness and frustration, her tour of Mr Pink's garden stood out as an oasis. How she had enjoyed being told the names of the plants, and even, once or twice, recalling—from her days at her father's house—the habit of a shrub or the uses for a herb of which Mr Pink had been unaware. Mr Pink was a man who, it would be fair to say, was closer to fifty than to forty years of age. No one but a person of very inelegant mind would speculate as to Agnes' age, but only a fool would suppose her to be less than forty. Mr Pink was small in terms of height—but still a head taller than Agnes herself—but rather portly. His hair was scant, his cheeks very plump and rosy, his nose snub and his eyes of a penetratingly bright blue. He was not what anyone would call a *handsome* man but he had a manner that was all gallantry and style, a loud, booming voice that Agnes found authoritative and admirable and, perhaps most pertinently of all, had taken a particularly marked interest in Agnes herself. That the two were matched in genteel upbringing, shared a clear-eyed—but not the less proud—understanding of their place, respected their betters and were disgusted by all things mean and vulgar was soon established as they toured the neatly hoed flower beds and minutely tended rows of vegetables. During this circuit he had told her—his speech punctuated by a series of coughs and false starts—of his role as deputy assistant chief clerk at the bank, made allusion to his 'personal portfolio of private investments', stated that he owned his cottage outright, mentioned that his half-day was a Tuesday and concluded by saying that he had been '*many* years' a widower. Agnes had been at a loss as to how to respond to these nuggets of intelligence, other than to say that she depended absolutely on the goodwill of the Talbots, had no family living and—with eyes downcast and a blush upon her cheek—that she had not been so fortunate *thus far* as to have secured a gentleman's affections.

Thus, in their hour amongst the flowers and plants, they had covered a vast deal of foundational territory. Mr Pink had handed Miss Trimble back into the carriage with particular grace and care and, as the carriage had turned, had boomed out with a significance not lost on anyone except Agnes herself, 'Until we meet again.'

One Tuesday morning ten days after the visit at Rotherhithe a knock at her door announced a footman with a parcel. 'This has been here a day or so now ma'am,' he told her, carrying it in and laying in on the table. 'Nobody else has had time to bring it up to you before this.'

'Why thank you, William,' said Miss Trimble. 'I could have fetched it myself, if I had known.'

'The house is in uproar,' the footman told her. 'Cook says she is a fortnight overdue at her niece's house. She was to have gone and looked after her, for her confinement. The housekeeper says she will never be able to get the summer works done at this rate, if her ladyship does not pack herself off to Brighton, as she was *supposed* to have done a month since. The kitchen maid has given notice and the groom says if the horses do not get put out to proper pasture soon they will be fit for nothing come the autumn.'

'Oh dear,' said Miss Trimble. 'Yes, I suppose we should all be elsewhere by now.'

The parcel bore Madame Planché's stamp, although Agnes had not ordered anything. Inside was a great amount of packing paper but nothing else. Agnes rummaged again through the contents. At last she found a letter, taped to the bottom of the box, addressed in a hand she did not recognise, to herself.

Dear Madam, I trust you will excuse this unusual means of communicating with you but it seems to me likely, from the intelligence you were so good as to impart to me at our last meeting, that some degree of discretion is required in relation to correspondence to and from your address.

My father and I were delighted to see you at Cuckold's Point on Sunday last. My father, in particular, enjoyed showing you his garden.

On my father's half-day, which is Tuesday, it is his custom to walk in one or other of London's parks. Now that the carriage-folklix have largely departed the city I find my own work hours less onerous and therefore am able to join him in this exercise. We—my father and myself—wondered if you would do us the great honour of joining us this Tuesday for this perambulation, the weather promising fine. We shall be at the Grosvenor Gate of Hyde Park at two o'clock.

Your servant

Petunia Pink

Miss Trimble consulted the clock on the mantelpiece. It was already noon! And having received the parcel so lately there would be no time to send a reply. It occurred to her that she ought not to go without Lady Jane's permission. But then she knew very well that if she were to ask permission, it would certainly be refused. She had no fear of Mr Pink; she knew he would be in all respects the perfect gentleman. Had he not arranged for his daughter's presence, that all might be respectable? Her fear was only for the great step before her—the door of possibility that had so unexpectedly opened to her. She thought of Mr Pink's little house by the river, the beautiful garden ... She thought of Mr Pink himself—a kind, gentle man, courteous in manner ... She tried to think of him in relation to matrimony—the intimate aspects of that holy institution. Her mind and her imagination failed her utterly. But nothing, she thought, could be as bleak or as awful as the prospect that lay before her otherwise. She had always been afraid of Lady Jane, even when they were at school together; but her fear had always been gilded with awed admiration. Of course she had been grateful for her place in the Talbot household, ambiguous though it was. But since Miss Willow's advent she had seen Lady Jane in her true colours: sickly shades of envy, spite and spleen.

She moved across to the little mirror that hung in a shadowed corner of her room and looked herself very directly in the eye.

'Agnes,' she said, 'we are going to the park.'

39

Lord Pokerham did call upon Miss Willow but not until some little time after the disastrous ball. He brought with him his brother, Lord Tonge, and his fiancée, Miss Charlton. Lady Virginia Shrewsbury was also of the party.

It appeared that whatever reluctance Lord Pokerham had felt towards his forthcoming nuptials had now been completely vanquished. He had indeed been most taken with Miss Willow, and had not been able to prevent himself from comparing her charms to those of Miss Charlton. It is not to be supposed that many—indeed *any*—young woman could bear such direct comparison and Miss Charlton, though an amiable girl, had never had any claim to beauty. But something, that calamitous evening, had shifted in Lord Pokerham's feelings for her. It may be that Gertrude's tears had moved him, or that, upon seeing the clamorous competition amongst the other young men for Miss Willow's notice, he realised that he could never hope to triumph with her. A bird in the hand, he may have told himself, is as good as two in the bush. He doubtless schooled himself that to renege on his troth would be ungentlemanly. If Miss Charlton chose to release him, that would be a different matter. But Miss Charlton, although patently unhappy, spoke no word, and it was soon understood that Captain Brimming's regiment had been deployed abroad.

In her unhappiness, Gertrude found that it was Lord Pokerham who could offer her the kindest, most gentle comfort. He was patient with her, quite ready to hear again and again the qualities of Captain Brimming that had aroused her affection and thus—knowing what she liked in a gentleman—he was able to emulate them. He developed a sudden passion for natural history—a subject close to Gertrude's heart—and as soon as she revealed to him her desire to go to Lyme to hunt for fossils he promised her that he would secure accommodations for their honeymoon in that locale as soon as ever she would name the day of their marriage. Little by little they learned to like, and then to love one another, and at the date of their visit to Grosvenor Square were as much in love as two young people can be.

All these things being so, the Sothertons' objection to the Charltons had been allowed to evaporate and they were warm in their declarations of affection for their presumptive daughter-in-law. Financial impediments had been swept away, the papers signed and the date set for the first week in July.

Once these things had been set in stone Lord Pokerham felt himself safe to fulfil his promise to Miss Willow, and called upon her one Saturday morning towards the end of June. Mr Robert Talbot was, as usual, in attendance and the introductions were made. Lord Tonge, on seeing Georgina, instantly lost all power of speech, and although he was present for the rest of the visit, he can be discounted as to any particular contribution as he spoke no word for the entirety of it. Lord Pokerham, on the other hand, conducted himself with a degree of self-control, being careful to give his fiancée the majority of his attention even though his dominant eye did find itself straying towards Miss Willow almost of its own volition. He got out a creditably articulate apology for the delay in doing himself the honour of calling, passed on his parents' regards to Miss Willow and Lady Jane and expressed a desire that both would be guests at Sotherton before the year was out. Having said as much he retired to the window alcove to join his limp and perspiring brother at the open casement.

With Lady Jane and the gentlemen present, it was not possible for the young ladies to take up their intimacy where it had been left off in the antechamber of Almack's assembly rooms. They made polite conversation for a few moments—Lady Jane taking more than her fair share of it, enumerating on her fingers the counts, dukes and marquises who had called upon them, the dinner engagements, the promenades, the soirées and at-homes that had occupied their evenings since the 'little party' at Almack's.

At last, taking advantage of Lady Jane's pausing to draw breath, Lady Virginia said, 'It is a very pleasant day outside, and the little park across the street looks rather pretty. Shall we go out and take some air?'

Everyone was amenable to this idea except for Lady Jane, who would rather have kept her illustrious visitors to herself, but she could not oppose two lords and accordingly bonnets and parasols were sent for and the party strolled across the paving stones and into the park. On the way Miss Charlton murmured a word to her fiancé and at her hint he offered his arm to Lady Jane, detaining her a few steps behind the young ladies and then guiding her off in a different direction so that the girls were permitted a few moments of free conversation.

'I have been eager to see you both again, after the ball,' said Miss Willow. 'I do not mind telling you that the half hour we spent in the antechamber was the pleasantest, to me, of the entire evening.'

'Dear me!' said Lady Virginia. 'If half an hour in the necessary[lx] pleased you the most, the rest of the time must have been miserable indeed.'

'You must know,' said Georgina, 'that I was not there by choice. Lady Jane has taken it upon herself to bring me out and I have no choice but to oblige her.'

'Lady Jane is the most disagreeable woman in town,' said Lady Virginia. 'Everybody says so. I would not be in your shoes. Thankfully, Baroness

Charlton is so preoccupied by Gertrude's nuptials that I am able to get away with a great deal.'

'You continue to meet with Mr Rex? But how?'

'Oh!' laughed Lady Virginia. 'It takes a great deal of ingenuity I do assure you, and some dexterity at climbing up and down a hydrangea that happens to grow around my chamber window. Gertrude has been my chief accomplice, and I have paid my maid to smuggle correspondence. But it cannot last. Once the wedding is over I shall be shipped off to some obscure country house where dear Johnny will not be able to get near me unless he reinvents himself as a peddler or disguises himself as a kitchen maid. I would not put *either* past him. He is such a rogue. It is why I love him. We are kindred spirits.'

Georgina turned to Miss Charlton. 'I perceive that your feelings about your marriage have undergone a change since the night of the ball, Miss Charlton. You smile very kindly upon Lord Pokerham now.'

'Oh yes,' said Gertrude coyly. 'I have made up my mind to it and I find the prospect not as bad as I once did. Pokerham and I have found we have more in common than we thought and, in short …' she allowed her eyes to look across the gardens to where her fiancé and Lady Jane were examining a display of roses, '… in short, he has won my affection.'

'I am very happy for you,' said Georgina. 'It is impossible to make any true assessment of a person on a slight acquaintance.'

'How slight is your acquaintance with Mr Robert Talbot?' enquired Lady Virginia. 'Does he make your ordeal slightly more bearable? He is very handsome, is he not?'

Georgina looked across the lawn to where Robert strolled with Miss Trimble. He undoubtedly *was* very handsome and, these past weeks, had made himself indispensable to her. He looked up and caught her eye, his face breaking into a smile, the light caramel of his skin emphasising the whiteness of his teeth and the dark humour of his eyes. His hair—straight, and as black as ebony—shone in the sun.

'He has been a true friend to me,' said Georgina. 'But we have known each other since we were children. He is like a brother to me. I could not think of him in any other light.'

The ladies strolled on and in a few moments had joined Robert and Miss Trimble at an intersection of pathways.

'Do keep your parasol up, Miss Willow,' said Miss Trimble. 'The sun is very strong today, and your skin is very fair.'

'Let me help you,' said Robert, relinquishing Miss Trimble's arm and possessing himself of Georgina's parasol. By necessity then, he must walk next to her, and very close. Georgina smiled up at him and in doing so saw, over his shoulder, across the park, a familiar figure. It was familiar to her—indeed, she would have known him anywhere—and yet so altered from her last sight of him that she doubted her own certainty.

She frowned, squinting into the bright sunshine. 'Is that …?' she began. 'Miss Trimble, that gentleman by the pool. Can it be Mr Balfour?'

Now the whole party turned to look at the figure that leaned on the stone parapet of the fountain. A tall man, but strangely stooped, his hat pulled low. In spite of the warmth of the day, he was swathed in a capacious cloak. He stared abstractedly into the shining waters of the pool, a figure of melancholy against the brightness of the gardens.

'I do believe so,' said Miss Trimble. 'But so changed that I should not have known him.'

'Oh do let us go and speak to him,' said Georgina. She turned to her two female companions. 'Will you excuse me? I must just …'

But Robert interjected. 'He does not look to me like a man who wishes to be intruded upon, Miss Willow. Leave him to his thoughts.' He slipped his hand beneath her elbow, and began to guide her in another direction.

'No, indeed,' she said, resisting. 'I am sure he would be distressed to know that I had seen him and not approached. There is no impropriety in it. We are very well acquainted.'

The figure by the fountain straightened, and the sunlight fell across his face. Georgina gasped, and raised a hand to her mouth. Mr Balfour it certainly was, but so transformed. He was perhaps some twenty or thirty yards from her but her eyesight *now*—without the impediment of her veil—was keen and she could see quite clearly the change in him. His face was thinner, his eyes sunken. And there was something else. She narrowed her eyes. Something about his cheeks ... What were they? Scars?

'He is an ill-looking fellow,' said Miss Charlton. 'One can never be sure, with men of that ... sort. I think you had better not go near him, Miss Willow.'

'What do you mean?' Georgina asked, turning to face them. 'Men of what sort?'

'*I* certainly shall not go near,' chimed in Lady Virginia. 'I have encountered him before. A most meddlesome person, I do assure you. I wonder he has the boldness to show his face here.'

'And such a face,' murmured Miss Charlton. 'Can he be a gentleman?'

'Because his face is black?' Georgina shook her head. 'How can you say so?'

'Yes. And because it is ravaged. He looks like a villain.' Gertrude retreated a step or two. 'I think I shall re-join Pokerham and Lady Jane.'

'Come now, Miss Willow,' said Robert, exerting again some pressure on her arm, 'let us *all* re-join the others.'

'No,' said Georgina, extracting herself from his grip. 'I *shall* go and speak to him.'

She strode away from them, across the grass, leaving Robert looking faintly ridiculous, holding her parasol. As she got closer to Mr Balfour the disfigurement of his face came more sharply into focus, but she did not falter.

'Mr Balfour,' she said, when she was within speaking distance.

He swung towards her but, at the same time, seemed to shrink within his cloak. He touched his hat but only to settle it more firmly onto his head.

'Miss Willow,' he replied, not meeting her eyes. 'I had no idea that you would still be in town. I thought you gone north by now. If I had known you were here, I would never …' he indicated, by a gesture, the park, the fountain and, across the square, the Talbots' house. Neither of them were unaware—how could they have been?—of the significance of the spot. Here, by the fountain, they had last seen each other. Here, on this very ground, she had lifted her veil that he might see her face. How searchingly she had tried to read his expression. How she had steeled herself to see the cold flame of avaricious craving she had seen in other eyes. Or the calculated appraisal of a connoisseur for a stone sculpture or, worse, that look of weak, mawkish adoration she despised so much. But she did not know now whether the unwavering light she had read in his eye was not more dreadful.

'But why ever not?' said Georgina. She was close to him now, right before him. She looked up into his face. One eyelid was puckered, pulled down by a livid weal. Other scars traced his cheek and his forehead, pinkish, raised, with ugly edges[lxi], as though some parasite had burrowed beneath the smooth, lustrous mahogany of his face. 'Oh Mr Balfour,' she burst out. 'What has befallen you? Have you been ill?' She raised a tentative hand towards his face, but he jerked it away from her touch.

'Yes,' he said, still not meeting her eye. 'I was … in Bristol … I was …'

'Miss Willow.' Robert had followed Georgina across the lawn and now stood some few feet away, her parasol raised aloft. 'Miss Trimble is most anxious that you do not catch the sun. Please come into the shade.'

Mr Balfour's eyes flicked to Robert, taking in his handsome features, his youth, his confident bearing. 'I should not detain you,' he said, bowing. 'Good afternoon, Miss Willow.'

'Oh, but do not go away,' cried Georgina, lifting her hand and placing it on his arm. 'Why do you not join us?' She gestured vaguely at the other members of her party then stepped closer, as though to hear his reply—

but in fact to enable her to say in a low voice, 'I wish you had called. I …
I have not forgotten you.'

Mr Balfour stiffened. 'Nor I you,' he said, and she thought for a moment
that his fixed, disciplined expression would melt. But no, he drew
himself away from her. 'I have not wished to impose myself upon you,
Miss Willow,' he said very formally. 'I have been unwell and, as I said
before, I thought you had left town.'

'I have *not*,' she declared. 'And it would have been no imposition.' She
glanced behind her, to where Robert still stood, compelling her to return
with him. As grateful as she had been to him these past weeks, *now* she
wished he would go away. She tried again. 'Mr Balfour,' she began,
speaking low and urgently. 'You see how it is with me now.' She raised
her hand and touched her face. 'And I thought … I wanted … I hoped
you might wish to see me.'

'I did not wish *you* to see *me*,' Amory at last burst out, his eyes anguished.
'Look at me! I am a monster!'

Robert was beside her, his hand again on her elbow, whole and hale,
whilst Amory was broken and ill. The contrast between the two men
could not have been more marked. Amory tore his eyes from Georgina's
face and regarded Robert in anguished horror.

'You must excuse Miss Willow,' Robert said. 'She is heedless of her own
wellbeing and I really must insist upon taking her out of the sun.'

Balfour bowed and turned on his heel. Georgina allowed herself to be
led away.

40

July came. The parks and gardens of London lost their freshness, becoming parched and dusty almost overnight. Madame Planché's premises closed for the summer, allowing Miss Pink to accompany her father on a fortnight's holiday in Weymouth. *The Georgina* was launched, and steamed down the Thames for her sea-trials with Arthur Harlish on board as engineer. Miss Gertrude Charlton became Lady Pokerham and departed for Lyme.

Georgina Willow greeted the season's end with relief. Surely, now, she had done all that Lady Jane required of her? Surely, now, she would be permitted to sink back into blissful obscurity? Not that she intended to go back beneath the veil. Those days, she believed, were over, and whilst she did retain a nagging fear that some injury could accrue to her mother, she had ceased to think of it with the kind of imminence that had so plagued her at the beginning. Whatever secret shame lurked in her mother's past, Georgina did not now believe that the exposure of her face could resurrect it. This, though a comfort, was a small one. Many other matters oppressed her spirits in such a way as to virtually obscure that small ray of relief.

Top-most in her basket of anxieties was her appearance. It might not be dangerous but it certainly was very disconcerting in terms of the effect it had on people. Why could people not see past it? At times she felt as though she was viewed as a work of art—beautiful, but inanimate, indifferent to the appraising stares and covetous evaluation of on-lookers. Did they think she had no heart? No feelings? Was she simply an object, to be looked at? She had harboured no very high hopes of society to begin with, but its shallowness had exceeded even her small expectations. Truly, the *ton* was a bear-pit of gossip and envy, resentment and spite. She hardly heard a good word of anyone unless they were within earshot. Then people could be sweetly sycophantic enough. The hypocrisy nauseated her.

Beneath this superficial layer was her confusion about Amory Balfour. He—who had seemed to her such a paragon of self-confidence and poise, whose sense of personal authenticity she had envied, who had prompted her to search for her own sense of self—this very archetype of self-assurance had been crushed. A few scars, the marring of his skin, had reduced all his assurance to naught. The memory of him, stooped and broken, haunted her. How far he had strayed from the well-lit path! He seemed to her to be as lost now as she had been, the night he had rescued her. She could not claim that they had swapped places; she would never be as impervious to opinion as he had seemed to be. But now it was *he* who hid and shied away from the light whilst *she* walked abroad *almost* without a care. The alteration in their circumstances was too severely contrary, too dizzying. She could not fathom it.

Last of all the matters that vied for occupation of her mind—darkly hidden because so troubling—was the increasing realisation that Robert Talbot was in love with her. Whilst her other gentlemen suitors had—mercifully—melted away to their country estates, to the continent and to seaside resorts, he had remained—coolly attentive, fraternally affectionate. He brought her news from France; that Robyn's recovery progressed well, and that a remove to England was looking more likely with every week that passed. He had found her a horse—a gentle creature with a soft mouth and a steady, reliable gait—so that they could ride together in the early mornings whilst the air was still cool. He was always at the house in Grosvenor Square. He might claim to have a dozen invitations to various country houses, to be sought after by several eligible young ladies, to be needed at his father's business, to be very much missed in Paris, but he never seemed to feel any of them very pressingly; day after day saw him lounging in the drawing room, tinkering on the piano, pretending to read a book, but absolutely at her disposal at a moment's notice. He was amusing, considerate and kind, always most assiduous in his care of Miss Trimble, and Georgina had dropped her guard. In the absence of her cousin, her mother and— yes—of Mr Balfour, she had learned to rely on Robert as her ally against Lady Jane, as her protector from the importuning of suitors. She was indeed very fond of him, but she did not love him. How alarming, then, to become cognisant of a deeper layer to his attentiveness, a jealous flame that had leapt up after her meeting with Mr Balfour.

'The impudence of that fellow,' Robert had spat out, even as he had all but frog-marched her away from the spot in the park. 'I wonder he has the temerity to claim acquaintance with you. I cannot think my father is intimate with him. You should not have approached him, Georgina. Indeed, you should not.'

Robert's arrogance—a quality she had not suspected in him before this—had surprised her. Afterwards she noticed that Robert increasingly adopted the *ton's* predilection to denigrate other young men, as though any weakness he could point to in them could only reflect favourably on himself. She disliked this trait in him; it made him no better than the rest of society. But when she gently suggested that there was no need to slander young men who would never have his advantages or charm, he grew peevish. She began to notice that he was always *looking* at her— purporting to read a book, for instance, but in fact regarding her from beneath his lowered lashes. Or she would suppose him absorbed in the view from the window, only to find that he had contrived to capture her reflection in the pane of glass. He threw her sidelong glances as they sat together playing duets, losing his place in the music and spoiling their rendition. It began to disconcert her to be always under his scrutiny, as it had not done before. Her sense of being benignly watched over by him evaporated. True, he did not drool and stammer as some other young men had done. Neither did he have a lustful eye. He did not flirt. He made no declaration. But he watched her, and she knew what his watching meant. It made her feel panicked and almost betrayed—that he had wooed her into a false sense of security. Was he a wolf in sheep's clothing, as predatory as the rest of the pack?

Georgina longed to hear from Cousin George, that he was on his way back from Paris and that they would proceed to Ecklington, or to the north country, as planned. But no word came.

41

Lady Jane had her own agenda, however, and announced it one morning at breakfast. Georgina was to begin preparations to remove to Brighton.

'We are long overdue,' Lady Jane remarked. 'The house was taken from June, and look how many weeks have gone by? The children will be carried there straight from school and we must have everything in readiness. Several of my acquaintance there have written to me, wondering what has become of me. Ah! But I have sacrificed myself for you, Miss Willow. You *would* wring every ounce of pleasure from your London season.'

'Excuse me, Lady Jane,' said Georgina, almost choking on her breakfast. 'I fear I must correct you if you believe that these past weeks have been for *my* benefit. You know very well why I acquiesced to them.'

'For whose benefit *have* they been then?' enquired Lady Jane, disregarding Georgina's final remark. 'I assure you I would much rather have been in Brighton.'

Georgina narrowed her eyes but did not contradict her. 'Your ladyship has sacrificed quite enough, then,' she said through pursed lips, 'and I will not trespass further. If it is all the same to you I had rather go to Ecklington.'

'Ecklington is quite out of the question,' said Lady Jane, motioning for the footman to replenish her coffee. 'If you have an invitation elsewhere, to Boxborough, for example, or to Lord Pyke's estate, I suppose I could forgo Brighton for a few weeks more.'

Georgina placed her cup very carefully onto its saucer. 'I have received no invitations that I care to accept,' she said. 'If I may not go to Ecklington I shall go back to Chanbury. My friends the Burleighs will not refuse me, I know.'

'Certainly not! You will undo all the good we have done, if you return *there*. Who in the world has heard of the Burleighs? We must build on our success if we are to achieve anything, and all the superior families are in Brighton, are they not, Agnes?'

Miss Trimble startled at the sound of her name, very loath to become embroiled in the discussion. 'I … I cannot say,' she stammered. 'Indeed, I have heard it said that Weymouth is considered more genteel, these days.'

'Weymouth?' Lady Jane thundered. 'Name me one family of note who spends the summer there and by all means, Agnes, we shall decamp to any house you choose to take for us.' She leaned over the table and directed a very withering look at her companion. 'Beggars, you know, cannot be choosers.'

Miss Trimble stifled a sob.

Georgina said, 'Come, your ladyship. I have done all that you asked of me, have I not? I beg you will not impose further. Let Miss Trimble and I go to Ecklington. That is surely where Cousin George will wish to take Robyn, when she is well enough to travel. We can give direction as to the opening of the house.'

'Impose?' shrieked Lady Jane, causing the cups on the breakfast table to rattle. 'You ungrateful girl! When I have all but prostrated myself for your benefit.'

'Forgive me, Lady Jane,' said Georgina, drawing herself up, 'but you misremember. It was at your own behest that I was brought out. Indeed, at your own insistence. I wanted nothing more than to be left in obscurity, but—you know—you brought much pressure to bear.'

'I still have, at my disposal, such information as could ruin your mother,' said Lady Jane very icily. 'Do not misremember *that*, Miss Willow.'

There was an awkward silence, whilst the footman lifted the lids on the dishes and discovered that more toast was needed, and so made his escape.

'Lady Jane,' Georgina tried, in a more conciliatory tone, 'I am quite sensible of all that is due to you, but I must insist on being left out of your plans for Brighton. I simply cannot endure it.'

'Endure? What has there been to 'endure'? You thankless wretch,' Lady Jane flung back, not at all moved. 'You speak as though I have been holding you hostage …'

'Indeed you have,' Georgina cried out. 'You know you have! Under threat of harm to my mama you have compelled me to accompany you into society. You have paraded me, like a trophy. Oh! It has been so humiliating. Had Cousin George been here, or had I any alternative whatsoever that you did not contrive to frustrate, I would have had no part in your scheme. Let us not pretend this has been for my good, or that you have not enjoyed every moment of it.'

'Well,' said Lady Jane, 'I will not pretend that I have not had some satisfaction from it. What sensible woman would not? I have simply done for you what any proper mother should have done. I have cured you of that ridiculous affectation of yours. I have introduced you to the most superior society, and given you opportunities for a match more advantageous than any you could have dreamed of. But it is clear to me now what your agenda has been all long. Do not think I am not fully aware of your reasons for wishing to go to Ecklington. You wish to assess your new domain! You have set your sights on my stepson and very cleverly have you reeled him into your net. But it will not do, missy. It will not do.' She sat back in her seat and folded her arms, a look of extreme superciliousness on her face. 'Consanguinity[lxii] is not permitted in marriage.'

Georgina jumped from her seat. 'I have no idea what you mean,' she said. In fact Lady Jane's veiled accusation had been clear enough, and of course Georgina comprehended very well the substance of it without at all admitting that it had the least basis. From the corner of her eye Georgina saw the door begin to open; the footman, she supposed, was returning with more toast. There was so much she wished to say, to ask, to demand, regarding her ladyship's concluding allusion. Had she, then, taken up once more her slanderous idea of some past liaison between Jocelyn and George Talbot? But in respect of the footman Georgina modified her stance and her tone, concluding only, 'You are wrong, quite wrong, if you suppose for one moment *that* is my intention.'

'Oh dear,' said Robert, strolling in behind the footman. 'In what is Lady Jane mistaken?'

'Never mind,' said Lady Jane and Georgina at the same time. Neither of them would meet his eye.

'Let me pour you some coffee, Mr Robert,' said Miss Trimble, reaching for the pot with trembling hands.

42

Robert Talbot had come to Grosvenor Square that day with the avowed intent of paying his addresses to Miss Willow. He was a man almost demented by love. The past few weeks had been part ecstasy, part agony for him. Yes, he had been daily in her company, permitted an intimacy of association that none of her other limp or lustful beaux could have imagined in their wildest and most febrile dreams. Others had been denied the radiance of her beauty altogether, or only allowed it in small, carefully controlled doses, but he had basked in the full brilliance of it. Publicly—in the carriage and in the park, and at elegant dinners—he had been the envy of every man as he handed Miss Willow in and out of her carriage, held her wrap, took her arm, and bent his head to catch her murmured remarks. Privately—on their solitary rides and in the sequestered exclusivity of the house—he had been her sole companion; trusted, in his father's stead and as her near relation, where no other man would have been tolerated. Who but he had accessed the breakfast parlour to see her fresh-washed hair still damp upon her neck? Or been allowed to watch the quiet repose in her features as she sat at her sewing? Who but he had enjoyed the privilege of handing her a candle and watching her mount the stairs at the end of the day? Oh! It had been glorious! A heady, elevating, almost religious delight. He had felt as though he had passed through the veil to the holy of holies. His sense of her divinity was mesmerising and there had been times when he had been forced to grip the back of a chair, or lean against a wall, to prevent himself from literally kneeling at her feet.

But, as often as he had seen her, it could not be often enough. And as much as he had seen of her, it could not be sufficient. Her beauty to him was like opium; delicious, intoxicating, transporting, but addictive. He could never be satisfied. The agony of parting with her each day had been acute; he could hardly bear, some nights, to leave the house. Though the butler yawned and the footmen discreetly blew out the candles, he would linger on, just in case … Sleep would not come to him. He had tossed and turned in his bed at the Oriental, breathless, heated, aroused, until at last he could tolerate it no longer. Then he had risen before the dawn chorus had begun, and woken the ostler, riding hard across Hyde Park in the blue light of dawn, the percussion of his horse's hooves in rhythm with the hard beating of his heart. Georgina Willow. Georgina Willow. Georgina Willow. The galloping feet and his own body had thumped out her name but still, when he returned hot and filthy, his ardour was unassuaged, his soul as full of her as ever.

And oh! The excruciating jealousy that had burned in his breast, as he had been forced to watch those other men come, with hot-house flowers, with beribboned boxes of confectionery, with their sweaty hands and jabbering inanities, to worship at the shrine that was his, and his alone. How had he borne it? There had been times when he had hardly been able to restrain himself. His hands had itched to punch their faces, to gouge their eyes, to stab their hearts; but all the time he had maintained a façade of aloof amusement, raising, from time to time, an ironical eyebrow, allowing himself a cynical smile. He had pretended to find it all so amusing whilst all the time wishing to tear them limb from limb.

On the whole it had seemed to him a very good thing that Georgina had been persuaded to forgo the veil, for how else could he have beheld her?

To have been denied sight of her would have driven him demented. But then there were times when he wished she would take it up again, so that other men might be deprived. In his heart he wanted her exclusively to himself. He fantasised about getting her into some quiet, sequestered room, of lifting her veil with his own hands, of keeping the privilege and honour and gratification of her superlative beauty, her great erotic potential to himself. He would keep her there and enjoy her again and again. He would never tire of looking at her. He thought of her as his personal idol, his own private temple. The idea of any other person intruding upon that holy ground drove him mad.

The only thing that had made it bearable was Georgina's own palpable indifference to them all. She could not have been cooler, be they dukes or marquises, owners of countless acres, their blood as blue as indigo. The conviction that he had no rival had assuaged at least a little of Robert's angst. But then had come Amory Balfour. For him, those crystalline eyes had lit up with bright, eager flame. For him she had shaken off Robert's hand and marched away. For him her serenity had given way to passion. She had shed tears as he had led her away that day. Only Balfour had disturbed the surface of her impervious tranquillity. Since her encounter with Balfour in the little park Robert had sensed an alteration in Georgina. She was distracted, troubled. He *knew* that Amory Balfour preyed on her mind.

It could not be tolerated; and so, Robert Talbot would act. He would stake his claim.

43

When the awkward breakfast was done, Georgina excused herself to go upstairs. Miss Trimble followed close behind her and Robert would have gone also, to loiter in pretence of perusing the papers until his star should reappear. But his stepmother detained him.

'I would speak to you, if you are at liberty,' she said.

'By all means,' said Robert, coming back into the room, for he had been all but out of it. 'I suppose we can send the servant away?'

Lady Jane nodded, and the footman left them alone.

'Do sit down, Robert,' said Lady Jane. He did so, but his step-mother remained standing. He recalled, then, that this had often been a ploy of hers, a way of placing people at a disadvantage. He sat, marooned, on a hard dining chair, whilst she had the freedom of the room.

'Have you heard from your father?' Lady Jane enquired, but went on without giving him time to reply. 'I have received word this morning. He is on his way home. He will be here by the end of the week but by that time I shall be in Brighton.'

'I do not think he will bring Robyn here,' said Robert. 'He is more likely to take her straight to Ecklington.'

'I think so too,' said Lady Jane. 'No doubt you will wish to go ahead and make sure everything is in readiness.'

Robert considered. His immediate scheme—to propose to Georgina—precluded thought of anything else. 'I had not thought of that,' he said. 'But surely a word to Mrs Banks will suffice. On the whole I have no idea of going there myself just yet.'

'I am astonished at you,' said Lady Jane, raising an incredulous eyebrow. 'I should have thought your sister's wellbeing your first priority.'

'Of course, I am very anxious that she should be well,' he replied. 'But as to the immediate future, my plans are somewhat fluid.'

'Ah, now,' said Lady Jane, resting from her perambulations and leaning over him, '*that* is what I particularly want to know. What *do* you plan, now you are home from your tour? Shall you join your father in his business? If you like politics, I am sure a constituency might be found for you. Or is,' and here she narrowed a gimlet eye, 'matrimony on your mind?'

Robert felt himself blushing. Was he so transparent? To cover his confusion he got up from his seat and walked to the window. 'What makes you ask that?' he got out.

Lady Jane declined to answer, but she threw him an arch look. 'If that is the case, Robert, let me give you some advice: Georgina Willow will not do.'

Stung, Robert said, 'If that *were* the case your ladyship, I think the lady should know it before *you* do. But, as a matter of curiosity, what is your objection to Miss Willow? You have been eager enough to ally her with countless other gentlemen of your acquaintance. Why should I not be as good as any of them? Why not better, indeed? It is my understanding that there have been, of old, ties between our families that would make such an alliance very natural.'

'*Natural* ties between your families?' Lady Jane burst out, highly amused. 'Yes indeed, you could say that.'

Robert frowned. 'It is no secret, I think.'

Lady Jane smiled, a cold smile that chilled Robert's soul. 'Oh,' she said, 'but it is.'

'What do you mean?' Robert's stomach knotted itself. Had his father not mentioned some secret? But surely that had pertained to Georgina's mother—an ancient matter, long-forgotten now? 'What do you mean?' he said again.

Lady Jane gave him a straight look. 'For such an apparently *distant* relative,' she said slowly, 'do you not discern a very *striking* family resemblance?'

Above the fireplace of the breakfast room was a portrait of George, painted many years ago, very soon after his return from India and his first marriage. He had been perhaps four and twenty years of age, not much more than Georgina was now. Lady Jane studied the picture and Robert followed her lead. His father had been a very handsome young man, classically beautiful, with dark hair curled across his brow, fine eyes—brown and very large, a full mouth … Suddenly Robert felt all the blood drain away from his face. A clammy hand ran itself down his spine. The knot in his innards untied itself and he felt his bowels loosen. He groped his way to the chair and sat down heavily upon it once more. 'You are not suggesting …?' he stammered out. 'You do not mean …?'

'I am suggesting nothing,' said Lady Jane carefully, but surveying the consequences of her interference with a high degree of satisfaction. 'I am the very last person to gossip, *you* know that, Robert. But I must say it struck me right at the beginning that there is a peculiarly close resemblance … It upset me greatly. I was quite ill, you may have heard, just after she came. But perhaps it is better that we say no more on this subject. Suffice it to say, you had better look elsewhere. Miss Willow will not do.'

44

From the breakfast room Georgina and Miss Trimble made their way by unspoken consent to Miss Trimble's little sitting room. It was cool—of course, at that season there was no fire—and the little window, flung open, admitted only the smells from the kitchen and wash-house below. Nevertheless the chamber had become a precious refuge to both women over the past few weeks, location of the too-occasional meetings that had been possible between Lady Jane's exhaustive calendar of social engagements. Agnes, released from her duties for Lady Jane and debarred from the august company assembled for the exhibition of Miss Willow, had spent many hours there, quite alone. But not *all* her hours; for, on several Tuesdays, she had had occasion to slip out.

'Do you think,' asked Georgina, when the door was securely fastened and the two were seated across the empty grate, 'that it might be possible to get a letter to the post *without* her ladyship knowing about it?'

Letters for the post were usually placed on the hall table, and taken to the post office by one of the lower functionaries of the house. But, as Georgina knew, Lady Jane was not above rifling through the post and extracting those she did not wish to be sent.

Miss Trimble wrung her hands, most loath to admit to any degree of subterfuge, but at last got out, 'Yes. I believe so. Indeed …' blushing furiously, 'it has been my *occasional* habit to visit the post office these past few weeks. I have … I have …'

'Miss Trimble!' cried Georgina, leaving her seat and kneeling beside her friend. 'What has transpired? Oh! I have neglected you recently. It has not been of *my* desire, I do assure you.'

'I know that, dear girl,' said Miss Trimble, fumbling for her handkerchief and dabbing her lips. 'I have been very wretched, watching you subjected to such *humiliating* exposure. But what could I do?'

'You did a great deal,' Georgina assured her. 'I know that it was you who sent for Arthur, that night of the ball. Miss Pink proved herself a true friend.'

'Oh! The Pinks are delightful people,' Miss Trimble burst out. 'And, with your usual perspicacity, you hit on *just* the quarter whence *my* succour has come.'

She reached to a low bookshelf where a number of trinkets and her tea caddy were stored. She lifted another box, the size and shape of a tea caddy but clearly utilised for another purpose, onto her lap. Inside were a dozen or so letters, bound up with a piece of pink ribbon.

'What are these?' asked Georgina, but making no move to touch them. She could tell that they were too precious to be handled by any but Miss Trimble herself.

'It seems very odd,' began Miss Trimble, 'really, most incredible to *me*, after all these years. But it seems I have … Really, Miss Willow, you will think me very silly and deluded, but I have read over these letters many times and there can be little doubt. In short, it seems that I have been so fortunate as to have aroused the affections of a gentleman.'

Now she raised her eyes to Georgina. They shone with happiness.

'Mr Pink?' Georgina breathed.

Miss Trimble nodded, and laid her thin little hand on the bundle of letters. 'We have been corresponding. And, a few times, when Miss Pink could be spared from the millinery to act as chaperone, we have met up. He is the most delightful man, Georgina: learned, refined. Mr Talbot thinks highly of him. Do you recall him saying so, that first time we went to Cuckold's Point? If he had *not*, you can be sure that I would not have permitted Mr Pink's addresses.'

'But this is wonderful news, Agnes,' said Georgina. 'Has he proposed?'

Miss Trimble nodded very shyly. 'In his last letter, here, he invites me to join them in Weymouth. Of course, I would share Miss Pink's accommodations. But he says quite clearly that if I can get away from Grosvenor Square he will arrange all the rest—the banns, I suppose he means, and a licence—and there will be no necessity of my ever returning here if I do not like.'

Georgina took her friend's hand. 'And, Agnes, *do* you wish it? For I will say this: if you do not wish to remain here, and you do not wish to marry Mr Pink, I can promise you a home with me, wherever that may be, for as long as ever you require. I am certain Mama will oblige me in this. I could not part with you now, unless you have some better hope.'

'I think ... I *think*,' said Miss Trimble taking Georgina's hand in both of hers, and allowing her tears to fall freely upon their conjoined fingers, 'I think that I love Mr Pink.'

Georgina sat back upon her heels. 'And he loves you. How could he not? And so it shall be. Oh my friend! How happy I am for you.'

The two sat in shared wonderment for a while, until Miss Trimble roused herself, dried her eyes and put away her box of love letters. 'But this is nothing to the purpose of *your* situation,' she said. 'You wish to write a letter and you wish me to take it to the post. I will fetch paper and pen. To whom shall you write?'

'I shall write, as I did before, to my friends the Burleighs. I certainly shall not go to Brighton with Lady Jane and it seems to me now—after what she said at breakfast—quite impossible that I should go to Ecklington. I am fond of Robert, but I must not allow my sisterly affection for him to be misconstrued by anyone. Before this I might have turned to him for assistance, but *now* that is impossible. Arthur is beyond my reach and we cannot expect Mr Pink to rescue *two* damsels. Therefore the Burleighs are my only hope. I know they will come for me if I ask them.'

Miss Trimble brought writing materials but before Georgina's note was commenced she said, 'You have *one* other friend, though, don't you? I mean Mr Balfour.'

'Oh,' Georgina shook her head, keeping her eyes fixed on the paper before her. 'No. I cannot write to him.'

Georgina wrote her letter and whilst she did so Miss Trimble penned her own short missive and directed it to the post office in Weymouth. When both were sealed and Miss Trimble was ready to slip out, it was discovered that she had left her shawl in the breakfast room.

'I will fetch it,' said Georgina. 'We do not wish to risk you encountering her ladyship just now. You go down the back stairway and I will bring your shawl to you there.'

45

It was some moments before Robert realised he was alone in the room. The remains of the ladies' breakfast lay across the table. On the sideboard, the spirit kettle spat and rattled. It had boiled dry. In a dream, he got up and extinguished the flame beneath it.

The breakfast parlour had always struck him as a very pleasant room. It was well-proportioned. The windows faced east; the morning sun poured in. The view across the street to the park was very agreeable. He went and stood in the window, looking out over the railings to the rose beds and lawns of the park. Through the trees he could just make out the stone fountain. The sight of it made his gorge rise. If he himself could not have Georgina it seemed likely to him that Mr Balfour—ugly, twisted man that he was—might well win her. The thought of those black hands on her exquisite white flesh made his skin creep. It would be sacrilege, an atrocity not to be borne.

Lady Jane could not be right in her speculation. And, what, precisely, *had* she hinted? That there was a likeness between his father and Georgina? So what? Dark hair, eyes of a particular shade of brown … what did that signify? There must be thousands—millions—who could claim the same.

Come to that, he could himself. It meant nothing. No, it was simply Lady Jane up to her usual tricks, meddling, spoiling things. She would not deter his intention. If she had proof, let her show it!

All the while he felt his father's image behind him, as vivid to him as the man himself. He dared not turn around and look at the portrait. He knew too well what it would show him. Why had he not seen it? Where had his reason been when he had laid his heart at Georgina's feet and pledged his soul in worship? His eyes had been on her, ever on her, drinking in the least detail of her beauty, venerating every hair, every pore. But he had been blind. In all his looking, he had not seen her at all.

He heard a footstep behind him and swung round. Georgina stood in the doorway. She was pale, solemn, nothing like the smiling, superlatively complacent young man who sat in the frame of the portrait. Nevertheless Robert could not help glancing from one to the other. The likeness was impossible to ignore.

'I did not know you were still here,' said Georgina haltingly. 'I came back for Miss Trimble's shawl.'

It lay on the back of the chair that Agnes had occupied at breakfast. Wonderingly, Robert crossed the room and picked it up. 'My father bought it for her,' he said. 'She told me about it. In the spring, when it was known that you were coming, and to save you from my stepmother, he arranged that Miss Trimble would have the care of you. And in order that she might not disgrace you—her words, not mine—he provided her with some new clothes. She was most grateful.'

'You father is all kindness,' said Georgina, taking hold of the shawl. 'I shall be sorry not to see him before I go.'

'Go?' he stood before her, the fringe of the shawl still in his hands, loath to relinquish it entirely, wishing to maintain the connection with her that it gave him. His eyes ravished her face but it was now, as it never had been before, a sinful enchantment. 'Oh,' he croaked out. 'I suppose you mean to Brighton. Lady Jane tells me that you are bound there before the week is out.'

'Yes, I believe that is her intention,' said Georgina. She spoke—they both did—with a degree of wariness that had not been habitual with them, as though in code. The words they uttered had nothing at all to do with what they meant to say. 'Although in point of fact,' she said, almost dreamily, 'I shall not be accompanying her.'

'No?' he asked as though it scarcely interested him. 'Where then, will you go?' He wondered if she planned to elope with Balfour. By God! He would scotch *that*, if he could!

To his surprise Georgina said, 'I had thought to go to Ecklington. But now, I think that will not be … wise.'

Robert dropped his hold on the shawl and tore his eyes from her, but only to fix them on his father's portrait. 'How so?' he asked, his voice tense and shrill. 'You are welcome to go there, if you wish. I can make the arrangements. Indeed, I believe by the end of the week my father and Robyn will be there.'

This seemed to surprise her. There was a pause. 'Is that so?' she said, continuing, almost to herself, 'If they were there already it might … but, as it is, no. I think I had better pursue my course.'

Robert cleared his throat. 'And what is *that*, if I may ask?'

She hesitated, perhaps wondering if she could trust him with her scheme.

'I hope …' he said, dragging his eyes from the portrait and fixing them instead on the table. He reached out a distracted hand and fiddled pointlessly with the unused cutlery that remained strewn about. 'I hope you can confide in me.'

'Of course,' she said. 'Miss Trimble is to take a letter for me this morning. She will take it direct to the post office …'

'You do not trust my stepmother not to interfere.'

'Frankly, no. I have written to my friends the Burleighs and I am certain that they will come for me.'

Robert allowed himself a small sigh, releasing the tension that had been building in his chest since she had entered the room. But he could not prevent himself from saying sourly, 'The Burleighs! I had supposed you to be sending to Mr Balfour.'

'Oh Robert,' Georgina said, and he could sense the frown in her voice. 'Your antagonism towards him is quite unjustified. Why should I send for him? He does not care about me.' Her voice cracked as she got out, 'He does not want to see me.'

Her emotion undid him. He swung round and snatched her into his arms. Perhaps she thought he wished to offer her comfort. She allowed him to press her to his breast, to soak her tears into his shirt. She stood quite limply within the circle of his embrace. He crushed her to him as though he would press her through his skin and into his body. He leaned down and kissed her, first her eyes, her brow, her cheeks, then her mouth. Her lips were full, yielding, sweet, as he had known they would be, but they did not open to his. She did not reach up and put her arms around his neck. She did not respond to his ardour but remained passive, as his hands tangled themselves in her hair, bent back her head so that he could kiss the alabaster smoothness of her neck, then swept the curve of her bosom, waist and hip. What was the matter with her? Why was she so cold? He kissed her more fiercely, pouring his passion into her, but she made no move, no sound.

'Why do you not love me?' he cried out, grasping her shoulders and almost shaking her. 'What is the matter with you? Oh you are cold. Cruel. Love me, Georgina!'

He swept her round so that she was pressed against the table. He found the neck of her gown and would have wrenched it open but small hands on his sleeve, a thin but surprisingly imperious voice at his side brought him to himself.

'Mr Robert,' said Miss Trimble. 'Let Miss Willow go.'

He stepped back, aghast at what he had done. Georgina, dishevelled and distraught, wilted against Miss Trimble. Her face was ashen except

314

around the mouth, where he had bruised her lips. Tears poured from her eyes but she did not cry as he had seen other girls cry. Her eyes stared from their sockets in stupefaction. He wondered for a moment if she was without a heart. But then he remembered Balfour.

'Oh forgive me,' he cried, falling to his knees and grasping her hand. He showered it with kisses. 'Forgive me. I love you, Georgina. Please, please marry me. That is what I came to say today. All the rest,' he indicated, by a wild gesture, their concourse of a moment before, 'I did not intend it. Only say you will marry me and all will be well. Oh Georgina! My love! My angel! I adore you.'

His hands were wet with his tears. Her fingers, like her body earlier, stayed cold and inanimate and soon slipped from his grip. He felt himself sliding down the skirt of her gown, lower and lower, until he reached its hem. He gathered the stuff of it into his hands, covering his face with it, sobbing, begging. But when he came to himself, his hands were empty, and he was alone.

44

The sea crossing from Calais to Dover, though short, had tired Robyn Talbot and her father decided that they would stay some four or five days in the port until she should be well enough to travel onwards to Ecklington. Quite apart from wishing for his daughter's comfort, *The Georgina* had put in at Dover to refuel and George wished most ardently to go aboard and hear from Arthur how she had fared in her sea-trials. Once landed and comfortably installed he wrote to Robert suggesting, if he was otherwise disengaged, that he might like to join Robyn and himself at the hotel. He did not expect to see his son until two days after his letter had been sent so was therefore most surprised to find Robert seated at the breakfast table when he descended the following morning.

'Robert,' he exclaimed, opening his arms to enfold his son in an embrace. 'This is well met indeed. I did not expect to see you until tomorrow at the soonest. You got my message, then?'

'Yes sir,' said Robert, sinking back into his chair. 'And came by the night mail. It is an execrable way to travel, such joltings and throwings about. I wonder anyone can tolerate it as a regular thing, even inside. Outside must be truly dreadful. I pity *those* poor souls. One fellow could hardly stand when we came in. Green about the gills he was. But still, he has worse to come I suppose, for he is to take ship to France within the hour.' As he spoke his eyes roved around the breakfast room but would not settle on anything. His father's direct eye he avoided altogether. It seemed to George that Robert sought to fill up the silence with inconsequential talk. Something was wrong.

'Your sister did not travel well,' George remarked, beckoning the waiter over. 'She too was an interesting shade of chartreuse when we landed. Have you ordered?'

Robert shook his head. 'Only coffee. I have not much of an appetite.'

George regarded his son. Robert was pale and hollow-eyed, more ill-looking than even a lost night's sleep and an uncomfortable ride in the mail coach should make a man of his age and vigour. He sat drooped in his chair, his stock poorly tied, a day's stubble on his chin.

'Let us take a room for you and order a bath,' suggested George. 'You have a change of clothes? My man can shave you.'

'Oh.' Robert shrugged. 'Yes, I suppose so. After breakfast and, perhaps, a walk. I feel as though I have been folded into a box all night. I need to stretch my legs.'

'By all means,' agreed George. '*The Georgina* is in port. We will walk down and look her over.'

Robert took a sharp intake of breath. His face—already pale—went a whiter shade still. 'Georgina is *here*?' he croaked out.

George wrinkled an eyebrow. 'The ship,' he said slowly. 'My new steamship. She is named *The Georgina*.'

Robert nodded understanding and pressed his lips together as though to hold back a torrent of words. 'Oh,' he got out at last. 'I see. I did not know you had named her that.'

George's breakfast arrived but a stone of anxiety had lodged itself in his stomach and he found he could not eat the food before him. Robert sat on at the table, staring at the cloth, from time to time reaching out for his coffee cup but finding it already drained. George indicated to the waiter to bring more, but when it came Robert shook his head. The flood of words that had filled up the silence earlier had been stopped up at the mention of Georgina's name.

Presently he said, 'If you are ready, Father, let us set out.'

The hotel was placed on the seafront about a mile from the docks, and the Talbot men bent their steps in that direction. The pavements were quiet, it being still quite early in the day. A shower of rain in the night had made the streets slick. A fresh wind blew off the sea presaging more rain to come.

George took his son's arm. 'I have been grateful for your letters,' he said. 'I am appalled at Lady Jane's behaviour in respect of our cousin. You can be sure that she will feel my displeasure when I see her next.'

'I think that will not be soon, Father, unless you go to Brighton. She departs for there today.'

'Does Miss Willow go with her?'

Robert shook his head. 'I do not think so. To be frank, I am not in Miss Willow's confidence. I have ...' he struggled for a moment, '... I have forfeited her friendship.'

George absorbed this information as they walked. 'I am sorry to hear that, Robert,' he said at last. 'How has that come about?'

Robert did not reply for a moment, but his expression of wretched distraction increased. The brisk wind on his face brought no colour to it. He walked with his head down, heedless of the view of the sea to their right, or the boiling clouds in the sky above them. 'I let my feelings overwhelm me,' he said at last in a low voice. 'I did not behave like a gentleman.'

'You did not impose yourself upon her?' George barked out, coming to an abrupt halt.

Robert continued a step or two before realising that his father had stopped. 'No,' he said, turning back and raising his eyes with difficulty to meet his father's. 'I made a fool of myself, but I did not compromise her. Indeed, she seemed quite unmoved by my display.' He spoke coolly, but then burst out in a fit of passion, 'I wonder if she has a heart at all!'

'Of course she has a heart,' cried George, continuing his walk and slipping his arm into his son's once more. 'She must care for you, or she would have screamed, called for aid ... She sought to lessen your indiscretion by making nothing of it.'

'I don't know,' said Robert, with an anguished sigh. 'I have thought of nothing else since it occurred. I have upbraided myself, you can be sure. These past weeks we have seemed to be very good friends. I flattered myself that she had become attached to me. I, certainly, have become most warmly attached to *her*. Father, I ...' He turned wide, tortured eyes upon his father. '... I am so entirely in love with her that I cannot eat or sleep ... She is *so* beautiful, is she not? I felt sure of winning her heart.' He fixed George with a penetrating look. 'Would it not please you, Father,' he asked, with heavy significance, 'if I were so fortunate as to make her my wife?'

Now it was George's turn to slide his eyes away. He made no reply, and the longer he failed to do so the more anxious and apprehensive Robert became. Surely, if Lady Jane's dark allusion had been simply malicious interference, his father would not have hesitated. But if there was, in her hint, some fragment of truth ...?

They had come by this time to the quayside, which was busy with stevedores and porters hauling crates and loading cargo. Several ships were in dock. Passengers milled about preparing to embark, wrapped in greatcoats, the ladies weighed down by shawls and wraps, for the warm, unclouded days of the past few weeks were a thing of memory now. Their expressions were apprehensive, sour and foreboding. The passage did not promise to be a smooth one. A horse—very reluctant—was being urged up the gangplank by two grooms. It lifted its tail and sent forth a spume of evil-smelling ordure. At the far end of the dock, away from the hurry and stress and mess, sat *The Georgina*, by far the newest and most impressive vessel to be seen in Dover that day, a beacon amidst the squalor.

'There she is,' cried George, hurrying his son along the quay. 'Is she not splendid Robert? We shall have a whole fleet like her! Let us see if we can find Arthur, to see how she fared.'

George loosened his grip on his son's arm and rushed ahead, eager to board his ship but just as eager, it seemed to Robert, to jettison their discussion of Georgina. Robert lingered, taking in the majesty of *The Georgina*. She was every bit as impressive as her namesake and he was overcome by a wave of jealousy, that other men should have the possession of her, that others should be more intimately acquainted with her decks and rigging and pulsing heart than he. He saw Arthur Harlish on board, leaning over the taffrail[lxiii]. How much better did he know Georgina than Robert did, both the ship and the woman? Did *he* love her? Robert felt himself engulfed with bitter, sullen rage, and although his father beckoned him forward, and Arthur waved a cheery greeting, he thrust his hands in his pockets, turned on his heel and walked away.

He walked amongst the stacks of cargo, past customs sheds and flimsy offices, with no idea of a destination, his eyes bleared by tiredness and tears, his heart as heavy as a stone. He seemed to walk for a long time, and for a great distance, but when he looked up at last he found himself back where he had begun, towered over by the massive hull of *The Georgina*, as though his fate and hers were inextricably linked, as though he would never escape her no matter how far he travelled.

His father came down the gangplank smiling. 'She's done splendidly,' he exclaimed. 'Steamed all the way down to the Bay of Biscay and back without breaking a sweat. Now they are to refuel and go north, to find some more testing waters for her. Would it not be fine to go with her, Robert? To Norway, perhaps? Imagine the fjords at this time of year!' George's eyes were alight with enthusiasm and Robert knew that he had only to say the word and Robyn would be packed off alone to

Ecklington and the next day would see the two Talbot men sailing round East Anglia. 'You did not answer my question,' he said.

'Your question?'

But Robert could read the prevarication in his father's eyes.

'About Miss Willow. I wish to know whether you would approve of her, for my wife.'

'Oh,' said George. He looked over his shoulder to where Arthur Harlish remained, half way up the gangplank. 'Of course, I recall. But just give me a moment, Robert. I have invited Arthur to dine with us. You have no objection do you? Only he would not agree to it until I had consulted you. He seemed to think he would be intruding.'

'It will be our first dinner together—just the three of us—since Paris,' said Robert, knowing he was being churlish but unable to suppress it.

'That's what *he* said,' replied George, amused. 'But it will not signify, will it? And I should like him to have a decent meal before he departs.'

Robert shrugged. 'You must do what you think is best,' he said.

George turned to Arthur. 'Come at seven,' he shouted up. 'We dine late. It is Robyn's continental habit.'

Arthur nodded and went back on deck.

The two men walked back along the dock, George discoursing on the ship's performance—coal consumption, rate of knots, manoeuvrability—attempting to dispel the portentous silence that seemed to surround his son like a storm.

At last his diatribe stumbled to a halt, and Robert said, 'Father. I must know, about Georgina.'

They had come to a ragged wasteland beyond the docks where, in the past, fires had been lit, leaving scorched circles in the scrub. Refuse, frayed ropes and broken crates lay discarded. It was a desolate spot, made more bleak by the grey cloud that pressed down upon them.

George turned and faced his son. 'I have been trying to think, all this time,' he said, 'how best to answer your question. I think I can only recommend that you look elsewhere, Robert.'

The expression on his son's face almost broke his heart. Robert's mouth opened in a maw, his eyes pooled with tears.

'No, Father, do not say that,' he croaked out.

George grasped his arms. 'Forgive me, son,' he said, very moved. 'But I must.'

Robert's mouth quivered. His whole face was woebegone and haggard. George looked sorrowfully into his eyes.

'Lady Jane said …' Robert faltered, '… that is, she suggested that the relationship was too near.' Again, he scrutinised his father's face, looking for some clue, some hint, some glimmer of a truth that neither of them, he suspected, really wanted to see.

'She said *that*, did she,' asked George darkly. And then, almost to himself, 'How has she found out?'

'Oh Father,' Robert burst out. 'Is it true, then? Is Georgina my sister?'

George's face softened and he applied pressure to Robert's arms that he hoped would be reassuring, comforting. 'No,' he said, and looked his son square in the eye. '*That* is not true.'

'Well then,' said Robert, swamped with blissful relief, his pain obliterated by hope, 'in that case, there is no impediment. If I can make her forgive me. If I can regain her trust.'

'Oh, Robert,' said George, shaking his head, 'if only that were true.'

'But you said …'

'I said she is not your sister, and she is not. But there is still something … Oh! How I wish I could tell you. But, as I have already explained, this is not *my* secret.'

'If the secret is that she is not cousin Jocelyn's legitimate child,' declared Robert boldly, 'I shall not care. *That* will not be an impediment to me. Georgina will never hear it from my lips for, I apprehend, she does not know it. Jocelyn need have no fear. Her secret will be quite safe with me.'

'That is not the secret,' George cried out, 'not really, and yet it is close enough to the truth. If it were *only* that.' George redoubled his grip on Robert's arms. He wished he could embrace him, as he had done when his son was just a small boy.

Robert's face had become stiff, immobile, betraying none of the confusion and panic that coursed through his mind, but his eyes could not shield it. In *them* George saw all his perplexity; a well of agony and denial and determination.

'Only that?' Robert prompted. 'So there is something else?'

George hesitated, swallowing. His mouth was dry. He summoned up courage but found only hopelessness and dilemma. 'Lady Jane is not entirely wrong in her supposition,' he said at last. 'Georgina is not my child but still her relation to you is too close, Robert. A marriage between you, even if you could persuade her to it, would not be permissible.'

'Not permissible by whom?' Robert challenged. 'If this is such a great and closely guarded secret, who is to know? I shall not tell if you do not. And cousin Jocelyn, I presume, will not wish to resurrect the bones of whatever skeleton she has hidden? She could not object without revealing the truth. And, in any case, it could all be done by the time she returns …'

'Robert,' George shouted, to stop his son's madness. 'It cannot be, I tell you. You must forget her. It cannot be.'

'But Father …'

'No.' George was adamant, now, and his grip so hard that Robert winced. 'If you love Georgina you will give her up,' George said slowly.

'Do you not see? She is already so fragile, so tenuously connected to her sense of self that if you cause her to question, even inadvertently, all she believes about herself, it will destroy her. Would you have that on your hands?'

The squall that had been threatening all day suddenly hit; needles of rain and flurries of restless wind swept across the wasteland. Robert, who wore no hat, was soaked in an instant. Water poured off his smooth black hair and down his ravaged face. The sound of the water on George's hat and coat, and on the rubbish that was strewn around, was loud enough to cause both men to raise their voices.

'I have told you, I will never let her suspect it,' Robert shouted into the teeth of the storm. 'Please do this for me, Father, or *you* will destroy *me*.'

'I am attempting to *save* you from destruction,' George screeched back. 'Can't you see? It will always be there, in your mind, lying between the two of you, a lie, indeed, at the heart of your marriage.'

'I shall have nothing to feel guilty about,' declared Robert.

'Oh but you *will*, son. Your conscience will plague you. You will know that it isn't right even if you do not know why.'

'It will kill me, Father, if I cannot have her,' Robert implored, his tears running unchecked and mingling with the rain that coursed down his cheeks. 'I promise you it will kill me.'

'Oh my boy,' George pleaded. 'It will kill *her* if you do. If you love her, you will steel yourself to this.'

'Then tell me *why*,' Robert shouted, angry now, as well as distraught. 'Tell me why, for God's sake! Is it because she is my sister?'

'No. No,' George sobbed out. His face crumpled and at last he pulled his son into the circle of his fierce embrace. 'God help me,' he cried, his voice muffled by the damp wool of Robert's coat. 'She isn't *your* sister, Bobby, she is *mine*. And God damn *both* our parents' souls in hell.'

45

Weymouth, September 1835

The season at Weymouth had been very pleasant, with fine, dry days enlivened by the occasional period of brisk wind. On these days the sea—normally glassy and very blue—had been whipped up into foamy peaks. Skiffs and leisure yachts had scudded across them, their greenhorn sailors hauling inexpertly on lines and shortening sails that ought to have been let out, racing each other and the gulls overhead and very often falling overboard as they criss-crossed the bay. On these days the broad promenade and smooth beach had been almost deserted, ladies and gentlemen preferring the coffee houses and reading rooms to the hat-blowing, hair-tousling breezes. Only a few hardy families and doughty nannies with their charges had braved the sands, although of actual rain there had been very little and the wind had not been cold.

These were the days that Georgina had preferred, of all her weeks spent in the elegant but quiet resort. Naturally, she enjoyed the empty streets and deserted beach. Though hardened to it a little, she would still much rather not be looked at. She thrilled to the sensation of the wind on her face, the freedom of her hair as it escaped its restraints and roiled in the stiff breezes. She liked to turn her face to the sun, to look about her at the shops' brightly coloured awnings and at the brilliant white stucco of the elegant houses. If people stared—and, naturally, they *did*—she turned her face from them and reminded herself of the words Mr Balfour had spoken to her on Hampstead Heath: that people were in general not cruel, or rude, only ignorant. They were to be pitied and, if possible, forgiven.

She had gone to Weymouth with Miss Trimble and the Burleighs. Her friends, upon receiving her summons, had gone at once to Grosvenor Square, finding her packed and waiting and resisting with all her might Lady Jane's imperious commands, threats and dire imprecations to enter the Talbot carriage and go with her to Brighton. Miss Trimble—very afraid but also very determined—had declared herself for Weymouth in the very gnashing teeth of Lady Jane's wrath and spleen, clinging to Miss Willow, to the door frame and then to the railings as Lady Jane bullied and harassed and latterly dragged her former companion towards the coach.

Mr Burleigh, of course, would stand for no nonsense of that sort, and had lifted Miss Trimble bodily from the grasping hands of her assailant and installed her without a moment's hesitation—even without quite knowing who she was beyond that she was manifestly a lady in distress—into the safety of his own equipage. At the sight of him—a large, imposing, angry mulatto—Lady Jane had erupted into hysterics, but Mrs Burleigh had been more than equal to histrionics of *that* sort. She was a diminutive woman who, at one time, would not have dared to so much as raise her eyes to so august a personage. But she launched in without the niceties of introduction or apology, boxing her ladyship's ears before bundling her, her maid and her elderly dog into the Talbot brougham and slamming the door upon the apostrophic cries of remonstrance that curdled from within.

Georgina threw herself into Annie Burleigh's arms and sobbed—with relief, with happiness, in expiation of all the treatment she had received at Lady Jane's hands. 'Oh,' she had got out at last, 'please take us home.'

Home for Mr and Mrs Burleigh was a pleasant and neat farmhouse on a not inconsiderable estate of land that they had bought from the late Mr Willow. Their children were at school just then but it had been arranged that they would go directly to Yorkshire, as soon as the term ended. Mr and Mrs Burleigh had decided not to accompany them north, perhaps in some expectation that Georgina might need to call upon them, an expectation that had been more than amply justified. On the journey to Wiltshire all Miss Trimble's hopes as regards Mr Pink—who awaited her arrival in Weymouth with all the nuptial arrangements in place—were explained to the Burleighs, and as they were at liberty for the summer it had taken a very short time for them to decide that a few weeks by the sea, in Weymouth, would be very pleasant indeed.

Mr Talbot had been written to, the letter being sent to Ecklington but not being opened for a week or so after it had been despatched, as he had been detained in Dover pending his son's departure abroad. Once it *was* read, however, and the prospect of Weymouth proving appealing to father and daughter, they too had repaired there and taken a house on the front not far from the Burleighs' lodgings.

Some few days after this, Miss Pink had been very astonished indeed to encounter her employer, Madame Planché, who had also just arrived in Weymouth and was residing in a very pretty but infinitely discreet apartment some roads back from the main thoroughfare. Madame Planché was a plump, good-natured woman in her early forties, of Afro-Caribbean heritage. She had come to England via Kingstown and Paris, where she had been initially owned by, then apprenticed to and finally married to Monsieur Planché, *modiste et mercier*[lxiv] to the *beau monde Parisienne*. His early death had left her the owner of a thriving business, which in time she had transferred to London. Madame Planché was well-liked and well-respected by the *ton*. She earned for herself a very comfortable living and owned a tidy little house in Chelsea known as Pear Tree Cottage.

Thus it transpired that on the day that Miss Agnes Trimble became Mrs Peregrine Pink she did so as finely trimmed as the combined expertise of Madame Planché and Miss Pink could make her. There was quite a crowd of well-wishers in the church. The trembling bride was escorted to the altar by Mr Talbot and followed by two bridesmaids, Miss Pink and Miss Willow, and a wedding breakfast more sumptuous than the bride could have expected or the groom afforded was enjoyed afterwards.

It was a very happy day. If there was a slight shadow of dented pride and offended beauty emanating from the direction of Cuckold's Point, no one took any notice of it.

The bride and groom departed immediately for their honeymoon, leaving Miss Pink in the care of Mr and Mrs Burleigh. That she would be required to return to her work at the millinery was beyond doubt, as Madame Planché declared she was quite indispensable, but that it need not be *yet* was made manifestly clear by that lady's extreme happiness at being in Weymouth, her delight in her new circle of acquaintance and in particular by Mr Talbot's insisting that she should not think of sending Miss Pink away—or of going herself—until Mr Arthur Harlish should appear amongst them. This he was contracted to do as soon as ever the north sea trials of *The Georgina* should be complete. By this time Mr Robert Talbot would be well on his way, trekking north-eastwards through the fjords of Norway, taking a long and very circuitous route towards India.

Georgina was sorry that he should have to make such a trip although she recognised and approved of his gallantry in taking it. She was glad to have been spared the protracted and perhaps embarrassing goodbyes that would have been required had he come to Weymouth first. Their last encounter had been one she would never forget. She was sure that he, too, would be haunted by it. But it was not one she wished to repeat.

By September most of the holiday crowds had left Weymouth to return to their estates for the shooting, or to London for parliament. Madame Planché had also repaired to town, where the *ton's* craving for new bonnets and haberdashery could be denied no longer. Alas, she did so without Miss Pink. *She* had been made into Mrs Harlish and carried off to Yorkshire, there to meet Arthur's parents before both should return to London in time to found Mr Talbot's new ship, sister to *The Georgina*, very likely—if Mr Harlish were again to be honoured with the naming of her—to be christened *The Petunia*. Mr Talbot had left Weymouth not long after Madame Planché—grim-faced, his loins girded for battle—to confront his wife. That there would be some reckoning—some break, some irrevocable severance—was beyond doubt. Robyn had gone with him, wholly recovered from her illness and ready to take up her paint brushes again, and most eager, on her brother's behalf, to witness the humiliation of Lady Jane.

46

Only the Burleighs and Miss Willow remained of the small but extremely affable circle that had been thrown together in Weymouth. Very soon Mr Burleigh's business would take him home to Wiltshire but it had been decided that Christmas would see them all at Tall Chimneys, in time for the return of Mr and Mrs Stockbridge.

What life would offer her after that, Georgina had no idea. She looked back on the past few months with rather mixed feelings. She was very glad to be free of the veil. It had been a hard—at times a cruel—lesson to learn, but she had ceased to feel the need to hide. No disaster had accrued to her mama, no curse befallen, neither shame, nor indictment, nor disgrace. She saw now that the dread had been of her own making, in the fevered crucible of her own pubescent imagination, an amalgamation of her mother's peculiar desire for privacy, the sudden loss of her father and the prurient behaviour of the vulgar, salacious clerk.

She was as she was, for good or for ill, and nothing could change it. What others made of it, and how they behaved in the light of it, was their affair.

In reaching this plateau of understanding, the hardest boulder to overcome had been the one posed by Robert Talbot. His behaviour in the breakfast room had resurrected—in all its vivid anguish—the conduct of the clerk in Salisbury. For some days afterwards she had suffered a relapse but was prevented from sinking very low by Miss Trimble's patient care, and the knowledge that the Burleighs would soon be on the scene. She had examined her conscience closely but found herself guiltless of any encouragement, any but a friendly, sororal partiality. Of course she was sorry to have caused him pain. She knew she had dealt him a blow from which he would not soon recover. She hardly knew how she would look his father in the eye but she told herself it was not her responsibility to pay the price for the feelings and actions of others.

Much, *much* did she have to be thankful for: the friendship of Mrs Pink and Mrs Harlish and also of Robyn Talbot with whom she had established an intimacy that was quite sisterly. She thought of her cousin George as a sort of father figure, and although she hoped in time to warm to Mr Stockbridge, she thought it no bad thing to have such a friend as George Talbot.

All these things Georgina pondered as she took her favourite walk along the esplanade. Mr and Mrs Burleigh were not far away, shopping for gifts for their children. Many of the stalls had been packed away now. The travelling performers had gone too, off to the continent to tumble and conjure, swallow swords and spew fire before crowds on the French riviera. The assembly rooms had closed their doors and in the distance she could hear the boards being hammered in place at the windows.

The beach was deserted, the tide very far out. A smooth, shining expanse of sand invited exploration and Georgina walked down some narrow steps, clutching her bonnet to her head with one hand. The breeze ruffled the skirts of her dress and tugged at the fringe of her shawl but she set her face to it and strode out to where the water lapped the sand into ripples.

She stood for a long time, looking out to sea, admiring the little boats that bobbed against their moorings, the way the sun made a radiant path across the waters to the horizon, the clouds that raced across the blue. So lost was she in her thoughts that a quiet cough and the sound of her name being spoken behind her was the first she knew of any companion. She swung around blinking. Her eyes, dazzled by the sun across the sea, now struggled to adjust.

A tall dark figure stood before her, hatless, the skirts of his light frock coat flapping in the breeze.

'Mr Balfour,' she cried, very pleased but of course also extremely surprised to see him. 'I did not know you were in Weymouth.'

'I have just come,' he said. 'Last night, in fact. I saw Talbot at the club two days ago and he told me … That is, he recommended it.'

Georgina eyed him. His scars were still in evidence but she believed they had faded a little from when she had last seen them. She thought she could discern a greater clarity in his injured eye. His demeanour was more upright; he had more of the proud and stately bearing she recalled from the spring. But he was not now *quite* as he had been then. There was still some shrinking in his manner. He did not absolutely meet her eye—as he would have done then—but stared past her, at the sea. But then she remembered that in the spring Mr Balfour would have been unable to see her eyes. He had only a sheer cascade of voile to look at. Perhaps he had been looking at *that* all the time she had thought he was looking at her, the *person* beneath the veil.

She turned and they looked out together. 'Weymouth is exceedingly pleasant,' she remarked, 'but I am afraid all the attractions have departed now. The season is over.'

'Not *all* the attractions,' Balfour muttered.

Georgina frowned. What did he mean? She let it pass. 'I hope you are much recovered, Mr Balfour. When I saw you last you were very ill. You had been taken ill in Bristol, I believe.'

'I was not taken ill,' he told her. 'I was attacked. Three cut-throats assaulted me, robbed me and left me for dead. Because I am not what the world recognises as a gentleman I was left to the mercy of the borough, nursed by a slattern in a hovel and left to live or die as I might.'

'That is very shocking,' said Georgina. 'I am heartily sorry.'

Balfour shrugged. 'It is in the past. I will rally. I *am* rallying. Indeed,' he touched his scars gingerly, 'I am literally making myself anew. And you, Miss Willow, I see that you have also made a new beginning.' He turned to look at her then, and she met his eyes. Again she searched for—but did not find—the light the sight of her face ignited in other men, the febrile illumination she had come to recognise as desire, the reverential gape of admiration, or the puerile, specious infatuation that was mis-identified as love.

'It was cruelly done,' she said, turning away, 'but, perhaps, in the end, not fruitlessly done. I suppose it is like having a tooth drawn. The pain before is intense, the extraction is agony, but the relief is worth it.'

'The relief does not come immediately, though,' he said. 'The pain takes a while to subside.'

'Indeed, and then, one must become accustomed to the gap. The everyday business of the mouth must be learnt anew.'

Balfour lifted his hand to his jaw and stroked it, nodding. He held out his arm. 'Will you walk with me a little, Miss Willow?' he said.

She took his arm and they strolled for a while without speaking. Georgina's pleasure in his companionship was shot through with confusion. What was he doing here? Had he come on purpose to see her, but, if so, why? She knew he did not love her.

'Shall you stay long in Weymouth, do you think?' she asked him.

'My plans are not fixed,' he said. 'Some days, certainly, if I find the society agreeable.'

'Society is much reduced,' she said, 'but I can answer for a warm reception from my friends, the Burleighs. They remain here for the next week but after that Mr Burleigh must go back to his stud.'

'And you will go with them?'

She nodded. 'For the time being. Until Mama and Mr Stockbridge return and decide on a house. But we are all to go to Yorkshire for Christmas, if the weather permits. I do not know if you are familiar with Yorkshire, Mr Balfour, but the weather there can be very fierce.'

'Notwithstanding the weather—indeed, perhaps *because* of it—you like it there.'

'Indeed I do. The snow, the wind, the rain; I find it fills me with energy, with passion. At one time I wished to remain there permanently. I believed I could live without human contact if I had the moors, the sky and the old house to shelter me. But it is very remote. I think, perhaps, it would not be good for me to live there all the time. I might slip back into my old ways of thinking.'

She felt him exert the slightest possible pressure on her arm.

Presently he said, 'I have spent the past few weeks believing that you would be married to that young man who was with you in the park.'

'Robert Talbot? Oh no. Three ladies of my acquaintance have been lately married, but not me. Mr Talbot has gone abroad.'

'Do you lament him?'

She shook her head. 'Very much, but not in *that* way.' She shot him a quizzical look. 'Forgive me, Mr Balfour, but is that not rather a personal enquiry?'

'You are correct,' he said. 'I have no right to enquire.' He sighed. 'Now, I know I have no business intruding upon the feelings of *any* woman. It is ironic. Before, when I had no interest in love, I think I could have done so in some quarters without the absolute expectation of rejection.'

They had come to the far end of Weymouth beach, where the sand gave way to pebble before meeting the enclosing arm of the cliffs. A number of large boulders provided perching places. He indicated one of these to Georgina and they both sat down.

'I think you still could,' she said, throwing her remark into the wind but feeling that, even so, it was indelicate of her to make it.

He laughed aloud at her—a cold, cynical sound. 'With these?' he said, indicating his mutilated face.

'You think yourself monstrous,' Georgina said, turning to him and allowing her eyes to rest upon his face.

'Do you *not?*' he replied. His eyes bored into hers. She could feel the heat of his body—its strength and solidness, also the tremor of his barely-suppressed angst—as his shoulder pressed against hers. She clasped her hands together lest one of them should find its way to his ravaged cheek.

'Some people might,' she said equably. 'But I do not. How could you think it? I, who all my life, have been cursed by an appearance that makes me different, that makes me an object of … Oh! I cannot even say what madness comes over men when they look at me. But I would be as bad as them if I looked at you and judged you by your injuries or by anything so utterly superficial as your appearance. Come to that, aren't we *all* scarred, one way or another? Yours are simply more visible.'

She turned away and looked across the bay. The sun was dipping. Soon, she knew, they ought to go back.

Mr Balfour, beside her, said nothing, but that she had given him food for thought was obvious. He stared before him, at where the toes of his expensive and highly polished boots dug into the shingle.

'You told me, once,' Georgina said, speaking so quietly that he had to bend his head to catch her words, 'that people are simply ignorant, and that we must try to forgive them; but that, for yourself, you strive to be the best iteration of yourself in spite of them. I have sought, since my unveiling, to emulate you.'

He must have got some sand in his eye. He pulled his handkerchief from his pocket and wiped one of them, but still he spoke no word.

'Perhaps we should go back,' said Georgina, rising. 'Mrs Burleigh will be wondering about me.'

He rose and they began the walk back along the beach. Now the sun was lower, and the tide coming back across the smooth sands. Georgina looked down to where their amalgamated shadows were thrown across the ground. They looked grotesque, unnaturally elongated and lumpen, and it made her think of the monsters that hid inside every human; monsters of bigotry and avarice, but also of fear, shame and self-doubt.

The breeze had strengthened and there was in it, for the first time, an autumn chill. Georgina gave a small shiver.

Abruptly, Amory said, 'Could you love me, Georgina?'

She smiled. 'Of course. But do not go where your heart does not follow. I know you do not love me.'

He stopped and turned her to face him. 'Why do you say that?' he asked incredulously, his brow furrowed, his eyes very intense. She could see his face in all its imperfection; the raised weals of his scars, the drawn-down skin of his eyelid, the slight bloom in his eye, the asymmetry of his jaw.

'When you saw my face, that night by the fountain, I saw no change in your eye,' she said. 'You continued to look at me as you always had done, as you had looked at me when you could not see my face at all. I could see that my face had not moved you, had not ignited you. There was no difference at all and so …'

He shook his head and one side of his mouth twitched into a smile. 'Because I did not show the signs of love *then*, does not mean I do not love you at all,' he said. 'Simply, that I loved you *already*.'

She looked up at him. 'You loved me *before*?' she said wonderingly.

He nodded. 'Yes. From the moment I lifted you into my arms in Lancaster Court.'

She lifted her hands and caressed his face—his beautiful, handsome face—and he bent his head to kiss her.

Epilogue

It took some weeks before Mrs Quince was able to look upon her new neighbour at all, let alone with any degree of forgiveness. How *should* she feel about the woman who, without any claim to beauty, after only the briefest of acquaintances, had purloined Mr Pink from beneath Mrs Quince's own very nose? Offended pride and a sense of having been rudely usurped made for a barrier quite as stout between the two households as the brick walls that divided them. But Mrs Pink had years of experience managing truculent tempers and inflated egos and, little by little, Mrs Quince found her resentment eroded. Being applied to for guidance and aid went far. Which washer-woman would Mrs Quince recommend? Which fishmonger did she patronise? What was the secret to such brightly shining brass? It was rather flattering to be constantly applied to. And then, Mrs Pink—for all her faults—was a lady, and against Rotherhithe's ever-encroaching tide of rough and low females, who else could such an ineffably genteel personage as Mrs Quince turn to for elegant companionship? To be sure, their tea-drinking was not always harmonious, for Mrs Quince must have the victory in all their conversational skirmishes. But Mrs Pink was quite inured to *that*.

Arthur's absence from Mrs Quince's house did cause her some temporary difficulty, however, for with two rooms unoccupied her finances were straitened. Some weeks after Arthur's departure, both Mrs Quince's problems were solved by the arrival of retired Commodore Winstanley Finch. Such were the immediate charms of the commodore that Mrs Quince did not perhaps make such rigorous enquiry into the validity of his credentials as she should have done. Mr and Mrs Pink wondered what a person of such elevated naval rank wanted with such lowly lodgings as those offered by Mrs Quince, but the lady herself gave it no thought whatsoever, so entirely bowled over was she by the commodore's gentlemanly manners and superior air. He took up residence in the house and had soon supplanted Mr Pink so entirely and effectively in Mrs Quince's heart that there was no further need for enmity of any kind to exist between the two households. Indeed, it was not long before the two women looked upon each other as dear and valuable friends.

After his marriage Mr Arthur Harlish established himself in a house in Wapping. That he and Mrs Harlish were supremely happy there goes without saying, or that their tenure was to be a short one. In time, as Mr Talbot had predicted, Arthur's character and expertise earned for him an excellent reputation and considerable wealth. From Wapping they removed to Chelsea—very close to Pear Tree Cottage—and not very many years after that they purchased a country lodge near Henley where they delighted to entertain their wide circle of friends, including Mr George Talbot and Madame Planché and Mr and Mrs Balfour.

Of Lord and Lady Pokerham it behoves us only to say that their marriage was long and happy if not always very passionate, and blessed by children who, though never notable for their prettiness, were at least spared the peculiarities that plagued other branches of the family tree. In defiance of their parents they made their home on the Isle of Wight, where they discovered many spectacularly well-preserved fossilised remains of prehistoric creatures well before it was generally accepted that such things had existed.

Lady Virginia married Lord John Wrexham as soon as he gained control of his estate, but forfeited the society of her mother and father in so doing, a loss she bore with remarkable equanimity. Lord and Lady Wrexham travelled a great deal, hiking in the Himalaya, thrashing through African jungles and navigating their own sloop through the islands of the Polynesian archipelago. Their early thirst for adventure and dangerous living remained with them throughout their long and perilous married life.

That Lady Jane and Mr George Talbot were effectively estranged for the rest of their lives was a fact well known amongst the *ton* but absolutely refuted by the lady. She claimed her husband's business kept him away, and, indeed, George continued to be involved in a multitude of projects, making money and friends, launching ships and shaping the new industrial age. But no one could believe that even so active a businessman as George Talbot could *never* find time to spend a night at his own home; he had plenty of time for his children, so long as they were away from it. Lady Jane's ascendancy in London society was so brief as to have made barely a glimmer in its firmament. Her protégé, the enigmatic lady in the veil later presented as a Miss Willow, was soon rumoured to have been an imposter—an actress, engaged to compromise eligible young men and insult their mamas. Lady Jane found herself firmly outside the charmed circle of superior families, omitted from guest lists and cut in public. She gave up the house in Grosvenor Square in favour of her son Rafe and took her daughter, Beatrice, with her to Brighton where she lived permanently, bitterly, until her early, unlamented death.

George Talbot did not remarry, but his deep and sincere attachment to a certain milliner, and her devotion to him, continued for the rest of both their lives.

Robert Talbot was seen at various places in Scandinavia—a lonely, brooding figure, not always well-shaven. He occupied himself for a while leading gentlemen on expeditions to hunt moose and reindeer, before tiring of this and moving on. He was known to have travelled as far as St

Petersburg and lived there for a time, fêted by Russian noblemen and courted by Russian noblewomen but showing no signs of settling permanently there. Indeed, he wrote to his father of a scheme to form an expedition that would cross Russia and explore the Altai mountains, circumnavigate the Taklamakan desert, come through the foothills of the Himalia and bring him at last to Nepal. He requested funds to be sent to await him at Kathmandu.

The funds were despatched as requested. A year passed, and then another. But the money was never collected.

At last George set out in pursuit, just as soon as the weather permitted safe passage, sailing to Suryapur and then making his way overland to Nepal. He could find no sign of his son. He had all but given up when a gnarled and weather-burnt mountain guide came to find him, purporting to know the young man's fate. He led George Talbot a journey of many days, via precipitous mountain tracks and sheer ravines, to a simple cairn on the top of a high and windswept peak. The guide pointed to the rough masonry, indicating that Robert lay beneath. When George asked what had killed his son the reply was simple. He had died of a broken heart.

Mr and Mrs Amory Balfour settled at Henley Court, and were happy. They lived in the world, occasionally—but not often—making appearances during the London season, and taking a few weeks by the sea in the summer, but liking most of all to be in the quiet privacy of their own home. They gathered around themselves a society of true friends, seeing a great deal of the Harlishes and the Pinks, George Talbot and Madame Planché, and from time to time—when she could be spared from her artistic endeavours—they entertained Robyn Talbot. In an artistic sense, Robyn Talbot was fascinated by Amory's face—the pink tracery of his scars, the drooped eye, the asymmetrical jaw—and made many sketches of him that might still be seen on the walls of public galleries and which are increasingly sought after by private collectors. What strikes the viewing public most forcefully about them—beyond the unarguable skill of the artist—is the essential pride, dignity and authenticity of their subject. He looks out of the pictures with an unwaveringly direct eye—stoical, long-suffering, undefeated.

The longer Georgina was married to Amory the more deeply loved she felt. Deeply, that is, in its truest sense. There was nothing superficial about Amory's affection for her. Of course, in appearance she was beautiful, and in time she came to terms with being beautiful, but her appearance had nothing to do with his most ardent regard and devotion. At length her physical loveliness did diminish. Her hair greyed and her skin lost its radiance, her eyes dimmed and her elegant bearing became stooped. But when she lay dying in his arms—a very shrunken, elderly and wrinkled figure—she knew that, to him, she was still a peerless beauty.

The house in Yorkshire, for all its new wings and improved chimneys, rarely saw any member of the family. Jocelyn Stockbridge found her old ties to it loosened by her attachment to her second husband. He understood the importance of it to her, but gently discouraged further visitations, citing the claims of the living; that is of himself, her children and her several grandchildren. Georgina, Amory and their children stayed there two or three times but, like her mother, Georgina had found within herself the security and shelter the old walls had formerly provided. Arthur and Petunia visited annually until his mother and then his father passed away.

His sister Betsy and brother Frank remained, living together in the old gatehouse with Betsy's daughter, a fatherless child whose provenance was never clearly established. They were adequately paid by Mr Talbot to maintain the buildings and the grounds; but their industry, year after year, could not hold back the dereliction of scouring wind, interminable rain and neglect. The drive became tangled with inveigling brambles, the garden grew into a meadow of weeds.

Local people began to believe there was something sinister about the place. Odd, echoic moaning sounds could sometimes be heard from deep in the combe. Ghostly miasmas were seen amongst the trees. Very few were willing to descend the drive but those who did—buoyed by drink or egged on by their dare-devil companions—reported that it had a sad, woebegone and very lonely air.

For fifty years more it remained abandoned, squat and sullen in its combe, its towering chimneys reaching in defiant challenge to the sky.

YOUR REVIEW MATTERS

Thank you for reading this book. As a self-published author I don't have the support of a marketing department behind me to promote my books. I rely on you, the reader, to spread the word.

A short review provides great feedback and encouragement to the writer, and is a helpful way for others to know if they might enjoy the book. Please write a few words along with your star rating.

AFTERWORD & ACKNOWLEDGEMENTS

The Lady in the Veil is a book about disguises and hidden identity. Conversely, it is about the authenticity of knowing and accepting who we are, the personal integrity that is part and parcel of contentment. Ironically, Georgina never does find out who she really is, and I leave it to the reader to decide if Jocelyn and George—and I—did her a kindness or a disservice.

In the troubled times we have been through we have all got used to concealing our faces behind masks, and this was my starting point for The Lady in the Veil. Like many people, I have witnessed the odd ways that people behave when wearing Covid masks. Some avoid eye contact and behave as though they are invisible, slinking along the supermarket aisles like foxes through the shadows. Others seem to feel that the masks act as gags. I have had some very comical 'conversations' using pantomime gestures, shrugs and head-nodding, but no words at all. These people seem to have felt that the masks have in some way dehumanised them. Others have felt empowered by the anonymity afforded by mask-wearing. They barge to the front of queues, ignore social distancing and hurl abuse at shop-workers, presumably safe in the knowledge that no one will know who they are.

There are many ways in which we disguise our appearances, even without face-masks. Make-up, hair-dye, sun-glasses, tattoos, cosmetic surgery, on-line avatars. Gregory Porter wears a hat to conceal facial scarring, a possibility I considered for Georgina. Gabrielle wears an eye patch, or covers one eye, because of a medical condition. Orthodox nuns cover their hair entirely. Other religious practices require the covering of the head, hair or the entire body. My point is that we all have our veils, even if not physical ones. We draw shrouds over painful things in the past, or colour them in brighter hues so that they sit more comfortably in memory.

Georgina's veil-wearing comes from a sense of feeling uncomfortable in her own skin, a notion assimilated from her mother and intensified by her encounter with the clerk in Salisbury. What interested me about it even more was the way the veil blurred her own vision of the world, of people, and of herself. Although The Lady in the Veil has a happy romantic ending, its triumph, for me, was that Georgina learns to love herself.

I'm sixty years old now, and the consequences of age on my face and body are sometimes hard to come to terms with. It's a shock to see myself in a mirror or on my daughter's Instagram. But the 'me' inside this wizening carapace is unchanged and that's the 'me' I'm holding on to. As Amory says, 'I am myself, the best iteration of myself that I can be. That is the only authenticity that really matters, I think.'

My thanks as always go to Tim, who encourages me to climb the attic stairs and get to work, and loves me, wrinkles-and-all. Thank you also to my daughter Abigail, who allowed me to talk through my dilemma—should I, or should I not, reveal the secret of Georgina's birth—and who helped me map out the conversation between Amory and Georgina on Weymouth sands. My editor, Sallianne Hines of Quinn Editing, treated my book with sensitivity and insight, and was patient with my confusion about hyphens. Any errors that remain are all my own.

ABOUT THE AUTHOR

Allie Cresswell was born in Stockport, UK and began writing fiction as soon as she could hold a pencil.

She did a BA in English Literature at Birmingham University and an MA at Queen Mary College, London.

She has been a print-buyer, a pub landlady, a book-keeper, run a B & B and a group of boutique holiday cottages. She taught literature to lifelong learners but nowadays she writes full time.

She has two grown-up children, two granddaughters, two grandsons and two cockapoos—but just one husband—Tim. They live in Cumbria, NW England.

The Lady in the Veil is her twelfth novel.

ALSO BY ALLIE CRESSWELL

Game Show

Relative Strangers

Crossings

Tiger in a Cage

The Widows Series comprising:

The Hoarder's Widow

The Widow's Mite

The Talbot Saga comprising:

House in the Hollow

Tall Chimneys

*The Highbury Trilogy inspired by Jane Austen's Emma,
comprising*:

Mrs Bates of Highbury

The Other Miss Bates

Dear Jane

[i] There is a distinction. Jealousy is a feeling of extreme possessiveness for things that we have, but do not wish to share. Envy is the same as covetousness—a desire to have the things that others own.

[ii] Pauline Auzou, (March 24, 1775 – May 15, 1835) was a French painter and art instructor who exhibited at the Paris Salon and was commissioned to make paintings of Napoleon. In the eighteenth century women were usually prevented from gaining an education in art but Auzou, influenced and encouraged by other women artists, became successful and, in time, opened her own art school.

[iii] 'Lady' is the formal title of the wife of a lord, a baronet, a laird or a knight, and is also placed, as in this case, before the first name of the daughter of a duke, a marquis or an earl. Even upon matrimony, she retains this title, so although George Talbot is plain 'Mr' his wife is Lady Jane Talbot.

[iv] Ranelagh was a pleasure ground opened by the proprietor of Drury Lane Theatre, where masquerades, concerts and entertainments were provided during the later eighteenth century. It is now the site of the Chelsea Flower Show.

[v] An annual event held at Eton, in honour of George III's birthday. George III took great interest in the school.

[vi] Nashoba Community, a two-thousand-acre stretch of Tennessee woodland, was set up to function without the use of any slaves. If it was successful, it could prove that slavery was not necessary. It also wanted to prove that all people, including slaves, could live happily through a system of labour sharing. Nashoba Community collapsed in 1828.

[vii] Opened in 1830

[viii] The City of London Club, opened in 1832, was patronised by city professionals.

[ix] The rope used to hoist a flag. 'Colours' is a nautical term denoting flags which were flown from ships to show their allegiance.

[xx] McAdam developed the Macadam road construction technique

[xi] Patented Portand cement (concrete)

[xii] Patrick Bell invented a mechanical reaping machine

[xiii] Pioneers of the telegraphic system of communication on which they were working 1830-40 but which was already in use for communication between railway stations and for signalling.

[xiv] The slave trade (the buying and selling of slaves) had been abolished in 1811 but the owning of slaves remained legal until 1833. The Factory Act of 1833 prohibited the employment of children younger than nine years of age and limited the hours that children between nine and 13 could work.

[xv] John and Robert Lord opened a cotton mill using water power from the Dean Brook which powered spinning mules invented by Samuel Crompton. The brothers built 13 cottages near the mill for workers. In 1830 Thomas Bazley and Richard Gardner bought and demolished the mill, replacing it with Dean Mills, twin six-

storey steam powered mills situated on the east side of the brook at the entrance to the village. They created a model village for the mill workers on the hill top accessed by a flight of stone steps, with rows of cottages, a shop and an educational institute.

[xvi] The weekday market known now as Petticoat Lane Market.

[xvii] Designed by James Walker, opened in 1835.

[xviii] The SS Great Britain was built in Bristol and launched in 1843.

[xix] A figure of Yorkshire legend. Her cave can still be visited today in Knaresborough.

[xx] Cardinal Wolsey

[xxi] The Thames tunnel was the first tunnel known to have been constructed successfully underneath a navigable river and was built between 1825 and 1843 by Marc Isambard Brunel (father of the more famous Isambard Kingdom Brunel).

[xxii] Agnes was right! The large 'leg-of-mutton' sleeves fashionable in the 1830s changed to sleeves that were tight around the upper arm and full below the elbow towards the end of the decade, and then went out of fashion altogether until a resurgence in 1890.

[xxiii] An ankle-length cape or cloak, often hooded, with slits for the arms, used as outer wear.

[xxiv] The Duke of Sutherland, formerly the Marquis of Stafford, was a politician, landowner and patron of the arts from the Leveson-Gower family. He was the wealthiest man in Britain during the latter part of his life. He remains a controversial figure for his role in the Highland Clearances.

[xxv] Stafford house, formerly Godolphin House, was situated close to St James' Palace. It was demolished by the Duke of York in 1825 and the exterior of the new house was built by 1826, followed by expensive work on the luxurious interior. When the Duke of York died in 1827 he was much in debt, but had not yet lived in the house. The government in 1828 sold the still unfinished mansion to the Marquis of Stafford (1758-1833), who proceeded to invest much more in its completion. It was not in fact completed until 1842.

[xxvi] By the 1840s cannabis was being touted as one of the wonder-drugs of the age, as doctors out in the Empire reported excitedly that it was a 'powerful and valuable remedy in hydrophobia, tetanus, cholera and many convulsive disorders'. The Provincial Medical and Surgical Journal seized on these reports and devoted its front page to the new medicine, and in subsequent decades the plant was used to treat everything from tetanus, to period pains and mental illness.

[xxvii] Tiny metal boxes holding a sponge soaked in vinegar and perfumed oils with a grille over the top to let the fumes escape, used if a lady felt faint.

[xxviii] Minute, unbreakable container of perfume, for when a bad smell was encountered.

[xxix] Each remove has taken Lady Virginia a step down the ladder of nobility, which descends from Duke to Baron via Marquis, Earl and Viscount.

[xxx] The oldest son of a duke takes one of his father's lesser title until he accedes to the dukedom. In this case, the marquis of Alton.

[xxxi] Buckingham Palace has a chequered history. Originally bought in 1761 by George III for his wife Charlotte it underwent refurbishment then, and again in 1820, when George IV came to the throne. Costs were exorbitant however and the architect was

dismissed in 1830 when the king died. His brother William IV had no interest in the place but the government took on the task of completing the works from 1833-1853. Queen Victoria moved in in 1837.

xxxii Literally the 'noble floor' where the state rooms are located.

xxxiii Recently voted the world's most awful colour. Also called puke.

xxxiv Romeo and Juliet Act I scene V

xxxv The cockney accent typically replaces 'th' with 'f' or 'v'

xxxvi Cockney omits the letters 't' and 'g' from the middle of words in what is called a glottal stop. Initial letter 'h' is usually dropped.

xxxvii At this point in time millinery did not refer exclusively to hats, but also to dress-making, but Miss Pink is in fact a hat-maker.

xxxviii Light was at a premium in all sewing, embroidery and lace-making industries. Those who were permitted closest to the light did the most detailed and highly valued work, so we can infer from this that Miss Pink is in a high managerial position.

xxxix Nowadays known as Queen's Gate.

xl A defensive weapon carried by gentlemen, looking like a cane or walking stick but concealing a blade.

xli These were the common treatments for hysteria at the time. Hysteria was believed to be specifically a women's complaint, caused by an excess of fluid in the uterus. Massage therapy involved stimulation of the genitals until a 'paroxysm' should be reached which would expel the fluid. Magnetism (also called Mesmerism) involved the laying-on of hands in order to draw forth the fluids by kinesis, similar to Reiki.

xlii This would be a hat with a large brim projecting forwards, preventing anyone not directly in front of the wearer from seeing her face.

xliii An open-topped carriage generally seating four passengers.

xliv The original home of the National Gallery. In April 1824 the House of Commons agreed to pay £57,000 for the picture collection of the banker John Julius Angerstein. His 38 pictures were intended to form the core of a new national collection, for the enjoyment and education of all. Angerstein's paintings were joined in 1826 by those from Beaumont's collection, and in 1831 by the Reverend William Holwell Carr's bequest of 35 paintings. The pictures were displayed at Angerstein's house at 100 Pall Mall, a cramped and notoriously stuffy facility, until a dedicated gallery building was constructed.

xlv Proverbs 30:17

xlvi The lavatories.

xlvii George was right, but it would not be until 1866 that the first telegraph line was laid between the US and Europe.

xlviii The increasing size of ships made Bristol less and less viable as a port. They had to contend with seven miles of winding river with strong currents and a very high tidal range. When the ships reached the quays and wharves they got beached in the mud by the tide and so loading and unloading was very difficult.

xlix Read *The House in the Hollow* for full particulars.

l A sauteuse was a turning dance for couples in 2/4 time with small leaping steps. Sauter means to leap or jump.

[li] These were in King Street, St. James's, in the heart of fashionable London, situated immediately to the east of Pall Mall Place. A ball and supper was held once a week for members, but I presume they could be hired privately on other days.

[lii] Feminine form of the Greek Adonis, the perfection of male beauty.

[liii] A gentlemen's club established by and for members of the East India Company in 1824. As a merchant with close connections to the east India Company George Talbot would undoubtedly have secured membership for Robert.

[liv] The Act of 1834 had made it illegal to buy or own a slave. Slavery was replaced by apprenticeships which were designed to guarantee former slaves the security of employment and an income and also to prepare them for life as free citizens. In practice, the apprenticeships were as cruel as slavery had been, and many former slaves ran away to Bristol and Liverpool with the idea of working their passage back to their families in the Caribbean, or stowing away.

[lv] Grave-robbing or body-snatching became illegal in the 1832 Anatomy Act.

[lvi] There was no police force in Bristol at this time. The 1835 Municipal Corporation Act would only just have given towns and cities the power to create their own professional police forces. Bristol was amongst the first cities in the country to do so. In the absence of any other law enforcement the magistrate would have overseen the investigation and consequences of crime in the city

[lvii] An Indian nobleman

[lviii] Two Greek Goddesses renowned for their beauty who, along with Aphrodite, competed to be named the most beautiful in a competition judged by Paris.

[lix] The name used by middle and working class people for the nobility.

[lx] Euphemism for toilet.

[lxi] What we would call keloid scars today.

[lxii] Blood relationship.

[lxiii] Handrail around the open deck areas.

[lxiv] Milliner and haberdasher.

Made in the USA
Las Vegas, NV
03 July 2021

25869353R00204